FORTUNE HUNTERS

Riley Masters

Lost Haven Press

First Edition

Published 2014 by Lost Haven Press

Cover design by: Lisbeth Harding Kassa

ISBN-13: 9780615956589
ISBN-10: 0615956580
Library of Congress Control Number: 2014902148
Lost Haven Press, Boston, MA

PRELUDE

Brookline, Massachusetts

Only a few are granted the wish to die quietly by the side of their soul mate. At the end of a lifetime of love, Phillip and Sarah lay back on the plush scarlet living room sofa, seated close to each other. Their heavy heads rested on the top of the soft fabric and tilted toward each other with their eyes joined in an intimate embrace. Two outstretched hands inched forward with fading strength until a few fingers touched. Two outstretched hearts embraced effortlessly as one, flowing intermingled in space and time in the way that mountain streams meet to find the sea.

Their home was dark and silent now. It was a large, old house, in a quiet neighborhood, the street outside still in the limbo that settles on such places after midnight. The ticking of a distant grandfather clock in the hall tolled the relentless march to eternity in a solitary watch over the old couple.

The throbbing pain in their bodies had faded, leaving them paralyzed with a growing numbness in their limbs from the alcohol and pills poisoning their failing flesh and blood. To fight off the fog that confused and obscured their thoughts, they gazed at each other as best friends will while a symbiotic past flashes by. Words could no longer come, so they spoke to each other with their eyes. After forty years, their minds flowed together easily with a look, and Phillip and Sarah saw each other anew.

She was more beautiful than ever, soft hair as black as the day they had first met, her eyes sparkling with the generous laughter of the party hostess. His receding gray hair still curled with traces of reddish brown, and below his eyeglasses, the lines of the face carved the features of a scholar king.

Gone were the agonies of hours before, the resentments, the helpless anger and denial, and finally the despair of failure. Questions remained, but they faded into unimportance as the couple flitted in and out of a faltering consciousness. Explanations and blame no longer mattered. In their search for a richer life, they had both given their trust. They had been foolish, and then careless, and then they had been betrayed. Everything they had worked for over the course of their years together was lost—present and future.

What was left was the past. And between people who have shared a long love, there was no more time for regrets, no need for apologies. All that was important was the inviolate comfort of love. For each other, and for their daughter. With no explanation, it would be very hard on her. There were some things that would remain unsaid, secrets that should never have been kept.

In the final moments, they each fought for life—not out of fear, but to keep faith with the other. Alone together as they had often been, with the one person each had been able to depend upon without reservation, they completed a life of sacrifice and commitment. They wanted to stay awake and be true to that commitment, but the narcotic of death embraced them tighter and tighter, calling the life partners to the long sleep.

At last, Phillip was gone. Sarah drank in one final, adoring look. Then, with no reason to hold her eyes open any longer, she closed her lids. As she went to the final rest of the sinner forgiven, her last thought was of Romeo and Juliet.

O, I am fortune's fool...

ONE

"Get the hell out of my office, McBain."

"Sure thing, Russell," the man across from him said. "Been a pleasure doing business with you."

He leaned forward in his armchair, picked up the envelope, and glanced inside. Satisfied, he slid it into the inside pocket of his blue pinstripe suit as he stared back at the purple-faced executive glowering across the broad desk. McBain stood up to leave.

"And just look at it this way," he said. "Don't think of it as backing down. Think of it as saving millions in lawyers' fees, your reputation, marriage, and business while doing the right thing by my client."

"I can't believe they haven't revoked your license," the fat man said. "I don't ever want to hear from you again, you piece of..."

McBain picked up his black overcoat and gray fedora, pulled the door back, and smirked. "That'll depend on you, won't it, Russell?" He left the door open.

After two quick phone calls in the building's lobby, McBain headed out into the heart of Boston's financial district. He buttoned his coat and hiked up his scarf as he walked, zigzagging through the maze of crooked streets that dissected the colonial architecture and glass-and-steel skyscrapers, weaving together historic Boston with modern financial culture. Cutting across the Boston Common, he strode briskly toward Beacon Street in the late afternoon chill to drop off the check. It had taken six long months, but this one was finally closed with a happy ending.

The receding grip of a hard, white winter clung to the park as he sped along the snow-lined pathways, taking in the view of ice-covered

1

branches and the skyscrapers looming over Copley Square to the west. The crisp taste of the air mingled with his cigarette as he angled uphill into the wind, holding on to his hat with one hand in defiance of the season. The days were growing longer in late March, and he still had light and time to spare. Get to the client's house, drop the check off, pick up his fee, and hit the office for a few minutes before cocktail hour. Life always felt fuller after wrapping up a case successfully, at least for a little while.

The sun's rays sliced through the fast-moving clouds to fall onto the facades of the stately townhouses along Beacon Street across from the north side of the park, and looking at the red-and-orange reflections, he imagined the windows of the Brahmin brownstones glaring down on him disapprovingly. McBain sauntered up to the front of a white limestone and redbrick apartment building on Beacon near the northwest corner of the park. The doorman called up and escorted him to the elevator. He pulled off his hat, scarf, and overcoat and straightened his maroon silk tie on the ride up, combing his brown hair in the polished doors. He noticed again with consternation the first strands of gray that were beginning to intrude.

Mrs. Parker answered the door in a little black dress that was entirely too friendly for March.

"Please come in, Mr. McBain. It's so nice to have you back again, and so soon. We weren't expecting your call. Andrew won't be here for some time." She pushed back the beach blond hair and invited him into the large drawing room with a practiced smile and a wave of French nails and diamonds.

"I take it from your call that you have good news?" she said, leading him into the parlor with classically uncomfortable furniture and a broad expanse of bay windows overlooking the Public Garden. "Has there been progress in your discussions with...that company?" She trailed off as she sat on the couch and crossed her long legs with a tone of condescension that McBain intuited was well practiced. "Please, sit down."

"The best," he said, landing in an armchair across from his hostess. "I just came from their offices. The company paid up this afternoon.

The case is settled quietly for the amount I promised you and your husband. Plus some."

The investigator watched as the woman's blue pupils dilated at the news. Though she remained composed as she leaned back on the sofa, it was evident she was trying to calculate the impact of what he had said. She couldn't have seemed more thrilled if he had just given her box seats to the next Red Sox World Series.

"Well...Mr. McBain, this is certainly wonderful news," she said. "Better than I ever expected...than either Andrew or I expected, I mean."

McBain couldn't suppress a smile at her new attitude and gave her a toothy grin.

"They came back in the high seven figures. I convinced them to throw in more than they owed you. Call it an act of contrition for all the emotional anguish they put you and Mr. Parker through over the past year."

Mrs. Parker might have been looking at fifty while trying to pass for thirty, but she was close to bouncing on the couch like an eager prom queen as she processed the happy news.

"Well...well." She caught her breath and clasped her hands together. "This calls for a drink, doesn't it, Mr. McBain?"

With admirable alacrity, she sashayed over to the bar and came back with two martini glasses that were suspiciously well chilled.

"Or may I call you Boozy, as your secretary did?"

McBain caught the change in tone he had noticed in one of their previous meetings. He took a sip as he thought that over. "She's actually more of a business partner than a secretary. Why don't we just stick with McBain, Mrs. Parker?"

She had already wet her whistle with a healthy drink.

"Oh, but McBain, please call me Kelly. After all, our business relationship is concluded now."

"Almost concluded, Mrs. Parker," he said. "Almost, but not quite. As I had hoped, I managed to settle this...misunderstanding without the involvement of the lawyers or the authorities, not to mention publicity. I think that probably saved you quite a nice percentage of the final balance, don't you? If you'll recall our retainer agreement, we should be able to do the math and wind things up with an exchange of checks right now."

With that, he pulled the envelope from his suit pocket and extracted the investment company's check slowly from inside. Out of the corner of his eye, he thought he detected a movement from the sofa, not unlike that of a badly trained Doberman flinching when her master throws a steak onto the floor.

"Of course." She brushed the hair away from her blue eyes and rose. "Let me just go into the bedroom and find the agreement and the checkbook. Unless, of course, you want to wait until Andrew gets home later."

McBain glanced at the white pearls that fell upon her chest, high up on the expensive winter tan, his face impassive. Too expensive, he thought. He shifted his eyes down to his watch. "I think it best we settle up right away so I can get back to my office before we close for the week. If you don't mind."

The socialite shrugged and offered him a "come hither" glance as she continued down the hall.

McBain wandered to the bay window looking out over the street to nurse his drink while he waited. The view of the Public Garden was quite pretty from on high, even at this time of the year. Friday afternoon traffic was beginning to build along Beacon and down Arlington Street, past the old Ritz-Carlton Hotel across from the park. The Ritz name and the piano in the lounge were both long gone, but the great willows by the pond, statue of a mounted George Washington, and ducks were still there to carry on the tradition and safeguard the warm memories hidden beneath a blanket of white.

After five minutes, he determined from the sounds in the direction of the bedroom that his client had figured out that her financial needs were the only ones the tall investigator would be satisfying that afternoon. The echo of heels clicking on the hardwood floor preceded her return. She was carrying a sheet of paper and the kind of checkbook really rich people used.

After looking over the agreement, she wrote out the check and handed it to McBain with a coy smile. "Here you are...Boozy."

He glanced at the number as he took it. When it came to getting paid, he was excellent at math. "This number is a little higher than the one I calculated. I think we'd better check your—"

"That's quite all right. Let's call it a performance bonus, shall we? We never know when we might be in need of your services again."

Never one to look a gift horse in the mouth, McBain nodded with a grin.

"Thanks, that's generous of you. I guess that means we can call this one closed. Be seeing you around town, Kelly Parker."

Satisfied, he took his leave before his baser instincts kicked in.

McBain used the extra adrenaline in his system to hustle straight down Arlington from Beacon Hill to Columbus Avenue and his bank in the South End. The account executive promised she would call the minute the check cleared and the cash was in his account. The investigator wasn't strong on trusting clients until after he got paid. He turned down the close, winding streets and was at his office before six o'clock.

The three-room office was on the upper floor of an historic red-brick building just off a small square full of bike racks and artist spaces on Tremont Street, with a back entrance available on Warren Avenue that allowed for discretion if visitors preferred not to advertise their troubles.

McBain opened the door to the front office and strolled in like the cat that ate the canary.

"Friday at six and the case is closed," he said. "That's how I like to start my weekend, Boston."

"Bullshit, McBain. You like to start your weekend with a martini."

The young redhead looked up from her computer behind the formidable oak desk on the far side of the room. The front office was spacious and furnished with a classic nineteenth-century New England elegance that presented clients with an air of success and confidence when it came to discretion in the handling of their financial problems. The walls were paneled with dark wood, and the Persian carpeting was a thick maroon. The furniture was comfortable and stately, the paintings colonial era.

5

"Money in the bank?" she asked.

He nodded. "Well, the check's in the bank. I told Alice to call you when it clears; shouldn't be a problem. I'm sure Russell's check will go through, so they've got plenty of money. At least until she starts spending again."

"That's Mr. Parker's problem. How did we do?"

McBain pulled out the stub from the investment company's check and handed it over to her, along with the bank deposit slip. She assessed the numbers for a moment.

"Looks like they overpaid a little," she said with an arched eyebrow.

He smirked as he shook off his overcoat and threw his fedora on a deep-brown leather couch by the far wall that bordered an elegant cherry coffee table and matching leather armchairs.

"Mrs. Parker was feeling generous and decided to give us a...what was her term...performance bonus for getting them back more than they hoped for."

"And how well did you perform?"

McBain feigned shock and threw open his arms. "Hey, I know the rules. Don't mess with the clients, even after the money is in the bank. Might be bad for future business. I have to be careful of our word-of-mouth reputation."

She laughed and waved the paper slips in the air. "And what does Mr. Jackson think of your reputation now? You think he'll be spreading the good word?"

McBain unbuttoned his jacket and loosed his tie, sinking into a chair across from the sea-green eyes and the freckles on her upper chest that always reminded him of a constellation. He thought back to a few hours ago and the tense showdown with Russell Jackson in his office on High Street. The executive had left no room for doubt what he thought about McBain. On the other hand, there was little chance he would be talking about the encounter with anyone important. In terms of potential business, that was a good thing.

"He threatened to turn me in to the police. I threatened to turn him in to the SEC. We called it even. Anyway, I guess our friend Russell will think twice before he tries to pump another client's investment account to boost his profits and support his fine standard of living. Or maybe he'll just clean up his loose ends so he's not so exposed next time."

"I thought the pictures were quite flattering," she said. "You older men always look better with a young woman on your arm."

"Very nice."

"Well, I'm sure he broke even. After all, he gets to keep his mistress, some of his money, his job, and his wife, and keep everything quiet. Though it would have been fun watching the two of them devour him publicly like lions going after an old zebra. But I suppose we can't have everything."

McBain shook his head as he looked her over, from cascading auburn hair to long, rough hands crossed on the desktop. The conservative black jacket and burgundy sweater barely concealed the curves and soul of a street cat. He admired how much she enjoyed going for the throat on cases like this one.

"From what you told me," he said, "the wife would have taken a blowtorch to his finances. She didn't sound like someone I ever wanted to cross."

"I thought you said she sounded like someone you did cross with once upon a time," Boston said. "I think your personal experience at these kinds of things probably helps you close the deal rather smartly."

McBain frowned and took off his tie. "Ouch. Thanks. Now I really do need a drink."

They went into McBain's office. He mixed them some Hendrick's martinis from the small bar set up in a rolltop desk, pulled out two chilled glasses from a compact refrigerator in a cabinet below, and plopped in an olive. He handed his partner a glass and raised his.

"Here's to another successful case, Boston," he said.

She touched his glass. "Well done, McBain."

Boston wandered over to gaze out the arched picture window into the twilight. Dusk was falling to inaugurate the weekend, and lights were beginning to glow in the bars and restaurants along Tremont, framing the snow-encrusted trees below. The massive Japanese elm that dominated the square still wore the cold mantle of New England in March. She sipped her cocktail, taking in the setting in silence for a minute.

"Just to remind you," she said, "our anniversary is coming up in two weeks. I want to go someplace new this year."

McBain leaned on the edge of his mahogany desk. "Sure." He thought for a moment. "Five years already?"

"Four. It just feels like longer sometimes."

"Ah, right. OK, I'll find something different, away from the waterfront this time."

Time was moving fast. It couldn't have been five years. Five years ago, he hadn't even been here. He'd been finalizing his divorce in New York, cursing the day he'd ever met his not-ex-enough wife. Thinking about quitting the city, not to mention the job that had paid for the grand style to which she was continuing to be accustomed. Thinking about quitting women, finance, and city life entirely and moving to a Mexican beach, a place where they had never heard of lawyers and he could spend what money she'd left him with on fishing tackle and cheap fish tacos.

Instead, he settled for quitting everything but the drinking. He moved to a new city and started over in a new line of work where greed, duplicity, and vindictiveness were stock in trade. It was then that he met Boston O'Daniel, so it couldn't have been five years.

He stared at his partner as she leaned against the frame, marveling as always at the difference from that night they had first met. One hundred and twenty pounds of Irish volcano smoldering under a demure, attractive veneer. She pulled back her hair, which framed high cheekbones set in an angular face with a graceful chin and a damaged Roman nose that hinted at her underlying toughness.

"Speaking of which, how is your dad?" he asked.

She remained still, her eyes cruising the street below over the rim of her martini. "He's good. He says hi. Thinking about retiring in a year or two, or so he claims."

"I hope not. His help comes in handy occasionally."

"I don't think help from the department is anything we'll ever have to worry about, Boozy."

He was getting uncomfortable with the changing mood.

"I'm sure you're right. Why don't we invite him to lunch next week to celebrate our case closing? I think we can afford it, can't we?"

She sighed and shook her head to snap out of her mood. Her face lit up again as she raised her glass to her lips.

"Yes, we're in pretty good shape, actually," Boston said. "The year is starting off strong. You closed the Parker case, our two other ongoing investigations are coming along, and I had another phone call today on a possible lead. We've got lots to keep busy on, so don't plan on any extended vacations to Costa Rica."

McBain finished his drink and stood up.

"In that case, I better enjoy my victory celebration tonight. If you'll excuse me, Boston, my bartender is expecting me."

His partner finished her own drink and walked to the doorway.

"Only one? Don't forget the aspirin before bed this time. See you Monday."

McBain lived in the South End, so the only challenging decision about finding a drink between the office and his front door was limiting the number of pit stops.

He was relieved to put the Parker case to bed. He would have been happier to do so literally, but Boston would never have forgiven him for that. She was tolerant when it came to his drinking; hell, she really had no room to criticize. But when it came to their business, she was as cold hearted as a crusty New England sea captain. She was smart as hell, and the first and only time he had crossed that line, she had been quick and angry enough to point out that it fed the ugly side of him, the one he had tried to leave behind in New York.

So instead, he spent the next few hours at some of his favorite watering holes, recalling his satisfaction at the look on Russell Jackson's face as he'd gone through the stack of pictures one by one. Savoring the tingling pleasure of the kill, watching Jackson sweat as he balanced the rage and growing fear in his mind, holding the cheater over the edge of the railing until he put his fat signature on the check. As the swizzle sticks piled up, past and present blended together, and he began to lose track of the players.

After too many drinks and several rejections, McBain got the sign from the last bartender. He paid his check and weaved his way home past the rows of brownstones and through the snowy lanes without slipping, using the streetlights as guideposts. He fell into bed, but the dreams played on for some time until they mingled and dissolved and he spiraled into the black hole of exhausted oblivion.

As usual, he forgot the aspirin.

TWO

With nothing to do the next day but nurse his hangover, McBain took his time coming back to life. He staggered out midmorning and picked up the papers to unwind and catch up on the week's financial news with breakfast at Charlie's Sandwich Shoppe.

Over bacon, eggs, hash, and coffee, he perused several stories bemoaning another day in the global markets. Terrible as usual, but then there was always an upside, and his good run of business was all he cared about. As somebody said, when the tide goes out, you really see the kind of garbage that's been lying under the water during the good times. And as far as he was concerned, he and Boston were in the waste-disposal business.

Since the market had begun to tumble, an entire era's worth of greed, incompetence, and outright fraud had opened up the corrupt and stupid side of a business that was made to separate people from their money, and for once he had been in the ideal position to capitalize on it. The trusted advisors of the boom had turned out to be not so trustworthy after all, and the angry and the betrayed were lining up by the busload in impoverished disbelief and outrage.

Madoff was just the tip of the iceberg. McBain had always thought it a shame he hadn't figured that one out ahead of time, like the Greek. Shaking down that old crook would have been a one-time lottery ticket to retirement in the islands. Oh, well. These days, there was enough sewage rising to the surface to keep them in business until the next bull market forgave all sins.

He sipped his coffee and rubbed at his throbbing temples as he read through a column lamenting another blossoming SEC investigation.

This one looked much like the first case he and his partner had undertaken. When he first moved to Boston, the markets had been booming, covering up a whole range of financial crimes and stupidity. Tony had suggested he get a private investigator license or become some kind of forensic consultant and work for one of the big firms to get back on his feet and forget New York. McBain had gotten his license and set up his own shingle instead, more to keep himself occupied and finance his drinking than anything else. It helped that he knew how the investment business worked, even more that he had contempt for those people who worked in the firms that built their fortunes on the back of their clients' money without a moral or ethical bone in their body. And that had given him an idea that led him to find some room between the wolves and the sheep, and take advantage when things went south in those relationships, which they often did.

As luck would have it, it hadn't taken long for the worm to turn.

Luck had been the reason that he and Boston had crossed paths those four years ago, though at the time they both viewed that luck differently. After an initial reluctance, they had become a pretty good team, more so after he came to appreciate that she was almost as cynical and bitter as he, with a mind as sharp as an accountant's pencil. And who wouldn't want to work with a woman with fists like an Irish cop? If McBain had a natural instinct for unraveling arcane investment transactions or corporate shell games, she was peerless at sensing human vulnerabilities, where to dig up the dirt, and how to go for the jugular. His marriage should have been so perfect a match.

McBain looked at his watch, wrote off the gym, and ordered more coffee from the waitress. Looking around at the hipster crowd, he appreciated how out of shape he was, but today wasn't going to be the day to turn over a new leaf. Good health would have to wait for a Monday.

On the other hand, thinking about the Parker case and payday cheered him up. Things were looking up on the financial front for the first time in five years. Maybe he'd consider a new car to go with his new apartment décor. If the timing worked out with these other jobs, a nice little summer spot on the coast might be in order; Nantucket or the Cape. Somewhere with sailing or deep-sea fishing to help him get his groove back. Maybe a little less tension to help him cut back on the sauce and get in shape. On the other hand, tension was par for the course in the line of work he'd chosen. A couple of good years, and he and Boston would be set.

McBain finished up the papers and took a walk through the maze of streets that people often characterized as Boston's edition of Greenwich Village. The sidewalks were still piled with snow, but the temperature was beginning to melt the icicles off of the eaves of the brownstones and townhouses, and the redbrick chimneys made him feel comfortable and at home the way only a good neighborhood can. On the other hand, the sky was turning gray and it looked as if more bad weather was coming on, so he decided against his stroll up to the Common and went home to clear his head.

By the time he climbed the stairs to his apartment, his neck and head were screaming *enough*. The kitchen took time to clean, but McBain treated the scrubbing as meditation to go with the rhythmic throbbing in his body. Most of his appliances and culinary work spaces were new, courtesy of flush times and last Christmas, and he wanted to keep them that way. He had just pulled out a stack of lunchmeats, mustard, and tomatoes when the door buzzer rang.

"I thought I gave you a key," he said.

Troy glided into the apartment, his head swiveling from side to side. The designer tossed his pea coat, snowboarder cap, and Cat in the Hat scarf on an ottoman.

"Just giving you the benefit of the doubt, sweetheart," he said. "I was hoping since it was Saturday afternoon, you might have a honey stay over for a change. She go home, or did you come up empty last night?"

"No joy this time. One bartender said I put a girl off when I slurred my words pronouncing her name."

"Imagine that," Troy said.

"Hey, I won another settlement for a client yesterday. I opted to share my good fortune with some of our neighborhood merchants."

"Which I'm sure they appreciated. I just thought maybe you'd find some young hottie who would appreciate your lovely new digs in a more personal fashion. I do fabulous design work, dear, but you have to supply the long-lasting touches. You know, a little exercise, some fine wine, a girlfriend."

McBain lit up the big-screen TV with the Singers and Swing music channel for background and straightened up the papers and clothes lying around his living room. Troy had done a magical job transforming an average space into a sophisticated adult apartment, but he had insisted McBain uphold the standards of the South End community. Exercising his *Queer Eye for the Straight Guy* license had cost McBain a bundle.

"Christ," McBain said. "Between you and Boston, my life is pretty complete. Why would I want a girlfriend? For what it cost you to decorate my place, I could have gone through another divorce."

The apartment appeared to have been lifted straight out of Tuscany, with faux-stone walls and subdued Mediterranean colors and furniture in beige and burgundy offset by alarmingly modern art from local galleries. The technology was discretely set back to minimize the intrusion of the modern world on his villa, visible from a long, soft couch and rustic brown leather armchairs. Troy had incorporated antique bookshelves to craft a professionally disheveled look that had previously just been chaotic.

"A man after my own heart," Troy said. "Spend it on yourself." He stood next to the fireplace and adjusted the lone photograph in a wrought-iron frame sitting on the mantelpiece. McBain and Boston were dressed in formal wear, gazing at each other while locked together on a dance floor. "Unfortunately for you, you're not getting laid by either of us. You go on and get out of the way while I finish touching up the mantel and trim here."

McBain went into his office and sat at his computer, surrounded by more walls of books and pictures. His spirits fell as he checked e-mail and the news. Then he checked his portfolio and cheered himself up. The joys of short selling never disappointed. It had taken him long enough to learn it after business school, but betting against the talent nearly always worked out well. In so many ways, his education had only begun five years ago when he left the street. And he was learning more with every case.

After a few hours, Troy shouted a farewell. McBain finished his sandwich and surfed through as many channels of sports as he could stand, and then he finally got around to the aspirin Boston had recommended and considered his options for the evening. With the Parker case closed, he could afford a little more relaxation on Saturday night. He was on his own, so the theater was out. The Sox had not started their season yet, and the Celtics and Bruins were out of town. The movies were all bad, and he wasn't the lecture type. There was always the old standby. He reached for the local guide to look up some music to go with his cocktail hour. The body was once again working its tragic healing power of forgetfulness. The weekend was still young, even if he didn't feel so.

By that evening, the weather had turned foul. McBain struggled against the driving wind and bone-chilling rain that pulled and wrenched at his umbrella like an angry spouse. He navigated around couples struggling down the wind tunnels of the South End, eyeing the brightly lit sign that swung in the wind outside the restaurant ahead that announced Holiday, beckoning him with the allure of a lighthouse across a raging sea. He forced his way through the door, shook off the drenched trench coat and soggy cap, and took up his corner seat at the bar. The room hummed softly to the engine of glass, ice, and conversation, with a side of Thelonious Monk provided by a piano and trumpet on a small raised platform by the street-side window.

McBain exhaled and relaxed. A couple of drinks and sets with no complications or disappointments would make for a nice, warm Saturday. The bartender slid his drink in front of him. He was settling into his chair and the martini glass was already to his lips when his eyes, lifting over the rim, chanced to fall upon the far end of the bar.

The woman was the most alluring creature he had seen in a long time. Her dark hair was pulled back to reveal steady, penetrating eyes that pored over the book in front of her. A shaft of white from the ceiling pin light fell onto a nearly empty martini glass that sat beside the book, brushed by the fingers of her right hand. Her left hand held a toothpick up to her mouth, the last of the olives captured lightly between her lips.

She appeared to be alone. For some reason, she reminded him of his ex. But that wasn't going to stop him.

McBain pushed back his full mane of hair and rubbed his unshaven chin for a moment, regretting the hangover-infested dash out the door that morning. After downing another ounce of courage, he could feel a force like the gravitational pull of Jupiter lifting him out of his seat and around the bar, almost against his will. So much for a quiet night.

In the time it took him to work his way through the crowd and around the bar, he drank in the sight of her like a tall glass of iced tea on a summer day. She was the definition of New England style and sophistication, the classy type that wouldn't be caught dead within a mile of a man like him. The red blazer followed the curves around her shoulders, chest, and waist like a Formula One track. A diamond pendant lay close to the collar of a white turtleneck. Her legs were folded under a black wool skirt that draped below her knees, touching the top of black leather, four-inch stiletto boots that were ready to step all over him on the way to the door if he wasn't careful. As he approached and eyed her studiously ignoring the men around her, he just knew that with her diamonds, looks, and brains, he was cruising for another night patching up a bruised ego.

But what the hell. If you're gonna strike out, better it be with a class act than some vacuous model wannabe. He slid in to the bar next to her seat and set his drink down.

"Not crowding you, am I?" he asked. When she turned her face up at him, he knew it wouldn't be the last stupid thing he would say that night. He had never seen eyes that were both intelligent and beautiful before. Their penetrating appraisal of him left him feeling a little unnerved as the silent seconds ticked by.

"It was a lot less crowded when you were sitting back in that corner chair," she said.

"Ah, I'm sure," he said. "But I couldn't help noticing your drink looks a little warm, even from there. Martinis should be drunk cold."

"And you would be the expert on that?"

He flashed a little charm. "I know a thing or two about it."

"You realize that normally such people are called alcoholics."

That wiped the smirk off his face. "Well, I didn't mean..."

She placed the olive back in her glass and took a drink. After a moment, she looked back at him. "Hmm, it seems you're right. I'm surprised a man your age has such good eyesight."

He was taking punches like an over-the-hill boxer up against a hungry youngster. He decided to play for time while he figured her out.

"My name's McBain, Boozy McBain. It's kind of a nickname my Wall Street friends gave me based on a consulting company by the name of Booz I used to work for."

"And my drink is warm," she said. "Did you come over to discuss literature, Mr. McBain, or mixology?"

"I thought maybe I could buy you a drink while you're waiting for whoever it is you're waiting for."

"Why do I have to be waiting for someone? Can't a woman enjoy a quiet drink, some jazz, and a book in a bar by herself? That seems a chauvinistic attitude."

At that moment the barman slid an icy cosmopolitan in front of her. McBain kept his irritation to himself.

"And as you can see, Michael takes care of me quite well," she said. "You might say I'm his number-one customer."

"And I thought I was."

"No. It's me."

She was a handful, all right—beauty, brains, and sass. Worst of all, she had that quality McBain disliked most in a woman: she was observant. All his senses told him to quit while he still had a shred of ego left. But then, his old man had said he never had shown much sense with women.

"So I guess that means you come in often?" he asked.

"Yet another original line," she said. "Better work on your repartee, Mr. McBain. You're running out of material."

"Sorry," he said. "Just that I come in here quite a bit myself, and I don't recall seeing you before tonight. And you're someone I'd remember. And considering you're customer number one—"

"Maybe you should be more observant."

She had a nice, steady manner of speaking that suggested she was a professor or, God help him, a lawyer. But the alluring siren of her voice, matched with that face and body, were beginning to put the hook into him even as she knocked him around. Never a winning combination.

"Mind if I ask your name?" McBain asked.

The woman took another drink as she shot him a deadpan look.

"And what do you do for a living, Mr. McBain?"

"You know you can call me Boozy."

"I don't think so," she said.

"I'm a cross between a private detective and an investment consultant. Sort of a financial troubleshooter, you might say."

"Probably more of a troublemaker, by the look of you."

"Coming from you, I'll take that as a compliment."

"I think you'd better," she said. "You're not likely to get another tonight."

This woman was really getting under his skin, but having thrown back too many martinis the previous night, McBain knew he was overmatched and in no shape to go many more rounds. He decided a tactical retreat was in order, checked his watch, and finished his drink.

"Well, on that note, it's been nice getting worked over by you. So long."

He was halfway to his corner chair when he glanced back over his shoulder. She was watching him, her face serene, lovely, and expressionless—except for those eyes.

They were laughing.

"See you next time, McBain." Her mouth turned up in a little smile as she returned to her book.

He nursed his ego and another martini, and immersed himself in the music, glancing from time to time up the bar to catch her eye. She never looked in his direction. For some reason, he felt all right with that. Sometimes a man just liked to enjoy a cold drink while someone else played the blues for a change.

THREE

The partners met Captain O'Daniel just outside Doyle's Cafe on Washington Street in Jamaica Plain. McBain wasn't really comfortable in Irish pubs. He had never found one that could make a decent martini. But Boston and her father loved this place, and whatever Tom O'Daniel wanted, he got. So instead of Hamersley's Bistro, they went to Doyle's.

"Hello, darlin'."

As usual, O'Daniel nearly crushed his hand when they shook, and he lifted his daughter off the ground with the other arm. At six foot six, he could have done the same with McBain, so he felt he was getting off easy with only a numb right arm. The captain may have been sixty, but he still had the energy of a linebacker and the hands of a blacksmith. His red hair was only now going gray, and his pockmarked face was still carved in stone, carrying the scars of his trade as a badge to go with his blues.

When the big man finally released his hand, McBain massaged it. "Hello to you too, sweetie."

Boston was almost a foot shorter than her dad, and she hugged his massive chest.

"I think he meant me, Boozy."

"I'll give you darlin', you shakedown artist," the police captain said. "Soon as you slap your cash on the bar."

McBain smirked. "As if you've ever bought a drink at Doyle's in your life. Let's go."

A few minutes later, they each had a Guinness in their hand and the warm glow of Jameson Irish Whiskey in their throat.

"Frank, one more time, and some menus!" O'Daniel said to the barman. "You're not too classy to eat at the bar, are ya', Boozy?"

McBain sat between them and looked around at his options. Polished wooden booths and checkered tablecloths were filled with locals, most of whom had the look of cops or firefighters themselves—off duty, of course. The walls were hung with the ghosts of Boston Democratic politicians and sports teams past, and the flat-screen TVs with the present. Doyle's was the real deal, with the history, bullet holes, and broken furniture to prove it, almost unknown to tourists and avoided by amateurs.

"'Course not, Tom. We all know Frank here has more class than me. Your daughter says I can drink martinis until they perforate my liver, and that won't change."

"My daughter is always right."

"Thanks, Dad."

They had another shot and ordered heavily, then swapped small talk and O'Daniel family gossip while they ate burgers, bangers, and mash. With the exception of potatoes and beer, vegetables were in short supply.

"So, how's business?" Captain O'Daniel asked. "I gather you two closed another case last week. Who'd you blackmail this time, or don't I want to know...as usual?" He chuckled.

His daughter gave him a little smile. "The guy who manages your pension money, Dad."

The captain's jaw dropped for a moment. "Why, you little...that's not funny. Better not be."

McBain chimed in between the last bites of his cheeseburger.

"So you really are talking about retiring? Come off it, Tom. You're too young to be thinking about that yet. How would Bureau of Investigative Services run without you? Besides, we might need your help again."

O'Daniel frowned as he eyed them. "Any more help for you two and I really might have to start worrying about my pension. Let's see, there was the first job three years ago when you were just getting going, that genius money manager with the sealed divorce court case. Then that master of the universe who couldn't trade his way out of a money market fund without losing his shirt. By rights, you never should have known about his scrubbed juvenile records."

Boston cut in: "Don't forget about the *shite* lawyer with the mansion up in Marblehead."

Her father drew on his beer. "I haven't. I should have put him in jail instead of giving him to you two. His victims may have gotten their money back, but he could still hurt other people. And I don't mean just financially; that guy is bent upstairs. I told you not to get too close to that one. I still think you got lucky he didn't flip out on you. You know, one of these days you're going to come across some real nasty type."

"We're very particular about our cases now, Tom," McBain said. "We'd never cross the line and put you on the spot. If any real trouble came up, we know our limits."

The captain's blue eyes drilled into him over the top of his glass until he put it down and lowered his voice.

"You of all people know that's not true. Sometimes we never know what we're capable of until it's right on top of us. Might be too late to back down, right or wrong. Events can take their own course and spin out of our control."

The investigator stiffened, sipped at his tumbler of whiskey, and set it back on the bar.

"So, we are who we are, huh? You don't think a man can change, learn from his mistakes?"

O'Daniel shrugged and looked around the bar. "Not that I've observed. But hey, who am I to say? I'm just a cop, not a shrink."

McBain nodded at the captain and played with his fork. After an uncomfortable pause, Boston broke the silence.

"That's my end of the business now, Dad. If anything like that happens, I'll be all over them. I've been aching to kick some ass and use some of this stuff. Brazilian jujitsu is my latest one."

Her father's face heated to match his hair color.

"And I keep telling you to stop taking all those classes. Your sisters and mother have just about had it with you muscling them around. And your cousin Timothy's arm will never be the same since you broke it practicing on him last Thanksgiving. I hear your girlfriends have given up on finding a man to set you up with. Why do you have to be so tough?"

She leaned across McBain and in on her father. "Because I'm a cop's daughter, and I'm not just going to know how to defend myself, but how to break bones and hurt people. Besides, what do I care what people think?"

The captain slammed his mug on the bar.

"I respect that you need to know how to defend yourself. But I didn't raise my girls to be street toughs. You're a lady, goddammit. Carry a nine millimeter like I taught you."

McBain pushed his partner back into her own chair and raised his voice to the bar. "Frank, another round for dessert.

"We're getting carried away here, guys," he said. "Tom, there's plenty of good business these days to keep us busy just straightening out scores for people who've been screwed by their broker or financial adviser or whoever. Especially people who had big money and just trusted somebody to do the right thing. If anybody started to get nasty, we'd come right to your boys. We can handle most of these financial crooks in our own style."

Captain O'Daniel grunted and jabbed his finger at them.

"Well, your style, as you call it, plays pretty fast and loose in the gray area of the law most of the time. You I don't care about, but I don't like you"—he eyed his daughter—"thinking you can make up your own rules to get your way."

Her temper flared again. "And where might I have learned that?"

Frank dropped off their drinks and retreated to the far end of the bar.

"Look, these characters are used to bullying and bullshitting people, Tom," McBain said, "and they do it for a living. Money is the air they breathe, and they don't give it back without a fight. They play a lot looser with the technicalities than she and I do, and they're always trying to blow smoke at our clients with what they think are complex explanations of how losing money wasn't their fault. You want to talk about finessing the law when it comes to separating customers from their cash? Some of them don't have an ethical bone in their body. And I'm not even talking about outright fraud, though there's plenty of that.

A lot of the time you have to motivate them to do the right thing. And if we end up helping people who have been basically robbed, isn't that a good thing?"

Tom O'Daniel was still in a staring contest with Boston as he answered.

"Yeah, isn't it the motivating part that worries me. From what I've seen, you stretch the meaning of the word robbery to its limits too. Rich people do stupid things with their money all the time, and they don't always need a lousy stock broker to lose it. And don't make yourselves out to be Robin Hood either, McBain. You make a nice buck on these deals."

"Better us than the lawyers," Boston said. "We get people their money back and offer them a better deal in the end, and they keep it quiet from the papers, their friends, and family. The only ones who get hurt are the people who deserve it."

O'Daniel shook his head and looked skyward. "Lord, if your mother could only hear you now. A redheaded daughter with a mean streak the size of the Charles is more than she deserves. Why couldn't you be a doctor like your sister?"

McBain pushed their shot glasses into their hands. "Because then she wouldn't be your favorite daughter and the woman we know and love. Here's to another successful, and safe, case closed. Bottoms up."

With the crack of the upside-down shot glass on wood, Boston excused herself, and McBain filled the captain in on the Parker case.

"So, Tom," he said as he finished up, "the investment company really was defrauding them. Not so much the company, but one of their top execs. He'd illegally moved their money around and into an account he'd set up for himself and stuffed them with some bad trades to make it look like their cash was lost in the market over time. It just would have taken a lot of time, money, and lawyers to prove. We took a shortcut when we found out Jackson was cheating on his wife with a pricey mistress. He gave us an opening, and we took it. We gave him an option, as they like to say in the investment business. And just maybe he'll think twice before he misplaces a customer's money again. I'll agree that sometimes our tactics are borderline questionable—"

"Borderline?"

"But they almost always get the right results. You know we don't just go after some money manager who had a bad year. Christ, your jail would be full."

"You're not convincing me, McBain. It only takes one mistake. You accuse the wrong guy or get caught turning the screws on somebody who snaps, you could be the one needing a good lawyer. And don't always count on me looking out for you."

"I won't, Tom. Just make sure you always look out for her."

The captain flashed a grin and a wink. "That I won't ever be retiring from."

McBain threw a bunch of twenties down on the bar as Boston returned.

"One more thing, Tom."

"Yeah?"

"Who is managing your pension money these days?"

Boston and McBain spent the rest of the day in the office going over their open cases and examining the three new leads that had been referred to them. Two of them looked promising.

"So which one do you want to go for first?" Boston asked across her desk. "The old-money philanthropist who says he was taken in by the so-called charity that wasn't so charitable with his money, or the actress who invested in the 'can't miss' derivatives fund that was guaranteed to earn double your money as the market fell? She's not too bright, but really cute. And really mad."

McBain was flopped on the couch enjoying his buzz, balancing the new cases against the others still to be finished. "Hmm, tempting. I like the idea of an angry drama queen going for the balls of the young investment genius. Don't you think she'll blow up on us first?"

She smiled. "You'd like that, wouldn't you? Break up your regular routine. I get enough drama with my own family, thanks. As you saw this afternoon."

He grimaced and adjusted a small pillow behind his head.

"Yeah, that was enough for a month of Sundays. You and Tom weren't always like that. When did that start?"

Boston remained focused on her computer. "He's feeling old with all this retirement talk. Plus he doesn't like me making mom angry 'cause she takes it out on him. And it upsets him, me taking all these street-fighting classes. Makes him feel like I'll never get married. And of course he does genuinely object to some of our methods."

McBain sat up and got his head on straight.

"It's one and the same. You heard him. He's just worried about one of the cases going south and having to bail you out of jail."

"You mean like the actress or the charity?" She toyed with her ruby pendant and laughed. "Hey, with millions of dollars at stake and people played for suckers, what could go wrong?"

"Exactly."

She scrolled down on her computer. "Anyway, I calculate that we've got room for two more at most until we finish up the ongoing investigations. So let's drop the third one as a low hit opportunity and stick with both of these."

"So they look like potential winners?"

"From what I've learned so far, they've got possibilities. And you heard dad. I'm just looking for someone to hit these days, anyway. Let's go for both of them and see what happens. I'll start with the bleeding heart; you start with the bleeding blonde."

McBain looked over at her, perched nonchalantly behind her desk like a bird of prey about to take flight. "Boston?"

"Yes, McBain."

"I just love you."

Her red hair and cheeks glowed back at him. "I know."

FOUR

April arrived a week later, and with it New England's annual fistfight between winter and spring. McBain strolled into Holiday at six o'clock sharp. The initial meeting with the actress had gone well, her case looking more promising than expected. At least it wasn't snowing again.

To his surprise, the class act from two weeks ago was there, sitting at the bar reading—in his corner chair. Her hair was down this time, framing her face as in a portrait, but he recognized her from the curves of her ivory sweater. Sober this time, McBain was itching for a rematch.

"I think you're in my seat, Ms...."

Her face turned up, and she looked up at him with those discerning eyes as if their last conversation had just ended.

"We discussed this last time, Mr. McBain. Who's customer number one?"

McBain pulled off his coat and settled into the chair next to her.

"For being number one, you certainly have been pretty scarce recently. Or maybe I've just been looking on the wrong nights. Mind if I sit down?"

"It's a public house," she replied.

"That's pretty funny," he said. "Wouldn't have pegged you as having a sense of humor, highbrow or otherwise."

"If that's your idea of highbrow humor, I'd better hold the Seven Sisters jokes to a minimum. Fortunately, your timing has improved. You've arrived in time to buy me that drink you owe me from two weeks ago."

Michael dropped off his own cocktail and grinned his wide grin. McBain took a long first sip and thought it over.

"Who says there wasn't an expiration date on that offer, Ms...."

"It'll cost you a drink, McBain."

"Michael, give customer numero uno another one of whatever she's having on me, would you?"

The investigator made a point of giving her an obvious once-over, from her black hair to stylish brown boots, and then settled in her eyes. Michael brought her a martini glass filled with the real thing. McBain liked that.

"Christina Baker," she said and extended her hand.

She had a firm, confident grasp. He liked her even more.

"Boozy McBain, at your service," he said, and took another sip.

"I'm happy to hear that, Mr. McBain, because that's exactly what I'd like to talk to you about."

"Come again?"

"Your service," she repeated. "I'd like to speak about hiring you."

McBain was mentally caught off balance for a moment.

"For what?" he said and laughed. But instinctively his stomach was already tightening in disappointment.

"You did say you were a private investigator in the financial business. 'Sort of a financial troubleshooter' I think were your exact words."

"Yes. So what?"

"Well, are you or aren't you? If you are, then I have trouble and can use some assistance and might like to hire you. If you were simply giving me a line as part of your not-so-subtle attempt to pick me up, you can find more room at the other end of the bar. I've had enough of liars."

McBain wanted to believe someone was playing a practical joke on him, but as he watched her produce a very full accordion folder from the large Louis Vuitton handbag hooked on her chair, his original optimism sank like a coin wasted in a wishing well.

Finally he sighed.

"I'm not a liar...Ms. Baker. At least not in this case. I do financial investigations for people. As it seems you confirmed since our last encounter."

"Yes, I know who you are," Ms. Baker said. "I did some investigating of my own and called around. Eventually I found a friend of a friend who had used your services to help her recover their funds. She was quite pleased that you had been able to help them in short order without any unfavorable publicity. You came highly recommended, though she did imply you were somewhat difficult to work with and unorthodox, whatever that means. But she said you got the job done. I have a similar problem I'd like your assistance with."

McBain continued to sip at his cocktail as he listened to his chances for an entertaining evening slip away. Now that she had a head of steam, Christina Baker was going to be difficult to derail. He tried to slow her down.

"Before you start telling me your problem, Ms. Baker, can I at least ease into the evening with my drink? It's after six, and I'm supposed to be off the clock. I just got here and started my cocktail hour. Can't we exchange small talk for a few minutes?"

She looked him up and down for a moment and then took a sip of her own.

"Fine, McBain," she said. "After our last meeting, I simply wanted to make sure I got your sober attention before you started slurring your words so you would at least remember the conversation tomorrow morning. You just let me know when you're reaching that point."

McBain took a belt, the heat rising in his face. The direct type—great. This was going to be a bigger challenge than he had anticipated.

"OK," he said. He put down his empty and waved Michael over. "We're on the express plan. You've got two martinis' worth of unpolluted attention. Shoot."

She placed her large envelope back on the bar and stared straight at him.

"My family has been robbed. I need you to help me get our money back."

McBain pushed some of his loose change toward her. "I know some cops who handle that stuff for free. Can't we just call them and get back to the small talk?"

She glanced at the change, then back at him.

"Are you going to listen? Or are you not interested in my business? Because so far, I'm not convinced you're worth as much as I heard you were paid."

McBain straightened his tie and smirked. "I'm worth every penny, sister. Look, I'm just trying to save you money. I'm happy to listen to your problems, but I'm guessing the police would be better suited to dealing with it." He was going to make it as tough as possible. "Please, go on. I won't interrupt again."

"I doubt that. You seem quite taken with your own wit."

"Please? I swear I'll at least listen to your whole story before commenting," he said, and put a smile on his face.

She looked skeptical but continued.

"I live in the city but grew up in Brookline. My parents have...had a house there where I was raised. They lived their entire lives in this area. They passed away about six months ago in an accident."

"I'm very sorry to hear that."

She paused to take a breath and a drink.

"Thank you. They were wonderful people, and it never should have happened the way it did. It shouldn't have happened at all. We couldn't understand it, really. At least not until the reading of the will."

Her rhythmic voice had a certain struggling quality to it. She was proceeding tentatively, and McBain sipped quietly as he let her go on at her own pace. She seemed hesitant now that it came to it.

"I should explain that," she said more firmly. "I'm an only child, Mr. McBain. My parents and I were very close. We did so many things together: holidays, birthdays, anniversaries of all sorts. We spoke every week, sometimes a couple of times. They had always been forthright with me about their affairs, their long-term plans and such, retirement—you know, things like that. It was all very abstract and distant, of course. They were in good health, and we didn't expect to have to face anything like this for decades. I certainly didn't imagine losing both of them at once."

McBain admired the way she was forcing her way through. He had been right: tough old New England stock.

"Well, I was quite familiar with their finances and plans. Or at least I thought I was. My parents had arranged their financial affairs so that everything was in trust—all their savings, their investments for me and their grandchildren someday—so that the money could accumulate and grow until it was needed. They had started a few years ago, and when we last discussed it, the money was growing into a nice amount. Then, when the will was read and the portfolio examined, it turned out there was almost nothing there. The investments were just a fraction of what they were supposed to have been only the year before.

"What's more, when I confronted him about it, the investment advisor my parents had been using for the past few years lied to my face about what happened. He said they made risky investments with the money. My parents would never have done that. I may not know much about the investment business, but I knew my parents. They were very conservative people with a puritan ethic. They worked hard for their money and would not have risked it that way. They always said it was too important for the future of their grandchildren, and they'd rather be safe than sorry.

"I don't know what happened, but I know their financial advisor had something to do with it. He robbed them somehow. I don't know what it was, bad advice or commissions or something, but I know it was him. They trusted him completely with their investments.

"It was very clear to us after we saw the will and the amount of their money that had been lost. When my parents found out he had stolen their money, they must have been devastated. They had saved their whole lives building that nest egg for their retirement and for our future. They simply couldn't take it. That so-called financial advisor is the reason they're gone. He's the reason they're dead."

McBain took another slow sip of his martini. It was always a good idea to keep his mouth busy while his brain sorted out the smart from the stupid before he opened it. Managing this situation in his direction wasn't going to be easy.

As her voice gained speed and rose, McBain took in her face. He knew that look; he had seen it often enough. There were no tears. Those were hard eyes, revenge eyes.

"I want you to get him, McBain," she said. "I don't know how he did it, but he stole everything from them. I want you to find out how and get the money back and send him to jail."

The one thing that McBain tried to get out of his head was: cocktail hour isn't supposed to work like this. Cocktail hour is supposed to allow you to wind down from a long day of wading through the human garbage, enjoy any number of drinks to help ease out of the tension, and with some luck pick up a beautiful, dark-haired stranger and take her home to your stylishly decorated apartment for the night.

"I'm very sorry about your parents, Ms. Baker."

"You said that already."

"Yes, well, it sounds to me like something happened to your parents' money; that's beyond dispute. You'll forgive me if I'm frank?"

She sat back in her seat and crossed her arms over her chest.

"Ms. Baker," McBain said, "surely you know what has happened in the markets over the past couple years. Has it occurred to you that just maybe this lost money could be a result of bad investment management by this financial advisor? I've seen lots of people lose their shirts through sheer stupidity, and believe me, most of the geniuses managing money aren't as smart as they think they are, even when they're not staring at a once-in-a-lifetime disaster. So combine that with some account churning—that is, making lots of trades to get commissions—and you'd be surprised how fast a large fortune can turn into a small fortune, and then an empty account. And it doesn't even have to be criminal activity. That's the sad reality many people found out in the past few years. Rich, retired, middle class, you name it.

"Second, you just told me yourself that your parents worked with and trusted this guy for years. And that you talked with them all the time. And yet you didn't know until the funeral that the account had lost its value. That doesn't make sense to me. If your parents thought this guy was robbing them, they certainly would have told you, or somebody, about it."

She objected. "I told you, McBain, they must have been too humiliated and destroyed by the loss..."

"Yeah, you said that, but I still think as close as you were, you would have heard something or picked up a tension, from them or a friend of theirs. And you said nothing about that. So I'm guessing that it was a gradual loss that had more to do with the market or bad stock picks than anything criminal.

"And third," he continued as she opened her mouth, "if this was some kind of real criminal fraud, you'd do much better reporting this man to the securities authorities than coming to me. Believe you me, those guys at the Boston SEC are doing a booming business these days and are in their glory. They love to hold press conferences with the word 'fraud' up in lights. And if you talked to someone about me, you know one other thing: I don't send people to jail. If that's what you really want, I think the feds are your best bet."

She turned back to the bar and looked straight ahead. "So you won't help me? Or are you saying you don't believe me?"

McBain knew he had to tread carefully at this point. So he took another sip of clever.

"I'm not saying either," he answered. "What I'm saying to you is that I've been through a couple of market meltdowns and researched dozens more. I'm telling you the odds of it actually being what you suspect. I'm telling you that it's unlikely. I'm trying to save you time and money when the most likely explanation is the simplest one. Look, our book is pretty full right now with four other things we're working on. And to get down to those four, my partner and I looked through dozens of other requests like yours that are just the result of bad decisions on someone's part. I know you're angry and upset and a lot of other things, but I'll tell you right now I don't think you have a case."

Ms. Baker remained silent, but it was clear from her expression she was struggling with her emotions. He could tell it must have taken a lot for her to approach him.

"Well," she said, then paused. She straightened and pulled the folder closer to her. "Well, McBain, I appreciate your listening to my—"

"But..." He slapped one hand on the folder, raised his martini glass, and tipped it her way.

"But?"

"All right, listen," McBain said. "I don't have much time, but as a favor—not as a client, but as a favor—to a fellow martini lover, I'll look at your file and do a little research at no charge. Especially since from the look of that thing, you already did lots of the heavy lifting. It's a lot of money to lose, so if there is anything in that file to suggest what you suspect is true, I'll poke around, ask a few questions, and determine whether you have any grounds to proceed. If you do, I'll take the case. Of course, then you have to realize we're talking about one chance in ten that we can actually prove anything or that you'll ever see that money again."

She finished her drink, rose from her seat, and extended her hand again. He stood up.

"I suppose that's all I can ask," she said as they shook. "My mobile phone number is in the file. Please call me when you've had a chance to find out anything. Good-bye. And thank you."

"See you around, Ms. Baker," he said and flashed a grin.

Her mouth almost gave him a smile back, and then she let go of his hand and left.

McBain cursed his luck and began to scheme as he ordered another martini. He would look into her case, all right. He would look into this case and find nothing to it as quickly as possible. There was no way in hell he was going to let this woman be a client.

FIVE

McBain was having a pretty good week. The actress was turning out to be an attractive client in more ways than one, though he was never really tempted. Drama in clients wasn't his cup of tea. Based on what he'd found out so far, Boston's instincts had been right—as usual. It had required very little digging to determine that she had been ripped off, and from what he had discovered about the young broker who put her into the investment, he wouldn't have to work too hard to put the screws to him or his firm for a sizeable refund. And commission.

During the day, he worked diligently to follow the threads on the case and research the personal and professional background of the whiz kid while finishing off his part of the two remaining investigations. Those only needed a couple of brainstorming sessions between him and Boston to decide when and how to bring the pressure to bear, and they too would be wrapped up neatly.

McBain had to work almost as hard to keep his partner from finding out about his moonlighting as he began to look through Christina Baker's file and do some homework on his nonclient without her knowledge. Boston was suspicious by nature, and he was such a creature of habit that anything out of the ordinary would tip her off. If she tumbled to the fact that he was using his time to "investigate" a case he never intended to take just for the sake of...well, he had seen her temper before.

As that was only a matter of time, he spent as many free hours as he could reading through the fat file at night. McBain kept the material in his apartment to avoid detection. As he made his way through the contents on Friday after work, he went through the motions of taking notes for future reference. If he was going to turn Ms. Baker down—and he was—it was going to have to be convincing.

Based on what he had read so far, it wouldn't be that tough an act.

The woman's parents had died about six months before. According to the doctor's report in the file, it was to all appearances a dual suicide. Ms. Baker had left that part out of her accident story. Understandable. They had been found together at home on the living room sofa in the morning by a housekeeper. The medical report confirmed the cause to be an overdose of alcohol and a mixture of drugs. There seemed little likelihood of an accident, especially as the couple had been found in each other's arms.

A casual perusal of the financial statements confirmed some of Ms. Baker's story. McBain thought of the old joke about getting a small fortune—by starting with a large fortune. Except this wasn't funny. Fifteen million dollars frittered away over the course of a couple years to almost nothing. He sympathized with the couple. He'd been on the receiving end of that kind of news himself, thanks to his ex-wife. But he had been young enough to start over. At their age, he was becoming convinced that their daughter was right. Getting the bad news would have been enough of a trigger to put him over the edge too. Hell, he had danced at the edge already.

The question, as always, was where the money had gone. Given the lousy and volatile markets over the past few years, it wasn't easy to tell right away why the account had lost value. Sometimes it looked steady, sometimes the balance had dipped, sometimes gained. A lot depended on where the money was invested during any given market move. There were stocks, bonds, mutual funds, ETFs, even options and futures accounts.

Another big question was: who was making the decisions for the account? Given the obscure nature of some of the investments, McBain doubted that the parents would have known how to even find them. They were college professors. The mother, a WASPY type, had inherited a sum from her side that they had used to build on. The father had published some kind of academic books. From Christina Baker's description, her parents had trusted this guy implicitly, so in all likelihood he had been calling all the plays.

McBain put down his wine and looked for one of the recent agreements—Richard Roche.

Ultimately, it seemed the bottom had fallen out with a vengeance as the market collapsed. It must have come as an ugly shock to the older couple when they'd seen the final numbers, and the notion had sunk in that it wasn't coming back anytime soon, if ever. That was not the kind of blow everyone could take. She was right; it had destroyed them along with their hopes for the future.

But that didn't mean they had been robbed. It just put them in good company. As McBain went back over the various investments in the statements, it wasn't clear that what had happened to the couple wasn't the same cataclysm that had destroyed millions of other portfolios. There were some curious choices there, to be sure, some obscure trading vehicles or options or futures, but there were also fairly normal and conservative choices. Or choices that might have been considered reasonably conservative in normal times by any other person managing money by the old rules. In that case, Mr. Roche was only another average incompetent, sticking his clients in the right places at the wrong time. Nothing criminal about stupidity, as Tom O'Daniel would have said. Maybe a little aggressive for an older couple, but who knew what the real story was there, despite Ms. Baker's protests. What went on between an investment advisor and his wealthy clients was their business.

It also wasn't obvious that he had raped them on commissions, which was always an interesting red flag and a less obvious way to fleece the sheep. A lot of those records were missing, but it appeared from some of the documentation that they had operated under a fee arrangement, so it would take some time to decipher who paid for what when.

As to his nonclient's argument that her conservative parents would never have agreed to some of the risky choices their advisor made, the file contained nothing that would confirm this one way or another. Presumably there was some documentation somewhere that delegated such choices to him. Every piece of legal paperwork he could find confirmed that the Bakers had given Roche all the power he needed to make the ultimate decisions on investments, using his own judgment. Sure enough, there were the authorizations for discretionary investing. The signatures of both Mr. and Mrs. Baker were pretty clear on all of the forms and matched their other documents. Mrs. Baker had signed the last two about a month before their deaths.

The files went back about five years, and like most accounts showed a pretty nice profit for the first three years. That was his first yellow flag. Ms. Baker had organized the statements chronologically, and Mr. Roche had been thoughtful enough to provide his clients with his very impressive performance numbers each quarter and year. A little too impressive, though nothing Ponzi scale. McBain may have spent much of the past five years in a stupor, but there was a part of his brain that knew the returns of every type of asset known to economic man during that time. And unless this guy was another Peter Lynch, his numbers looked a little better than they should have. Probably explainable. He'd dig into some of the investment picks over the weekend.

More return equaled more risk; that was for sure. But unless he had access to some kind of agreement governing the risks the guy was allowed to take, the investments he was allowed to put their money in or any guidance, all he had was Christina Baker's word that her folks were the careful puritans she had painted them to be. And the investigator didn't see many treasury bonds or CDs in the mix. By the time he finished the file, McBain concluded that with the encouragement of their advisor, they had agreed to swing for the fences when the market looked invincible and got caught unawares and unprepared for the collapse. It was the rare money manager indeed who didn't mistake the market for his own talent. More than a few had doubled down assuming it was a great buying opportunity and lost it all in the meltdown.

McBain scribbled away over his zinfandel. He was quite comfortable with his plan to report back to Christina Baker in the next week that, sorry as he was to have to say it, there really was no basis for her suspicions.

In some ways, his job was much easier without clients who were still breathing. McBain would finish up the noncase with a little research on some of the investments, then a cursory checkup on Roche himself. Then he could focus on delivering the news to her in a manner that reflected most favorably on himself.

He woke up Saturday in a pretty good mood for a change and hit the Sports Club/LA early before he settled in for his research. Come Monday he would check out Mr. Roche with some of his contacts, but for now he'd let his fingers do the walking.

Predictably, the financial advisor wasn't exactly the talk of the town on the Internet. Roche pitched himself as an old-school professional to wealthy clients who would be looking for something tony and exclusive. As part of his cachet, and because he was successful enough, he worked alone rather than for some large investment firm. He would be one of those who consciously avoided having his name bandied about the web. McBain smiled at the coincidence. Unlike McBain, however, he did appear in some of the high-society references, a man with all the right social credentials.

Roche was somewhere on the far side of sixty, having graduated from Princeton and Columbia and gone into the business right after college. He had the usual track record at the typical firms where you punched your ticket to build a resume in investment management, but he had set up his shingle in Boston from New York some years before and begun to pitch his services to high-net-worth individuals. The timeline was a little spotty, with gaps here and there, but unemployment was a given for job hoppers. There wasn't much out there about the man's personal life outside of the social scene, no mention of wife and kids. Also no traces of family money, though Ivy League degrees didn't grow on trees.

McBain made a note of questions to call Ms. Baker about later in the day, including a description of the man, along with any information she might have about hangouts, fancy clubs, golf memberships, and such. It wouldn't hurt to try to see if he was living beyond his means, but the investigator was pretty confident, based on what little he had seen, that this guy had plenty of means already. Besides, he wanted to let her know he was working hard on her behalf, diligently tracking down the scoundrel who had ripped her off.

In the stream of Monday-morning commuters filing through the streets of the Financial District, the memories came flooding back. New York had been much worse, of course, but a couple years outside the mines had created an aversion to rush hour of any kind. McBain emerged from South Station into the bright April sunrise, floating along with the crowd to pay his first visit of the day. To his right, the Federal Reserve Bank of Boston rose up across the street on Atlantic Avenue, an eerie, futuristic building looming on the edge of the maze of brokers, mutual funds, banks, insurance firms, venture capitalists, and hedge funds that pumped the lifeblood through much of the financial world outside New York. Like some kind of Transformer, it stood ready to come to life and crush everything in its path.

He crossed Atlantic on Congress Street and made his way through Post Office Square and into the canyons to Arch Street and the offices of the Securities and Exchange Commission.

McBain checked in with security, got his pass, and made his way up to the twenty-third floor. At the back of the crowded elevator, he straightened his rep tie and brushed some lint off the shoulder of his gray pinstripe. There was a receptionist expecting him just outside the elevators.

"Mr. McBain to see Dave Thomas," he said.

The money cops of the Enforcement Division of the SEC hovered behind a bank of windows looking out over the Financial District. Dave Thomas had ten sleuths reporting to him and a nice corner office to help monitor the firms in the region.

"A little early for you to be up on a Monday, isn't it, McBain?"

The office was well organized, with the overflow of Iron Mountain file boxes stacked neatly under Thomas's raised feet or under a table away from the windows. Dave Thomas was less organized. The regulator had refined the rumpled look and boring demeanor to a T. Even to start the week, his tie was loose and beige shirt wrinkled. He needed a haircut badly and a workout more. Horn-rimmed glasses slid down his nose and showed off the premature worry lines around his eyes.

"Look at you," McBain said. "Surprised you even bother coming in yourself, Mr. Boss Man. With all these underlings you've got, you should be going on junkets to the Caribbean, wasting the taxpayers' money."

Thomas's face lit up like the man in the full moon. "Just making sure a couple of the new ones get properly trained and learn to be afraid of me first. Plus there's a new political appointee coming in as head of enforcement in a couple weeks. I've got to bring her up to speed and get her comfortable in the job. Then I'll be off with rod and reel. Working remotely, of course. Lots of crooks still out there to prosecute."

"Don't I know it."

"Which I guess is behind your special Monday-morning house call."

"Nah. I just wanted to put on a suit and tie and pretend for a while." Thomas nodded his head out the window.

"Pretend what? Every time I talk to you, I always get reminded how you hated that routine."

"Not that. Pretend I'm a legitimate fed snoop catching financial crooks like Madoff and sending them to prison for life."

Thomas frowned at him. "Saying that name out loud here isn't going to win you any friends," he said. "Better close the door."

McBain did, then lifted his grocery bag and pulled out the coffee and bagels.

"Hopefully these will," he said. "Just like your deli used to make. Fresh from that bakery you love in the South End. I remembered how bad your coffee was here."

Thomas took his feet off the boxes, and they got to work on the bagels and cream cheese.

"Now I know you're after something. OK, let's have it while we eat. I've got a meeting at nine."

"Fair enough. I'll give you one, and I've got a couple questions on new ones."

McBain filled the regulator in on the actress who got played and the Parker case.

"The Parkers are satisfied with the settlement, so you don't have to bother with this one."

"But you're telling me because..."

"Partly because I took a real dislike to Jackson," McBain said. "But mostly because I don't trust him to learn from his experience."

Dave talked with his mouth full.

"You think he'll try to make up his lost fortune somewhere else?"

"I like the way you think, Dave."

"You think just like I do."

McBain just smiled. "If I had half your brains, I'd be rich. Pity those poor suckers who sit down across from you and smirk at your round, innocent face and off-the-rack suit. Oh, to be a fly on the wall when you start explaining the flaws in their financial models to them."

"But you were rich."

"Thanks for reminding me."

"Sorry, man," Thomas said. "Just bad luck on your part. You'll get it back."

McBain jammed his thumb toward the window.

"With their help, you bet I will," he said. "Speaking of which, before I go, I've got another one you might be able to help me with." He had some coffee and shrugged. "Probably nothing to it, but I'm checking into it to ease the mind of a friend of mine."

"What's her name?"

"I'm getting that predictable, huh?"

"Shoot."

McBain took out his notes and handed a page to Thomas. "Here's the guy's name."

"Roach? Really?"

"I think he probably uses the French pronunciation, but go with it," McBain replied. "From what I found out over the weekend, he manages money for high-net-worth individuals."

"Oh, them again."

"Pretty exclusive and low profile. Works on his own, but I'm sure he has a license. Credentials tick all the right boxes, as if that means anything. Hangs out with the right people, mostly old money I'm guessing, but who knows."

"What's your take so far? What do your instincts say?"

McBain had to think that one over.

"My friend thinks he's dishonest. I think he was just incompetent, like the rest of them. But she lost a lot of money, so you can guess how she feels."

"What do you know about that part?" Thomas asked.

"She had a pretty thick file of statements and other documents. I looked at the track record on the account. Nothing stands out except maybe he looked a little too good during the fat years. I haven't finished all the forensic work yet, but I'll know more once I follow the big losses and see where they lead."

Thomas looked at his watch and finished his coffee. "What does Boston say?"

McBain suppressed his smile behind a drag from his cup.

The regulator shook his head.

"I'll make sure I don't call the office on this one."

He stood up and they shook.

"I don't recognize the name off the top of my head, so he probably doesn't have a history with us. I'll have one of the minions do some checking. Give me a chance to see the quality of his work."

"Thanks, Dave. As always, I owe you."

McBain stayed in town the rest of the morning, making some house calls on his friends at brokerage houses and banks to check out the broker who had ripped off his actress client. Dave Thomas had given him some insight into the firm where the kid worked, jogging the investigator's memory about their track record before he had arrived in Boston. His strategy for bringing that case to the table was beginning to become clear already, and it wouldn't take much time.

By one he was ready for lunch. He met Dee Dee Franklin by the burrito cart on Washington Street, not far from the *Boston Business Journal*'s office. More than an editor and columnist at the paper, Dee

Dee was their resident encyclopedia. McBain considered the Internet a second-rate desk reference compared with Dee Dee's memory. She had worked her way up from the projects in Dorchester to become one of the most successful unknown African American women in the world of business news.

"You really know the way to a woman's heart, McBain," she said after the first bite. She was careful to hold the tin-foil wrapper away from her crisp red blazer and white blouse.

They sat on a slab of concrete near Macy's and enjoyed the taste of hot sauce and spring. The aromas from the food carts filled the air like a culinary UN.

"Well, Dee," he said, "most of my dates don't have the good taste for value you do. If I could find the woman who enjoyed a burrito like this over an expensive dinner, I'd keep her. How's the family?"

"Pretty good. Big one's been accepted to Bentley in the fall," she said. "He wants to be an investment banker."

"Sorry to hear that. But he's a good kid and smart. The business needs more like him. Put me out of business in no time."

"That'll be the day. What do you have for me this time?"

McBain fished out his notebook and went through the two cases they were wrapping up and the actress.

Franklin shook her head. "It's amazing how they just keep coming. Good times and bad, up market and down. Some of these guys aren't satisfied with a good six-figure salary and secure job. They just have to take more. I guess they can't help themselves."

"Yea, go figure. But when the only product in the factory is money, the temptations are just too much for a lot of them. That's how they keep score. Anyway, here are the facts on the first two for your files. They're just about put to bed. Boston and I will wrap them up in the next couple weeks. She is looking into another one, the kind you really hate."

"Charity scam?"

"Exactly. And this one with the actress and the derivatives fund shouldn't be too big a deal. But it's Drysdale Securities again."

"Not again. What is it with those guys? Don't tell me: another young, good-looking salesman and a cute girl with some money to burn."

McBain finished his chicken burrito and washed it down with water.

"Of course. More money than brains, same old story. I may be able to talk to their chief investment officer and get a refund pretty quickly after I show him what I've got. Otherwise, I may need to let your name drop, OK?"

Franklin's name and influence in the investment community was one of the most powerful tricks in McBain's magic bag. Most crooks making a living off their name and reputation were willing to do anything to keep them out of print. Even if the young broker didn't appreciate it, his boss would.

"Not a problem," Dee Dee said. "With Drysdale's track record of filings over the years, I'm betting they'd do almost anything to keep from showing up in my columns again."

"I appreciate it," he said. He handed her another page from the notebook.

She brushed off her jacket and read: "Richard Roche. Who's this one connected to?"

"He's new. Probably nothing, but I'm checking him out for a friend who lost some money. Seems to keep a pretty low profile and mix with high society. Good reputation among the old-money set, but I couldn't really find out much online or asking around."

"Pretty boy?"

"Well, if you like the sixty-year-old Robert Wagner look, maybe. Not my type."

Dee laughed. "May be mine. I could use a rich husband to put these boys through college. All right, I'll see what I can find out."

"Thanks, Dee," he said. "I'll be buying you burritos all summer. Let me know when you've got something."

"Sure, McBain."

"Oh, and Dee?"

"Yes."

"Don't call the office on this one..."

SIX

cBain called Christina Baker and asked her to meet him at the usual spot that Thursday. Over the next two days, he finished up his examination of her file in connection with his Internet research and typed up a quick summary of the conclusions to hand to her. By late Wednesday, Dave Thomas and Dee Franklin had both checked in to report they had come up empty. He was pretty confident his cursory "investigation" would support his findings to Ms. Baker well enough. The challenge was how to frame the disappointing news in a more favorable light.

With one eye on his partner, in between phone calls he worked out the best way to present the bad tidings and was still thinking through the all-important delivery as he strolled to Holiday that cool April evening after work. He had hurried home to put on one of his finest blue Armani pinstripes for the occasion, with a burgundy Hermes tie to highlight his white shirt and matching smile. Boston was still at the office finishing up some work, and he had promised to help with the filings that would close off their two ongoing investigations by the following week. But he didn't plan on being in the office too early on Friday morning.

The restaurant was relatively crowded and filling up, but there was still room at the bar to talk in private. While he was waiting, McBain slipped the piano player a twenty along with a request for some soothing, romantic jazz selections. As expected, the punctual and lovely Ms. Baker arrived on time. Her hair was pulled back, and she wore a conservative gray wool suit that fit her like a glove, her neck draped with a silk scarf and her ears adorned with delicate diamond earrings that punctuated her style like exclamation points.

He helped her out of her coat. "You look exquisite."

"Thank you, McBain," she said with a slight upturn of her lips. "I just came from a book auction for some rare volumes. I don't usually dress this way at my shop. You're looking surprisingly respectable this evening. Almost like a banker."

He waved to Michael. "Thank you, I think. Didn't think I had it in me, did you? Your shop? I'm sorry, I didn't even ask what you did for a living last time we met."

She produced an elegant bone-white business card from her jacket. He took the card and smiled as he read it.

Ivy Covered Tomes, Christina Baker, Proprietress.

"A bookstore. I might have guessed," he said as he pocketed the card.

"Or you might have done some investigating," she said. "However, I'm so very glad you haven't been wasting your time checking into my background. I hope you have been more diligent with my case and the file I gave you. I gathered from your call that you've found something. That was rather faster than I'd expected."

He eased into his chair and martini.

"Well, like I said, we're pretty busy these days. But since you're a special favor to a fellow customer, I put all my extra time into looking over your file and doing some research. Also called in a couple favors from some people who were able to check into your guy to see about him. I know some folks on the more official side of fraud investigation and with the feds, not to mention quite a few in the business of managing money. I've spent the better part of the last week and weekend investigating Mr. Roche, digging up everything I could find on him either online, in the business library or news archives, or through people who know about these things. I've also been trying to piece together the financial trail from your parents' investment records, statements, and the account documentation you gave me."

Ms. Baker absorbed all this with a soft and steady gaze as she nursed her own drink. If she was eager or anxious to hear his report, it was not evident in her manner. Every bit the unflappable New Englander, she listened patiently and awaited the verdict.

"As far as the investments themselves went, I looked over the types of securities this guy had your parents in—you know, stocks and bonds and such. The idea is to build a kind of paper trail of how the investments in their statements did over time and match it up against what the market did overall. You gave me a pretty well-organized path going back five years, but I had to put in some heavy-duty searching to rebuild a map of how he should have done versus how he did. This is including the fees he charged and trading commissions, as well as how often he was trading. You with me so far?"

She nodded her head. "Yes, please go on."

"By comparing the record of the investments on your parents' statements against the actual verifiable track record of those types of securities over time, we are able to see if anything unusual sticks out in any of the transactions. You know, like if money was siphoned off or deliberately placed into losers instead of winners. Or if the account should have been gaining value when in fact it was losing money. It's also helpful to compare his performance with other, well-known money managers just as a benchmark, though results are often all over the place.

"Given what you told me about your parents' style, I also wanted to see how aggressive he had been over the years with their money, especially when the market was real hot just before it tipped over the cliff.

"I also needed to see what kind of documentation there was that allowed Roche to make these investments and what kind of authority—or discretion, as we say—he was given to pick and choose where to put their money."

"And what are your conclusions based on all this?" she asked.

"In your folder I found some documents that indicated that he had a great amount of latitude in where he could invest your parents' funds. The signatures appeared to match those you provided for both of your parents. What I couldn't find was an agreement that would guide what kind of approach he should have taken and what his limits were. In other words, was Roche supposed to restrict himself to the conservative investments you say your folks would have preferred, or was he allowed to get aggressive? In most large investment firms, this is standard documentation and required by the executive who opens the account. In this case, given that Roche seems to have operated independently, it may have been more informal."

"So you didn't see anything that would have given him permission to take a lot of risk with their money?" she asked.

"No, but so far that doesn't mean much here. After looking through the portfolio and the types of things he bought over the years, there was no conclusive evidence that he took too much risk. Sure, I saw some unexpected things that a conservative advisor shouldn't be putting a senior citizen in—"

"Doesn't that prove anything to you?"

"No, because I also saw plenty of indications that he had them in good old American blue chips much of the time," he said.

"I just don't understand. Then how could they have lost so much money?"

McBain took a sip for dramatic effect. "One word."

"What do you mean 'one word'?" she asked.

"The most terrible word in the English language—margin."

"What?"

McBain pulled out the summary of his investigation from his briefcase, turned it over, and began to sketch some numbers on the blank side.

"In a nutshell, this is what seems to have happened," he said. "Things were going pretty good in the market for a while. From what I can see by his performance, it looks to me like Roche impressed your parents with his results so much that he must have persuaded them to supercharge their money. In effect, after a while, he began to use borrowed money to multiply the positive effects of their good investments."

Her eyes were saucers. "But why would he do that?"

"My guess: because a lot of other people were doing it, and with the market going gangbusters, it seemed like a safe bet. And that's just what it was, a bet. A gamble that a lot of supposedly smart people took that the party was never going to end. Your parents probably looked at how well their money had done for the first couple years under this guy and decided they could really move up the time frame for retirement and the size of your future trust fund while things looked good. Since they were still a little far from retirement, it may have seemed like a risk worth taking in order to strike gold while the market was hot.

"And there is one other thing. The account agreement states that Mr. Roche was paid a fee in terms of a percentage of assets. That means the more the account was worth, the more he got paid. So it was in his interest to see the value of the account go up faster."

Her first drink went down very fast.

"But...but how could it all have vanished?" she asked. "If you say there were good investments, and the account kept going up..."

McBain kept sketching out the figures. "Here's the thing most people, even some professionals, don't appreciate. Margin is a wonderful thing—when the market is going up. When the market goes down, it's like a great relationship turned ugly. And when the market collapses in a matter of months, unless an investor is very alert and disciplined, it is merciless. Because you have essentially borrowed money you don't have from the house to gamble, and that money has to be repaid. Even worse, some investors aren't experienced enough to know when to cut their losses and run. They look at big drops as an opportunity to buy more, like a Vegas player doubling down to make back his money. Over the long term, that often works if you're dealing with non-margin accounts and can afford to be patient. But with market crashes like the one we went through, it's a siren song to disaster. You end up buying and watching it go lower and lower until there's nothing left but debt."

While he was talking, he drew a zigzagging line heading down at an angle and then drew it straight down. He pointed to the figures with his pen.

"To be plain, here is the account's original investment amount. Now add this borrowed amount, and it looks good. But the money was borrowed to double the bets on good stocks, not to mention some of the leveraged exchange-traded funds he had your parents invested in. Now, those are a kind of mutual fund that many traders use to make money fast. They're inappropriate for most non-professional investors, that is true. And they accelerated the losses. But they aren't illegal.

"The punch line, I'm afraid, is that Mr. Roche may be stupid and incompetent, but he didn't steal your money."

McBain put his pen down on the bar and took up his drink. He felt the warm satisfaction of a lawyer who has just put forward an impenetrable closing argument. He watched as Michael returned with Ms. Baker's second martini. It was hard news, and he wouldn't be surprised if she needed a couple more stiff belts to handle the disappointment, along with a strong shoulder and sympathetic ear. He had felt the same way when his ex had cleaned him out with her lawyer. He waited and watched Christina's face to try to determine how difficult it would be for her to accept the news. She had suppressed her initial amazement and now showed little outward sign of distress. Her eyes were thoughtful, her face almost calm in demeanor.

He was surprised. He hadn't expected any tears. But despite her upbringing, the pent-up thirst for revenge he had detected in her eyes the previous week had suggested a deep-felt desire for retribution.

She finally spoke: "I disagree."

McBain had been prepared for her to argue back, question his conclusions. But there was nothing but certainty in her tone.

He nodded. "I know how you feel, Ms. Baker...Christina. I was hoping to find something, anything in my investigation to suggest there was some line worth pursuing, some indication that this slime ball had lured your folks into any kind of Ponzi scheme or fast-buck shakedown. I really did consider every angle that I've ever encountered in the business. But what I've laid out for you is the facts as best I can determine them. I know it's difficult to accept, but I can't honestly recommend you pursue this any further. I would just be wasting your money. Based on my long experience, it's best to come to terms with the loss and move on. I can assure you that millions of people have had to make the same hard decision over the past year or two."

"I don't believe this," she said. "There must be something in there. He must have done something to persuade them to borrow this money. It just wasn't their way to take those kinds of risks."

He pulled his chair closer and lifted a glass to her, lowering his voice and looking her in the face. The music he had requested began playing right on time.

"It's a blow, I know. Both in terms of your own future and especially in connection with this terrible tragedy that you've faced with your parents' death. And you may be right. The stress of this discovery might have been the trigger for their actions. But you're young and beautiful, with your own business and a lifetime ahead of you to recover. You have to focus on what you can control now and not let this become an obsession."

An icy determination and growing resolve were written on her face.

"You didn't know my parents, McBain," she said. "Something just isn't right about what happened. There has to be something else that wasn't in the file."

He reached out his hand and put it on top of hers. "Look, I wasn't going to mention this before, but I see how hard this is for you to accept. I've been in exactly the same boat as you, Christina. I've had my savings wiped out too by a seemingly avoidable series of decisions, and had to face the future and start over. It was a horrible period in my life, and every day was difficult to get through. In the end, I found it was helpful to focus on other things. Try to take my mind off it one day at a time."

She took her hand out from under his and lifted her glass.

"You're wrong, McBain," she said. "I don't believe this was simply an unfortunate case of bad investment advice. Surely there must be something else that can be looked into. I just know there's something improper about this."

McBain shrugged and frowned sympathetically.

"I agree. It just isn't right," he said. "And I'm sure what this guy did might not have been ethical given your parents' age and plans. But unethical isn't the same as illegal, as I learned in this business early on. I've looked high and low for any thread that I could follow to prove illegality here—"

"Try harder," she said. Her eyes were steeling up and narrowing again. "You're forgetting my parents died over this money. Because of this bastard."

She took another hard drink from her martini. The noise in the bar was picking up as more people wandered in, but her voice was rising. The piano player finished his first request and segued seamlessly to Erroll Garner's "Misty."

"Please, I know you're upset," McBain said. "You need some food in you before you drink any more. Let me buy you dinner."

"I don't need any dinner. What I need is justice."

He was preparing another pitch when he became aware of someone sliding into the seat to his left. There was no need to look. He had grown fond of that perfume over the years.

"Sorry I'm late, McBain," she said with a smile.

He was caught.

She extended her hand. "I'm Boston O'Daniel, Mr. McBain's partner. He may have mentioned me. You must be Christina Baker."

They shook hands.

"No, I don't think he..."

McBain could only look at his partner like a deer staring sideways into an oncoming semi with glittering green headlights.

She put her hand on his arm with a most reassuring tone. His partner was the epitome of elegant professionalism, a set of delicate white pearls resting gently atop her gold cashmere sweater and tailored Chanel suit. Her red mane was pulled back behind matching pearl earrings.

"I know I said I'd be able to get done with that mountain of paperwork an hour ago," Boston said with exasperation, "but those two cases are really proving to be a lot tougher than I thought."

Ms. Baker seemed impressed for once, and her scowl and attitude changed visibly.

"It's a pleasure to meet you...did you say your name was..."

"Yes, it's a long story, but it stuck, so I use it formally as well."

"Well, I think it's very stylish, especially in your business. I take some comfort from knowing there are two of you looking into my case. It sounds like you are terribly busy. I appreciate your making the time."

"I'm sorry I'm not familiar with all the details of your case," Boston said. "McBain kept meaning to fill me in, but I've been a bit overwhelmed by some of our other work."

Ms. Baker chastised him: "You should get Ms. O'Daniel a drink. Where are your manners? I'll fill her in while you get Michael's attention."

They spent the better part of a half hour going over the background of the case. Ms. Baker told Boston about her parents, their home in Brookline, their plans for retirement and the future, their untimely death, and finally about Richard Roche. McBain tried his best to put on his game face while he described what he had found out with his research to determine there wasn't really any reason to believe there was fraud involved.

Boston listened patiently while she sipped her gin martini, all the while skewering her olives with the toothpick.

"And I disagree with McBain," Ms. Baker said. "I still think there must be something we haven't found out. Maybe this fellow is really clever. I've heard things about offshore accounts and such."

He shook his head. "Listen, I've done what I can based on the available information in the file, and what is publicly available. I don't think—"

"That's an intriguing idea, Ms. Baker," Boston said. "I think McBain's point is that we don't typically have access to a level of personal account information that might help follow a trail overseas. As I'm sure my partner explained, we are private financial investigators, not government employees."

"Exactly what I was—"

"On the other hand," Boston continued, staring him in the face, "since I can tell this is a special case, there are additional steps that we can take to pursue the inquiry a little further than we normally would at this stage."

McBain could see he was going to pay for this one.

"Such as what?" their new client asked.

"I have some ideas, but we will need your help," Boston replied.

"Anything I can do to help you uncover this theft will be my pleasure."

Boston put a firm hand on her partner's shoulder. Somewhere he felt a nerve tingle.

"My colleague here checked all the public information he could, I'm sure. And I'm also sure he went through the records you gave us thoroughly. What we'll do now is some first-level research."

"What does that mean? What can I do?"

"I understand you spoke to your parents all the time and didn't know about the loss of the money. Please don't take offense if I suggest that perhaps we might discover something from talking to more people. If you could give us the names and contact information of as many people who might have been close to your parents as possible, McBain will be able to interview all of them to see if they know anything about this. It's a long shot, but well worth our time. Often people know something without making a connection. That's what we do best. Put the puzzle together and see if there is the beginning of a trail to follow. As a literary professional, you'll excuse me if I mix my metaphors, but you see what I mean."

"But—" McBain said.

"And we should talk to your parents' psychiatrists or physicians as well. If they were stressed, they might have spoken to one of them confidentially about the reasons. We'll need your permission for them to discuss such things with us. They may not want to violate a patient confidence."

Ms. Baker was brightening at the prospect of the new leads.

"And he will want to talk to Mr. Roche as well. Casually, of course, to get a more personal read on him. We always find it interesting what a face-to-face conversation can trigger. Nothing confrontational, just some probing questions and gut impressions."

Ms. Baker was nodding enthusiastically. "Yes, exactly. I think that's an excellent idea, Ms. O'Daniel. You should look him in the eye, McBain, and get him to defend himself. Let him try to lie to someone who knows what he's talking about."

He forced a smile and nodded in agreement as he saw his next couple weeks of free time circling the drain along with his evening plans for Christina Baker.

"Thank you both," she said. "I know it is more work for you, but I really feel there is something here. Somehow I owe it to my parents to keep following this to the truth."

He was amazed. For the first time since they had met, she was actually getting emotional.

Boston reached over and patted her hand.

"I'm so sorry to hear about your parents, Ms. Baker," she said. "From what you've said, I can tell they were the finest sort of people. We don't often come across their like in our line of work."

"Thank you, Ms. O'Daniel."

"Please, call me Boston."

For the first time that night, their client smiled. "Thank you, Boston. That's nice of you to say. I'm sure many of your clients are of the finest quality; otherwise, they wouldn't need your services."

"Yes, but we rarely take on clients under such tragic circumstances."

Boston ran her finger around the rim of her glass. "By the way, Ms. Baker, you must feel so fortunate to have Mr. Hilliard to rely on during this difficult time. I come from a big family myself. I know you're an only child, but I'm sure he and his family have been a rock to lean on, and to remind you that you aren't alone in dealing with this."

"Do you know David?" she asked.

McBain didn't like the sound of this. He glanced over at his partner and recognized that expression he had seen on her face countless times before. It was the look the bull saw just before the matador plunged the blade between his shoulders to finish the game—the coup de grace.

"Who?" He turned to his right.

Christina Baker's eyebrows lifted. "My husband."

"Ah," he said, smiling broadly.

"It's a shame he couldn't meet with us this evening," Boston said.

Ms. Baker looked down for a moment and paused.

"David wasn't interested in joining me, Ms....I mean Boston," she said. "I'm afraid he is of the same mind as McBain. He doesn't believe there is anything further to be gained by continuing this matter. He thinks I'm just wasting my time in an effort to cling to the memories of my parents."

The investigator chimed in. "You know, he's probably right. Even with these meetings—"

Boston talked over him. "Be that as it may, we'll turn over every possible stone until we're absolutely convinced there is nothing further to be done. I have to warn you that in the end, we may still find nothing; he may be right. But you will have known that you did everything possible to find out the truth. Then you and your husband can put this tragedy behind you and move forward with your lives."

Ms. Baker sighed. "I hope you're right. It has been a source of some friction between us, and I feel much better now having spoken to you tonight. Maybe it will help us to move on. Thank you so much."

"Well," Boston said. "Perhaps we can all have dinner together, the four of us, once this has all been resolved."

McBain ordered another drink, happy to see the lights in the bar dimming. The piano had been joined by a trumpet and bass, and they were very much playing the blues.

SEVEN

Friday dawned a crisp April day, and a little too early. It wasn't often that McBain felt nervous opening the door to his own office, but he knew what was coming this morning. Boston let him get two steps into the room.

"What the hell were you thinking?"

She was dressed in black, leaning on the front edge of her desk like a boxer itching to leave his corner. He held up his palms defensively.

"You're angry, I understand," he said. "You have every right. I only—"

She was angry, and not cold, silent-treatment angry. Irish redhead angry.

"For one thing, I have been working my ass off to get these two cases documented and closed over the next week so we can get paid."

McBain opened his mouth to respond.

"Shut up," she said. "For another, using your time and our connections to work on something that has no opportunity for us to make any money, and something you don't want to tell me about, is a waste of time and an insult to me. Why the hell do we bother going through these requests to see if there is any merit to them, anyway? Maybe we should just hang out in bars or outside discount brokers and see what happens.

"Worst of all, trading on our business reputation to try to get laid is about the worst thing in the world you could do to us. We've spent the past four years building this business with word-of-mouth references from satisfied clients. You know how important this is to me. You're lucky I showed up when I did. She looked like she was about to just walk out on you. And maybe tell all her friends about what a shit you are. Just think of what that could have set us back."

McBain had been working on his defense half the night, and it made no more sense now than it had at three a.m.

"But I really did look into it on my own time," he said.

Her eyes only got wider and greener. "Really? Well, if you had so much free fucking time, why didn't you spend it in the office helping me clean up these last two clients so we could get paid faster? You know, paid? That is why we do this, isn't it?"

"You know, I did take it seriously. How was I to know there was nothing to it until I looked at the file?"

He could tell he was just digging deeper from the way Boston was fingering the stapler on her desk.

"It's not like I went from bar to bar. Sure, I had hit on her before. And got shot down. But I was minding my own business when she came up to me with this story about being robbed."

"Oh please," she said. "I saw what she looked like. And I've seen you in action before. If she had been a day over forty with one gray hair, you would have been out of there halfway through your first drink. So don't try to sell me on your damsel in distress story. What the hell was wrong with our standard answer? Thanks, but I'm too busy right now helping my partner on other cases."

She was walking back and forth now as she read him the riot act, waving her hands, which were empty for the moment. McBain threw his arms up in surrender.

"What was I supposed to do after she told me about the dead parents? And she didn't even mention the part about it being a double suicide. After that, I had to do at least a little something to try to put her mind at ease. Which, as you saw, is going to be extremely difficult anyway."

Boston stopped and glared over at him.

"Which is something you should have been thinking about when she first approached you. Our clients are emotional enough about losing money. And you have to take on one overcome with grief from dead parents? What were you thinking? As if I didn't know exactly what you were thinking. And it serves you right to finally find out the punch line to that little scam anyway."

He sank into the red velour chair in front of her desk, a disciplined schoolboy with his hands folded in his lap. Looking up, he took advantage of the icy lull that filled the room.

"And by the way, how did you know she was married?" he asked. "I didn't see any ring on her finger."

"How did you not?" she said. "You moron. You didn't even bother to check the obit for the parents, did you?"

McBain swallowed hard. His ability to make such a rookie error notched up his sense of guilt, reddening his cheeks further.

"This is why there is a rule." She was jabbing her finger at him. "You act stupid and unprofessional. And remember why the rule is in place. Because the first time you violated it, you cost us over two hundred grand in a fee that should have been a slam dunk. I knew you were up to something. That's why I used my key to check your apartment. Then I called Dave and Dee. You've got some nerve asking them to keep things from me. Don't ever do it again."

Boston walked back to her desk and sat down. Her eyes sizzled with anger leveled at McBain. There was nothing beautiful about it.

"Your penance is to finish investigating her case," she said with finality.

"I did investigate it," he replied. "There is no case. I looked over the file, the investments. I had Dave and Dee check him out. The guy was just another loser in the market."

"I mean a real, full investigation. On your own spare time, not our clock. Until you're sure this guy is clean and there is no other lead to follow. Then you give her a full report. Then you say good-bye. Maybe if you're lucky and do a good job, she'll introduce you to her husband for good measure."

McBain threw out his hands again in objection.

"You just said there's nothing in it for us. Why bother?"

"Because I said so." That was hard to argue with. "And because I like her. And because you owe me for the hours I put in here without your help while you were working your social life."

Game. Set. Match, Boston O'Daniel.

"OK, OK. What do you want me to do? What will satisfy you?"

She shook her head. "It's not me you need to satisfy, it's Christina Baker. Ms. Baker to you, since she's a client. And you can go down the whole laundry list I did at the restaurant last night. Friends, relatives, physician, and finally the suspect himself."

McBain already knew the conversation was over. There would be no Red Sox games at Fenway for the foreseeable future.

"You realize how much time this could take?"

"Yep."

He thought for a moment and tried one last appeal. "But what about helping you with the closes and the other case with the actress?"

"Not a problem," she said. "You can do the interviews in your own abundant spare time. Then, if it takes longer and we don't get any more paying business in the meantime, after you're finished with the actress and Drysdale Securities, not to mention my philanthropy scam. *Capiche?*"

"You're not Italian."

He got a red eyebrow in return.

"Don't try me today, McBain. I might get mad."

The Bakers had been very popular. When McBain checked his inbox later that day, he found a short e-mail from Christina Baker with a file attached. For an only child, she certainly knew plenty of people. The file contained dozens of names, addresses, phone numbers, and e-mail information for friends of the family and acquaintances, thoroughly catalogued and organized. Most were in the Boston area. Some lived and worked in other towns or states that were accessible in a day's drive.

The family had lived in Brookline for decades, but they got around. According to her note, both Phillip and Sarah Baker had been teachers at Wellesley College. He had been a professor of English literature, as well as random and obscure classes in Celtic and Anglo-Saxon languages. His wife had taught both French language and French poetry courses. The list reflected a wide range of friends and academic colleagues.

McBain grumbled as he read through the pages, trying to decide where to start and how to proceed. Just his luck. Whatever happened to the reclusive academic?

For a nanosecond, his mind settled on the notion of visiting only those people he could reach easily within the city. Then his common sense kicked in. Boston was mad enough already, and she would be checking up on him with random phone calls of her own.

He looked over the addresses closest to home first. The Bakers had a large number of friends in Boston. This meant visits to Beacon Hill, the South End, the North End, Charlestown, and Back Bay. After that, he would have to work his way outward around the city in a spiral, starting in Brookline and moving through Cambridge and other adjacent neighborhoods. Then there were the suburbs, such as Wellesley, Newton, Natick, and more to the west of the city. Finally he would have to drive to Connecticut, New Hampshire, and Rhode Island. The end of the semester was fast approaching. Some of these college types would no doubt be heading out to summer homes on Cape Cod, the Vineyard, or Nantucket. And so would he if he didn't hustle. If absolutely necessary, he decided, he would call on the few in New York.

For the better part of ten days, McBain spent his evenings paying visits to these people. Each person he was able to contact was all too happy to meet with him and talk about the Bakers. Unfortunately for him, that meant just about everyone on the list. Only a few did not respond to his calls or e-mails. So first by foot and the T, and then by car, he methodically sat with each of them to ask a few polite questions and hear them talk about Phillip and Sarah Baker for hours.

In a way, the conversations were quite touching. Like attending a wake for a beloved person who would be long remembered and missed. Many of the memories were fresh and vivid. Most of the comments laudatory and gracious. A few of the stories quite long.

In their early sixties, the Bakers had been married for nearly thirty-five years. Although they both came from old New England families, the couple hardly lived up to the image of the stiff and self-contained WASP. They had been gregarious and friendly, open and generous with their time to both friends and associates, eager to go the extra mile to help out a struggling student. They threw parties on a regular basis, both in their Brookline house and in impromptu settings, as befitting the scholarly eccentrics. Phillip loved wine and would go on endlessly about its place in literature, both fictional and among writers. Sarah regaled guests with French poetry late into the night. Above all, they were devoted to academic life, their students, and their college.

For decades they had lived in the house in Brookline. They had inherited a little money, but nothing to retire on. As Christina Baker had pointed out, they built their savings largely through thrift. They had each had successful careers, publishing works in academic journals as well as books in their field, but none of them had exactly been movie material. By all appearances, the marriage had been an archetype of professional, literary, and personal success.

One thing everyone agreed on: they loved their daughter with the passion of an artist for his greatest creation.

It was hard to imagine what might have pushed these people to take their own lives, money or not.

He could understand how their deaths would have appeared out of the ordinary. After weeks of evening tea and bad drinks, McBain could almost recite the family history by heart. All of these people were telling him wonderful things about the Bakers, but that only made the investigator even more certain of his initial findings. Not one of them had known or suspected anything about any money problems or trouble of any kind. And those who knew his name or had met him had nothing but glowing things to say about Richard Roche.

The day after one of his visits, McBain expressed to Boston the predictability of continuing these interviews, hoping to cut things short.

"The only thing that's getting me suspicious is the fact that these people were so well thought of by everybody. I would have expected at least a couple would have been lukewarm or deliver some backhanded compliments. Academics aren't usually afraid to bring out their stilettos when talking about their fellows. I guess when your colleagues are deceased, it's another matter—never speak ill of the dead and all that. I hope people are as generous with me when the time comes."

Boston simply looked at him, divining his intent.

"Well they better not ask me anytime soon. I'm more than happy to write your obituary myself, warts and all."

Picking up where he had left off, he went back to work with an eye to finishing up his interviews as soon as possible and getting his evenings back.

Yes, the Bakers were too good to be true and didn't seem like the type to just give up, even if they had been wiped out in a crash. So maybe there was something else they hadn't been telling anyone, even their daughter. They didn't have a psychiatrist, priest, or rabbi. That left one good possibility. McBain looked at the last few names on the list, cross-checked them against his scheduler, and then picked up the phone to schedule an appointment with a doctor.

EIGHT

Rush hour on Beacon Street heading out of Boston proper can resemble a Roman race packed with amateur charioteers. McBain accelerated near Coolidge Corner and began looking for the road to take him into the maze of Brookline Village. The red and orange of the late afternoon haze blurred his vision as he tried to locate the turn on the directions with one eye on the traffic. A chorus of blaring horns and curses followed him as he turned his forest-green Range Rover onto Harvard Street, and, after ten minutes of searching for parking close to the address, found the doctor's shingle near the street entrance. A white, one-story office with black shutters was attached via a glass-enclosed walkway to a redbrick and stone house. Both were set back off the street and shielded for privacy by a high hedge. The pathway of granite slates led from a driveway to the entrance on the right. He stopped for a moment to smell the early buds of roses growing in the flower beds bordering the doorway steps.

His watch read five thirty, and the front door was locked. McBain looked through the glass panes and saw a lean, middle-aged man in a white coat sitting behind the reception desk. The investigator studied him briefly for a moment before ringing the bell. The doctor jumped a little, then came quickly over to the door.

"Yes?"

"Hello, Doctor Lehmann, I'm Mr. McBain. I called earlier, and you said I might stop by to talk about Phillip and Sarah Baker."

The good doctor took off his wire-frame glasses and smoothed back a head of slick black hair. "Yes, of course, Mr. McBain, come in. I thought maybe it was an unexpected patient. Let's go back in to my office so we aren't disturbed. Sometimes I get walk-ins who aren't watching the clock."

The two exchanged pleasantries while they walked to the office. Lehmann had a friendly manner about him, perhaps cultivated to offset his appearance. Not a large man, the doctor had the misfortune to carry certain Mediterranean facial features that might have elicited some uneasiness from strangers. A narrow face with small eyes and nose, dominated by thick black eyebrows and a dark complexion, gave him a somewhat seedy, lower-rank Mafioso look. When he smiled, his thin lips transformed into more of a sneer.

The office was warm, but professional and orderly. Comfortable, modern chairs sat across from the desk to allow for frank consultation. A phone and computer monitor filled the right side of the desk, and several steel file cabinets stood between bookshelves and the bay window looking out on the rose bushes. The office walls displayed several degrees and certificates prominently, along with an array of pictures of the doctor posing with men and women at gala events, golf outings, or other society gatherings. Presumably these were high-profile patients, their presence intended to reassure or impress the clientele. McBain recognized a few of the faces from the pages of magazines or newspapers. He didn't see any former clients or targets.

He took a chair and watched Dr. Lehmann get comfortable, crossing his hands on his desk.

"Thanks for agreeing to see me, Doctor. I know it's after hours, and you must have some paperwork to do. I hate paperwork."

The doctor smiled his thin smile. "Christina Baker called me to confirm that you were looking to speak to me at her request. I'm more than happy to help you in any way I can, though I'm not quite sure what this is about or how I can be of service. The Bakers were patients of mine, but I considered them friends as well. And naturally Christina need only ask."

McBain pulled his notebook out of his suit jacket.

"Thanks, Doctor; I appreciate it. I'm sure that as both physician and friend of the family, you are aware how devastating this whole incident has been to Ms. Baker. It may not seem rational to you, but she's asked me to try to tie up what she considers some loose ends surrounding the deaths. It may help her with some closure and give her the chance to get past this tragedy. You understand."

Lehmann sighed and said: "This is about the money, isn't it?"

McBain nodded and smiled sheepishly. "I'm afraid so. You're not surprised."

The doctor shook his head. "Yes, a number of us who were close to the Bakers have talked about this with her from time to time. Ever since their death, she has been fixated on the subject, perhaps understandably so. But I was hoping that by now, Christina might have come to terms with the loss of the money and any connection with the tragedy."

"Well, in a way I'm here to talk about that," McBain said. "Ms. Baker may think it's about the money, but between you and me, I think that's just the thing for her mind to focus on in place of her parents' death. She has asked me as a financial professional to look into the matter, and I am. What I'd like to do is put the money issue to rest if I can so she can move on. To do that, I need your help understanding the larger issue."

The doctor's eyes narrowed again. Under those protruding eyebrows, it wasn't a good look for him.

"The larger issue?" he asked.

"I'll be frank, Doctor," McBain said. "I think Ms. Baker has to come to grips with their deaths. I've spoken to many of their friends and acquaintances, and I'm a little troubled by something that seems inconsistent to me. As an investor, I've lost money and worked with people who've taken a real bath too. So I know what that kind of stress can feel like, old or young. Phillip and Sarah Baker just don't strike me as the kind of people who would have...how can I phrase it delicately...taken that kind of a way out of financial trouble. You said you considered them both friends as well as patients. That puts you in a unique position."

"I'm still not sure I understand what you're asking, Mr. McBain."

"Ms. Baker thinks that it was the stress of losing their fortune that pushed them over the edge. I'm asking you if there was something else. Some kind of medical condition that might have been fatal or painful. Something they didn't even tell their daughter about. Perhaps because it was sudden or awkward. Maybe so debilitating that they didn't want her to carry any burden of caring for them since they'd lost so much money."

Lehmann looked at his computer screen, then down at his desk before answering. He looked uncomfortable.

"Mr. McBain, I know you're here at Ms. Baker's request, but I'm not sure I can give you any confidential information about my patients. I don't want to be the cause of any undue stress on her part."

"Doctor, it's hard for me to imagine her being in any greater state of distress than she is now. And medical ethics aside, as an act of humanity, shouldn't we be more concerned with the health of the living?"

The doctor leaned back in his chair and considered this for a minute.

"I can tell you there was no major medical issue with either Phillip or Sarah," Lehmann said at last.

"Then as their friend and doctor, you can't think of any reason that would have pushed them over the edge? Why two perfectly healthy people would have decided to end their apparently happy lives? Was all this happiness just a public front, then, for two people who were ticking time bombs of depression? Because based on all I've been hearing about them, they put on a pretty good game face if that was the case."

"I didn't say that." The doctor stared at his hands. "Look, Mr. McBain, I didn't want to come forward with this because I agree with you. Christina should move on. And what happened is clearly preventing that."

"What do you mean?"

He ran his hands through his hair and leaned back, closing his eyes to the ceiling for a moment.

"It may be that she is right about the reason for their suicides."

McBain put his pen in his pocket and crossed his legs. *Uh oh.* "Go on."

The phone on Doctor Lehmann's desk rang, breaking the silence. He started for a moment at the intrusion, then hit a button to send it to voicemail.

"You have to understand something about the Bakers," Lehmann said. "They were the kind of people who liked to have a lot of fun. They threw parties. Went on exotic vacations. Helped out a friend or student occasionally. Those things, the lifestyle they enjoyed, cost money. They both enjoyed playing the well-to-do literary aristocracy. But academics don't make a lot of money.

"Phillip came to me shortly before it happened. He said he had to talk to someone confidentially, that I couldn't tell anyone about the losses from the investments. But the stress on both of them was frightening. He said they had been doing so well for a while, and then it was gone. They had taken some risks to try to cement their winnings, as he called them, and retire early. They kept up a brave face for everyone after they found out. Christina is correct, poor girl. And I should have seen it tearing them apart. But as you said, they were such upbeat people. They were both still working. I thought they would get through it in time. I never thought..."

Damn. This was going down a road McBain didn't want to take.

"So they blamed Mr. Roche for—"

"Oh, no," he said, waving his hands. "I didn't mean to imply they placed any fault with how he managed the money. Neither of them ever said a word against him to me or suggested any wrongdoing. I wouldn't know anything about that part. I just know they were utterly destroyed by the loss. Everything was going to suffer. Their style of living, their future. They thought even their relationship with their daughter might be affected. Phillip was so convinced she would be terribly disappointed in them. They had always been so careful. Then they took a risk at the wrong time and were left with almost nothing in the end. He felt like such a fool."

McBain did not want to hear this. He found it hard to believe that his instincts had been wrong. He tried one more time.

"And as their doctor, you're certain that there might not have been something else wrong with one or both of them? I mean, hell, I've known people who lost relatives suddenly, even at a young age. Things like fast-moving cancer or something. Maybe you didn't even know?"

But Lehmann was already shaking his head.

"I thought of that, Mr. McBain. I thought of it right away. That's why I was involved in the autopsies so closely from the start. I thought perhaps I had missed something. But nothing of the kind was found. As it happens, neither of them had had a physical for nearly a year. At his last, Phillip and I discussed what I diagnosed as a potential heart problem, but it was in its early stages. We hadn't even begun to treat it. They were receiving regular medication for minor ailments, hypertension, and cholesterol, but nothing immediately life threatening, I assure you."

McBain exhaled and stood up.

"OK, thanks for your time, Doctor," he said as they shook. "I guess we'll just have to deal with the facts, unpleasant or not."

"I'm sorry I couldn't be of more help," the doctor said. "I hope you can put this matter to rest, for Christina's sake."

McBain put his overcoat on. "I've got to stop by and see the financial guy himself just to get a few final points down to help me explain this to Ms. Baker, but I don't expect we'll need to cover anything else unless something new crosses your mind. If so, please give me a ring. You take care."

The investigator looked up at the wall of pictures again. "Maybe see you around sometime."

The next afternoon, McBain took a long walk to have some tea at the Bristol Lounge. He didn't really like tea, especially after consuming so much of it over the past week. He had been to the Bristol a few times on business for other clients. The Public Garden was finally starting to blossom into spring as he window-shopped his way up Boylston Street past Hermes and a few other high end boutiques across from the park. At last he arrived at the classic redbrick façade of the Four Seasons Hotel. He recognized the doorman in the top hat and gray overcoat and slapped a twenty in his hand as he passed by, then strolled through the elegant modern lobby and into the lounge.

Saturday-afternoon tea at the Bristol was a tradition for many people, so the restaurant was fairly crowded with regulars, well-dressed clientele who might reasonably be expected to fit the demographic of "high-net-worth individuals."

Sure enough, he found the man he was looking for seated at one of the choice tables by the street window looking out on the Public Garden, reading and sipping tea. His legs crossed, looking down a pair of half glasses at the weekend *Financial Times* in a high-backed wing chair, he was the picture of cultured refinement. McBain hardly needed the description Christina Baker had provided. The man was right out of central casting, from brown shoes and creased khaki slacks to button-down pink shirt, blue blazer, and Hermes tie from the store down the street. His full head of dark hair was streaked with traces of silver, but just enough to project a distinguished and experienced wisdom. The tailored clothes fit his lean figure, trim and fit from regular workouts. The investigator couldn't get the image of Cary Grant in his later movies out of his head. In which case there was no reason he shouldn't play Bogart. Showtime.

"Mr. Roche," he said with a smile. "I'm Mr. McBain. How are you today?"

The face that turned up at McBain made him like the man. Not so old as to seem grandfatherly, it radiated a warm personality who could be comfortable with anyone, regardless of social class or background. For a few seconds of silence, they both smiled pleasantly at each other, taking in and processing a world of information. Judging.

Richard Roche put his newspaper aside and took off his glasses.

"You have me at a disadvantage, sir," he said in an affable voice. "You seem to know who I am, but I'm at a loss. I'm quite sure we've never met. I would have remembered."

"Quite right, sir," McBain replied. "Sorry to interrupt your Saturday afternoon tea. I'm actually a friend of a friend of sorts. I was hoping to talk to you for a few minutes. I promise I won't take up too much of your time."

"Not at all, Mr. McBain," he said, and waved his hand to the chair across the table. "Please sit down. May I ask what friend referred you to me?"

McBain threw his coat over the back of the chair and sat before he answered.

"Actually, Mr. Roche, I'm here at the request of David Hilliard. He is married to Christina Baker."

The older gentleman just nodded. Otherwise, his visage changed not a bit.

"I see," he said, then: "I think I understand. Are you an attorney?"

McBain let out a chuckle. "Oh no, Mr. Roche, nothing like that. I'm just a friend. I know this could be a bit awkward given the circumstances. I'd be grateful if you'd give me just a bit of your time this afternoon. I'm sure you know the subject."

Roche extended a manicured hand and poured himself some hot tea from the elegant blue porcelain pot.

"Can I offer you some tea while we talk, Mr. McBain?" He glanced up at the young lady who had been standing next to their table for a half minute. "Deborah, please bring a cup for this gentleman if you would. Thank you."

He turned to McBain with a look of such understanding that he was reminded of the last time he had been in confession thirty years ago.

"Yes," he said solemnly. "I can imagine the subject. Though I'm not sure what else I can say about it that I haven't discussed with David, or with Christina herself. I suppose she hasn't changed her thinking. How is she?"

"To tell you the truth, she's still pretty preoccupied by the whole matter. That's why I'm here. Her husband has asked me to try to help him provide some kind of closure so that they can move on with their lives. He thought, based on my background, that I might be able to explain how these things work. He seems to think his wife just doesn't understand the many ways people can lose money in the market, and if you and I chatted, I might be able to translate in a way that helps her to accept that part of it and let go. It would mean a lot to them both. What do you say? Are you willing to talk to me about what happened?"

"Of course," Roche said, nodding reassuringly. "By the way, do you have a first name?"

"McBain is OK."

Roche smiled. He seemed to like that.

"Of course, McBain. I'm sure you can imagine that I've had to have many of these conversations with clients over the past year or so, not just with Christina Baker. Though of course none in connection with such a tragic outcome as this. But might I ask what makes Mr. Hilliard think you might be able to put her mind at ease. Who are you? A financial planner? Relaxed but appropriate weekend attire. Confident, firm manner with strangers. Quite comfortable strolling into the Four Seasons on a Saturday afternoon. I would have guessed investment banker, but you aren't that pompous."

McBain smiled and laughed. He was beginning to like this guy.

"I guess that's why I gave it up," he said. "I was with Morgan for a few years in New York. Traded lots of markets, made some money, had some fun. Hit all the right vacation spots and clubs for a while. But the fit wasn't really there long term. Eventually both sides figured that out. You know how it goes."

"I do indeed," Roche agreed. "I myself worked in New York for years on the money management side."

"I figured. You don't get to be a successful manager of rich people's money without playing in the big leagues. Harvard?"

"No. Princeton, actually. Then I spent time at some fine firms. Shearson, Merrill, a few other private firms with a more select profile. But after a time, I found the pace in New York a bit too intense. There have been so many changes in the business over the course of my life. No more exchanges, so much electronic trading, algorithms, and such. You might say that, like you, I didn't quite fit in with the monolithic mindset of those firms and where they were going. I found I could build a much better business up here with the kind of relaxed clientele that appreciated a somewhat more independent and personalized approach."

His expression fell as he shook his head.

"Unfortunately, nothing in my approach or experience prepared me for what we faced over these past few years. As a trader, I'm sure you understand what I mean. All but the most bearish investors I know suffered to one degree or another."

"Yes, I do know what you mean."

"I hope you didn't lose too badly in the collapse."

"No, I'm actually one of those bearish types you mentioned," McBain said. "My friends tell me it's a personality defect. Just lucky, I guess."

Deborah placed a cup and saucer in front of McBain. Roche poured him some tea.

"Luckier than most, no doubt. For the vast majority, both our luck and training failed us. And this, if you'll allow me to get to the heart of our talk, is what I tried to make Christina understand. These markets were so unusual that it wasn't just her parents' portfolio that suffered, but nearly every person I know, with the exception of those who were either as savvy as you or had their money in cash. I used every bit of my knowledge to try to meet my clients' goals. Every bit of standard investment technique or trading strategy that we had been taught to use. In the end, nothing worked. They had been leveraged too highly.

"And if I might confess to you what I admitted to Christina and David, in the end that means I failed the Bakers when they needed me most."

"How so?"

The older man stared out the window on the greening Public Garden, but with a look of sadness born of many springs.

"I'm not that old, McBain. But I should have been wise enough to know what could have happened. I gave them what I considered sound advice based on all the experiences of my professional life. But at one point they came to me and said they wanted to be more aggressive. They had been reading up on markets as they watched other people make a fortune, and they wanted to find ways to make more money faster. Initially I told them it wasn't a good idea, but things were going well in the market, and I got too comfortable. I was overconfident in my own ability, and I got blindsided. Just like everyone else. But that doesn't make any difference to them now, does it? It's hard to say everyone else was doing the same thing when two friends are dead because I failed them."

Roche turned from the view of the park and looked at McBain.

"So in a way, Christina is correct. Sarah and Phillip died because I didn't do my job right. I should have seen what was happening and saved as much of their money as I could."

McBain didn't know what to say. So he just shut up and listened.

"I tried to explain this to Christina," Roche continued. "I suppose it sounded like excuses. I told her about some of the major investors who thought they were smart, jumping in to buy at what they imagined were bargain prices and still getting wiped out when they kept dropping. I showed her the articles, the names of people and historic investment firms that went under. Sovereign wealth funds, investors with brilliant track records. I admitted I made some of the same mistakes in thinking there were rare buying opportunities on the way down. I told her I had done everything I could with her parents' consent every step of the way. She didn't want to hear it. All she could say was it was my fault.

"I'm not admitting there was any legal liability. You and I both know that isn't the case. And I never suspected it might have led to their death. But in some way, at some level, I do feel responsible for what happened to Sarah and Phillip."

It was exactly what McBain had determined. And the last thing his client would want to hear. He had really been hoping this guy would be an average asshole of the kind he usually came upon: arrogant, stupid, and full of his own sense of superiority. The last thing he had expected to hear was common sense and an admission for once that a money manager had been in over his head and played the fool in the end. And, twisted as it seemed, he had really been hoping for the cancer or heart attack angle.

He sipped at his tea and thought for a minute. There really wasn't much more to cover.

"Their daughter keeps insisting they were good old puritan types who would never invest in anything but T-bonds or mutual funds."

"When I first met them," Roche said, "that was indeed the case. But over time, as the market kept racing ahead, they looked at their returns and saw themselves losing out compared to others. They did some Internet research, as amateur investors often do, and came to me hoping to do much better. It's just that simple, I'm afraid. And of course if you knew the Bakers, you'd know they liked to spend money freely. A difficult combination, to be sure, even with the money that they had inherited."

"How long did you know them, Mr. Roche? I understand you had only been their financial advisor a little over five years."

Cary Grant smiled ruefully, taking a walk down memory lane.

"True," he replied. "I was introduced to them at one of their parties. We became friends, and they seemed to be in the market for a new investment planner. I think maybe even then they might have been thinking about their aggressive new strategy."

Roche paused for a moment and looked directly at the investigator.

"I'm guessing you've looked at the statements and the paperwork related to the portfolio over time. With your background, you've been able to evaluate the various types of investments Phillip and Sarah were in. You can trace the change yourself from a fairly conservative book into a wider range of securities, some of them increasingly risky. The more the strategy paid off, the more enthusiastic they were about their decision. And then, as you know, things turned very quickly.

"When I finally sat down with them and confronted them with the extent of the losses, they were devastated. But if I'd known the depth of their depression, their despair...I might have found them counseling of some kind. In the end, it's only money. It's not worth taking your life over. When I found out they had poisoned themselves...well, I was just sick, and I felt terrible. Nothing like that has ever happened to me."

After a respectful moment of silence, McBain stood up and offered his hand. "Thanks for your time, Mr. Roche, and for the tea. I'll speak to Mr. Hilliard and his wife and see if I can help provide her with some answers. Maybe see you around town sometime."

Roche rose and grasped his hand firmly and with warmth.

"I'm sure I haven't been of much comfort, Mr. McBain. But I'm afraid there isn't anything to be said that might grant me any forgiveness from Christina. Sarah and Phillip were good friends, and I hate to think that this is the lasting legacy left to their daughter. They deserved better."

The investigator put on his coat and gazed out on the park, the return of spring heralding the season of renewal and hope of new life. "They almost always do."

Doctor Lehmann said good night to his receptionist at ten minutes after five o'clock. At five thirty, he locked the front door to his office, put on a black raincoat and Red Sox cap, and biked down to Beacon Street, where he caught the Green Line to the Kenmore stop near Fenway Park. A few minutes later, he found the store he needed not far from the CITGO sign.

By six thirty, the doctor had purchased two disposable cell phones at the T-Mobile store. He waited at Starbucks until seven o'clock and then walked out on the street to place his call. It was picked up after three rings.

"Yes, good evening," the doctor said. "I know we haven't spoken in some time, but I needed to contact you."

Lehmann listened for a minute.

"Of course I remember our agreement, but we need to talk. I received a visit yesterday from someone asking about the Bakers. I thought you should know."

The doctor kept moving along the sidewalk, his eyes patrolling the sidewalks and storefronts in the fading light as he spoke.

"I'm not getting nervous, not at all. But I thought this would have been finished after all this time. This man was curious about the Bakers, about their health and state of mind. He had some idea that there might have been something else behind their suicides, like a terminal illness. I told him there was nothing of the sort. I confirmed what happened was related to stress and depression...."

"No, he didn't seem suspicious after I was done talking with him. I believe he is just going through the motions, maybe as a friend or for a paycheck. He didn't ask me any questions about any money. But he said he was going to see—"

He pressed the phone close and placed his finger in his other ear to keep out the noise from a passing garbage truck.

"Of course I did...I explained all that. I didn't want him coming up with any new ideas that might lead to more questions...no, I assure you...no, nothing can be proven at this point."

Another minute went by.

"Well, I hadn't spoken with her in two months, so I assumed there was nothing more to say. But it seems I was wrong, since she asked this fellow to research what happened to the investment money.

"She still seems quite agitated about the whole thing," Lehmann continued. "I don't understand why this should be coming up now. It's been six months. There was no evidence of any wrongdoing by anyone. I thought this was all resolved. Instead, she won't let it go."

He listened for another moment.

"Yes, I know, but—"

He started nodding aggressively at the phone.

"All right, all right, yes, I understand," the doctor said, "but this is still troubling. What if this man comes back again? Or what happens if she hires an attorney? I don't want more questions, especially now. I cannot afford...What?...But I may need to reach you if something else comes...very well, but it better not."

The doctor listened to the silent phone in frustration and then took off his baseball cap and slicked back his hair. There was no reason for any of this to come up again. It should have all been finished months ago. He pulled out a pack of Dunhill cigarettes and smoked one halfway down before throwing it to the ground. He walked his bike briskly back to the station. Just before he reached the Green Line, he crouched down to tie his shoes. He glanced around, flipped the phone into the sewer, and took the T back to Brookline Village.

TEN

It was a beautiful evening to do a thankless job. Newbury Street had emerged from layers of winter clothing, and the promise of spring filled sidewalks with shoppers and strollers even as the shadows of the brownstones lengthened along the street. Music and chatter filled the air from passing cars and open doorways of the boutiques and restaurants on either side of the street from Arlington and the Public Garden west. McBain enjoyed the walk, the warmth, and the view. He took his time, being in no hurry to deliver his news. But as Boston had pointed out yet again that morning, he had gotten himself into this, and there was only one way out.

Midway between Fairfield Street and Gloucester, he found the shop above a manicured garden and wrought-iron fence. He looked at his watch and then glanced up the stone stoop to the sign above the entrance: *Ivy Covered Tomes* was indeed bracketed by pale marble and vines of ivy, a ladder of tendrils climbing the brick facade of the four-story brownstone. McBain took off his brown fedora and held the door for two silver-haired ladies who passed him on their way out, then entered one of the most intimate bookstores he had ever seen.

The room stretched back into a warren of narrow aisles that formed a small maze, heightening the illusion of a larger store. Well-ordered shelves reached from floor nearly to the high ceiling with seven or eight rows of books climbing to the recessed lighting. Small bronze plaques at the head of each row indicated categories and headings. Strands of ivy interlaced with a variety of plants and ferns among the ranks of books, lending an air of antique mystery—and to his mind, a vague sense of the room as a living thing. He stepped to one side and looked down through two glass panes into a locked cabinet that held some very old but well-preserved bound volumes. A sign read First Editions—Do Not Touch. He assumed that meant people like him.

At the front of the shop, checking out a customer from behind the counter with a cheerful demeanor, was Christina Baker. Another woman, older with ash-blond hair, was working beside her, chatting with another customer in hushed tones.

He stood quietly, watching and listening to Ms. Baker work. McBain was struck by her rapport with her customers and her encyclopedic knowledge of literary subjects. Once again she was dressed in her casual but conservative style, with white blouse, gold silk scarf, and tweed jacket. Her smile was businesslike and pleasant, but genuine in its professional communion. The woman seemed thrilled with her purchase. He was certain every customer left her store cherishing the special find she had taken the care to unearth for them. By the time she looked his way and smiled, McBain had a full-blown librarian fantasy underway.

She turned to her assistant. "Karen, can you finish up with the register while I take care of this last customer? Then I'll lock up. Thanks."

Christina came around from behind the counter and beckoned with her finger. "Come along, sir, this way."

"Sure. You don't by chance wear glasses, do you?"

She glanced at him curiously. "No, why?"

"No reason. I just thought in the book business, they might be handy."

He followed her into the maze and pulled some sheets of paper from his coat pocket to help him focus on the job at hand. The narrow library aisles didn't help. She finally stopped and turned in the section labeled Spiritualism and Personal Transformation.

"Well, McBain, it's nice to see you again after all this time."

"Good to see you too, Ms. Baker. Nice place you have here. It's a pleasure to see you in your element. You're almost like a different person."

"Should I take that as a compliment or an insult?"

"I'd never insult a woman as beautiful and smart mouthed as you."

The corners of her mouth curled up in satisfaction.

"Thank you for coming down to the shop so we can talk," she said. "It saves me some time. And I would much rather we discuss your investigation without drinking."

"That makes one of us."

"You do like your martinis, don't you?"

"I drink manhattans too."

"I've been meaning to ask, why do you drink so many?" she asked.

"They're what some of us have instead of children. Shall we talk about what I found out?"

He handed her the first sheet of paper. "Here's the list of people you gave us. I've checked off all of the ones I've been able to contact and meet with. I've included the names of Doctor Lehmann and Richard Roche for the sake of completeness."

Christina Baker looked over the list.

"This is very thorough, McBain," she said. "I am impressed. You managed to cover quite a bit of ground in ten days."

"As you can see, I was able to track down and talk to all but three."

She followed the names with her finger, then paused and looked up at one of the shelves for a moment. One book was an inch out of alignment with the others. Standing on her toes, she pushed it into place. She looked at the list again and nodded.

"Oh, of course," she said. "Professor Sheldon is on sabbatical working on his book, researching Gallic sociology somewhere in Ireland, I think. Dennis Abbott has been traveling abroad for nearly a year now on an extended vacation. He's recently retired. I'm not sure about Mr. and Mrs. Caruthers. They are retired as well and tend to come and go between Cambridge and Europe. I wasn't able to contact any of them about the funeral. I'm afraid they are all going to be terribly upset, especially Dennis."

"Why's that?"

"He used to be so very close to both my parents. They drifted apart in recent years, but I know he would have wanted to be there. I'm certain he would have told you some wonderful stories about them."

"I'm sure he would have," McBain agreed. "Everybody else did. Your parents must have been great people, Ms. Baker. Everybody I spoke to thought highly of them. Made me wish I'd known them myself. Like my partner said, we don't meet their kind much in our line of work. But then, I might have guessed that already."

She tilted her head. "How so? You had only read about them on paper."

"I've already seen a sample of their work."

She returned his stare, but not without warmth.

"Thank you, McBain." She held up her left hand and wiggled her fingers, one of them now adorned with gold. "Do try to remember this."

"I haven't forgotten, Mrs. Hilliard," he said. "And just so we're straight, I couldn't care less about jewelry when it comes to that subject. But you're a client now, and I'm here on business."

"Fine," she said. "So let's get down to business, shall we?"

"Yes, let's."

The investigator pulled out several typed pages and glanced at them. The easy part of the conversation was over.

"OK, here's the long and short of it. One, everybody I talked to loved your parents and had nothing but great things to say about them. They also said they socialized whenever they could and were generous people. You translate that however you like. They were certainly the life of the party." He paused for a moment and considered a wisecrack, but thought better of it. "I'm sure you attended more than a few of them growing up.

"Two, nobody seemed to have any idea of the stress they were under from these investment losses, so they kept it pretty close to the vest from everybody, not just you. And we're talking about people who knew them well and spent a lot of time with them over the years, both individually and together.

"Three, only a few knew anything about Mr. Roche, and they had only positive things to say. No one can recall your parents ever criticizing him or complaining about him. In fact, several of their friends remember them going on at length about how well they were doing. Considering the stress they were under at the end, I consider that a minor miracle in itself, but there it is. Certainly nothing came up about any suspicious activity or stealing.

"Four, combine that with a clean bill of health he got from my contacts in the business. There's no record of unethical behavior on file with the financial regulators or anyone else who keeps track of complaints."

McBain kept going to push through to the end.

"And finally, after speaking with Doctor Lehmann and Roche himself, I've got nothing more to go on in the way of evidence that this was anything more than a case of bad investment decisions at the worst possible time. Roche as much as admitted that himself, and he's sticking with the story he gave you already."

He handed Christina Baker the pages.

"I've typed up these conclusions for you to review and think about. Given your argumentative nature, I wanted to give you a chance to comment before I told you your ideas were wrong again. Except that it looks like you weren't totally wrong."

She pulled her eyes up from the paper.

"What do you mean not totally...?"

"The punch line seems to be that you were right about their state of mind," McBain said. "It looks like the stress of the investment losses pushed them over the edge. I was really hoping it was something else. I even ran a couple of ideas past Doc Lehmann in the hopes that it was."

"What did Doctor Lehmann have to say?" she asked. "What ideas?"

"I thought there was a chance there was something wrong with one or both of your folks that they might not have been telling you about. Something medical, maybe even potentially debilitating or fatal."

"That's ridiculous," she said. "They would have informed me about anything like that."

"OK, OK," he said. "Looks like you were right, and Lehmann agreed. He said there was nothing of the kind. I just thought there was an off chance that they wouldn't want to burden you with the responsibility of a terminal illness. The doc says no, that nothing out of the ordinary had come up in their last few visits. He said nothing came up in the autopsy either."

"You see."

"And he also said that your father admitted to him not long before they died the kind of pressure they were under, and that it was because they had gambled with their investments, and that the depression was driving them further down. The doc said that they were afraid that maybe it might even damage their relationship with you. They felt they had let you down. He regretted that he didn't see just how bad things were and where they were going and head it off somehow."

Ms. Baker started to push several books around on a couple of the shelves, and she pulled a cart loaded with others over toward her. She began to place them while she talked.

"So, he confided to you that they were depressed. Did he mention anything about Mr. Roche? Did my father speak to him about that?"

"Not in so many words. He didn't seem to know anything about that one way or another. I think he felt bad that he wasn't able to spot any warning signs about how far out on the limb they were. You were right about them feeling so humiliated about losing all their money. Probably felt even worse after talking up their success during the good years. That would explain why they kept putting on the brave face for you and their friends. Since they didn't have any therapist to talk to, and they weren't inclined to dump on anybody else, I suppose Lehmann was the closest thing to a confidante in this situation."

She scowled and pulled over a rolling ladder and continued her sorting on a higher shelf. She slapped a book onto a ladder step.

"And you spoke to Roche as well?" she asked.

"Yes. I met with him and went over the case. He seemed straightforward. Didn't deny he failed your parents as a financial advisor. Told me that they started out conservative like you said, but they wanted to be more aggressive once they saw other people making money as the market went up. Claims it was their idea. And based on what I've learned about their lifestyle and financial plans, I have no reason to disagree. I've seen it happen before. People sometimes change their approach when they start to make big money in the market. The money looks easy and risk free, and they see themselves getting richer on paper by the day. There's even a term for it: we call it the house money effect."

The bell at the front door rang twice as Karen left for the evening. Christina stopped working for a moment and looked down at McBain with daggers.

"Well, it sounds to me like you two got on just fine. You don't have to sound so impressed with him. I don't think it takes any great courage to admit you ruined two older people who trusted you. I should have known you two would like each other."

McBain leaned against the shelves and took two deep breaths. If she was going to continue to be so stubborn, he might as well have been drinking while they went through this again. The actress was a sea of tranquility compared with this one.

"I didn't say I liked him," he said. "I said that he came across as one of the more frank money managers I've met over the years. Most of them are young or arrogant pricks who can't admit they were wrong. Instead they just make up excuses. This guy didn't. He admitted he blew it on the market. But like I told you, that doesn't leave you with much of a case."

"Even after what Doctor Lehmann said?" Christina asked. "The doctor as much as told you that bastard drove them to it. Hand me that stack of books."

He moved around the ladder, grabbed a pile of thin, leather-bound volumes from the cart, and began to hand them up. She shoved another few books into a shelf. Christina operated like a filing machine with hands and eyes that worked fast and knew exactly where to place each one without thinking.

"As for all this talk about taking risks, well, I just don't believe it. They never said anything to me about this. He's lying, I tell you."

"You know, Ms. Baker," he said, "maybe they wanted to surprise you with their success and the size of their stash at some point. I don't recall you mentioning any detailed conversations on investment strategy with your folks."

She climbed to the top of the ladder with an armful of volumes and pushed them into open spaces, moving others to the side.

"Hand me those red-bound books," she said.

McBain grabbed five of the old volumes off the cart and lifted them up.

"You know, McBain, I've been around him when he turns on the charm, and I think he just did the same with you. He has a way with people; I saw it with my parents. He must have played on your common background."

He frowned up at her. "I don't think so. You're not listening, as usual. The statements show the investments going up and then tanking with the market in a pattern that confirms what he said. Roche admits he screwed up. There's nothing on file anywhere to suggest he's a swindler. That means there's nothing for us to go on, regardless of how badly it worked out."

She shoved another book into a tight spot on a higher shelf, then pulled out another to replace and slammed it on the ladder step.

"With everything Doctor Lehmann told you," she said, shaking her head, "how can you not suspect that Roche didn't try hard enough? I'll never accept his excuses just because everybody else lost money. I think everyone was wrong about my hiring an attor—"

In her irritation, Christina Baker leaned over too far to reach the highest shelf in the next section. She pulled at a book until it was almost out. One tug more and...

She lost her balance and came off the ladder like an angry comet as it rolled the other way. Hearing her yell, McBain barely looked up in time to avoid being flattened. Instead, he managed to reach out and catch her in a bear hug as they both tumbled to the floor. They were chest to chest, faces inches apart. For a few seconds, neither of them said a word. Christina lay on top of him, wrapped in his arms, both of them breathing heavily.

McBain looked up at her, and his lips curled up.

"You know, for an uptight, New England WASP bookworm, you have an incredible body."

Her heart pounding, she pushed against his chest with her hand to get up. He held on and narrowed his eyes.

"Wow. It seems your thermostat runs a little hot too," he said. "Interesting. You must be quite a furnace to lie next to at night."

"Let me up, Mr. McBain."

He released her with a chuckle, and they both rose in the aisle.

"Anything you say, Ms. Baker."

Christina smoothed out her clothing and arranged her dark hair. McBain handed her the report again. Then he picked up his hat and coat from the floor. There wasn't much more to say, and no reason to remain any longer.

"Look, Ms. Baker," he said, "I wish there was something more to go on here, something I could follow up on. But I just don't have anything to use against him. If even one person had voiced a suspicion or mentioned something negative your parents told them...But I think we've run out of alternatives. I'd give anything to be able to stay on this, believe me, I would, but there isn't a case."

She walked him to the front door.

"Thank you for your efforts, Mr. McBain," she said. "Please tell Bos...Ms. O'Daniel that I said thank you as well. I appreciate your time. Good-bye."

Their eyes met for several seconds. McBain wanted to say something to make it right. In a way that he never had in the past few weeks, since that night when he first took the file, he really wished he had found something to prove she was right, to help get her money back. To make up for the loss of something money could never replace. But he could see a softness starting to grow in those beautiful, tough eyes. And he knew he had to get out now and leave her alone.

"You're welcome, Ms. Baker," he said. "Good-bye."

McBain pulled the door closed behind him. Boston had said they made sure only the people who deserved it got hurt. For a moment he wished that were true.

ELEVEN

Christina Baker was finished crying. Since the death of her parents over six months before, episodes had come upon her when she couldn't hold the anguish or the sadness inside, when the open wound of grief tore away time's healing scars. At such moments she made sure to be alone, or with her husband.

McBain had said there was no way to prove that Richard Roche was responsible. She had been angry at the investigator, but not really surprised. David had said the same thing months ago, as had her friends. She had dared to get her hopes up that a financial expert might be able to unearth something they had not, some evidence that a novice might not detect. Then, when she had by chance encountered McBain, her heart had imagined that he could be that person, despite, or maybe because of, his scandalous temperament and selfish intentions.

Proof or not, she remained certain that something had gone wrong. There were secrets her parents had kept, to be sure. It was true she hadn't discussed the details of their investing with either of them. Mainly that was because they both knew of her dislike for Richard Roche and any discussion of him. Something about him had always felt insincere, though her parents had chastised her for saying so. Maybe they were right that she felt slightly jealous at the comfort level their relationship with the financial advisor had reached. McBain was correct about that as well; her parents had never had a cross word to say about the man they considered a good friend.

In the months since the funeral, Christina had come to realize that this was the thing she held on to like a life preserver, giving her the certainty that she was right about him. The thing that made her persevere. No true friend would have allowed them to gamble and lose their money for any reason, especially one who knew his business. She was convinced Roche was simply a disingenuous fraud. Somehow he must have made money at their expense. In a way that even a trained eye wouldn't detect without a great deal of effort. Why couldn't anyone else see that? And was there any means left to discover how?

Perhaps not. She might not be able to prove anything, but that didn't mean she couldn't threaten him. Maybe a lawsuit wouldn't resolve questions or bring her parents back, but it would be a small compensation to make his life miserable, for a while at least, in payment for the misery he had brought to her, and them.

What she wasn't sure of was whether her marriage could stand the strain. Upon returning home to Beacon Hill last night, she had shown David everything that McBain had reported. Of course he had agreed. He had insisted all along that an investigation would produce exactly those results. They had argued. He had been patient all these long months, helped her to make calls and ask questions, and comforted her during her moments of grief and rage. When she had gone silent and turned inward, he had said nothing and waited for those spells to end.

But last night had been the final straw. Her husband had stood by her through many ups and downs, but after McBain has completed his investigation and found nothing, he had made it clear that her obsession was damaging their marriage. The absence of joy and passion in their lives had strained their relationship. He had argued that it was time to move on and to seek counseling if necessary.

Fresh from the encounter at the bookstore, Christina had let her emotions get the better of her and replied that a lawsuit would provide all the therapy she needed for some time. David had reacted logically and angrily to that idea. He was right that such an action could stretch on, possibly for years, and would be the focus of their lives.

Now, after another sleepless night, Christina was undecided. At an intellectual level, she knew she had to get on with her life. At an emotional one, she was certain she was right about Roche. But David had made it clear that this was a critical moment. She knew she had to make what could be a life-changing decision in the next few days.

But first she wanted to gather some facts. Maybe there were still things she didn't know. Before she spoke to her attorney, she needed to hear what Doctor Lehmann had told McBain. He had never mentioned the conversation with her father about his anxiety and losing the money. Maybe there were other unrevealed thoughts that her parents had confided in the doctor. If there was anything that might help her, she had to find out what he knew.

Christina was finished crying. With her teeth clenched, she dressed in a suit, grabbed her trench coat and keys, and headed to the parking deck under the Boston Common.

The reception area held several patients, but the force of Christina's emotions would not allow her to wait.

"Good afternoon, Elaine. I don't have an appointment, but I need to speak with Doctor Lehmann right away. It's very important."

"Well, all right, Christina," the receptionist replied with hesitation. "He should be finished with a patient at any minute now, and I'll see what we can do. What seems to be the nature of the emergency?"

At the same time, a white-haired woman with a metal cane ambled around the corner from the examining rooms in the back. Doctor Lehmann was just behind her, writing on a form on a clipboard. When he looked up and saw Christina Baker, he paused and then finished writing and handed the form to Elaine.

Christina rushed up to him before he could say a word. "Doctor, I need to speak with you. This won't take but a few minutes."

Without waiting for his assent, she strode into his office, leaving the physician slack-jawed, along with several irritated patients in the outer room.

She was already seated across from his desk when the doctor came in and quickly closed the door behind him.

"Christina, this is highly unusual," he said. "I have patients to see and several appointments after the office closes. Can we schedule some time over the next few days to talk?"

"Doctor Lehmann, I need to know some things before I make an important decision. I'd like to know what you talked about with Mr. McBain the other day. And I want to talk to you about my parents again."

Lehmann stood behind his desk and ran his hands through his hair. He took his glasses off and cleaned them with a tissue while he talked.

"Well, I...what did he mention to you?" the doctor asked. "Did he have anything to say about his investigation? I know you asked him to look into your parents' investments; he mentioned that. Did he speak to Mr. Roche?"

"Mr. McBain has finished his work for me," Christina stated flatly. "I'm considering hiring an attorney to pursue this now. But before I do, I'd like to know anything my father or mother may have said to you about this. I didn't realize that they had confided in you about how distraught they were over losing their money."

Lehmann continued polishing his glasses, and then he put them on and paced back and forth beneath his wall of pictures.

"Christina, I knew I shouldn't have mentioned that to him. I really didn't want to upset you. I don't think it serves any purpose now to go on about something we can't change. I'm sorry I didn't see it sooner. We've talked about that before, but I don't believe anything we can do or say now—"

"Are you sure that my father never said anything about Richard Roche to you? About what was happening with the money? If he was so depressed, maybe he mentioned something. Perhaps a disagreement over his financial advice or certain decisions that had been taken. Please, think back. My mother? You knew them so well."

"Yes, yes I did," the physician said. "And that's why I'm asking you to reconsider this lawyer business. Please, for your own peace of mind."

"Doctor, did they have any concerns about him? Did you talk about that?"

"Well, I...I can't recall, other than the time I mentioned to your friend Mr. McBain...maybe...I don't think...please, this is very awkward... I'm not sure I can discuss this..."

He was becoming very agitated and uncomfortable. She rose and put a hand on his shoulder to stop him.

"I'm sorry, Doctor," she said. "I don't want to involve you in this going forward. But you have to understand. I'm convinced this man did something wrong, and I'm going to do what I have to in order to find out what it is. I know that as a true friend of my parents, you want that too. You know I don't blame you for not seeing what was happening. They kept it from all of us. I just want to know if there are other things they might have said that I can use in court. Or perhaps with the securities authorities."

Lehmann sat down behind his desk but continued to fidget with several files that lay there.

"In court?" he said. "No, Christina, I don't think there is anything I can talk about there. I only met Mr. Roche once or twice at events at your house. I couldn't really speak to their relationship. I know your father and mother were both extremely depressed by what happened, but I'm sure I wouldn't know...that is, I can't recall any specific anger toward Mr. Roche. Of course your father was upset about the losses, and well, with Mr. Roche as their advisor, how could he not be? But I don't recall anything specific. I mean other than maybe some outrage over the whole market disaster. Certainly not any accusations of any misconduct that I am aware of. I'm sorry. I couldn't add anything to that, not in court."

Christina thought for a moment.

"Well," she said. "Maybe that will be enough. I'll speak to the attorney and mention it to him. He will probably want to interview you about what my parents spoke of with you. The timing also. When did you say this was?"

"I can't say right now," Lehmann replied. "Sometime a few months before they passed away. Let me check my records to be certain of what and when. I'll get back to you."

"All right, do you think you might—?"

Doctor Lehmann rose from his seat. "Please, Christina, I really do need to see these people outside. I'll try to remember more if I can as soon as I'm free. I will look up the files in my computer this evening and talk to you tomorrow. That might jog my memory about anything specific. I promise, tomorrow."

Christina nodded and put on her coat.

"Very well. Thank you, Doctor. I'll look forward to hearing from you. Anything you can provide me will be helpful in any lawsuit. Please phone me if you remember anything else. I'll be staying at my family's house. You can call me there."

He ushered her out of the office with a consoling hand on her back.

In the courtyard, Christina mentally placed herself in the office and tried to imagine that day her father had confessed his anguish to Doctor Lehmann. It was obvious the doctor didn't want to get involved in a legal action, but she couldn't help feeling that there were other conversations he hadn't yet recalled that might be helpful. She had the distinct sense that her father or mother had said something about Roche. Either way, it was time to pay the charlatan a visit. Christina hated the thought of being in the same room with him. But this time, she wouldn't be a bystander to her parents' decorum. This time, he would be the one to lose something.

The crowds and traffic were beginning to herald the afternoon rush hour in the financial district. In concert, even faster-moving clouds from the west urged people to hasten home with the threat of a looming deluge of April showers, as the weather reversed direction back to a cold gray to compensate for the early taste of sun and warmth.

Walking against the stream, Christina Baker smelled spring rain in the air as she zigzagged along the pathways of Post Office Square on her way to High Street. She found the building in a few minutes and took the elevator up to the sixteenth floor.

Richard Roche was not expecting her when she opened the door to his office. The room was spacious, with a spectacular view between adjacent buildings of the Boston harbor through the glass behind his desk, the streaks of cloud casting shadows on the ferries and tour boats that plied the water below. Off to the right was a small meeting area with a cherrywood conference table and chairs. An antique credenza with glass doors and a small bar stood by the other wall. It held a number of diplomas and framed pictures, along with financial books and copies of the *Economist, Financial Times,* and *Wall Street Journal.* A flat-panel television broadcast the day's financial news from the wall just above.

He rose from his chair in a charcoal-gray suit and greeted her with a smile.

"Hello again, Christina. How are you?"

The cold-eyed beauty looked him up and down for a moment in contempt. Her anger left her nearly speechless. Nearly, but not quite.

"Outraged, but not surprised," she said. "I didn't want to see you at all, but wanted the pleasure of telling you in person that this isn't over. You might have been able to charm the man I sent to speak with you about my parents' money. We'll see how well you do in a legal investigation."

Roche took the news in stride, nodding his head as if humoring a young student.

"I suppose I should have expected this. Surely Mr. McBain informed you of our conversation. I explained what happened, and he agreed that there was nothing I could have done under the circumstances. We financial professionals do our best, but we can't be held liable for the decisions of our clients or unforeseen market circumstances. I had hoped you might understand that better if he explained it to you."

"We'll see how liable you are when my attorney begins to review your performance for the lawsuit I'm going to bring. I'm going to ask him to take my case to the securities authorities."

"I'm sorry to hear that, Christina," he said. "However, I do appreciate your willingness to tell me this face to face. You always were direct."

She narrowed her eyes and crossed her arms.

"Not always. I should have been more direct with my parents, before it was too late. They were always impressed by you, for reasons I could never understand. But your charms were wasted on me. You'll come to appreciate my directness more in the months ahead. Sooner or later, I'll find out what you did and how you convinced them to trust in you."

The older man showed no sign of anger, no hint of confrontation. He merely shook his head in resignation.

"You seem quite determined on this course of action despite everyone's better judgment and advice. I don't suppose there's anything I could do now to convince you I've done nothing wrong."

"Certainly there is. Return my parents' money."

Roche sighed and sat down. "Good evening, Christina. Take care of yourself."

She inhaled and stared at him one last time, then turned on her heel and left the door open. Actually seeing Richard Roche again, hearing the sweet poison of reason in his voice, had helped harden her attitude even further. As the elevator doors opened, Christina Baker was more determined than ever to see her attorney the next day.

She returned to Newbury Street, but after a few minutes, she decided to have Karen close the bookstore that evening. She needed to calm down and consider carefully what she would do next. She drove west on Newbury with the traffic and then found her way to Beacon Street. As always when she was troubled, Christina returned to her family's Brookline house to think. Somehow she always seemed more at peace and able to gather her thoughts in the home she had grown up in.

But this was also the place where her parents had died. The house was quiet, and it now felt hollow and claustrophobic in its emptiness, both larger and smaller without them. With her emotions raw, the memories of their times together were overwhelming in intensity. At first she tried to focus and write down her thoughts in a diary, but soon found she needed motion. Christina flitted from room to room, grasping at memories as she caressed picture frames or furniture. Several silent hours passed by without any peace or sense of resolution as she leafed through scrapbooks and sorted through dresses, pants, and jackets that hung in their closets. Part of her remained sure they would return at any moment. That she would hear the front door opening downstairs, run to meet them, and fly into their arms. She lost track of time but could not lose her anxiety.

Finally she sat down at the desk in the library, took out paper, and penned a letter to her attorney. In irritation she addressed and stamped it and turned it over in her hands.

Then, overcome by the need for action, she was peeling off her work clothes. In a few minutes, she had changed into her running gear and stretched. She placed the letter inside her pink weatherproof jacket and zipped it up. By the time the first raindrops began to fall, Christina was out the door and running.

In the brisk night air, she started at an easy pace and hit her stride after the first mile. Several minutes later, the first echoes of thunder rolled in from the distance. As she picked up speed, the rain increased its own pace in response.

Christina soon entered a familiar rhythm. She was home, in the neighborhood where she had been raised. Her feet followed roads she had known since childhood. She had forgotten how good it was to run in the rain. How it felt to be happy.

As the lightning flashes grew brighter, the rain intensified and thunder boomed closer, riding the wind. In response, she ran even harder, recalling how often she had done this as a girl. Just as in high school, she was finally alone with her thoughts, her body on autopilot in a smooth pattern of automated adjustment in tempo as the hills rose and fell, and she glided between asphalt, dirt pathways, and tall grass.

She loved this place and missed it. The neighborhood, the brick and stone Victorian houses and tree-lined streets of Brookline that intersected chaotically, the small parks and hidden walkways. At times she ran with the traffic and at times against, dodging oncoming headlights and horns carelessly.

Stands of trees, black wrought-iron fences, and ponds rolled by. The skies opened up, the downpour blotting out sound and sight until the next brilliant flash illuminated the skyline of Boston to the crack of thunder. Christina let go of time and immersed herself in the all-consuming force of nature, of the thunderstorm and the physical boundaries of her legs and lungs as she pushed them to their limit. She ran to forget, and for that time she did.

After two hours, she felt the cleansing simplicity of exhaustion. As she crossed the railroad tracks, she sprinted the last two hundred yards, nearly home.

She tore across an imaginary finish line and slowed to a walk to cool down. The rain continued to beat on her, and she reveled in it. The cooling drops pelting down were a welcome massage, soaking her body, mind, and spirit.

Her consciousness clear from hours of escape, random thoughts began to reappear. The conversation that day with the doctor. The confrontation with Richard Roche. Memories of her parents, of their friends and happier times.

For a moment, Christina thought of the bookstore the previous afternoon and McBain, then the fall from the ladder and the aisle. She had been both angry and embarrassed at her clumsiness. It had been rude not to thank him for breaking her fall. But something about his pleasure in that embrace made her not want to give an inch. McBain was transparently selfish, a strange contradiction of the direct and the conniving. On the other hand, he had done everything within reason to investigate her case, just as he had said. Part of her anger had come unrequited when she realized how much she didn't mind lying on top of him after the spill. For a brief moment, it felt entirely too comfortable, and that was wrong.

As she recovered her breath now, she allowed herself to feel a wave of flattery from his attention. She had never met a man quite like him before. He did not seem the kind of company she kept or worked with, but Christina suspected there were things about him that might surprise her. Certainly he had chosen a strange line of work for reasons she could only guess at. He had been nothing if not honest at last, in both his intentions and his diligence. His partnership with Boston O'Daniel spoke well of him too, despite himself. She wondered about their relationship, which was clearly rich with chemistry of some kind.

Bastard though he might be, it had been a long time since she had felt a strange man's eyes devouring her with such unabashed sexual intent. Though she would never act on such a thing, it had been a nice feeling.

A little smile graced her lips. She was almost to the mailbox on the corner near her house; now was the time to decide. Christina felt the envelope inside her jacket, but after the run and the time to think, she was unsure. Drained of obsessive energy, her anger had cooled and her reason was guiding her in a new direction.

Perhaps she should listen to them and let it go. There seemed little to be gained and much that might be lost if she continued.

Maybe it really was time to move on with her life.

The roar of another set of approaching tires ripping up wet asphalt finally pierced her concentration as the sound of the rain peeled back momentarily. She was sore and tired but moved as quickly as she could to get out of the street as her shadow lengthened along the pavement. At the curb, she turned to glance over her shoulder.

The headlights were the last thing she saw.

TWELVE

McBain started the day making a few notes on the history of Drysdale Securities, which was none too savory to begin with and certainly would not be improved by bad publicity from an aggrieved client with a fan base active in social media. By noon he had enough material for leverage and drew up a quick summary of the situation with the actress and the young salesman, accompanied by a short history of the firm's troubles with the SEC and associated headlines. After checking his research files, he dialed up the head of the investment division of the firm and made an appointment through his administrative assistant for that week.

It was almost April 15, ensuring a good amount of stress for everyone involved and helping him turn up the heat at just the right moment to get some cooperation and a fat refund. With the right pressure, he would pick up a check soon after while the young hotshot picked up a pink slip. Maybe he'd have better luck in real estate.

McBain picked up his hat and jacket and walked past Boston on the way out to lunch. He had filled her in on the results of his research on the Bakers and his final conversation with their daughter. Now that they had put his little indiscretion behind them, his partner seemed to have returned to speaking terms, penance exacted. She was on the phone, listening and scribbling quickly with a pen but staring directly at him with a peculiar look of consternation on her face. He mouthed "want anything?" and pointed to his watch.

She held up her finger. "Yes," she said into the phone. "Yes, I've got the room information. Thank you for calling us."

"Another lead?" McBain asked. "Excellent."

Boston pulled her hair away from her face and looked at her notepad.

"Not a new one. That was about your other client, Ms. Baker. From her husband, actually."

His appetite ruined, McBain pulled on his coat and grimaced.

"She's not a client, Boston. I told her several times there's nothing to her case. I finished up the interviews, went to her bookstore, and told her the truth, that there's nothing there. I never want to see her again. You win; you were right."

"Oh yes, that's right," his partner said. "Well, you know that client you don't have? She's in the hospital. Somebody tried to run her over."

They took Boston's red Shelby Cobra GT through the midday traffic to Mass General Hospital. With her shifting and McBain hanging on, they reached the parking deck near the Charles River in fifteen minutes. The reception desk was on the tenth floor, where David Hilliard was waiting for them, speaking with two of Boston's finest. An NFL-sized officer wore sergeant stripes on his sleeve, the seams bulging beneath the chevrons as he took notes. His younger partner had on an Irish scowl, befitting the bad cop role.

Both officers took their caps off when they saw them—or, more specifically, the redhead in the black thigh-length leather jacket and Jimmy Choo boots.

"Hey, Boston, how are you?"

"Hello, Miss O'Daniel."

She shook hands with the big one, then his partner. "Hi, Clarence. Hi, Roy. How have you boys been?"

"Pretty good," Clarence said. "Nothing much new. Didn't expect to see you here. A bit off your beat, isn't it? You know these folks?"

McBain shook hands with both men. "A little. We haven't actually met Mr. Hilliard yet."

He had been hoping against hope that the guy would be some old academic stiff with a bad goatee and receding hairline, a chip off the old Ivy League cliché. Once again he was disappointed. The lean, dark-haired young man greeted them with a sincere and solid handshake and a look of deep concern on his face. He was tall and good looking, with probing eyes that looked directly at a person from behind horn-rimmed glasses when he spoke.

"Ms. O'Daniel, Mr. McBain. I'm David Hilliard. Thank you both for coming."

"Sure thing," the investigator said. "Though I'm not certain what we can do or say. I'm sure Ms. Baker told you about my report. I'm a bit surprised she had you call us in connection with the accident after that."

"I didn't want to involve you anymore, but Christina insisted," Hilliard said. "Considering the accident and her heightened emotional state, I was hoping you could spend a few minutes with her and help calm her down. She was adamant about speaking with you."

"Not a problem, Mr. Hilliard," Boston said. "Why don't you and the guys fill me in on the details of the accident while McBain goes in and talks to your wife."

McBain nodded and looked at David Hilliard.

"What kind of condition is she in now?"

"Pretty upset," Hilliard replied. "But in her calm, determined way. I think the timing of this just pushed her further into her obsession over the business with her parents' death and Mr. Roche. You'll see for yourself, but you should be prepared for another argument."

"How badly was she injured? Is she able to talk?" McBain asked. There was a trace of hope in his voice.

"Oh, yes."

McBain sighed and walked over to the door. "Wish me luck."

Boston watched him enter the room and then turned back to the two policemen.

"So, Boston," Sergeant Davis said, "what brings you two into a little traffic accident like this in the middle of a busy day?"

"Well, to tell you the truth, I'm not sure, Clarence," she said. "I gathered from Mr. Hilliard here that his wife was pretty upset and banged up. She seems to think that maybe her accident wasn't totally an accident."

"So she said a few minutes ago. What's your interest?"

"We've been looking into a little disagreement for Ms. Baker having to do with some investment business of her parents a few months back. Sadly, they passed away about the same time as the financial problem came to light. A substantial amount of money seems to have been lost, and we've been trying to determine whether there was anything illegal going on."

"Mr. Hilliard told us about her parents," Clarence said. "Didn't know about the money. So anybody in particular have a reason to try to run over the young lady?"

"Not that we can determine. We pretty much finished up over the last few days. Talked to a lot of people who knew them. McBain's take is it was just the wrong advice at the wrong time. Unfortunately, as tragic as it was, there doesn't seem to be anything we can do about it. No case."

"That's what I told her, Ms. O'Daniel," Hilliard said. "But she insisted on pursuing it. As I said on the phone, she spoke to both Doctor Lehmann and Mr. Roche yesterday. She didn't want to give up. I was very concerned that she was going to push on despite what you and Mr. McBain told her."

"Hmm. I'm sorry to hear that," Boston said. "You boys check out the scene? What did you think?"

Roy opened his notebook. "From the look of things, there's nothing to suggest anything deliberate," he said. "It's a through street leading to a main drag, and poorly lit. Not uncommon for people to zip through that neighborhood in a hurry day and night. Plus it was late and dark, and it was pouring rain. Between that and the flashes of lightning, the driver could have easily missed seeing Mrs. Hilliard."

"No skid marks," Clarence said. "And no other damage. Given the road conditions, it's just as likely the driver lost it for a moment. Didn't hit anything else but Mr. Hilliard's wife. She's just lucky she was close to the mail box. Driver must have seen it before he saw her and swerved to avoid it. Clipped her pretty good and kept going. I think she got flipped into the air by the blow and hit the mailbox and sidewalk pretty hard. Our best guess: it was probably some drunk on the way home in the rain who never even saw her."

"Any witnesses?"

"None that we could find, Ms. O'Daniel," Roy replied. "We checked the neighbors, and no one saw or heard anything. No other drivers around, either."

"Who called the ambulance and you guys, then?"

David Hilliard shook his head. "We're lucky she managed to stay conscious long enough to reach her cell phone. Christina was barely able to speak when I picked up."

"Tough girl, your wife," she said. "Sometimes it pays to be hard nosed."

Clarence smiled at her. "Yea, we know the type."

"That's how they make us up here," Boston said. "You guys should be used to it by now. Maybe more of us will join the force and add some spice."

"You ready for that kind of cut in pay?" the big cop said. "It's not all glamour, you know. Anyway, the docs say Mrs. Hilliard will be OK. She's pretty banged up now and will be limping around on pain-killers for a couple weeks, but nothing broken or smashed up inside. Scars heal. She'll be all kinds of colors for a while, but her reflexes might have saved her skull, or her life. We've got to go, Boston. Give us a call if you find out anything we should know."

The officers left, and David Hilliard was about to depart when something occurred to Boston. She stopped him. "Excuse me, Mr. Hilliard, but you mentioned your wife was still going to pursue this case. What did you mean by that? And why would she think this wasn't an accident?"

Hilliard put on his trench coat. "Even after you had finished your investigation and told her there was nothing, Christina was still convinced there was something we didn't know. That night, she argued that she should see her attorney and start legal action against Roche, maybe go to the securities authorities with her case. She went to see Doctor Lehmann and Mr. Roche yesterday. She told Roche she was going to sue him. So now she thinks..."

"Got it," Boston said with a nod. And she did.

McBain closed the door softly and approached the bed. In the filtered light with the blinds down, Christina Baker appeared to be asleep. He took off his coat and stared at her for a minute. He swallowed hard while he pushed down a familiar rage. Hospitals bothered him, he didn't like being there, and he hated what he saw even more.

The covers were pulled up, and her head lay back on the pillow. The left side of her face was bandaged from the scalp to her jaw. Her forehead was slashed with scars, the skin raw and pink, even though her face had been cleaned up. Black-and-purple bruises spotted her exposed cheek and chin. The black hair was pulled back away from her face, and he could see that her eyes were swollen like a boxer who had taken a beating for twelve rounds.

McBain wondered if she was sedated. Just as he was turning to go, she opened her eyes, raised her head slightly, and looked up at him. A private moment passed while their eyes met. He drew a breath.

"Buy you a drink?" he asked.

She didn't laugh, but she did blink twice, and McBain thought that was just as good. He grabbed a chair and pulled it over by the bedside.

"I won't ask how you're feeling. Do you want to talk now, or should I come back?"

Christina pointed to the water bottle on the tray as she sat up. He handed it to her.

"Can you open the blinds a bit?" she asked in a gravelly voice. "We need some light."

"You sure that's a good idea?"

"Afraid of what I look like, McBain?"

"You look great."

She used the bed control to raise her position while the room brightened.

"Thank you for coming. I do want to talk to you."

"Your husband called us," he said. "We got here as fast as we could. He said you wanted to speak to me. Sorry to hear about the accident."

Her head moved back and forth on the pillow.

"It wasn't an accident. That car came right at me. Someone tried to kill me."

He glanced over at her and smiled.

"Sure, why not?" he said. "I only met you a few times, and I wanted to kill you too."

"That's not funny."

"Sorry. Well, we know how accident-prone you are. Look, your husband gave us a quick update over the phone. You were running in the dark, in the rain. The police report says you told them the car swerved. It was probably some drunk."

"It wasn't," she said.

"Are you sure you want to talk now?" he asked. "You're in pain, and probably have some good drugs in your system too. Maybe we should have this chat when your head's a little clearer."

"I am in pain, and I do want to talk now. And that car did come at me deliberately. I was dizzy and confused when I first talked to the police. I'm not sure what I said or remembered. I've been rerunning it in my head. I am sure now."

The investigator folded his arms. Yeah, she certainly was returning to her old self already. "OK, I know I'm going to regret asking this, but why would someone want to kill you?"

"I've been thinking," she said.

"Uh oh."

It was hard to give him the evil eye when both eyes were puffy, but she managed. "After you told me the results of your investigation, I went to talk to Doctor Lehmann, then Roche. I told Roche that I would be hiring a lawyer to start legal action against him and go to the securities authorities."

McBain groaned. "Why did you do that? I already told you it would be a waste of time and money."

"So you said," Christina replied. "And by the time I was done running last night, I have to admit I was almost ready to agree with you."

"So what's the problem?"

"Don't you see?"

"No."

"First you start asking him questions. Then I threaten him with legal action. That same night someone tried to run me down in the rain near my parents' house. If someone tried to kill me, that means...that means that there must be something more to this than I thought. That maybe my parents didn't commit suicide...it means it's possible he had them killed to keep them from..."

McBain stood up and backed away from her bed with his hands out.

"Whoa there!" he said. "Wait a goddamned minute. Now you think your folks' financial advisor swindled you and them out of the money and then killed them to shut them up? Listen, Bernie Madoff robbed thousands of dupes and stole sixty billion dollars, and the only one who ended up in danger was him. Someone in South Boston is more likely to get killed over five bucks than a wealthy person over millions. That's just how it works, lady."

The door swung open then, and a nurse rolled in a small cart. "Time to change your bandages, Ms. Baker," she said.

McBain reached for his coat. "I'll just come back when—"

"Shut up and sit down," Christina said. "We're not finished talking yet. Go ahead, nurse."

The nurse paused for a moment, looked at him, and then shrugged. "All right, if you say so."

McBain pushed his jaw shut so he could grind his teeth. As a token act of defiance, he stood behind the chair instead of sitting. He averted his gaze while the nurse pulled the covers back. Christina Baker rolled onto her right side with a grimace.

"What's the matter, McBain?" she said. "Squeamish? Or are you just not used to looking at women this way?"

His fingers gripped the back of the chair while he shook his head at her. "You really are some kind of pain in the ass. Anybody ever tell you that?"

"I'm an only child. What do you think?"

He didn't turn away then. His eyes followed the nurse's hands as she shifted the hospital gown strategically and changed the dressings along Christina Baker's left side from her face to her knee. The bruises were ugly and thick, shades of pain from black to puke green. They were fresh and would get worse before they got better. McBain recognized them. That was the problem.

She stared at him while he watched, but otherwise they remained silent. The nurse finished her work and gave Christina pain medication. McBain held his tongue until the door closed behind her.

"Look, I'm sorry," he said. "But there was an autopsy of your parents. There always is with suicides. They weren't murdered by anybody. It was an overdose of pills and booze. You know this."

"So," she said, "you think it's just a coincidence that the day I threaten Mr. Roche with legal action I almost get killed at night by a speeding car that disappears without stopping? Is that it?"

"Head injuries do strange things to people," McBain said. "And accidents happen."

He rubbed his jaw and sat down again. He wanted to believe he was a sucker for a beautiful, wounded woman. But that wasn't it.

"Answer me."

"It's the most likely explanation." But he said it without conviction.

He was taken aback when he glanced over at her. It must have hurt, but she was trying to smile.

"You don't believe that," she said. "You don't believe that because you are a good detective. And because you are a numbers man and you know the probability of them not being connected."

McBain leaned closer to her and narrowed his eyes. "Nobody likes a know-it-all."

She was breathing heavily again, getting tired. "With you or without you, McBain, I'm not going to stop asking questions."

Questions. He had talked to lots of people. He had asked all the right questions and gotten all the right answers. So why was an annoying sense of guilt needling the back of his mind? And the answer echoed back as the thought evolved. Maybe they weren't the right questions. He and his partner were used to having all the information at their disposal before they made a move. During the past two weeks, it hadn't occurred to him that maybe there was something else going on here that was out of their normal calculation. Then he heard Boston's words ringing in his ears again: treat it like a real case. And the nagging suspicion that somebody—maybe Roche, maybe not—had played him for a sucker began to creep under his skin. Maybe he was still making rookie mistakes here and not even realizing it.

McBain stood up and looked down at his damaged client, her eyelids fighting sleep.

"OK. We'll do some more investigating, but under one condition."

"Which is?" she asked.

"You leave it to us, cooperate when we ask, and otherwise stay out of it."

"I'm not sure—"

"It's not negotiable, Ms. Baker. It's a yes or no. I'm no only child, but Boston and I have our own rules for doing business."

"Do I have any choice?"

"Sure you do," he said. "Like you said, you can limp along with us, on our terms, or without us."

Christina pressed the button to lower her bed to a comfortable position and then closed her eyes. "Terms accepted."

He walked to the door.

"Thank you, McBain."

He walked back over to her bedside and gently pushed the black hair away from her bruised eyes.

"You know, you can call me Boozy."

"I don't think so," she whispered.

McBain closed the door and walked back over to the reception desk. Boston was alone talking on her cell phone. She hung up when he reached the desk. He took one look at her face and frowned.

"Well?" Boston asked. "What did she say? How is she? Did she remember anything, or see anything? What do you think?"

He threw his hands in the air. "She's one big mass of bruises. What do you think she said? What do I think? I think she hit her head on the sidewalk. In her case, that just shows how hard-headed the woman is."

"That hard head may have saved her life. And it may just be onto something."

The minute the light bulb had gone off in his head McBain had guessed Boston to be two steps ahead of him. Her instincts about people were clearer than his.

"Maybe there's something there, maybe there isn't. In any case, you can try not to get so excited about our client turning up black, blue, and purple in the hospital."

"What do you mean?" she asked.

"For one thing," he said, "you can stop bouncing up and down inside like a kid on Christmas Eve. We've worked together four years. I know that look in your eye. You're getting excited over nothing. It's probably nothing."

"Something's going on. This was too much of a coincidence for my taste. You pay visits to all those people, then she talks about seeing a lawyer, then she meets up with the front of a car. There's something here that we haven't seen before, something new. And we've never had a case with a death involved."

"You're right, I don't believe in coincidences either. And I've started thinking about something that's bothered me the last two weeks—"

"You mean other than the fact that you weren't going to get to sleep with Ms. Baker?"

"Besides that," he said. "Too many people had wonderful things to say about the Bakers for my taste. I'm not saying they weren't great people and loads of fun, but nobody's free of warts like that. This has all been too easy to wrap up."

"It does stand out in contrast to what we usually find out about people, doesn't it?"

"But that means there are a whole bunch of other, harder questions we should be asking and getting answers to. Like, why do two seemingly happy, relatively healthy people end up dead at the same time as a bunch of money goes down the rabbit hole?"

Boston nodded and ran her finger around the gold chain on her throat. "Which leads me to wonder: if, by some chance, Christina Baker was right, why would anyone be afraid enough of an ongoing investigation to try to have her killed? I admit that's a big 'if.'"

"I'm still not convinced it is Roche," he said. "I talked to a lot of people. Somehow it looks like maybe we put a stick in a hornet's nest and woke somebody up. If something is going on here, we'd better start from scratch with what we do know. Let's not assume anything yet."

He put on his coat and straightened his tie. "Somebody lied to me, and I don't like that."

"I think maybe it's time for you to drop the nice-guy routine and be the asshole I know you can be."

"I think you're right, partner."

They walked down to the parking deck, each quietly calculating.

Boston spoke first as they reached the car. "Whatever is going on, there was no hint of it in the investment file. That means we have to start somewhere else. Dig through everything we can and build our own file on the Bakers. Then maybe on Roche if it starts pointing to him. Otherwise see where the trail leads."

He nodded. "I already talked to Ms. Baker. As soon as she's back on her feet, she can help us pull everything together from her parents' stuff. What do you have in mind?"

"The usual: the will, credit card history, receipts, phone records, bank statements, insurance policies, any correspondence or diaries. Schedule books for as many years as they've got them, any time away or trips, hotels, vacations, and travel for work. And I'll want to look at that list of colleagues and friends again, including the ones you didn't talk to. Where are you going to start?"

He didn't skip a beat. "Their previous advisor, if they had one. And I want to talk to the doctor again. I'm already curious about a couple things. Like why the doctor was the only one the Bakers spoke to about those investment losses when they had so many friends. Also, he may be able to give us more detail about the autopsy report from those suicides on the unlikely chance something else did actually happen to them. And I want all their medical records and bills."

He opened his car door.

"Hey, Boston, considering what we don't know, maybe you had better fill Tom in and keep him updated, just in case."

"That's what I was doing when you came out of her room."

She opened her door to get in behind the wheel, but he stood with his hand on the car.

"I just had a thought," he said.

"What is it?"

"Maybe it was the husband."

Boston rolled her eyes. "Give it up, McBain."

THIRTEEN

The morning after Christina Baker was released from the hospital, Boston and McBain drove to the house in Brookline. Boston was armed with her portable organizing system, laptop computer, and notepads; McBain with a couple of whiteboards for mapping out connections and some smart remarks. Upon their arrival, he noted with some trepidation that their client was apparently well enough to move around the house and assist them, and eager to get started.

The first order of business for the partners was to set up a workspace in the large formal dining room just off the foyer. The massive mahogany table proved an ideal location for spreading out and arranging what Boston expected would become an epic amount of paperwork that had to be gathered, organized, and interpreted. McBain removed several portraits from the wall and commandeered the spots for the whiteboards on which they would make their notes, sketch out connections, and brainstorm their ideas.

Christina stood in the entryway to the room observing them, leaning on her walking stick with both hands. In her wool jacket, boots, and shawl, she appeared ready for a stroll in the countryside. A polished wood-and-bronze staff served as a stylish improvement on the cane the doctors had given her.

"Well, Boston. You two certainly do seem to need quite a lot of room. Do you really think you'll require all of this space?"

Boston looked up from her laptop, with one eye on McBain's redecorating efforts. Household skills were not his strong suit.

"Absolutely, Ms. Baker," she replied. "We have a very particular system that works well for us in each investigation. Your case is somewhat of a first, but I expect to use every bit of this room if not more of the house."

"What do you mean a first?"

"You understand that normally we devote our time and attention to the potential target of our investigation, the person we suspect of fraudulent behavior in cheating our clients. McBain and I try to dig up information about our suspects without tipping them off and put together an idea of how they did it. Then we see if there is a way to apply pressure on them to return the funds. This is going to be different. In this case, we need to assemble every piece of paper and scrap of evidence we can about your parents in order to understand them as a starting point. We'll see where that leads us. Hopefully we can discover material in that short history that gives us something to go on."

"But how will you know what to look for?" Christina asked.

"At first we won't," Boston replied. "That's why we need everything we can get. With your help, we'll construct a story that tells us about Phillip's and Sarah's lives and habits, as complete as possible. There are regular patterns to how we live and what we do each day that cement themselves over time in our routines. Once we have a firm grasp of those patterns and rhythms, the hard work begins."

"You mean you look for changes in the patterns," Christina said.

"Exactly," McBain said as he finished hanging the boards. "We start to look for anomalies or unexpected behavioral divergences that might suggest something new in their routines. Then we look for an explanation, a reason for the sudden change. In our normal work, we can then observe our target covertly and gather more information in order to decide how to proceed. We have to do it quickly in this case, since the trail is six months old."

Christina looked confused. "But I don't understand. We already know when Richard Roche appeared in their lives. It was five years ago."

Boston was going to reply, but her partner beat her to it.

"After your car...accident...Ms. Baker, we don't want to start off by assuming anything. Maybe Roche is involved, and maybe he isn't. If he is, something will emerge from the pattern. Until that happens, we don't want to rule anybody or anything out. If there is as much trouble here as you suspect, we want to get up to speed with the possible source of it before we come to any conclusions and move in one direction or another. If someone was serious enough about stealing this money to try to run you down, they'll very likely stand out in our investigation at some point.

"So to use Roche just as a hypothetical, we'll want to see how your parents' decision making might have changed when he appeared on the scene. For example, I want to know exactly how their spending habits and investment decisions looked before and after he took over. If and only if something looks suspicious, we'll start over again looking at the statements and at Roche himself. But until that time, we keep an open mind."

Christina winced ever so slightly and shifted her weight to her right foot. The swelling around her eyes had receded, and though the left side of her face was still lightly bandaged, the bruising was almost gone. The investigators knew she had to still be in pain, but her ability to conceal it and control her limp was impressive.

"Well, you've set yourselves quite a task in that case," she said. "You already know how many friends my parents had. If you start casting that wide a net, it may take some time to narrow your focus to Mr. Roche."

"Possibly," Boston said. "But you'll find we can move very fast once we've identified the information we need. And based on what we find here, we can start asking people questions again to see if we can shake out any new leads. We've learned how to dig for answers from some of the best in the business. It helps to start by assuming everyone is lying to you."

"That seems a disappointing way to approach people," Christina said.

McBain laughed. "No. In fact, we're rarely disappointed."

Boston frowned at him. "More helpful to say that there is a time to be cynical. After what happened to you, I think now is that time. Don't you?"

"I suppose you're right," Christina said. "What next?"

Boston looked at the table then around the room. She checked the windows.

"How is your security here, Ms. Baker? Normally we do this at our office so there's no danger of anyone tampering with our material. This time it's best we just assemble everything here and work in this dining room."

"Not very good, I'm afraid," she answered with a shake of the dark hair. "We always felt safe in this neighborhood. People didn't really worry about crime, so my parents never saw the need to put in extra security. Sometimes they wouldn't even remember to lock the doors. They were quite old fashioned in that regard."

Boston jotted down another line on one of the whiteboards. "We'll have a new one installed tomorrow, just in case."

She dug into her weathered leather briefcase and looked at her notebook. "Right," she said, pulling out three identical sheets of paper. "Here's one for each of you. This is the initial list of what we are looking for. McBain, you start at the top of the house, then tackle the library. I'll take the middle floors. Ms. Baker should get whatever she has and the contact information for the credit card and phone companies and any others we might need. Hopefully, your parents kept some of their records here in good order. Otherwise we will need your authorization to reach out to the companies for back records."

Christina examined the list. "I have a few of these on hand, such as the will and insurance documents. But I'm afraid I haven't taken the time to assemble all of their boxes and sort out the rest of this. I kept putting off going through their things. We may have quite a chore ahead of us. I just don't know what is here and what isn't. All of the investment records were in the library."

"OK." McBain scanned the page and took a deep breath. "Let's get started."

The three spread out throughout the house and began to comb each room for any kind of paperwork, record, or document that might prove of value.

The Baker house in Brookline was no mansion, but it was old enough and large enough for a sizeable family. Built in the early 1920s, the Victorian-style dwelling was a formidable challenge, with three full stories of rooms, closets, cupboards, crannies, and storage areas, as well as an attic and basement where a person could store small boxes or hide private treasures.

McBain climbed a spiral staircase to the attic. It proved to be more of an extra work space, full of shelves and trunks. He dug through racks of old magazines and newspapers, then came across cardboard file boxes labeled Wellesley, organized by decade. For hours he sorted through the piles, making notes of the contents and lugging the most relevant finds downstairs.

Boston spent the better part of the morning tearing through bedroom closets, dressers, cabinets, and storage rooms. By noon she had hauled over a dozen boxes down to their table.

As McBain entered the dining room with the last of the college boxes, she sighed. "Shit."

"What is it? Oh."

Each of the cardboard boxes Boston had placed on the table was full. The contents had been tossed in and heaped at random, with no sign of any organization or order other than that suggested by the age or condition of hundreds of slips of paper. McBain could see worn American Express card receipts, old utility bills, printouts from registers, and assorted scraps of paper with words and numbers scrawled on them. "Worst-case scenario?"

Boston took a sharp breath and looked up at him as she sat back and crossed her arms and legs. "No. A worst-case scenario would mean we had nothing to work with. This is the second-worst case. A total fucking mess."

He was forced to agree. Christina joined them with her collection of legal documents and a list of contact phone numbers. For the rest of the afternoon, the partners sifted through everything the three had collected, did an inventory, and came to one conclusion.

"All right," McBain said. "That takes care of the obvious stuff. Now I'll start banging around the house looking for the real gold."

"What is that?"

"The critical items," Boston said. "Personal correspondence. Diaries. Notebooks. I don't see any sign of them in what we found so far. Do you have them?"

"No, I haven't had the heart to look," she said. "I never saw them, but knowing my father and mother, I'm sure such things exist. If they weren't in their bedroom, they are probably all in the library. I didn't see anything lying about."

Daylight faded and lights snapped on while Christina helped Boston sort through the boxes and begin to bring order to the chaos.

Meanwhile, McBain went painstakingly room by room, searching with flashlight and a set of tools for any possible hiding place, without success. But in searching the house, he began to get a more personal sense of Phillip and Sarah Baker, staring at pictures and wandering through their possessions like a tourist in a ghost town. He thought perhaps his client had been exaggerating, but in some rooms, a thin layer of dust confirmed she hadn't touched a thing since their death. It was another reflection of her obsession that the house still breathed their presence, from the clothing in the closets to fragrances on a dresser and the unique scent of age. He found nothing but memories.

Finally he was left with the library.

"If there are secrets, there is always a special hiding place. You know, like porn or drugs."

McBain's eyes wandered around the vault-like room, trying to gauge the best place among the walls of bookcases, shelves, and nooks to place a secret compartment or hide something personal from casual view. A large desk sat in front of two French doors looking out onto the garden, now lit up with floodlights. Deep, comfortable chairs littered the room, some stacked with books. One corner was filled with two squat easy chairs with ottomans; their worn, rustic leather shone brightly from floor lamps and torch lights arcing down from the lofty ceiling.

"I don't know anything about those things," Christina Baker said dryly from the doorway.

With his back to her, McBain just bit his lip and took a moment. After exhaling, he said: "No, I'm certain you don't. So let's think in terms of legal documents or diaries instead."

The library had been their favorite room; it was obvious. The space had that lived-in appearance and feel that reflected both attentive care and frequent use. They were all book people. They had done their reading and, more importantly, their writing in here. McBain mentally catalogued a variety of literary paraphernalia, from letterhead with the

Baker name and address in elegant typeface to a somewhat dated desktop personal computer with wires leading to a network connection and printer.

He sat down at the desk in front of a beautiful black Smith Corona Sterling typewriter. The antique machine was in pristine condition. "I didn't know anybody still knew how to use these." Looking to his left, he tapped at the keyboard of the computer. "Or this. How old is this computer? Any chance they used this to keep their private thoughts?"

"My parents only used it to print out documents for work and for e-mail. When it came to their personal lives, they were rather attached to old-fashioned ways of communicating and writing."

McBain thought that over. "Have you gone through their e-mail accounts?"

Christina shook her head. "No, I didn't see the need. I don't even know their passwords."

"No problem," McBain said. "You write down their addresses, and I'll take care of that later."

McBain started on the drawers and soon hit pay dirt. "Hello. Here's something." He pulled out a stack of black Week-At-A-Glance schedulers from under some loose newspapers and examined them. "His and hers calendar planning, going back one, two...ten years. This will make Boston happy. Might give us some help in putting timelines together too. About time we caught a break. Most people do this stuff electronically these days."

That prompted another thought, but based on what he had seen, he already knew the answer.

"I saw a phone bill for the house service. Do you have any cell phone records?"

"I'm afraid not," she said. "I kept trying to persuade them to get at least one mobile permanently for emergencies. Once in a while they would try one of those temporary disposable ones, but said they didn't use it enough to rationalize the cost of a regular number. My father and mother were social people, but they rather enjoyed their quiet and privacy. They didn't approve of technology and these social media trends, as they called them."

McBain swiveled around and took a look outside through the French doors. The backyard was well manicured and lit, with a weathered, red-and-white wooden shed beside several rows of earth and fitted stones tiered up to a concrete wall. The barren garden had survived a brutal winter, the soil turned up and fertile with the expectation of spring. He suspected his client had been exerting herself there as well.

He walked around the bookcases, examining the sturdy frames and backs for any sign of a latch or compartment. From time to time, he plucked a book from a shelf and opened it to remove some scrap of paper and determine its relevance to their search. He was always careful to replace the volume in its proper place. At the second bookcase, he stopped at eye level in front of a set of red classic volumes and looked closely at the names. His fingers ran back and extracted a worn red linen text that appeared to wear the years of its owners. He opened it and caressed the frayed pages for a moment.

"Is this *Le Petit Larousse*?" he asked.

"Yes, my mother used it for...what did you say?"

He replaced the book. "Don't faint. I'm only a part-time Neanderthal. I used to eat in a lot of expensive restaurants, some of them in France."

"*Pardonez moi, monsieur.*"

"*Pas de problem, madame.*"

The investigator smiled and pressed on. Several of the shelves served as filing areas. There he found the bank and investment records he was looking for, dating back years before Roche had come on the scene. McBain pulled them out and stacked them on the desk.

"We'll add these to the statements in the file you collected. I'll want to talk to their previous financial advisor after I go through these."

"I don't believe they had one," she said. "After my mother's estate lawyer passed on, I never heard them mention a specific name before Mr. Roche. I think they just left everything in a mutual fund account or two. They said they didn't want to pay for the fees. That was one of the reasons I was surprised when my father first told me he had hired him."

McBain kept browsing the shelves with his eyes and hands as Christina followed close behind, straightening books in his wake.

"Yeah, us financial types do like our fees," he said. "While we're on the subject, you and I haven't discussed our business relationship yet. Boston and I will follow this through regardless of whether we find anything or not. If in the end we still come up empty, there's no charge. If you were robbed and we can prove it, we get a percentage of whatever we recover for you. Our standard rate is twenty-five percent of what we get back. You in turn save a bundle by not paying any lawyers. And unlike them, we only get paid for results."

"Boston already told me it was fifteen, but she would accept ten in my case."

McBain ground his teeth and then turned to face her. "By the way, I hope you won't have any...ethical objection to how we get your money back if it comes to that. I wouldn't want to offend your Puritan sensibilities."

To his surprise, Christina didn't flinch. The corners of her mouth turned up. "Did you want to look at those bruises on my body again, McBain?"

He held her gaze. "I'm beginning to like you, Ms. Baker."

"You mean you didn't before I got hit by a car?"

"I'm funny that way."

"Well, I'll try to keep you entertained as the case progresses. Sorry, but I don't have any ladders in the library."

"I'm sure you'll tumble into some new way of getting into trouble," he said. "Ever since that first night in the bar, I suspected there was a part of you that was looking to start a fight. Part of the attraction, I guess. I should have known you were too good to be single when you showed up that second time sitting in my seat."

"Thank you," she said. "And it was my seat. I'm just glad we were able to get over that little impediment to your working on my case. Or perhaps I have Boston to thank for that."

"Partly," he said as he continued moving. "I don't make any apologies for my behavior or intentions. But that's in the past. I wouldn't be here if I didn't believe there was evidence to support your argument, circumstantial as it might be. I'm a numbers man, remember. Not to mention your persistence in the face of the known facts and a speeding car has me intrigued. You're my client now, limp or no limp."

"I'm really not normally this single minded," Christina said. "I understand that I can be stubborn at times, but I've never been in trouble before and don't go about disagreeing with people as a matter of principle. My friends tell me I'm quite pleasant and fun to be around."

McBain thought discretion the better part of valor.

"I'll bet you are," he said. "On the other hand, we haven't seen your husband today. Will Mr. Hilliard be joining us in the hunt?"

She fidgeted with a couple of books before answering.

"I don't believe so," she said in a formal tone. "David still thinks we are wasting time and that we won't find any evidence Roche stole any money. He and I argued again about the time and distraction involved with pursuing this. I'm afraid it is still a point of some contention between us. He thinks I'm obsessed."

"What do you think?"

"I think that it is worth finding out the truth about what happened to my parents' money," she said. "If that requires time and patience, then I'm willing to do whatever it takes. I told you that at the hospital. This is more important than anything right now."

"More than your marriage?"

"I love my husband, if that's what you're asking."

"Nope. Just wondering what's more important to you, your marriage or the truth. You seem to be pursuing this despite the obvious lack of need for money."

"I'm pursuing this," she said, "for a reason that's apparently beyond your ability to perceive through any of your investigative intuition."

"Revenge?"

"Love. You know, McBain, love?"

"I've heard about it."

Christina drew her battered frame up, and a fierce authority grew in her eyes.

"Let me tell you something about love. Once when I was in college on the gymnastics team, I fell and was hurt. Nothing bad, really, but I was in the hospital when a friend called my father. My parents drove eight hours at high speed through a raging blizzard of snow and ice to reach me without regard for the law or their lives, blind to any thought but that of their daughter in pain. They meant the world to me, and I miss them more than you can imagine. I would have done anything for them when they were alive. I won't do any less now that they're gone."

McBain looked her up and down for moment and then nodded with a little smile.

"That's good," he said. "I just wanted to make sure you were in this for the right reasons. Revenge is a bad reason to do anything. And it's especially bad to sacrifice valuable things over, like a marriage or the rest of your life. Just keep that in mind, and you'll be OK."

Her expression softened, and she looked puzzled.

"You're a strange man," Christina said.

"All part of the service we offer, ma'am." He looked at the last of the bookcases. "I don't see anything else here. Let's get this stuff back to Boston. Then she and I can head home for the night. We'll be back tomorrow to start following the trail."

The two investigators did return early the next morning. Thirty minutes and two cups of coffee later, a van pulled up in the driveway, and a team from a private security firm installed a home security system.

For the next two days, Christina and McBain poked and delved into every corner of the house again, alternating this with turns sorting and organizing the mountains of paper into Boston's system. Each day UPS and FedEx delivered packages of documents from the archives of credit card and phone companies. Mapping out notes on the whiteboard, Boston and McBain methodically assembled a history of the Bakers' habits, routines, events, and schedules. They separated the paperwork, first into categories and then chronologically, poring over phone records, credit card bills, travel receipts, purchases, vacation plans, random notes, and bank statements.

When the paper stacks had finally been sorted, they began the tedious job of working their way through the material, beginning with the first of the schedule books going back ten years. Boston and McBain pored over the dates, while Christina perched on their shoulders or answered specific questions about people or meetings. For hours they talked out the meaning of various items that seemed to stick out from the norm. They cross-referenced any large or unusual outflows of money against particular events on their paper trail or their client's formidable memory.

McBain listed the names of people who were mentioned repeatedly and anything that seemed out of the ordinary on the wall. The list of questions grew.

"As we go through these," Boston said, "let's note any appointments with Roche, or anyone else who you think is financial in nature. I'd also like to list any visits to Doctor Lehmann or any hospital stays, as well as see their medical records."

"Why?" Christina asked. "Don't you trust Doctor Lehmann's word?"

McBain shot her a look that said: *You poor, naïve kid.*

"Because Boston wants to see if we can chart any spikes in stress or something that reflects medical issues. Doc Lehmann told me your father admitted the stress to him, but he didn't give me a specific date. I also have a few new questions. We're not counting out the possibility of some kind of medical fraud, either. It's more common than people think. Since he's shy about returning my calls this week, I want to have more information when I see him again."

Together they spent the days and nights immersed in the case. Their client was amazed at the speed at which the two investigators processed information and worked, as well as their knack for unspoken communication and apparent knowledge of what the other was going to focus on or say next. Christina smiled at them for a moment during one of their working lunches.

"What's so funny?" McBain asked.

"You two. Sometimes when I listen to you together, it's hard to distinguish between your thoughts. I guess that comes from working as partners for so long."

Boston rolled her eyes. "Yes, a convenient side effect of all the quality time we spend with each other on this type of research. Of course, there are times when any given case can generate some creative tension in the room. Or if there is a minor disagreement between us."

To break the tension in the Baker house, they listened to a continuous stream of show tunes from a stack of old record albums and a turntable that the Bakers had maintained in immaculate condition. McBain enjoyed them but considered musicals a poor substitute for the piano at the Holiday. He had not had a martini for several days and had received a hard look from Boston after suggesting a quick trip to the "store" for supplies. Boston, for her part, considered it the equivalent of keeping a carrot just out of reach of a running horse as motivation to finish the race during their workday.

The Bakers' historic tax returns arrived on the morning of the third day. McBain added them to the bank and investment statements so they could examine the financial history of the late couple in context.

One by one, Boston and McBain tossed out ideas for potential leads or trails to follow. They talked about the names of the people who appeared on the board repeatedly. They followed a trail of bank payments here and unexplained spending there. Each questionable meeting or trip was double-checked and investigated. And one by one, each question mark on their whiteboard was scratched out, either through logic, explanation, or sheer lack of further detail.

Despite the casual demeanor they affected, Boston and McBain couldn't hide their disappointment at each dead end. If there was anything to this story, they would have to find it in documents that had not yet appeared. Perhaps something private that had not come out. All they had so far was conjecture and organized data. If there had been any wrongdoing, it was not evident in the guesswork and assumptions that evaporated after hours of probing and testing. The mountain of material they had labored to accumulate yielded only loose ends, random theories, and long-shot hypotheses. They needed more. They needed proof.

By the third night, they were exhausted and frustrated. After three days of searching the house, assembling the paper trail, and talking out the story, they had completed a portrait of the Bakers, but there was little indication of where to turn next or of a thread to follow.

Christina cooked them a dinner of roast rosemary chicken, asparagus, and baby red potatoes. At a temporary impasse, they turned over each idea again, one after another, while they cleaned up the kitchen and emptied a bottle of French Burgundy in the living room. The two investigators decided to take Christina up on her offer to stay the night so they could continue to talk it out before retiring.

"I don't think there's any place left to look," McBain said. "We've turned the house upside down poking around."

Boston swished the wine around in her glass.

"Well," she said with an audible exhale, "we've been through the library, the bedrooms, the attic, the garden, the garden shed, the basement, hall closets, kitchen, garage, living room, and every other space we could find. We've sounded out echoes in panels and drilled through walls. We need insight into their lives from their own thoughts and words. Both your father and mother were prolific writers. There should have been personal diaries going back decades. It doesn't make sense that they don't exist, and that makes me more suspicious than ever. But I'm out of ideas. Is there someplace else? Maybe they kept something at their offices at the college? If there was anything at all here, we should have found it by now."

"No," Christina Baker said firmly. "I never saw them, but there has to be something. You're right, Boston. I know they're here somewhere."

"We looked all over the house," McBain repeated. "Unless your parents were master spies, there's nothing here. What do we do next, dig up the garden? X-ray the walls?"

It was rare that Boston allowed her exasperation to show in front of a client.

"If we have to. This is bad. Why isn't this shit here...sorry, Christina. Without anything that gives us insight into their thoughts and decisions, our picture is incomplete. Anything else we guess at might lead us to a dead end."

McBain emptied the last of the bottle of red wine into his partner's glass.

"It's worse," he said. "We're out of wine."

"No, we aren't," Christina said. "There's more."

"I took this one out of the wine cooler in the pantry. It's the last bottle. Sorry."

"There are hundreds of bottles in the wine cellar," she said.

Boston brightened and sat up. "You have a wine cellar?"

"Yes, of course we have a wine cellar. Strangely enough, it was my parents' favorite room."

"I thought the library was their favorite room," McBain said.

"No. They both spent most of their time at home working or reading in there, but the wine cellar was their sentimental favorite. They built it themselves twenty years ago. The basement leads to the wine cellar."

McBain and Boston looked at each other. An acrobat could have walked the tightrope between their eyes.

"Let's go have a look at your collection, shall we?" she suggested.

He grabbed two large flashlights from a shelf near the door to the stairway, handed one to his partner, and followed the women down into the dimly lit cellar.

Sure enough, on the far side of the long basement lined with concrete pillars, was a doorway that led to another section of the floor. McBain cursed himself for assuming it was to a utility room. When Christina opened the door, they entered a brick-walled chamber that was cooler than the rest of the floor. Boston threw a switch to an overhead light, and they surveyed half a dozen rows of shelves packed with bottles leading back to a wall of reddish brown bricks where the foundation should have been. She and McBain scanned the walls and wine racks, bloodhounds on the scent.

Christina examined one of the racks. "Did you want another Burgundy, or something different?"

"Something a little bigger, if you don't mind," McBain said. He continued to poke around the room and between rows of dust-covered bottles with his light.

After a few minutes of searching vainly for a space in the back wall, he exhaled his disappointment. "I don't see anything here where something could be hidden."

Boston examined the length of the wall he had just passed with her flashlight. She focused on one spot for a moment, touching the seams between several bricks with her free fingertips. Then she disappeared out the door for a minute and returned with a cast-iron chisel and a large hammer.

"Step back," she said. "Only a useless city slicker wouldn't recognize twenty-year-old mortar from new work. McBain, hold the flashlight beam on that spot there."

She eyed the brick for a moment and then attacked one spot with the hammer and chisel with a lust and precision that would have warmed the heart of a stone mason. In a few minutes, she had removed a half dozen bricks from the wall. McBain held the flashlight over her shoulder. His partner reached around the inside of a small enclosure for a few seconds and then pulled out something with both her hands.

When she turned to them, Boston was holding a dirt-covered metal box.

FOURTEEN

The box sat in the middle of the kitchen table, bracketed by half-empty wine glasses on three sides. The container was made of green porcelain with a floral design of vines and orchids tracing the lid and was large enough to store jewelry or small mementos. Or a large book.

The three of them alternated glances between the box and one another for ten minutes before anyone spoke, questions brimming on the tips of their thoughts and lips. Christina was the first to break the silence, her voice barely above a whisper.

"I've never seen this box before," she said. "And I don't understand why either of them would feel the need to hide it behind a wall in the cellar. It looks like something my mother would buy. But then, why would my father make a place for it in the wall? They had nothing to conceal from each other."

"Like I mentioned in the library," McBain said. "There are hiding places because there are secrets. Whoever they belong to, I think it's about time we opened this up and find out what those secrets are about."

He reached for the box.

"Wait." Boston stopped him. She looked over at Christina. "Perhaps McBain and I should take a look without you."

"Why?" Christina asked.

"Like my partner said, there probably are secrets in here. They may or may not have anything to do with our investigation. It might be something very personal that one of them kept from the other. But I suspect whatever is in here may be something one or both of your parents didn't talk to you about. Why don't you let us evaluate it first? Then, if it has no bearing on the case, you can examine the contents privately."

"She's right, Ms. Baker," he said. "There are lots of reasons people hide things. We can look at what's inside and rule it out quickly if it's nothing."

"Thank you both. But the box is in the open now. Whether it has anything to do with this or not, I want to know what was important enough to one of them to seal up behind a wall in the wine cellar. We're all in this together. Open it up, and let's face it."

The lid didn't open easily. McBain took out his switchblade and edged open the top. He placed the box in the middle of the three of them so they could all look.

The box was filled with letters on the Baker letterhead. Boston carefully lifted them all out of the container and placed them on the table. The pages were in good condition, covered in an elegant, handwritten script.

"Do you know which one of your parents wrote these?" she asked.

Christina paged through the stack to see if they were all the same. "Yes, it's my mother's handwriting."

McBain was puzzled. "There's no salutation on that letter." He examined several others. "Or on any of them. No dates either."

Boston took the first two pages off the top and scanned them. "This is a romantic letter."

Christina and McBain did the same with the next two letters.

"So is this," she said.

"And this one."

Boston gave their client another glance. "Are you sure you want to do this with us now? You can always wait and look at them later."

Christina nodded, but didn't speak. They watched as her face fell along with her heart. There was no need to say it. No need to ask.

Boston left the room and returned with three notebooks. "OK, let's get started. Each of you take a third and keep them in order. Let's hope that despite the lack of any dates, they are laid out chronologically. As you go through, make a note of anything you think might be relevant or help us figure out who she was writing to and when."

Well past midnight and two more bottles of cabernet, they were still reading and writing. The letters opened a door into Sarah Baker's heart and soul. As they had all suspected, the letters were not to her husband. The affair appeared to have been long and passionate, and Sarah had not been reluctant to recount their moments together in explicit sensual detail. Occasionally, Boston or McBain would hear a small sound and glance over at Christina, but there was nothing to be said.

The letters painted a vivid and eloquent portrait of old New England towns and cozy bed-and-breakfast hotels, rocky Maine beaches and pine-scented clearings in the woods of Vermont, long, hot summer nights and naked passion by the fire in winter. Sarah Baker had been a sensuous woman, and that eroticism flowed out in her writing. They passed the letters around as they finished them so that all could see the full set. From what they could tell from the context and references in the letters, the affair had lasted somewhere between two and three years and had been carried on recently. There was no indication of any trouble or sign of termination in the relationship. The last letter simply stopped without any explanation.

The correspondence was full of details about the affair and her feelings for the man who was not her husband, but there was no name mentioned and no indication of who or what the man might have been. That search would begin the next day.

One by one, they left the kitchen and went to their rooms.

"OK, Ms. Baker," McBain said. "Any ideas?"

They had risen early and started the day together in silence over a large breakfast of asparagus, onion-and-cheese omelets, bacon, home fries, and toast. Cooking kept Christina's mind focused, she had insisted. Now, over coffee, it was time to discuss this new, difficult subject, uncomfortable or not.

Their client was at the kitchen table in an ivory wool sweater and blue jeans, but her eyes were far away. They were red and tired. Her hair was pulled back, dark and wet from the shower. She sipped at her coffee.

"She never said anything to me."

Boston and McBain sat with their coffee as they waited for more.

"I thought perhaps since the letters were in that box, they were never sent. Maybe they reflected some fantasy on her part that was never realized. My mother did love to dream."

Boston tried to think of a way to ease the conversation.

"I'm afraid not," she said. "You see, those are just copies of the originals. I've seen too many not to recognize that. And the comprehensive detail was...well, regardless of how fine a writer your mother was, I think we can be reasonably certain they were based on actual experiences."

Christina stared down at the table. McBain knew this territory.

"I'm sorry, Ms. Baker," he said. "There's never an easy way to find out about these things. I don't know what you're thinking right now, but I can tell you I know it hurts like hell."

Christina lifted her eyes to him with questions.

"That's right. I've been on the receiving end myself. Five years ago."

Boston's eyebrows arched, and she bit her tongue. McBain never discussed his ex-wife with clients. In fact, he generally never discussed her at all without the comfort of a vicious comment and a drink close by.

"And based on my experience and the fact that the letters were walled up in that cellar, I'm guessing that since you never knew, Phillip never knew either. Maybe that's small comfort to you, but if he died without knowing, that's a big piece of hurt he never endured. Whatever happened, Sarah didn't want to cause either you or your father any pain."

Christina Baker's eyes teared up again. After a minute, she shook it out and nodded.

"I hope you're right." She wiped her eyes with a tissue. "To answer your question, I'm not sure yet. No one comes to mind immediately, but my mother knew lots of men, both professionally and socially. I don't think it was a colleague, though. Nothing in the letters suggests they were both at the college. Perhaps a friend or someone she met at one of the parties. There were a couple of men she was close to, but I never made anything of it at the time."

Boston put the list of names that McBain had used for his interviews on the table.

"We can start with this and see if it provokes any thoughts," she said.

Christina dabbed her eyes with a tissue again, took a deep breath, and straightened up. Line by line, she examined the list, carefully circling a name here and there with a pencil. Then she handed it back to McBain. He looked it up and down as he made mental notes.

"Yes, I recall these men," he said. "I talked to all of them. Except for this one. Dennis Abbott isn't around. Remember? You told me he was on a long trip to Europe or somewhere. Recently retired, I think you said."

"Yes he was, for the past year. A few days ago, I received a message from him while I was in the hospital. He said he had just returned from Central Asia and found out the news about my parents, and about my being in the hospital. I called him back, and we talked for a few minutes. We'll get together for dinner next week sometime."

"Interesting," McBain said. He leaned back in his chair, balancing on the rear legs. "Did he say when he got back?"

Christina shook her head. "No, he didn't say exactly. I'm sure it was in the last week. He would have called me as soon as he heard about my parents."

He exchanged a glance with Boston. "Funny. Another coincidence rears its ugly head in this case."

"Don't be absurd," Christina said. "Dennis couldn't have anything to do with this or what happened to me. And he certainly couldn't have anything to do with the missing money. He wasn't even in the country when my parents died."

Boston looked up from the list. "Then why did you circle his name on here with the rest?"

Christina shrugged. "I suppose because for years he was closer to my parents than anyone else. I doubt it was him, but if my mother was going to have an affair, I would have hoped it would be with a man like Dennis. He is a wonderful, kind, and giving person, and he loved both my parents. For as long as I could remember, he was a part of the family, and I think he is the kind of man reflected in some of the things my mother wrote in those letters."

McBain's worst instincts were in play. Something about another coincidence made him uneasy and aggressively suspicious.

"But you said they parted ways a few years ago. For people who were that close, it seems odd. Do you know why?"

She sipped at her coffee for a moment before answering.

"It was never really clear. At first, my father said something about changes in schedules and meeting new people. But they never made a big deal out of it. Dennis just gradually stopped coming around. To be honest, I was preoccupied starting the bookstore during the time it happened, so I didn't really press the matter. In hindsight, I wish I had found out more. That's why I circled his name. Now that I consider it, I imagine that he might have been capable of having an affair with my mother. Perhaps that explains why he stopped being part of their lives. Maybe my father found out about it. I hadn't thought about it until just now."

McBain folded up the list and put it away. "In that case, Ms. Baker, why don't you give Mr. Abbott a call and tell him I'll be paying him a visit today. According to this, he doesn't live too far from me in the South End. Don't tell him anything. Just say that I'm helping you out with some important family business. Maybe he can provide us with a few answers or give us some insight. What do you think, Boston?"

The redhead nodded and downed her coffee. "Based on the timeline we sketched out from the letters, it could fit, I suppose. It's worth a shot. Besides, I'm tired of having nothing but questions. My guess is at the very least Mr. Abbott could help fill in a few blanks, even if it wasn't him."

Christina expressed surprise. "About the affair, perhaps. But that has nothing to do with Roche or the money or my attack."

Boston smiled as she reached over and patted her client's hand. "Remember, Christina, no assumptions at this stage. Let's see where the conversation with him leads us."

McBain didn't have the heart to tell Christina Baker about the insidious mental clockwork that lay beneath his partner's charming, lethal smile.

FIFTEEN

McBain and Boston left Brookline and spent a few hours at their office catching up with other business. Their two longest-outstanding cases were ready to settle. Boston continued her due diligence on the philanthropy scam, while her partner put on a dark-gray suit and paid another visit to Drysdale Securities' chief investment officer just before lunch.

McBain's blood was up from the new revelations and suspicions that had emerged at the Bakers'. This, coupled with the actress's recent confession regarding her intimacy with the Drysdale salesman and his peculiar sexual proclivities, had the investigator torturing the investment executive with double entendres and innuendo regarding bonds, stocks, and exotic instruments throughout the meeting. By the time McBain was through, the CIO didn't feel much like eating anything but his young salesman's beating heart ripped fresh from his chest. He grudgingly suggested he would call in the next few days with a settlement offer.

After digesting that appetizer, McBain headed back to Columbus Avenue in the South End for a late large lunch at Charlie's. He enjoyed a cheeseburger and turkey hash, then strolled across Harriet Tubman Square to Pembroke Street, counting the medieval turrets on each brownstone as he looked for the number. He rang the doorbell three times. After a minute, Dennis Abbott opened the door and welcomed him in.

In that first encounter, McBain dispensed with the pleasant pose of the disinterested friend he had used with Richard Roche. He assessed Dennis Abbott visually, searching his bearing for some sign of evasiveness; some signal that he was involved in what was going on. And he wanted Abbott to be aware of it. As Boston had suggested, it was time to drop the nice-guy persona and start rattling some cages.

Perhaps forewarned by Christina Baker, Abbott seemed not to notice or take offense. He was tall and lean, in good condition for a man of almost seventy years, slightly stooped with the bearing of a man who has not slept well for some time. A full head of unkempt white hair sat atop a pleasant tanned and rugged face, though to McBain's eye, the crags wore the marks not so much of age but of prolonged sadness or depression. His greeting was polite, but he did not smile, and his handshake lacked enthusiasm.

McBain had the scent of something. Finally there was a trail to follow in this case. Despite what they had told their client, he suspected the affair had some relevance to what they were investigating. Maybe that was wishful thinking on his part after coming up craps for days. More important, Boston felt it too. McBain had been aware of it the moment he had seen her fanged smile at the breakfast table. Whether Abbott was involved in any way was something he wanted to flush out at this meeting.

His host led him down the hallway of the brownstone to the rear of the building. The air in the house was close and stale, untroubled by fresh air from the spring breeze outside. They passed a living room and dining room thick with dust but uncluttered and sparely decorated in New England country themes and natural colors. Some of the furniture was covered with white sheets. As they walked through the kitchen, McBain observed that Dennis Abbott was also a fastidious man who liked to cook, though the stove had not seen much use recently. Unopened boxes and packages with overseas shipping labels were stacked on a long wooden side table and island alongside unstored groceries, but otherwise the kitchen was orderly and clean. The white lace curtains were pulled back, and large windows looked out onto a small yard enclosed by a tall wooden fence that preserved the solitude of the owner.

There, beneath the shade of two large oak trees, they sat in a landscaped garden that was beginning to see the first buds of spring. McBain was reminded of the contrast with the barren garden out back of the Baker house in Brookline. It was quiet in the garden, though they were just a football's throw away from Columbus Avenue. The chirping of birds in the surrounding trees, climbing ivy vines, and scent of flowers carried them outside of the city.

Dennis Abbott poured two cups of afternoon tea from an English tea set on the cast-iron table between their chairs.

"I trust the timing is OK for you, Mr. Abbott," McBain said. "I wasn't able to give you any notice. I hope Ms. Baker filled you in."

His host showed no sign of nervousness, just weariness.

"It's not a problem, Mr. McBain. Christina told me you would be stopping by to ask some questions related to Phillip and Sarah. I took the opportunity to make us some tea to help me stay awake. I'm still adjusting to being back in Boston and this time zone, I'm afraid."

"That's right. You were somewhere overseas for the better part of a year, I understand. Where was that?"

"Oh, a number of countries," Abbott replied. "I took a long trip to celebrate retirement. One of those trips-of-a-lifetime one plans for and constantly puts off. Parts of Africa, Europe, the Middle East, and finally some countries in Central Asia you probably haven't heard of."

McBain had heard. "You mean Genghis Khan, Tamerlane, Mongol hordes, that sort of thing? Kazakhstan, Lake Baikal, Aral Sea, Tajikistan, around there?"

"I'm sorry, I didn't mean to offend."

"None taken, not everybody gets around. That's a long time to be away. I'm sure you're jet-lagged. When did you get back? Six, seven days ago?"

"Seven days," the older man said.

"I gathered that was the first time you found out that Phillip and Sarah Baker had died." McBain focused on the eyes to see how Abbott reacted with the sound of each name in that quiet garden. "You live by yourself here? No one contacted you overseas?"

"Yes, I live alone," he answered. "It was one of my goals to immerse myself in the culture of each place I stayed. I had no need to contact anyone back here. For the first day or so after my return, I just slept. I only found out after I checked my answering service and picked up my mail. There were messages from Christina and many of our friends. I called Christina right away. David told me she had had an accident and was in the hospital. I hope she is recovering well. I can't wait to see her next week."

"She'll be her same old self and back at the bookshop in no time," McBain said. "She was lucky. The car nearly killed her."

Abbott shook his head and sipped from his cup.

"I know that street very well. People are always going too fast down that road on their way to Beacon. And the driver didn't stop? They have no idea who it was?"

"Nope. We're working with the police on that."

"The thought of losing Christina would be unimaginable after what happened to her parents."

"Yes, she is something else," McBain said. "Everyone I talked to can't stop going on about her. I've been working with her for a few weeks to help sort out some confusion in her parents' affairs, if you'll pardon the expression."

Abbott shifted in his chair and took a sip of tea. "Confusion? I'm not sure I understand."

"That's OK, neither do we yet. But we're getting there."

He took his notebook from his jacket for effect.

"You mentioned 'our friends,' Mr. Abbott. But my understanding is that you hadn't really been in touch with Sarah and Phillip for a number of years."

"Five, to be exact," Abbott said.

"Hmm," McBain said. "I'm not sure you'll be able to help me, then. The problems seem to have arisen since then. On the other hand, Christina says you and her parents used to be inseparable. I gathered she has missed you since then. What happened?"

The older man shrugged and gazed up at the tree limbs overhanging the back yard with their young leaves.

"Life happened, Mr. McBain. People grow and change, they get busy. They go on to new jobs and meet other friends. They get old. Some relationships just wear out."

"Like Sarah Baker?"

"All three of us, actually," Abbott replied. "We drifted apart. It was sad, and I missed them, but I'm afraid it's as simple as that."

McBain bored in on the old guy.

"Actually, in this case, it isn't quite that simple," he said. "We've been investigating the possibility that the Bakers might have been swindled before they died. Now we've come across letters written in her own hand suggesting that Sarah Baker cheated on her husband with someone. We thought the two might be connected somehow. That someone wouldn't be you, would it?"

The blood drained from Dennis Abbott's face and lips. Moments passed while McBain worried he had caused his host to have a heart attack. The man's blue eyes were swimming along with his mind and emotions. He seemed disoriented and confused, his breathing labored. McBain gave him all the time he needed but observed him closely, hoping that he hadn't just killed his only lead in this case.

Finally, the older man reached for his tea and took a drink. McBain was betting he wished he had something much stronger.

"Ye...yes," Abbott said in a hoarse voice. "I did have an affair with Sarah. No one else knew. After it was finished, I never spoke of it to anyone. We thought it would never come out. To my knowledge, Christina was never supposed to know about it."

Bingo.

Abbott took a deep breath and looked straight at the investigator. "But you mentioned something about letters. There were never any letters."

Damn.

"What do you mean no letters? Are you saying Sarah Baker never wrote to you?"

He shook his head firmly. "No, we never wrote to each other. We saw each other on and off for many years. Our friendship had just evolved into something more. When Phillip found out about it, we broke it off. Neither of us wanted to hurt him. Your guess was correct. That was the reason I stopped talking to the Bakers."

McBain frowned and listened to the birds for a minute in the quiet of the garden. Just when he thought he had someone cornered...Now this thing was on the edge of becoming more complicated rather than less. Abbott may have been lying, but his investigator's instincts said no. Abbott's responses to all of this—his explanation, his tone of voice, his body language—didn't quite add up, but they didn't point in that direction.

"Any idea who else it might have been?" he asked. "We're guessing the affair went on sometime over the past few years. Maybe Sarah Baker moved on, knowing she wouldn't be able to see you. I can tell you it seemed pretty serious."

McBain was well beyond the point where tact and sensitivity for hurt feelings were going to stand in his way.

"No, Mr. McBain, I have no idea. As I said, I broke off all contact with both Sarah and Phillip when they told me to. As far as I know, there was no one else at the time. I would have hoped that the two of them could reconcile and find happiness with each other instead of some stranger."

McBain almost smirked at the thought of a former lover wishing the cheating spouse well and a couple picking up the pieces after years of unfaithfulness. What a nice thought.

"Well," he said instead, "maybe they did in their own way. After all, they died together, in each other's arms. Christina didn't know about it until we found the letters, and there's no indication Phillip said anything about an affair. Maybe she took her secret to the grave with her."

Dennis Abbott looked away. He wiped at his face with his sleeve. The investigator wondered which memories he was choosing.

"Mr. McBain," Abbott said. "You mentioned that your investigation was connected with some potential swindle involving the Bakers' money. What were you talking about?"

McBain considered this for a minute while he measured Abbott's level of interest. Why not?

"The Bakers seemed to have lost most of their money in the market during the collapse. Their daughter thinks there's something suspicious about the way the money was handled by their financial advisor."

"Richard Roche?"

"Yes, you know him?"

"No," Abbott said, "not personally. I know of him. He met the Bakers and became their investment advisor while I was still speaking with them."

McBain pictured Roche in his head for an instant. On a hunch, he made a leap.

"He's a good-looking man. You think he might be the type Sarah Baker would have an affair with?"

Abbott's eyes dipped for a few seconds, then he shrugged.

"I really couldn't say. I only met him once, at the party where Doctor Lehmann first introduced him to Phillip. I never spoke with him myself, so I can't really tell you anything about him. Certainly Sarah never said anything to me about him or any other man."

McBain kept his eyes on the page.

"So you know Doctor Lehmann?"

"Yes, of course," Abbott said. "He's...had been the Bakers' physician for nearly eight years. I saw him at social events of theirs from time to time. He had become a good friend to both of them, so for a short time I knew him as well, though only through their acquaintance."

"And you're saying that the Bakers met Richard Roche through him?"

"Yes, at a party at the house in Brookline. Why? Is that significant?"

McBain flipped his notebook shut. He needed to process and talk to his partner.

"Who knows at this point?" he replied. "We're still piecing together the details of what happened to the money. Like I said, this is a private investigation, and very preliminary. Let's not start trashing anybody's reputation. Thank you for your time, Mr. Abbott, and for the tea. I'll be in touch. Here's my card. Please give me a call if anything comes to mind."

"Anything for Christina," the old man said.

McBain refrained from rolling his eyes, but the thought occurred to him that the way things had played out, Abbott's phrase could just as well serve as a theme for this case. Despite the disappointment over the apparent dead end with Sarah Baker's affair, the conversation had unearthed one new revelation that had the hounds straining at the leash. The dog had just barked.

McBain almost ran back to his office. Boston was not there. He looked at their scheduler and caught a taxi across the bridge to Charlestown. He got out of the cab at the Navy Yard and then walked to the gym near her apartment where Boston trained. Even though they knew him, he paid a guest fee just so he could walk in with a suit and tie. The dojo was on the third floor. He watched his partner finish her Muay Thai session while he munched on a bag of pretzels. He took off his shoes and met her in one of the empty training rooms so they could talk while she finished practicing.

For some people, the sight of a man in a business suit holding a heavy bag in a gym would seem out of place. For others, watching a beautiful redhead kick the crap out of a suit was an inspirational experience.

"You're hitting a lot harder these days."

"New teacher," she grunted.

"Sure it's not your adrenaline from this new case?"

"'Course not."

She spun and landed a vicious kick where his throat would have been. McBain steadied the bag again and thought about Boston's agenda since he had left the office.

"Anything else? What happened with the nonprofit-investment whiz?"

The force from Boston's next kick nearly took down the heavy bag on top of him. She backed off for a minute. Her breathing had barely picked up.

"The little shit actually thought he could charm his way out of it," she said with a smirk. "He pitched the same pile of bullshit he gave our client. The punk ripped off a charity and didn't bat an eyelash. I'm sure he thought I was just some dumb twit who worked for the trust."

"Uh oh."

"Yeah, the prick came on to me toward the end and tried to put his hand on me. I'm going to enjoy costing him his job. For good measure, I might just agree to go out on a date with him, break his knees, and accuse him of attempted rape."

McBain steadied himself and the bag. When she said things like that, he needed to cool her down and change her focus.

"All right, partner, let's hope it doesn't get to that. In the meantime, I've got some news that will help take your mind off that asshole for the moment. I met with Dennis Abbott a little while ago."

Boston put up her hands and hit the bag four times in a second. "Yeah?"

"He admitted to having an affair with Sarah Baker."

Boston's face brightened, and she stepped back. "Sweet. Progress. Did he confess to—"

"But he said the letters weren't for him. He claims that he and Sarah carried on for years but that there was no correspondence. Phillip found out, they broke it off, and he cut off all contact with the Bakers about five years ago, end of story. If true, that means there was another affair after theirs."

Boston took some deep breaths and then hit the bag again several times. He held the bag steady.

"That's his story," she said. "What's your take on Abbott? Any chance he's lying?"

"I've been thinking about it on the way over," he said. "I'm not sure what's going on there. I think I believe him about the affair. But the way he reacted? There's something he's hiding. Maybe just the newness of it all, maybe not."

"Shit, back to square one." She put her hands up again and focused.

McBain smiled. He liked drawing it out.

"On the affair, maybe," he said. "On the other hand, as the economists say, something new came up in conversation that might be of interest."

He held out for a moment, but with Boston already hungry for red meat, he didn't take chances. McBain mentioned Dennis Abbott's comments about Richard Roche and how he met the Bakers. His partner digested the information for a moment while she bounced on the balls of her feet. She stepped back from the bag and looked at him.

"I thought you said the doctor barely knew Roche," she said.

"So he said."

"Didn't you say Lehmann seemed a bit jumpy when you first paid him a visit?"

Smash.

"I did. Didn't think too much about it until this week. I'm jumpy around doctors too. I figured he didn't want any part of trouble. But he's been dodging my follow-up calls, which pisses me off. That got me thinking maybe it wasn't just his poor bedside manner. Now I'm wondering if he doesn't feel responsible for putting the Bakers together with Roche to begin with. Or maybe there's more to the story."

Smash.

"Maybe he was the one having the affair with Sarah Baker," Boston said. "Abbott said Lehmann was friends with both of them. Maybe he got nervous with you asking questions about the Bakers, having betrayed Phillip and all. A guilty conscience makes most people uneasy, especially when their friends end up dead."

Smash.

"And he was their doctor. For all we know, Phillip found out his wife was having an affair with the one guy he had trusted with his depression. Might have been the thing that pushed them over the edge."

McBain didn't want to imagine Sarah Baker with Lehmann. He couldn't picture the doctor as the Romeo portrayed in those letters.

"I hope not," he said. "You didn't get a look at him. But, like you say, everything's on the table with this case until we prove otherwise. I'm thinking we should pay him a visit early tomorrow. There's a whole new round of questions I want to buttonhole him on. Let's see how high we can ratchet the pressure. Maybe suggest a new autopsy on the Bakers. From what I've seen, if he's hiding something, he might crack pretty easily."

She shook her head. "Much as I'd like to, I can't make it tomorrow. It's Saturday, and I'm going up to Rockport for a family wedding. You hit him tomorrow on his day off, and I'll follow up on Monday to put more pressure on him during office hours."

Boston began bouncing again as she rubbed her taped hands together.

"I thought this would make you happy, partner," he said.

"I didn't say I was happy about it."

"You don't have to. I can tell. Whenever you get that bloodhound scent of the trail, your nostrils flare and your tongue sticks out just a bit between your lips."

"It does not."

"If you say so," McBain said. "It's almost cute."

He never regretted the bruises he got that afternoon.

After the workout, the investigators returned to Brookline. Christina Baker was alone in the living room reading through the letters again. McBain relayed the gist of his conversation with Dennis Abbott and his confession. With her inscrutable patrician's face, it was hard to know what to think. Finally she spoke.

"I think I need a drink."

"That's my line," McBain said. "Maybe you should open a bottle of..."

Boston glared at him as she sat down on the couch next to her.

"Let me ask you a question," Boston said. "Aside from Richard Roche and your husband, who else knew you were preparing to take legal action in the case?"

Their client thought for a moment.

"Well, I had been to see Doctor Lehmann just before I went to Roche's office," she replied.

"That's what I thought," Boston said. She looked at her partner.

Another piece fell into place. Boston led them into the planning room. A minute later, she had the new connections mapped out on the whiteboard.

Christina was puzzled. "Why have you moved Doctor Lehmann's name on the wall?"

"McBain is going to pay the doctor a house call tomorrow," Boston said. "We'll know more then. But right now, he's moved up the list of people whose names keep popping up repeatedly in our search. So as the connections to different people accumulate and thicken, he moves closer to the center of the picture."

"Ms. Baker," McBain asked, "did you know that it was Doctor Lehmann who introduced your parents to Richard Roche?"

They could tell by the expression on their client's face that this was a news flash. "No," she replied. "When...how?"

"According to Dennis Abbott, it was at one of your parents' house parties some five years ago," Boston said. "We thought it strange that it hadn't come up until now. We need to find out why, and if there is more to the doctor's involvement with your parents than he's led us to believe."

"Surely you don't think he could have been involved with my mother? Or with Roche?"

She shook her head and tapped a pencil on the planning table. McBain presumed that for her, this was the equivalent of an emotional outburst of distress.

"We interviewed all of the people on the list," he said. "As far as we know, they all spoke candidly about Richard Roche—those who knew of him, anyway. Lehmann is the only one who we know has lied to us...at least so far. We want to know why."

McBain turned to his partner, whose fingers were blazing away on her phone.

"In the meantime," he said, "Boston, can you take care of one other thing before we call it a night?"

His partner put down her phone and turned to him.

"Already done," she said. "We should have a copy by Monday."

Christina looked back and forth between them. "What are you talking about?"

Boston looked at McBain, who nodded. They had discussed some darker scenarios on the drive over from Charlestown.

"We need to talk to the police about the death of your parents," she said in a calm voice. "Given the new prominence of the doctor in our inquiry, I'm going to get hold of the police report from that day, as well as any information we can from the coroner and the autopsy. It's probably nothing, but we want to cover all bases."

"We already asked our friends on the force a couple questions," he added.

"And we thought that given everything you've told us," said his partner, "and all that we've learned about them, it was unusual that there was no suicide note."

"Statistically speaking, that doesn't normally indicate anything," McBain said. "But..."

"For two people who would rather write than breathe?" Boston said. "It doesn't make sense. We told you we look for deviations from patterns. This is a big one."

When they left the house a minute later, their client was gripping her stylish walking stick much tighter.

SIXTEEN

McBain was pissed. It was Saturday, and he hated working on Saturday morning. This hour of the day was usually reserved for a hangover and a leisurely breakfast. But he had called, left messages, and been put off for a week. Since the good doctor had conveniently colocated his office with his home, McBain saw no reason why there should be any patients around at this hour to come between him and the subject.

Aside from the brush-off, the investigator was beginning to take a real dislike to Doctor Lehmann. At their initial meeting, he had observed how nervous the doctor appeared. The man's face and body practically screamed a second language. His gut told him the guy was untrustworthy, but maybe that was just his general aversion to doctors and advice about health. McBain's suspicions had been heightened by his growing sense with each passing unanswered message and new discovery that Lehmann knew more about the Bakers than he had revealed at their first meeting. It wasn't a stretch to imagine he knew something about the affair as well, though his skin crawled considering even the infinitesimal possibility that it could have been the doctor himself. Dennis Abbott's revelation that the doctor might be more familiar with Richard Roche than he had admitted was just the last straw.

Now he had had to stay relatively sober on a Friday night in order to get up early and remain focused for Saturday morning. Lehmann was going to find out just how big a prick McBain could be under these conditions. By the end of this house call, the doctor would have plenty of reason to feel agitated.

McBain was going to find out exactly how close Doctor Lehmann was to the Bakers. If Phillip Baker had confided in his physician about money stress, maybe he would have told him about any suspicions of his wife's infidelity as well. Just for good measure, while he was at it, he wanted to ask about the autopsy process and hint at the possibility of a new one. And the doctor was going to be more forthcoming on his relationship with Richard Roche, one way or another.

As he strode up the walkway to the house, McBain noted a new, white, high-end Mercedes C-Class in the driveway and made a mental note to check into how much cash a doctor made these days. In this neighborhood, probably a pretty good nickel, but it was worth a look.

He tried the doorbell to the house three times. There was no response. There were no other cars in the drive. Lehmann could be out for a walk or visiting friends, but on the off chance he was seeing patients today, the investigator wandered over to the office entrance and looked through the glass panes in the door. The receptionist was not at her desk, but he tried the door anyway. It opened right away, and he stepped into the office.

He looked around. It was quiet, and McBain called down the hallway to the back rooms, then he yelled up the walkway toward the house. There was no answer. Well, since the doc wasn't at home, there was no reason to let a perfectly good Saturday morning go to waste. He might as well take a look around the doctor's office to see if those file cabinets held any notes of interest to their investigation.

He almost had his hand on the door handle when his nose registered the scent.

McBain jerked his hand back and recoiled from the office door.

The olfactory memories flooded back. The day he had walked into the living room and found his mother and uncle in the corner, waiting for him and for the ambulance and police, standing as far from the body as they could but unable to look away. He never wanted to remember his father like that again. And he would never forget the sight. Or the rancid, sickly sweet smell of decay that pervaded the room.

McBain's mind raced along behind his pulse. He focused on listening for a full minute.

There was no sound except those distinct noises from the world outside.

He stared down the hall again. Then past the receptionist's desk to the enclosed walkway to the main house.

Nothing.

He forced himself to take some deep breaths to control his breathing. Hell, it was a medical office. Who knew what they kept here. Maybe he was wrong. He reached into the pocket of his brown leather jacket and found a package of tissues. Taking several out of the pack, he used them to turn the handle and enter the office.

Inside the dimly lit room, the stench filled his nostrils and mouth. The doctor was at his desk. His head was on the desk. The thick curtains on the windows to the office were drawn, but enough light seeped into the room from the open door for him to tell that the man wasn't sleeping. McBain moved toward the drawstring to open the drapes but thought better of it. Instead he found the light switch and used his tissues to flick it on.

The office had been turned over. File cabinets were askew and drawers sat open, their contents disorderly. Lehmann's head lay sideways in a pool of drying blood. His slick black hair was matted and sticky on the left side, where McBain guessed a bullet had gone in. The doctor's glasses lay smashed beneath his face. McBain sniffed the air again. The good news was that aside from the rotting smell of dead flesh, he didn't detect any cordite in the air. So whoever had put a bullet in the doctor's skull was long gone. Probably.

But McBain's body was screaming with tension. He had to make a decision, and fast.

The investigator was in over his head, and he knew it. His fear was almost overwhelming his ability to focus and think clearly. He had to push it down and concentrate. He pulled his eyes off the head of Doctor Lehmann and looked at an open file cabinet. His mind could only grasp at two things: they were now well past the point of coincidence, so there was no question that the dead body in front of him was related to his investigation, and in this situation, there was no way he was qualified to do anything clever in this room. That may have worked for amateurs in the movies, but it was stupid and dangerous.

He reached into his jacket, pulled out his phone, and placed a call.

"Tom, how are you?"

"McBain?" Captain O'Daniel answered. "I'm up to my eyeballs in shit. I've got to sort out crap on the damn car insurance and then get in to the office to work for a few hours. Then we're out of here for a family wedding in Rockport. I'm too busy to talk now."

"You're gonna get busier, Tom."

The phone went silent for a moment.

"What's going on? Is my daughter OK?"

"Yeah, she's fine," he replied. "She's not with me. And it's not what you think. But you know that stuff that you were talking about at lunch a couple weeks ago?"

The investigator's words were few and to the point.

"Where are you?"

McBain gave him the address.

"Don't move. I'll have a car there in minutes. I'll be there myself in thirty."

"Don't worry; I'm not going anywhere. I just hope nobody else is here."

"Hold the line." The connection was quiet for fifteen seconds. "A car will be there in four minutes, McBain. Stay calm. Keep your ears and eyes open. Hold on."

"Thanks, Tom."

He hung up and stood rooted in the morbid silence while his mind cycled through his options. The doctor had been killed. That meant something important. When the police arrived, the office would be sealed off to him. Should he take the time to look around? To try the computer or rifle through the files? The man had been dead for a while. There wasn't really a danger that anyone was still here. His brain and instincts were screaming at him: *there had to be a connection with his case.* This was his only chance to find anything in the office.

McBain heard the approaching siren in the distance in two minutes. The car screeched to a halt in front of the house in three with lights flashing.

Still standing in front of the desk, he took another deep breath and let it out. The case would have to play out on its own for now. He stared at the blood-encrusted head of Doctor Lehmann once more as the officers eased their way through the front door with weapons drawn. Boston was going to be mad that she wasn't here.

Boston was mad, but by the time the Shelby pulled up near the house, she was the epitome of professional poise. The officers milling around outside the office wouldn't have stopped her in any case, but she was wearing a drop-dead, royal-blue party dress and diamond pendant under her coat, looking like a million bucks.

When McBain saw her come through the door, he remembered she must have been halfway to Rockport when she got the call. Pretty good time, even for her.

It was also clear from Captain O'Daniel's face that he wasn't happy to see his daughter under these circumstances. McBain hoped they could both keep it under control for the sake of the soul of the recently departed and those within earshot.

The two converged in front of the receptionist's desk, with McBain in the middle.

"So," she said coolly to her father, "who is going to give me the story? Or would you prefer to start off with an 'I told you so'? Either way, with my business partner at the center of a crime scene, I'm involved."

Even in the midst of a murder scene...Jesus. McBain swallowed his smile so hard it hurt his dry throat. After all this time, his partner still had the ability to amaze him.

Captain O'Daniel seemed torn between her chutzpah and his pride.

"OK, you two," he said. "I told you so. Just like I told you to stay put in Rockport an hour ago. While we're finishing cordoning off the premises, McBain, you can start giving me the background on how you manage to walk into the room with a murdered doctor in a quiet neighborhood. You can fill in your partner with the particulars as you give them to me."

The investigator gave him the basic outline of the Baker case and their client's suspicions about unethical activity.

"She also claims that her car accident last week might not have been a car accident," he said. "Personally, I think she's crazy...or at least I did until an hour ago."

"In any case," Boston broke in, "what happened here may not be related to our investigation at all."

Her father narrowed his eyes and smirked as he towered over her. "Who do you think you're kidding? If you really thought that, you'd be in Rockport right now, and he'd be nursing a hangover as usual. Why are you working on a Saturday morning?"

"A hunch," she replied ahead of her partner. "And don't snort at me. You know where I learned to trust my instincts. The Bakers are dead. Lots of money is missing. The more we dig, the more questions keep emerging, and this guy's name keeps popping up as a common denominator. He was our only lead, so McBain decided to interrogate him a little more."

"And now he's dead," the captain said.

"Not because of us," McBain replied.

"We'll see about that."

McBain laid out his every step since arriving at the house that morning.

"The only things I touched were the door handles and the light switch."

"And you got in here how?" O'Daniel glanced at his daughter.

"Front door was unlocked," McBain said and pointed with his thumb. "I figured he was open for business and seeing patients, so I walked in."

The captain still looked suspicious, but he nodded. He noticed a homicide detective waiting for him inside the doctor's office and went to confer with him.

McBain watched the detective talk for a minute but couldn't hear anything from where he stood. He turned to Boston...and did a double take. Her expression wasn't what he was expecting.

"Are you OK?" she asked. "I was worried when Dad called me."

He nodded. "I am now." The arrival of the police had barely helped his calm. Part of him felt silly that he only felt better once his partner was by his side.

"You aren't mad?" he asked.

"Of course I'm mad. Now I wish like hell that we'd done this together this morning. But I can't blame you for that. You asked."

"That's uncommonly reasonable of you. Care to buy me a drink to help soothe my nerves? You don't even have to change."

"Don't push your luck," she replied with a coy smile. "We'll get one at Doyle's as soon as he lets us go. It may take us time to get out, though. The neighborhood's getting crowded."

McBain looked out the window for the first time since the police had arrived. Violent crime was rare in Brookline Village. As a result, the house and grounds were packed with local Brookline and Boston uniforms, patrol, detectives, and emergency units. Thanks to the evolving wonders of gossip technology, word had spread like wildfire, and with everyone home on a Saturday morning, the crowd of bystanders trying to peer through the hedge from across the street or upstairs windows was growing by the minute.

"It would have been handy if they had been a little more curious when a loud bang went off in the middle of the night at their neighbor's house," he said. "This isn't exactly South Boston or Dorchester, for Christ's sake."

Captain O'Daniel returned.

"Well, we think we know why," he said. "Detectives found a pillow at the doctor's feet. Looks like whoever pulled the trigger used it as a silencer and to keep any residue contained. Not sure if the doctor was already incapacitated when they shot him. We'll know more after the Crime Lab Unit and coroner get a good look."

Boston decided to press her luck. "On the off chance that this isn't connected to our case, any ideas what else might have happened here?"

"Whether it is or isn't connected, parts of the house, the office, and the files were tossed. I'm guessing the killer or killers went through the place quickly. The detectives think it took place in the wee hours this morning, so either they found what they were looking for or got out of here before the area got busy with early-morning types. The boys say his computer doesn't seem damaged, so maybe they didn't have time or the need to focus on that. We'll take that and the file cabinets back and start going through them."

His daughter looked around his shoulder and into the office.

"I'm curious," she said. "This looks pretty messy compared with what we're used to. Aside from the fact that the doctor shouldn't have been connected to the fraud at all, our suspects are usually more subtle about their thefts. We've never encountered any kind of violence before, and I wouldn't have expected to see it here. White-collar criminals don't resort to this kind of thing. Got any hunches of your own yet?"

Tom O'Daniel had a little blue gleam in his eye. McBain recognized the glow of diagnostic cunning. Now he saw where she got her bloodhound smarts. It was interesting watching the two of them go head to head.

"I just got here, remember," the captain said. "I'm still playing catch-up with you two pirates. But if I had to hazard a guess, I would say there's more to the doctor than meets the eye. This wasn't an unhappy patient. And it certainly wasn't any robbery. More likely he was into something besides his day job, with people he shouldn't have been. We'll know more after we start asking questions and digging into his background. This was quick, violent, and calculated. The doctor was fully dressed in the middle of the night. He probably knew his killer. He was executed deliberately. They knew what they were looking for. Maybe something he owed them or something that identified who they were in some way. Let's hope they didn't find it."

McBain listened closely. He wanted to get out of there, get back to check on their client, and start asking some questions of his own. For the second time in two days, their best lead had turned into a dead end, this time literally. He and Boston had to find another one fast. Events were picking up speed for some reason, and they were still behind. Their white-collar crime had taken an unexpected red turn, maybe even because of their investigation. He wasn't comfortable with that thought.

"So," he asked, "you need anything more from us, or can I go?"

"Yes," O'Daniel said. "I do need something from you."

"What?"

"Go home. First you started with two suicides and some fraud allegations. Then you moved on to an alleged attempted assault with a car. Now you've graduated to a violent killing in the middle of one of the safest neighborhoods in the city."

"What's your point?" Boston asked.

"I don't like the way this is going, and I want you out of the way. Next thing I know, you'll be starting a bloodbath in the lobby of the Ritz-Carlton. Stick with the money angle. If you come across any leads that might contribute to this murder investigation, let us know right away."

"Fine," she said. "Same to you."

Her partner's eyes popped open.

Tom O'Daniel put his hands on his hips. "What's that supposed to mean?"

They were beginning to lean in toward each other—and McBain—a little more as they spoke.

"We have a client and an investigation into possible securities fraud and intend to pursue it. We're happy to help out any way we can, share information, and keep our eyes and ears open. But if this does happen to be connected to our case and we don't get any assistance, I can't promise anything. We'll just have to follow where it leads."

McBain could tell where this exchange was heading by the escalating volume of their voices. Heads were beginning to turn.

He pulled his partner's arm along as he headed for the door. "Thanks, Tom, we're going. We'll keep you posted."

In the end, it took them almost an hour to get out of the neighborhood and down to Doyle's. On the way, McBain called their client and persuaded her to meet them there without telling her the reason, which, considering the location, was half the battle. When she arrived, it was almost one and they were sitting in a booth near the back of the bar area, already two stiff drinks in. There was no way to put it delicately. Well, there was, but he beat Boston to the punch.

"Ms. Baker, Doctor Lehmann was murdered last night."

Boston ordered their client a drink while she absorbed yet another piece of distressing news. Boston's preference would have been to break this latest turn of events gently. Her father had been right. The intensity of this case continued to escalate, and given the close personal nature of cascading revelations, their client would be under considerable strain. And they needed her New England resolve to stay steely. But McBain was still rattled from his encounter and was by nature short on tact. He spilled out the morning's events in between a shot and a beer.

"I don't understand," Christina said. "What does it mean? Why would anyone kill Doctor Lehmann?"

Boston pushed a glass in her direction. "We don't know yet, Christina. The police are only beginning to gather information. But I think one thing we can be certain of is that this is tied to our investigation somehow."

"But...how can that be? It must be an awful coincidence of some kind. Perhaps it was a robbery."

"That's unlikely at this point," McBain said. "The doctor was dodging my calls and refusing to see me for a week. Then last night, someone he was meeting with killed him in cold blood and went rummaging through his home and office looking for something. All that on top of his relationship with your parents. We're ruling out coincidence until we know more."

Their client finished her drink more quickly than she might otherwise, a habit she was developing in earnest the more time she spent with the two investigators. The three of them sat without talking while she regained her composure. The bar was getting crowded. McBain glanced back and forth at the two beautiful women sitting across from him. He had noticed that their booth had become the center of attention for a growing audience of admirers around the room. He felt pretty smug about that, and it helped him regain his own composure and to think.

"This is unbelievable," Christina said and exhaled. "The thought that a murder is connected to my parents' death is bad enough. The idea that the doctor could be involved in this is hard to accept. What do we do now?"

"We have to regroup and examine what we know and believe about our findings up to this point," he said. "With the doctor dead and no idea whether your mother's affair is related to this at all, we don't have any leads. We need a fresh start."

"First of all," Boston said, "I think we all have to agree that something really bad is going on here. The signs are pointing to a more complex investigation than we first guessed. They are suggesting some kind of involvement by Doctor Lehmann and pointing away from Richard Roche for the time being. At the very least, it seems more and more likely that your original instincts were correct: they were probably robbed. We just don't know how, how much, or by whom. While we wait to hear from the police, we need to know more about Lehmann. Is there anything else you can tell us?"

"Only what I know from casual conversation with him and from my parents. He was their physician for eight or nine years. They became friends as well, so he was a frequent guest at the house. He was well liked by everyone we knew. A bit shy perhaps, different from most of their friends in the neighborhood and at college. He wasn't particularly literary, so he seemed nervous at times around everyone."

"Do you know where he was from?" Boston asked. "Anything about his background or education?"

"I seem to recall he was from Miami originally," she replied. "A very good Jewish family there, where practicing medicine ran in the family. He had lived in a number of places before he came here, including New York. He said he liked Boston because of the size of the city and the people. He enjoyed being in Brookline very much and appeared to be doing well here. From what my parents told me, he didn't have much of a personal life to speak of. He wasn't married and had no children or family here. I'm afraid that's all I know."

"His med school diploma on the wall was from some college I didn't recognize in Saint Louis," McBain said.

Boston was taking mental notes and leaping ahead. "Let's check there first and see if they can tell us anything. We can also talk to some of your parents' friends again and catalog what they have to say. I'd give my left earring to get a copy of his patient list and some time on his computer, but that may take some doing. I doubt the police will want to give that to me."

Her partner smiled at her. "That would be a first."

Boston wasn't laughing. "This one is going to cut both ways, McBain. Normally we could count on a certain level of assistance. In this case, Dad's going to be watching us like a hawk to make sure we're not getting into any more trouble. He's going to have the guys on a tight leash when we call. My challenge this morning may get us updates on the investigation, but that's about it. We may have to improvise."

McBain lowered his hand after waving the waitress down for another round and a check. Doyle's was noisier now and filling up with the sports-lunch crowd and a busload of people waiting for a tour of the Sam Adams brewery.

"Which brings up another important subject for discussion now that Ms. Baker is here."

Boston nodded. "I know."

Christina swiveled her head between the two of them. "What do you mean?"

"Whether you want us to continue this investigation aggressively or hand it over to the police and the SEC," he said.

"We're willing to keep pushing, Christina," Boston said. "But Doctor Lehmann's murder changes things in a big way. Dad was right that whatever is happening seems to be escalating. If his killing is connected to your parents' deaths and the car trying to run you down, you may want to rethink your approach. The police are involved now. This is getting public, and serious. Someone didn't want the doctor talking to us."

"You hired us as financial investigators," McBain said. "That's what we do, and we're ready to keep digging to find and follow a money trail. But this is getting dangerous for you, and we're not cops or trained bodyguards. I don't know what we stumbled into this morning, but for your own safety, I want you to think seriously about giving this up. You've got a life to live, and we don't want to see anything happen to it. If a killer didn't think twice about running you down or putting a bullet in the doctor in his own office in Brookline, he can easily pay you a visit again. He knows where you live."

They could see the answer forming on Christina's face even before he had finished.

"Thank you both for your concern. But as I said before at the house, this is about my parents. I'm more convinced than ever that they were cheated. I won't stop until we find out what happened to them and to the money. I'll understand if you want to drop the investigation. You could be in just as much danger as I am. You might easily have walked into that office at the wrong time."

"I knew you cared," he said.

"She means both of us, McBain."

"I'll follow your recommendation to work with the police and financial authorities if you say so. You've already done enough by showing me that there really is something to my case. But if you are willing to continue, I want to go on with you."

The two partners looked at each other and nodded. The waitress arrived. They raised their glasses to their client.

"You've got a lot of guts, Ms. Baker," McBain said. "In which case you're at the right table. That's just what my partner wanted to hear. Not only did you get her out of going to a family wedding. You've made her day."

Christina's glass met theirs. "What do you mean?"

Boston threw back her shot of Jameson. "Here's to our first murder investigation."

SEVENTEEN

The initial thrill of a murder investigation soon dissipated back into the methodical drudgery of forensic accounting. From Doyle's, McBain and Boston stopped at their office for a few things and then went directly to the workroom at the Baker house. Christina returned to the bookstore to catch up on her own business before meeting her husband for dinner. When she arrived at the house that night, the whiteboards looked as if they had been commandeered by chemists or software engineers, Boston's elegant block lettering interlaced with a barely discernible cursive scrawl.

The main table was still organized like a toy village, but there was a difference in the ways the piles of paper had been rearranged. Now they provided a tangible reflection of the names and boxes on the whiteboard. Sarah Baker's original letters occupied a central position on the table, alongside an empty black plastic inbox labeled The Doctor. The stacks of bills and telephone records stood to one side in orderly fashion, while new columns had appeared with titles such as Questionable Items, Further Research, and Cash Flows. There were also several black binders on a side table standing alongside a copy machine and duplicate stacks of the love letters, all on different-colored stationary.

"You've had a busy day," Christina said. "What's this?"

Boston finished writing on the board with a blue marker. "Yes, we've had to reorganize a little, but we think we've scrubbed it down to a new plan of attack." She pointed to the center of the dining table with her marker. "We're going to follow two main threads for now and see where they lead: Sarah's affair with the unknown man and Doctor Lehmann's involvement with your parents."

"What about Mr. Roche?"

"We're keeping him as another party of interest at this point," McBain replied. "Mainly because he was in charge of the missing money in the picture, and also since we still have to determine how well he knew Lehmann. But right now we have two other crucial mysteries to go along with the money—the affair and the murder of the man who was personal physician for Phillip and Sarah, both of whom died prematurely."

"Before, we just had to find a money trail," Boston said. "Now we not only have to do that, but discover if and how these things are interconnected with one another. So we'll start with the assumption that they are and start looking for clues. By the way, we were just about to have dinner. Are you hungry?"

Christina shook her head. "No, I had dinner with David, thank you. But I'll be happy to open a bottle of wine with you."

McBain led the way into the kitchen. "Not necessary. I took the liberty of doing a little food pairing from your cellar. We're having Italian. I hope you don't mind."

"Why no, not at all," Christina said as they walked. "You're welcome to explore the cellar as long as you're here. I only ask that you not finish the...oh goodness."

As they sat down at the kitchen table, she was appalled to see two boxes labeled Pino's Pizza at Cleveland Circle stacked next to a dust-covered, thirty-year-old Bordeaux.

"Interesting pairing choice," she whispered. "You were saying?"

In between slices, they brainstormed ideas.

"Isn't pizza the greatest?" McBain said. "We have to start digging on the doctor and stay out of the way of the police while doing it. Monday morning, I'll contact the school in Saint Louis to see what they can tell us. We also have some contacts in Miami who can do some investigating to see if we can track down the family or any trace of Lehmann there. I'm not optimistic either one of those will turn up anything."

"Why not?"

"We've been thinking about it all afternoon," Boston said. "At this point, it wouldn't surprise us if this guy's background was fraudulent. Everything you've told us suggests no one knows anything about his life before he showed up here in Boston. We'll check with your parents' friends again, but I doubt they'll have anything to add. While we're doing that, we can construct a partial list of any of them who were patients of his, and that may lead us to more. Who knows what kind of people he was involved with, and what he was into?"

McBain swirled his glass with one hand while he contemplated another slice of pepperoni with the other.

"I want to quiz Roche again too. I'm sure he's heard the news by now. I want to ask him about his relationship with the doc. Give me a chance to read him a little more. Who knows? If by some chance he's involved with the same people and really did rip off your parents, he could be rattled by seeing the doctor end up dead. You never know what a little pressure can bring to the surface. Speaking of which, there's something else we'd like you to consider."

His partner shot him an eyebrow. "I thought that could wait until we found out more. We don't have to discuss this tonight."

"What is it?" Christina looked back and forth at the two investigators.

"It's rather delicate," Boston answered. "And it has to do with your parents, so let's wait and tackle it next week."

"You want them exhumed, don't you?" Christina asked. "You want a new autopsy for my parents."

McBain cocked his glass at his partner. "Like I said, she's pretty smart."

"We'd like you to think about it," Boston said. "I'm going to speak to the coroner's office on Monday, but from what we've learned and seen so far, I think we have to question the original conclusions of the autopsy. The doctor's involvement taints everything, and his murder suggests the worst. No matter what we find out about Sarah's affair, that alone means he was killed to prevent anyone finding out more about him, and them. His position as their physician gave him unlimited access to their healthcare. Not to mention knowledge of any medication that might have triggered a fatal overdose. We also need you to get all of their medical records as soon as you can."

Christina was calm as she listened. McBain watched her and saw the toughness again. Sipping at his wine, he felt the stir of something he vaguely recognized as affection mingled with respect. He knew she was going to agree even before Boston finished explaining their logic. The woman had been a rock in the face of the apparent suicides of the two people she most loved in life. She was very cool and controlled for someone who was beginning to come to grips with the reality that her parents might have been murdered. And while she was as irritating as she was beautiful, she was a damn good client. He liked her a lot.

"Of course," Christina said. "Whatever you think is best. I'll speak to my attorney and see what steps we have to take to get it started."

McBain noticed her eyes roam around the kitchen where she had grown up, eaten, and learned to cook, and linger on the things her parents had known and loved. The parties they had thrown had been hosted here, holidays planned and celebrated. Surely the countless late-night conversations they had shared together echoed in her thoughts at this very table.

"I just cannot imagine why Doctor Lehmann would have wanted to hurt my parents. Or why he would have stolen from them. He had a good business and reputation in this neighborhood. I still feel there must be some kind of mistake. I'm hoping his killing has nothing to do with us. But we have to know for certain. If a new examination is the only way, so be it."

"Thanks," he said. "Boston and I know it's a difficult thing to think about. If we can in any way avoid it, we won't ask. Let's see what the police come up with first. Until then, we'll just lay the groundwork."

"By the way," she said, "I'm curious as to why you made so many copies of my mother's letters."

Boston smiled as she wiped her hands on a cloth napkin. "As we said, in the meantime we're going to do our best to track down the affair under the assumption it's connected to all this. So while McBain is focusing his efforts on the doctor and the financial records, we're going to try to match up any information we can decipher from Sarah's letters with any records we might have from receipts and such. Then I get to take a few road trips to see if I can find any of the places in New England she refers to and locate someone who recognizes her picture. Maybe we'll get lucky and come up with a description of her Romeo. Sorry."

"Right," McBain said. "And we'll be going through another set of copies to build a profile of the stranger to help Boston out. It's long shot, but if I give you some material, it just might jog your memory. You never know. We'll continue to dig for clues in that mountain of paper in the other room."

McBain and Boston operated from a simple premise. There were any number of ways to cheat someone in the world of finance, but in general, there is always one key element involved: trust. Sometimes that trust is tied to credibility or reputation. Other times trust is extended based on references from others. Sometimes it relies on a system that is in place, like paperwork or faith in the law and regulators doing their job. But in every case, the fox gets in to the hen house because he is able to win the trust of the victim. Then, when they least suspect it, comes the betrayal.

Without the help of the Bakers themselves, Boston and McBain were on their own for the first time in their four-year business as financial sleuths. It was a strange feeling sifting through the paper history of someone else's life. At any given time, people hated the drudgery involved with facing their taxes, paying bills, or filling out forms. Now the two partners were forcing themselves to do the same tedious work multiplied exponentially, working backward without the aid of memory or help from the victims. It was an odd way to learn about people. They had done some strange things and burrowed their way into private lives and secrets before without the slightest scruple or hesitation. But there was something eerily discomforting about reconstructing the lives of two dead people.

Computer algorithms profiled lives every day in seconds, and better. But that was a luxury they did not have. And because the Bakers had been so traditional in their way of life, in a way it would have desecrated their memory. In defiance of technology and treasuring a way of life that was almost archaic, they had kept their thoughts and secrets on paper, and not in a digital safe.

As brutal as it was, McBain and Boston had to resurrect the Bakers with the help of their daughter in order to find a path to the truth. The letters and knowledge of the affair had been a painful beginning. There would be more pain to come, of that they were certain. As McBain had said, there were secrets. Once they started to come out, people were going to get hurt. They already were.

The partners explained to Christina Baker that the key was some-where in the records of their financial transactions. Money always told the tale of a life. So beginning on Sunday, they went over them—all of them. Then they went through them again. Page by page, month by month, McBain and Boston rebuilt the history of the Bakers' financial lives, finding paperwork that followed and confirmed every bank deposit and payment, every bill charged and paid, every cash withdrawal and every investment statement that they had received going back ten years.

The fact that Phillip and Sarah maintained separate bank accounts and credit cards complicated matters. Boston was also flummoxed that there were statements from a number of bank accounts that seemed redundant. Christina explained that her parents often failed to close out unused accounts or credit cards out of sheer absent-mindedness, getting around to them after months or years of delinquency notices from the companies. She recalled at least twice when a bank itself had closed them out after several attempts.

The records had been a mess, but, guided by Boston's discipline for detail and organizational mania, over three days they brought order and coherence to the map. *Damn academics,* she kept repeating under her breath. As the paper mountain gradually became less chaotic, most of what they needed emerged.

When they had finished with the medical bills, there was no evidence of any suspicious billing or unnecessary activity. Without access to the doctor's files, that closed out that route. The insurance company might be able to tell them if any questionable payments had been made, but that would take time, even with Christina Baker's authorization. The medical records arrived on Monday, but they would need to rely on an outside expert to determine how to proceed, especially if a new autopsy was involved.

It was late Tuesday morning when McBain found the first thread and put together a mismatch in cash flows involving transfers between the investment and bank accounts. With an eye to large withdrawals, he noted that cash movements out of the accounts sometimes spiked during times when the market was moving up in years past. In most cases, money had shifted directly to a bank account. But as he began trying to match up all the withdrawals and deposits, it became clear that a number just disappeared. While none was sizeable enough to attract attention given the scale of the assets, when he totaled up the individual payments, his eyes sparkled with the first signs of discovery. The numbers were the beginning of a path.

"Just over a hundred grand," he told Boston. "It's not the missing millions, but it's a start."

"And you don't know where it went," she said.

"Down the rabbit hole."

"Do you know who and when?"

"The withdrawals are from the investment account over time. Some of them are accounted for in the bank statements. But quite a few of them aren't. They just disappear. None of the amounts is particularly large, so it looks like the intention was to keep it steady and low profile enough that it wasn't noticeable or could be explained easily. Looks like both of them, but mostly Sarah. The last one was a few months before their death."

Her green eyes lit up as she sipped at a cup of coffee.

"Know what I think?" Boston asked.

"Usually."

"Where are they?"

He handed her a stack of withdrawal authorization forms. "Let's take a look."

Their bloodshot eyes and sore backs were rewarded that afternoon, when Boston was finally certain of what she was looking at.

"You see it?" she asked.

"I do now. I didn't catch it the first three times around. Damn."

"It's good." He could hear the admiration in her voice. "I'm no expert, but if I'm right, it's the best I've ever seen. In fact it's so good we should have Dee Dee check it with her guy just to make sure we aren't wrong."

"You're not wrong," he said. "You can see it with the small *r*'s in the names. Your eyes are younger than mine, but I see it too. It's frequent enough that whoever did it must have gotten lazy. Maybe things were going so well that he or she got sloppy with overconfidence. When you compared the stream of signatures with some of the handwriting from the letters, it became a little more obvious. But you're right. Check it out with Dee."

"I'll see her on Thursday just before I hit the road for Vermont."

McBain rifled through a stack of notes on the table in front of him. They had made progress and could call it quits for the day and head back to the office.

"OK," he said. "By the way, here is the list of hotels in the region that fit the profile and some of their credit card receipts over the last three years. You can use them as a starting point for your road trips. Along with Sarah's picture, the few descriptions we have from the letters might help find someone who recognized her and any guests."

"Fine. I'll match up what I've gleaned from the letters with the hotels and restaurants and start setting up a patterned search. You have a profile of him yet?"

"Almost. Damn, Sarah took a lot of trouble to make sure she didn't identify him. There are some things in here about him, but no description and not much detail. I still wonder if it wasn't one of their friends. She writes like she is afraid they might be discovered. Maybe she was worried about her letters falling into the wrong hands, like the guy's wife. I'm sure a divorce lawyer would kill for these. The woman should have worked for the CIA."

"That would be a pattern, wouldn't it?" Boston said as she shrugged. "You couldn't get much closer than Abbott. Maybe that's how affairs evolve. Isn't that how it worked with Melissa?"

"Quite the opposite. I only wish she had cared enough about my feelings to be this discreet. Mel pretty much shoved it in my face in the end, like she was spiking the ball or something. And hard as it may be for you to believe, I have no experience from the other side, so I have no idea whether there is a common pattern."

Boston leafed through the stack. "So why do I have receipts for both of them? That's a lot of extra ground to cover, even for me."

"Because they were lumped together in a mess, and I didn't want us to miss anything by accident. And considering Ms. Baker's newsflash about how flighty her parents could be about accounting, I figured they might use each other's credit cards once in a while too. I separated them by hotel, date, and geographic category, not person. When I could, I marked them with a *P* or an *S* so you can skip over the ones that aren't relevant. Besides, sometimes there are matches, which means they had both used their credit cards at the place at different times. You can ignore those for now. I may not know much, but if she was that concerned, I doubt she'd go to a place nearby that knew Phillip. You'll just have to pick out Sarah's in context and keep them in order as you go."

She paged through the pile, shaking her head.

"For a college professor, she sure seemed to get plenty of time off to take extended trips. Vermont, New Hampshire, Maine, Nantucket, the Cape, the Berkshires. You'd think she was already retired. Nice work if you can get it. This could take a while."

McBain grinned at his partner as he packed up his briefcase. "Well, you've been talking about taking a trip all winter. And how I've been getting on your nerves....Bon voyage."

Boston grabbed her own leather bag and patted her partner on the cheek with her free hand.

"What will you do without me when I retire?"

"Probably start drinking."

EIGHTEEN

Wednesday was turning out to be a profitable day. Boston and McBain had each collected a check from two outstanding investigations and filed the cases under Winners. A follow-up call to Drysdale Securities just before noon was about to lead to another satisfied client.

They were considering where they would celebrate over an expensive lunch when Boston took a call from her father.

"Thanks, Dad, we'll be there at one." She hung up.

"Where will we be at one?" McBain asked, his voice sinking.

"Down the street at the office. Dad is going to fill us in on the Lehmann investigation. He says he has some interesting background on the late doctor. So lunch will have to wait."

McBain straightened his tie and pulled on his jacket. If they were going in to police headquarters, both of them were going to look professional and expensive. He wore a gray pinstripe, while Boston dressed in black cashmere and pulled her hair back in a ponytail.

They took a cab down Tremont to One Schroeder Plaza in time to pass through security and grab the elevator to Captain O'Daniel's office in the Bureau of Investigative Services. The headquarters of the Boston Police Department was housed in a modern, white building on the edge of Roxbury, with state-of-the-art facilities and one of the leading crime laboratories in the country. After working his way up through the districts in the greater Boston area, Tom O'Daniel had been promoted to the role of a free-floating supervisor in the Bureau. In that position, his mandate put him in touch with the formidable resources the Boston PD deployed in any murder investigation, from homicide detectives to forensic science.

The two partners put on their game faces as they walked through the hallways and waited outside the captain's office at 12:59. His office was not large, but it was busy. Although they both knew a number of the detectives on a personal basis, Boston and McBain were aware they were in new territory, and they merely nodded politely. None of their cases had ever involved violence, let alone murder. On this terrain, they knew to be all business.

A minute later, two hard-looking detectives sauntered out of the captain's office. With a glance, his secretary urged the partners in. Tom O'Daniel was seated behind his desk, speaking on the phone. His uniform was immaculate, the tie notched in a perfect triangle at the top of a black strip that sat upon a crisp, white shirt. He pointed to the chairs across from him while he was talking. McBain had never been here, and he took the opportunity to glance around. One white wall was lined with shelves holding plaques with citations, trophies, and sports memorabilia or pictures with department personnel and city or state bigwigs. The other was covered with framed photos of the captain, Boston's mother Margaret, and the five girls at various ages. It was easy to make out the youngest daughter in every picture—the one with energy exploding toward the camera. He always had a hard time reconciling the shots of Boston as a child with the woman he had grown together with over the past four years.

The captain hung up and leaned back in his leather chair, arms on the rests. There was a nice view looking north to Cambridge over his wide shoulders.

"OK," he said, "what do you two have for me on Lehmann?"

Boston crossed her legs and flipped open her notebook.

"It's what we don't have," she said. "We checked with the college in Saint Louis and our friends in Miami. There's no record of anyone with his name graduating from med school. No one knows anything about the guy. Even the people and patients we talked to from the Baker case had nothing to add. No one seemed especially curious about him. Nobody had an inkling of his personal life or background. He was their doctor and an occasional social contact, but not close enough to anyone to generate questions. Nada. Which means he was probably a phony."

The captain nodded. "Makes sense. Most of our checks into his background produced fraudulent credentials. We came to the same conclusion."

McBain leaned forward. "I would have thought that if he was legit, we could have tracked him down through the Jewish community in the Miami area, but even down there, no one connected him to any of the families named Lehmann."

"That's because he wasn't Jewish."

"Who was he?" Boston asked.

"Doctor Lehmann, as he called himself here, was from Brazil," the captain replied. "The detectives have started piecing things together from the records we found. They also contacted the medical boards and certification authorities here, in New York, and DC. It seems our man had good reason to move around so much. He had been caught practicing medicine without a license several times. I talked to one of the lead investigators in Washington who was very familiar with the man we know as Lehmann. He was intrigued to finally find out his guy had resurfaced here and what name he was operating under."

McBain said: "For how long?"

"About twenty years all told, here in the States. Five in Brazil."

Boston seemed less surprised than her partner. "Did you talk to anybody else about him?"

Her father's lip curled up reflexively. "Like who, for example?"

"Like maybe anyone in Brazil?" she said. "Was he guilty of anything except medical malpractice, or whatever they call it? Any chance he was connected with any kind of scam or untimely deaths?"

"As a matter of fact, I did speak to a few other people, including some in Brazil. Apparently your man left the country in a hurry all those years ago. He has former associates down there who engage in some of those very unsavory practices you mention."

McBain saw it. "And you think the boys from Brazil decided to visit their old partner in America. Why?"

The captain shrugged. "Too early to tell yet. Interestingly enough, when we took apart the file cabinets, we happened to find a file taped to the back of one drawer. Whoever went through the files missed that, since the cabinets were too heavy to move if you were in a hurry. The file contained some bank account numbers that we're running down now. The guys are pretty sure they are offshore accounts. This may be the connection with your case. We should be into the computer files by this afternoon."

Boston took her pen off the notebook.

"I don't suppose our suspect Richard Roche has come up in any of your investigations yet?" she asked.

Her father shook his head. "No, and I wouldn't count on it. It's only been a few days, but this is beginning to look more and more like some kind of organized-crime killing, probably over money or some bad history down there. I had Roche checked out too, though, since he's a money man. He looks pretty solid. Unlike the late doctor, his credentials are for real, and he's squeaky clean with the securities regulators. Manages money and lives well, but not too well. You want to help me out, you can put your skills to work sorting out whether Lehmann was ripping off the Bakers somehow. Check out their medical bills or something for bogus activity. You know Medicare fraud better than we do. See if they loaned him any money, voluntarily or without knowing it..."

"...that he might have sent back to Brazil?" Boston said.

"Or not?" McBain added.

"Exactly," O'Daniel replied. "And that's it. Let me know what you come up with. Stay away from Roche. And don't let me catch you at the airport. I'll update you as I get more. *Capiche?*"

Boston smiled as they stood to go. She nodded politely. "Understood."

The two left the building through the front entrance on Tremont.

"You heard him," Boston said, buttoning her coat and arranging her scarf.

"Yep," he nodded as he lit a cigarette. "I'll see you at the Baker house for dinner."

McBain waited for the market to close before calling on Richard Roche at his office on High Street. The financial advisor welcomed him in with collegial warmth, and the two eased into comfortable wingback chairs looking out over the harbor sipping eighteen-year single-malt Scotch.

"I appreciate the fact that you came by in person, Mr. McBain."

"Not at all, Mr. Roche. I figured you saw the news, but I wanted to stop by myself since this was yet another person who knew the Bakers. And I thought maybe he was a friend of yours."

"No, I wouldn't say we were friends. Still, it does hit close to home when someone you know personally is killed, especially in their own home in a safe neighborhood. It's not abstract, like watching the news."

McBain sat back in his chair. "Oh, I thought maybe you and he were acquaintances. I came across someone who mentioned that Lehmann introduced you to the Bakers five years ago."

"Yes, I knew Doctor Lehman for years. We met on a golf course not long after I moved to Boston. Come to think of it, he did introduce me to Phillip at one of their parties. But we were never close. Still, I wouldn't have suspected anyone would have reason to kill him. I wonder if it was a robbery of some kind, perhaps drug related."

McBain scrutinized Roche's face for any sign of nervousness.

"It turns out it may be more complicated than that. It might even mean the end of your potential legal troubles with Christina Baker. I spoke to the police. Can I trust in your discretion?"

"Certainly."

"There's a chance the doctor was a fraud, and that he may have been involved with organized crime in Brazil. Did you know that's where he was from?"

"Brazil? No. I thought he was from Florida."

"That was a lie, like much about the late doctor. It seems he was practicing medicine without a license—that is, practicing to be a real doctor someday. Maybe practicing on the Bakers too, both medically and financially. The police are raising questions about his relationship with Phillip and Sarah. They're going to begin looking at the financial angle with us to see if the man, whatever his name was, fleeced the Bakers somehow in connection with his ties to some crime gang. They may want to talk to you to see if you noticed any suspicious transfers or money movements out of the investment accounts over time. I told them I hadn't seen any evidence of it, but, you know..."

Not a blink. Roche shook his salt-and-pepper head and sipped at his cocktail.

"This is incredible," he said. "How could this be possible in Brookline? He seemed like such a stalwart member of the community."

"It's a good thing you weren't close to the doc," McBain said. He brushed lint off his pants. "If the police turn up anything bad on him, it's going to reflect poorly on anyone associated with him. You're right; a murder in Brookline is pretty high profile."

"Yes, I'm sure you're right."

"Aside from the scandal, I'm interested in seeing if there is anything wider going on. If someone had the *cojones* to put a bullet into Lehmann in the middle of the night in Brookline, they won't stop at cleaning up any other loose ends, if there are any."

This time Roche walked his glass over to the bar and refilled it with a steady hand. To McBain's eye he didn't look nervous, but he didn't look particularly comfortable either. He brought the bottle of Macallan back to the table and poured more into the investigator's tumbler. He put the bottle between them.

"My God," he said as he sat down. "They don't really think this is some kind of conspiracy, do they? That there is some assassin on the loose in Boston?"

McBain shrugged. "I guess if we learned anything in the past few years in our business, it's that anything is possible."

"Of course," Roche agreed. "Speaking of which, I discovered a bit more about you since we last met. It seems you're not exactly a financial planner. Like a good trader, Mr. McBain, you were playing your position. I have to say you were being somewhat economical with the truth in our last conversation. You have your own thriving private business."

The investigator smiled modestly. "Well, I'm also a financial planner."

"I did an online search on you and didn't find much."

"I'm not on the web. Not exactly the kind of business that advertising pays off for. Word of mouth is fine. I'm sure you understand."

Roche laughed as he dropped more ice in the glasses.

"I should have known Christina would have gone looking for the very best assistance she could find. I presumed it would have come in the form of an attorney, as she suggested here in this very office. And in a way, I'm flattered. From what I've heard, you appear quite successful at getting results for your clients. One has to respect that kind of reputation. But for the record, I assure you that our previous conversation regarding the Bakers' investments reflects the full truth of the matter. I am quite happy to answer any questions you still have. However, my reputation also is a matter of public record, and I stand by it. And I assure you that my personal life is boring enough that you shall find little grist for your mill there."

McBain had to give Cary Grant credit. He did his homework. He still felt warmly toward the guy, even if he wasn't about to let him off the hook just yet. Christina Baker was right; Roche could really turn on the charm in the way McBain had seen countless slick Wall Street salesmen lure in trusting suckers. Unfortunately, most of those people actually were incredible bores, despite the size of their paychecks and egos. So unless Roche was somehow involved with the Brazilians, there probably wasn't going to be much to use against him. On the other hand, that hadn't stopped him before.

"Mr. Roche," McBain said as he raised his glass, "if I thought you were even remotely responsible for what happened to the Bakers, or connected with anything unethical, I wouldn't be here now. I'd have turned over all I've got to the SEC and the cops. This is a murder investigation, and the police are handling everything. I'm just here as a courtesy."

"And I appreciate the consideration. It's a welcome change at the end of another disappointing day in the market."

They exchanged views on certain stocks and the economy, along with their expectations for the coming year, then McBain finished his drink and left.

He savored the taste of that good Scotch as he emerged into the lobby and the bustle of the rush-hour crowd. Shards of sunlight reflected off the glass atrium and filtered into the broad landscaped lobby.

Shift change, he observed, as the nightly cleaning crew marshaled to replace the white-collar tide issuing from the elevators and heading home into the spring sunset. McBain smiled, made a mental note, and remembered how good it was to have a drink liar to liar. It was always good to remind himself why he was in this business.

NINETEEN

Boston was anxious to get on the road north. She woke at six, finished a quick workout, and dressed in jeans, white sweater, and leather jacket for a long day in the car, her blood and thoughts pulsing with the thrill of the hunt. But with traffic still clogging the arteries around the city, she decided to make a quick stop downtown. She left her car in the parking garage on Post Office Square along with a threatening, ice-cold stare at the manager and staff. It took only a few minutes to hike down Federal Street and get to the offices of the *Boston Business Journal* by eight.

Dee Dee Franklin was waiting in her office, dressed in a dark-green suit and leopard-print silk scarf. She gave Boston a hug and a mug of Italian roast coffee.

"I was surprised to get your call, girl," the editor said. "You don't usually travel down here at rush hour. Must be important."

By the time Boston had finished talking, Dee Dee's mouth was as wide open as her eyes. The springs on her swivel chair squeaked as she leaned back and whistled.

"You're not kidding me about this, are you, Boston?"

"No, Dee. We weren't sure before. The doctor's murder sealed it."

"And you're certain his killing is connected to the Bakers?"

Boston sat back and folded her arms.

"Are we one hundred percent sure? No; how can you be? But the sequence and timing of events is beyond circumstantial. I've approached everything the way you taught me—with a skeptical eye. We've thought about everything that's happened here, beginning with the Bakers. We've constructed the story, done research and background checks, talked to friends. We've considered alternatives and looked at events from different directions. I can't tell you how long it took us to assemble and organize all the old receipts and records we found. Really, are all academics the most disorganized people in the world? Is there some kind of absent-minded-professor requirement for the position?"

Dee Dee shook with laughter. "My God, I think I created a monster. Go on."

"There are too many coincidences and connections in this case. And the more questions we ask, the more trouble seems to result. We can't prove that Richard Roche is involved, or that he cheated the Bakers, but we know that he was introduced to them by Doctor Lehmann, and now Lehmann's not only been killed but revealed to be a total fraud. My gut tells me that Sarah Baker's affair is connected somehow too. She was incredibly secretive about it, and we don't know who he is yet, but she took an awful lot of trouble to hide his identity. This is looking bigger and bigger by the day. If Roche was the money man, I know we can find a way to connect him to the investigation. Then we can tie him to any organization that Lehmann was a part of."

Shaking her head, Dee Dee pulled out a slim file from her top drawer and threw it in front of Boston.

"I don't know, B. McBain had me check out Roche a few weeks ago. As far as I can tell, he's clean and respectable. Has a nice little business managing money for people, some rich, some not so rich. Moderately successful and likes to socialize with the right crowd, but he's not a particularly high roller. No complaints to the SEC or anywhere else. I don't like coincidences any more than you do, but unless you find his fingerprints on something, sometimes a cigar is just a cigar."

Boston was grinding her teeth. She hated to admit that McBain's social conniving had actually produced something useful in this investigation, especially if it contradicted their suspicions about the financial advisor. She filed away the intention to hold it against him regardless of how the case turned out.

"Maybe," she said. "But given the turn of events and money involved, we're not prepared to count him out yet. Meanwhile, we'll focus on what we do know and have, and keep poring over the Bakers' financial records."

Dee Dee's face widened into a broad smile. Boston could see that familiar look of omniscience in the newspaperwoman's eyes as she placed the file back in her desk.

"Sounds to me like you two have everything under control," Dee Dee said. "You are so good together. As a team, I mean. I don't think I would have done any different based on what you have to work with and what you told me. So what can I do for you?"

"We need your help on this one, Dee. I don't think I can rely on my contacts in the department. I think dad's going to cut us off from anything they have on the doctor."

"Of course he is. If you are right, this isn't just another one of your investment scams. The more he senses the murder may be connected to your client, the less likely he is to want you involved in any way. He's your father, for Christ's sake, not to mention the man in charge of a murder investigation."

"I really need access to his financial information," Boston said. "Not to mention his client list. I'm probably not going to get it, though. If you can dig up anything connected to him and his track record...Dad says it goes back twenty years, both here in the States and in Brazil. That would help speed things along. The plan is for McBain to try to dig further here and see if we can tie the doctor to Roche. Meanwhile, I'm going to run down the list of places we identified as potential hideaways for Sarah Baker and her Romeo."

"I doubt I can get much of that stuff," Dee Dee said. "I don't have that kind of pull in Homicide. I can have my guys do some research to backstop your investigation and get some more info on Lehmann and Roche. Might give you more threads to pull. Anything else?"

Boston handed a brown accordion folder to Dee Dee across the desk.

"A couple days ago, we found the first signs of some money being drained away from the account over several years. When we went over the withdrawal authorizations, I found what looked like some signatures that didn't match up with the handwriting samples from either of the Bakers."

"Forgeries?"

Boston nodded. "We both think so. But it would help to have a hand-writing expert confirm it. We need to be as certain as possible before we can use it as evidence of anything. If they have a guy this good handling the paperwork, the sky's the limit on what they can pull off. We could be looking at a pretty large operation, with a lot of other victims out there."

Dee Dee rifled through the folder for a few minutes while Boston refilled their coffee mugs. The editor hummed as she reviewed the pages from Sarah Baker.

"This is pretty racy stuff. I'll have my John Hancock do the work. He should be able to give you some answers by tomorrow."

"Great, thanks. If I'm not back, he can call McBain when he's done."

"Where to?"

Boston slid into her black leather jacket. "Vermont for starters, probably a lot of other places until I find anyone who saw Sarah with her man. The letters go back a few years, and there are lots of them. I didn't know a woman could have that kind of energy at her age."

Dee Dee stood up.

"You know," she said, "that means you could be looking at a pretty cold trail. With your main lead lying on a slab, if you don't move fast, or if the cops don't find Lehmann's killer, you'll probably lose the scent for good. I hope you come up with something, for the sake of those poor people. Not to mention my own interest. This could be a once-in-a-lifetime story."

Boston smiled and nodded once. "I thought of that. If this thing turns out to be what we think, you get an exclusive with as much inside background as we can deliver. That ought to be quite a lead item. This isn't a shakedown for a slice of the pie, Dee. We're going to get this one."

Dee Dee Franklin hugged Boston. "You just be careful. Much as I want a good story, I want my protégé back safe and sound. Don't let that temper or cop's nose get you into trouble."

Boston feigned a look of surprise. "Trouble? *Moi?*" She patted the Louis Vuitton handbag slung over her shoulder. "You know what a safety-first kinda girl I am. See ya, Obi Wan."

An hour later, the red Shelby was blowing north past the sign that read Welcome to Vermont on highway I-89 leaving New Hampshire.

She checked her watch and eased up on the pedal, allowing the car to slow to seventy from ninety. Boston had not been to the Green Mountain State in two years, and rarely in springtime. Her eyes scanned the panorama of green, brown, and white rising before her. It was beautiful at this time of year. Her body settled into the seat like a cockpit, and she stretched out her arms. Then her mind slipped into that meditative zone that allowed her eyes to absorb the passing scenery while she processed the agenda for her trip along with Sarah's letters.

The Shelby rolled past mile after mile of forest and hills, the steaming landscape rising like waves before the prow of a ship as the sun reached into fields and ravines to burn off the last traces of a late-morning fog. Fresh snow fields at the higher elevations in the distance hinted at ski resorts and residual drifts from the persistent winter. She turned off the music and opened the window to breathe the cold mountain air rushing by. The scent of relentless ranks of pine took her back to college and the ghosts of ski trips past.

Boston weaved her way north for almost two hours. Just after Montpelier, she saw the signs for Exit 9 and Middlesex. She turned south toward Route 100 and the Mad River Valley. The countryside was picture-postcard Vermont, studded with red farmhouses and silos, rolling hills rising to mountains, and a distant monk's scalp of a tree line. After fifteen minutes, she turned left just before Waitsfield Village and then, with a series of right and left turns on country roads, found the driveway she was looking for.

Sarah Baker's pen had been eloquent, but her description of the Inn at the Round Barn Farm barely did justice to the aura of rustic, romantic tranquility that the grounds and buildings exuded. While not quite two hundred miles from the city, the investigator already felt emotionally transported farther away from the stress of her job and city life than she could remember having been in a long time. The sensory overload of peace, silence, and simplicity on a bright spring morning was intoxicating to the spirit.

It occurred to Boston that she didn't get out enough.

Parking was not a problem at the twelve-room country inn. Boston felt a little sheepish and hoped no one was watching as she locked her car, but as she told herself: *you can take the girl out of the city, but...*

The grounds were landscaped and well manicured, with a white wooden rail fence separating the entry road from trees, grass, and flowerbeds that were just beginning to erupt in color. The two old farmhouse buildings were two stories high in an L-shaped design. To the left of these stood a large barn in the shape of a hexagon painted the same soft yellow with a dark-charcoal roof punctured by windows that gave it the appearance of a medieval castle keep.

Walking in through the front door, Boston's olfactory senses were steeped in the aroma of fresh baking from somewhere in the house, her hearing caressed with the soft strings of classical music. The entryway was decorated in rustic but elegant New England antique furniture and bucolic oil paintings.

Closing her eyes, she inhaled deeply.

"Just like your mother's kitchen, I'll bet," a woman's voice said.

Boston turned to observe a middle-aged woman with light-brown hair and a wide, pleasant face emerging from a sitting room. Rather than the farmhouse wife look that she was expecting, Boston was impressed with her professional demeanor, trim figure, gray jacket, and black wool skirt. The only surprising nod to the bed-and-breakfast surroundings were the pale gold slippers on her feet.

"You never ate my mother's cooking," Boston replied. "I should have grown up here. Hi, I'm Ms. O'Daniel."

"Jennifer Pierce, the day manager," she said. "Oh yes, we've been expecting you, Ms. O'Daniel. I saw a note that you would be visiting today. You made very good time coming from Boston."

Boston smiled back. "Yes, I usually do."

"So, how about I give you a tour of our inn and the grounds? I can answer your questions as we walk. Unfortunately, the cookies won't be ready for some time."

"Absolutely. And don't feel you have to hurry."

Mrs. Pierce led her guest through the house, showing her through two of the master-sized bedrooms, the game room, and sitting areas. They walked outside, along the garden that led down to a pond, strolling past the ducks and the occasional staff member or groundskeeper. Distant meadows rose up the hillsides spotted with cows and horses.

"Are those real cows?" Boston asked.

Mrs. Pierce paused for a moment and then got the joke.

"You don't get up to this part of Vermont much, do you, Ms. O'Daniel?"

"To tell you the truth, Mrs. Pierce, I don't get out much beyond the Boston city limits that often. That's why this is so overwhelming to me. Almost like falling into a *Twilight Zone* episode."

The woman's laugh was genuine and refreshing.

"We get that a lot from city people. Some of our longtime guests come from Boston, New York, New Haven, even as far away as Washington. Yes, those are real cows. The farm is a working business and completely organic. We grow many of our own vegetables, and most of the ingredients for our meals are grown or raised locally."

They walked through the barn, inspecting the soaring oak beams and ceiling and paging through several books with pictures of weddings, parties, and large events. Boston read through a portfolio of articles and portraits from bridal magazines.

"It really is fabulous," she said. "You'll have to forgive my ignorance. But I wanted to do something special for my wedding, and my girlfriend's mother told me about your inn. She said she stayed here a couple of times in the past few years. Her name was Sarah Baker. Do you remember her?"

Mrs. Pierce rubbed her chin. "No, I can't say I recall the name. I know most of our regulars and repeat customers, so perhaps she was only with us once or twice."

Boston reached into her jacket and pulled out a photo Christina Baker had given her. It was Sarah, sun-browned and smiling as she gardened at the Brookline house. Mrs. Pierce looked at it only a moment.

"Oh yes, Sarah. I never knew her last name. I do remember her, but we haven't seen her for some time. Please give her my best and tell her to come back soon."

Score, first time going to the basket.

Boston smiled and pulled at her earring. "Yes, I will. I'll be stopping by next week to see her and...um, what is it...I can never remember his name...um...you know..."

Mrs. Pierce put her finger to her lips. "You know, I can't really say who she came with. I never saw her with anyone, but since I didn't see her name in the book, I've simply no idea who her companion was. Isn't that strange? Hah."

Yes, isn't it? Boston pursed her lips.

She thanked Mrs. Pierce profusely and promised to call her to make arrangements as the happy date approached. She stood by her car and took a last look around, feeling more of the tension drain from her body. Despite her disappointment with the news about Sarah, she was possessed by an almost physical urge to stay and book a room as relaxation spread through her nerves and muscles like a massage.

"Jesus, if the rest are like this one, this is going be a long day. I gotta get out of here."

She did, but not as fast as she normally would have.

The other four resorts that she visited that day were like the Round Barn Farm to one degree or another. If not quite as agrarian in their motif, each in its own way possessed a unique pastoral elegance that would appeal to any romantic couple looking for some remote hideaway from the cares and pressures of career or family—of course, the kind of hideaway with personalized services and the breadth of amenities that came with a price. As with most places, paradise didn't come cheap in New England.

At each location, Boston assumed her persona of the enthusiastic bride-to-be in search of the perfect wedding or honeymoon destination. In only one other mountain inn, however, did she find anyone who remembered Sarah. In that case also, no evidence of a beau was to be found.

The investigator booked a room for the night at her last stop in Vermont, the Windham Hill Inn, where she also came up empty. Over a bottle of merlot, she had a steak and salad at the bar in the restaurant while she chatted up the barman. The bartender was friendly and had worked there for years but did not recognize Sarah Baker's picture or name.

She strolled outside for a few minutes before turning in. Exhausted and frustrated, she gazed up into a dazzling half moon and sweeping canopy of starlight. In a dark mass, the Green Mountain National Forest rose into the night sky. The air was clear, clean, and cold. Boston thought about many things.

She thought about the investigation and the events of the past few weeks. Despite her initial fury at McBain's underhanded machinations, this case had evolved into the most challenging experience of their partnership. Though she would never admit it to him, she had to concede the sheer luck of stumbling into something this complex and intriguing was a stroke of good fortune that had spiced up their lives, even beyond the thrill of winning. The thought of Christina Baker relentlessly pursuing the truth for months on her own, with no sisters to provide support and no real hope of an answer, still astonished her. She felt a kinship with her client born of her own dogged determination in the face of adversity over the years.

She tried to imagine Christina Baker's grief, and the idea of losing her own parents. She thought about Sarah and how happy she must have been at all of these idyllic resorts, and the moments she had shared with her companion far away from her own suburban, academic world. Whoever he was, whether a part of a scheme or not, he had taken her to romantic places, both physically and emotionally. Boston had read and reread the passages and now pictured those moments more vividly in her head than she had envisioned them scanning the words on paper. He had made Sarah feel special, and loved.

Boston wandered back to her room aimlessly, breathing in the mountains and woods as a sleeping draught. Inside, most of the other lights were out, and the inn was quiet except for a few tardy diners in the restaurant. She closed her door, pulled off her clothes, and showered. She cried once, softly, then fell asleep.

TWENTY

McBain glanced at his watch as he strode up Berkeley Street on Friday afternoon. The sidewalks and streets of Back Bay were filling up as people used the weather as an excuse to start their weekend early. Not that Saturday or Sunday meant anything to him these days. The professor, however, might have other plans.

He turned left on Commonwealth Avenue and crossed over the street to the tree-lined promenade of Commonwealth Mall that divided the eastbound from the westbound sides of the avenue. Spring was coming on with gusto down the long stretch of broad expanse as he headed west with the outbound traffic. Commonwealth often brought back memories of Paris, which irritated him because he didn't want to think about Paris anymore. He would take the seacoast and the Charles over that noisy city and dirty river any day. Along with the gardens encircling Boston with an emerald necklace, the long, broad views of the avenue exuded an air of architectural history of open urban spaces that he rarely saw anywhere else in America. The mall seemed endless, flanked by turn-of-the-century brownstones and townhouses, and each seemed unique in its design or rooftop flamboyance, its own tribute to Boston history.

On this afternoon, that view was challenging to maintain in the face of skateboarders and a spider web of annoying extendable dog leashes, but such was the price of civilization. McBain wanted to take time out to smell the flower beds and landscaping waving invitingly in the afternoon breeze, but the longer he tarried, the less likely he would make his appointment. The one problem with Commonwealth Avenue was that it seemed to go on forever, and he was not sure how far down the address was.

At Dartmouth Street, he stopped for a moment and took off his hat, paying his respects at the memorial to the Boston firefighters who had died fighting the Hotel Vendome fire in 1972. Two blocks later, he tipped his hat to the statue of Samuel Eliot Morison, the great naval historian, and still the trees marched on. He looped around the Boston Women's Memorial, avoiding the lecturing bronze eyes of Abigail Adams. The ranks of four- and five-story brownstones went on and on, and as he neared Massachusetts Avenue, he wondered if he had missed the house. It took him another five minutes of brisk walking to locate the number on the north side of the street.

He pressed the buzzer to an apartment at street level three times and thought perhaps the professor had started his own weekend ahead of schedule. Finally, a wizened and bespectacled face peered between the red lace curtains of the doorway.

"Professor Gartner?" he asked. There was no answer, and the old gent seemed not to understand English. "Professor, my name's McBain. Mrs. Franklin sent me? I called."

The elderly man pushed up his glasses to examine McBain and jutted out his lower lip in challenge. The face expanded into lines and crevasses until the expression brightened and the door popped open.

"Ah, now I remember," he said. "Please come in, Mr. McBain. Forgive me, but I was immersed in a document."

The professor led him to the right of the entryway, where light streaming in from the south-facing windows illuminated a room that was a pack rat's dream and a fireman's nightmare. Though all was orderly and organized, paper and books filled the walls, tables, sofa, chairs, and floor. At the front of the room, flooded with late-day sunshine beneath the bay window, stood a broad pinewood architectural desk pivoted at a low angle. The drafting table was bordered by lamps and magnifying glasses, with a high stool of fraying plaid cloth pushed back from the front.

McBain thought about Boston's comments about academics. Despite his penchant for organization, the man certainly had nailed the look, from worsted wool pants and tired brown shoes to corduroy blazer hanging off the stool. The gray hair and goatee were thinning, but his penetrating eyes shaved decades off his appearance. The tall host turned and leaned on a wooden walking stick while he scrutinized the investigator, who was busy looking around the room in wonder. The guy either had a photographic memory or an incredible indexing system, or not. It was like stumbling across a cave filled with ancient treasures. He hoped his samples had not disappeared like a bad Indiana Jones finale.

"Do you live here, professor?" he asked.

"No, this is just my office. I was ready to leave for the weekend. Sorry, I'd forgotten you were coming. I'm afraid I get a bit distracted when I focus on a project." He opened a wooden cabinet drawer next to the work table and pulled out two small tumblers. "I was about to have a drink to start. Can I offer you one while we talk?"

"If you insist."

The professor filled the glasses with whiskey.

"I don't drink while I work," Gartner said, "I assure you."

"That's a relief. Me neither."

"But I've finished looking over your files." He tapped the folders on the desk. "Interesting challenge, I must say. A bit like a game, picking out the real person from the imposter, so to speak. I did enjoy finding the forger's work randomly spread throughout the files and documents."

"So you're a forgery expert?" McBain asked. "Nice line of work."

"Not exactly. We prefer the terms graphologist or forensic handwriting examiner." The professor talked with his hands, including the one with his glass. "They are, to employ a joke we use, more accurate. Heh heh. In fact, I also happen to be a qualified forensic document examiner as well, which is a forensic science that focuses on suspect documents of every kind. That is why Mrs. Franklin has need of my services from time to time. I imagine that's why she sent me your material, although apart from the financial documents in the file, the letters themselves were truly absorbing."

"What's the difference?"

The professor reacted as if he had just been asked the difference between Chinese and English. McBain held out his glass.

"The short version please."

"Well, as a graphologist I can discuss issues with handwriting itself and compare subjects to see if they originated with the same person. On the other hand, a document examiner will help you determine whether a document itself is legitimate or questionable. I often get called in to court cases for both types of work, not to mention my assistance to Mrs. Franklin and the police. However, you should realize that most findings in graphology are not particularly useful as evidence in court."

"You're pretty handy."

"Of course, I prefer the challenges of handwriting analysis myself. Document analysis can be intellectually challenging, but you learn so much more about people from their penmanship than you could imagine."

McBain sipped his whiskey and considered their mountain of documents.

"So you can tell me things about the author and the forger based on their handwriting?"

"You have to understand, some of the claims that are made about what we can do are a bit outrageous, I will grant that. As long as you limit your expectations and allow for a margin of error and skepticism, I do believe it is possible to diagnose certain things about a person or, more accurately, personal characteristics or temperament from an individual's penmanship."

"Such as?"

"For example," the professor said as he pointed at the top of the open file, "this note of yours that accompanied the documents. From your handwriting, I can deduce that you are a strong, confident person; however, the flow of the script indicates a high degree of impatience. I would almost suggest barely restrained energy that often borders on anger. You are lively and physically active, yet filled with an unspoken romanticism that is probably restrained in public. You attended at least twelve years of Catholic school, maybe more, where you were taught how to write properly. You are intelligent, analytic, detail-oriented, and inquisitive, but not overly educated in a formal sense, say at a master's level. In all likelihood, I would guess you are a sports aficionado, someone who would prefer a Celtics game to a night at the ballet. Close enough?"

McBain frowned at him.

"That's not my handwriting. It's my partner's. And he is a she."

"Ah, quite a woman, I suspect. What is the expression—a handful?"

"You have no idea."

The older man poured a dash of whiskey into both of their glasses as his face brightened.

"Would she be available?" the professor asked.

"For what?"

"Why, a social engagement, of course."

McBain's jaw hung open for a second.

"She's twenty-eight years old, Professor."

"Wonderful."

"Let's look over what you've got. I'll put in a good word for you."

"Well," Gartner said, "to answer your original question, I can't really tell you much about the person who copied the signatures of the victims. I would be stating the obvious to suggest that they themselves have excellent writing skills and elegant handwriting. They attempted to mimic Mr. or Mrs. Baker quite closely when signing forms, but there do not seem to be any examples of complete sentences or extensive copying, so there were rarely instances when the individual's own style showed through. I regret that there is not enough for me to work with. What I can tell you is that the attempts were very good. I'm impressed that your partner caught them. But I agree that it seems that a few of the more recent ones are sloppy compared to the quality of the others I found. He, or she, is quite adept, but I can confirm that the signatures are forgeries."

"We suspected that," McBain said with a nod. "Whoever it was hadn't been caught, so they might have gotten lazy over time. Could you tell how many?"

Gartner sat at his table and pulled the files over. He handed McBain a blue folder that opened to reveal a clean and organized summary of his findings. The investigator almost shed a tear in gratitude at the high quality and meticulous organization of the work.

"I started by analyzing the source individuals from their handwriting samples," Gartner said. "It is very clear that both of the Bakers were people who thoroughly enjoyed writing by hand, a rarity in this day and age. That was helpful in identifying the forger's work. As good as he or she was, once I knew what to look for, it became a fairly simple task to spot the real from the fake. On the other hand, there was some trouble from time to time differentiating from some of the real author's penmanship. That was until I began to suspect that a fair number of those real signatures were in all likelihood applied when the writer was intoxicated. Most people tend to hurry and distort their natural handwriting when they are under the influence.

"After that, I went through your forms and documents. I found questionable items on everything from withdrawal forms to authorizations to set up additional accounts. There were several on discretionary authority and permissions for types of investments or transfers between accounts as well."

"For both of them?"

"Yes, I found discrepancies for both original parties. Oddly enough, the majority of the earlier ones were for Mr. Baker, and the preponderance of my later discoveries tended toward Mrs. Baker's signature and forms. I'm not sure why that should be, but there it is."

McBain frowned and took another hit from his glass. "Our best guess is that the swindler worked on Mr. Baker's trust first then wormed his way into Mrs. Baker's good graces to cover his bases and avoid suspicion."

"As to some of the forms or documents themselves," the professor said, "I would have to spend more time comparing them to other source material. There's no way to tell if the documents themselves are illegitimate. Is that important?"

"Not yet," McBain replied. "I'm thinking that once he had their trust, they didn't pay too much attention to what forms they were getting. Most people don't. At best, they just check the highlights that say my account went up or down in value. Especially if they let a professional take care of their decisions about money and don't understand anything about the business. In my line of work, people usually acquire an interest after it's too late, if you know what I mean."

"I do indeed," Gartner said. "Myself, I keep what money I have in a money-market fund. Our profession is an interesting one, but not terribly lucrative. I suspect that, like yourself, I have trust issues."

McBain smiled and picked up his files and the summary folder.

"Nice doing business with you, Professor Gartner," he said. "Thanks for the quick work."

The graphologist put on his corduroy jacket and led him to the door. "Oh, and you will mention me to your partner?"

McBain held up the blue folder with its sterling organization.

"Maybe I'll just hand her this and send her over as a surprise," he said. "She'll love it. Besides, I have a feeling we could be doing a lot more business together. See you around town."

Light flooded the windows over the square from the west as the setting sun broke through the last bank of gray. A massive cloud front was retreating overhead, driven by brisk, high-altitude winds as the horizon augured another change in the weather after a soggy day. Boston threw open the windows. The air was already cooling down outside and the temperature dropping.

She toyed with her watch. McBain would be back by six, leaving time to head over to the Baker house for a few hours of catch-up. After several days away, she was eager to tell him about her trip across New England. His phone call on Friday in the wake of the visit to the professor had piqued her interest, and she wanted to hear more. After describing his insightful analysis of her note, her partner had suggested it might be worthwhile for her to meet Gartner and discuss his findings in person. Maybe this new contact would be willing to teach her more about his craft. It could certainly come in handy in the future. She shut down her computer and locked up the credenza for the evening.

When the front door opened, she had her coat in her arm ready to go.

Tom O'Daniel strolled in with windburned cheeks and a look of curiosity on his face as his eyes wandered around the office. For a moment, she was dumbfounded.

"Dad. What are you doing here? This is quite a surprise."

"Can't I stop in and see my girl at her place of business if I want?"

She walked over and gave him a kiss on the cheek and a quick hug to warm him up.

"You can. You just never have."

Backing up to her desk, she sat on the edge and folded her arms. Her father took off his blue overcoat and wandered over to the door to the conference office.

"Nice view. Especially at sunset. I always liked this neighborhood."

"I imagine it's changed quite a bit from your day in the precinct."

He grunted. "Hell of a lot pricier, that's for sure, and a lot tougher to park. But I guess it's true what they say. The gays really do raise real estate values after they move into an area, don't they?"

"I like it for the restaurants and shops," she said. "And the fact that it's not downtown. Not as noisy."

"Been busy?" the captain asked.

"Not so much." Boston shook her head. "I actually got away for a few days. Did some driving and hit some spots in Vermont and New Hampshire. Real pretty up there."

He clapped his hands and lit up with a broad smile.

"Good for you, baby. About time. You haven't taken a vacation in more than a year. I'm glad to hear you're taking my advice for a change. You could use a lot more time off, you know."

She smiled and walked to the door of McBain's office.

"We've closed some cases in the past week; peacefully, you'll be happy to hear. So I have a bit more free time on my hands. McBain has been looking after the Baker file while he checks out a couple leads, and we were waiting to hear something from you on the Lehmann angle. Do you want a drink?"

Her dad shook his head and sat down in one of the red chairs in front of her desk.

"Nah, I've got to get home to your mother. But that's why I stopped by. I have some news for you. Is McBain around?"

"Not yet. He should be here soon, but you can fill me in."

She walked around and sat at her desk across from her father.

"It's been pretty productive," Captain O'Daniel said. "I just got back from a trip to the country too. Up to Maine."

He had her attention. "Maine? You almost never leave the city for work. Where?"

"Nice little town up near the coast about three hours north of here. Turns out our victim had a vacation house up there, a nice secluded spot in the woods. We turned it inside out with the assistance of the locals. Quite a jackpot of information, too: documents, bank statements, payment orders, authorization slips. Looks like his associates either didn't know about the place or didn't get there in time. We found lots of financial stuff that's been keeping the fraud guys busy."

"Accounts?"

"Yep. We found something else too. Something you may be interested in."

Boston waited in silence, letting him enjoy his pace.

"Another vehicle registered to Lehmann. A late-model, gray SUV with a dent in the left front hood, along with what turned out to be traces of dried blood behind a headlight. Care to guess who it belonged to?"

Her eyes flickered for a moment as a smile crept along her lips. She shook her head at him, leaned back, and folded her hands on her lap as the light bulb went off.

"Christina Baker."

"Smart girl. Christina Baker. We confirmed it with the doctor at the hospital who treated her after the accident. Only it appears your client was right all along—it wasn't an accident."

"Score one for our team. So we were right. The murder is tied to our investigation."

He nodded. "Oh, you were right, all right. We found a whole trail of accounts that weren't in his regular computer files from the office.

Looks like he had been putting money into a secret stash and sending it offshore for years. Pretty fancy footwork, too. The amounts never triggered red flags at the banks. Routed through the Caymans, then someplace I can't pronounce, then back to Brazil. When the fraud boys finish mapping out the network on this end, they'll contact the Treasury guys and the authorities overseas so we can get authorization to track it to the end.

"So it's beginning to look pretty clear cut," he continued. "Lehmann soaked the Bakers, probably like he did lots of others. Maybe they got suspicious or found some missing money and confronted him. He must have gotten spooked and poisoned them somehow. Not too hard to do since he was their doctor. I'm going to have our forensic people contact the ME's office to talk about the case and reopen it. When your client started making a pain of herself and told him she was going to get a lawyer to go after the financial advisor, he got scared again. Either he, or more likely one of his friends, tried to take her out at night. That would have sealed the leaky operation. Instead he missed. So they decided to seal it another way."

She looked at the ceiling for a minute and then back at his satisfied smirk.

"How much money are we talking about? That you've found so far."

"About two million bucks."

"That's it?"

"Not exactly the treasure chest you were hoping for, eh? What was the Baker girl's number—fifteen mil?"

"Well," Boston said, "you've just started pulling the accounts apart. There could be more, lots more. We can meet with your fraud guys this week, show them what we've mapped out and compare notes..."

Her blood started rising with every slow shake of his head.

"Not gonna happen, kid."

"What do you mean? Why not?"

"I can't give you access to anything from this," the captain said. "This is a murder investigation that's turning into an international case. Lots of other agencies are going to be involved now. We're turning the material over to them. And it's pretty clear now that the guy you wanted was Lehmann, not Roche. I told you, he checks out with a clean bill of health. So while your client was right—her parents got ripped off, and she was a target—she had the wrong guy."

She leaned forward and folded her hands on her desk, playing with her ring.

"You can't be certain of that yet, Dad. You're talking financial fraud. Lehmann didn't have the brains to pull this off. The kind of complex money movement and camouflage you're talking about means there had to be a smart money guy. It still might be Roche. And besides, even if it isn't, you know we're as good as anyone you can put on this."

"You said you checked with other patients of Lehmann who were friends of the Bakers."

"Right. So?"

"Any of them use Roche as an advisor?"

"No, but that doesn't mean anything," she replied.

"Of course not," the captain said. "It never does."

Boston narrowed her eyes.

"Look," he said, "it's just a coincidence that the Bakers lost money in the market when they were being shafted by their doctor. Everybody lost money in the market. And you told me yourself McBain went through the paperwork and gave Roche a pass."

"Based on what we saw at first, yes," Boston said. "But we need more information. If we had a full list of Lehmann's patients, we could ask some more people and take a broader survey. You said yourself this went on for years. We can help you track down the other victims. If Roche is part of this group, he could have helped launder money for them. You know that."

"All I know is that you're pretty much accusing a guy with no track record of criminal or unethical activity of being an accomplice to a murder. Without a shred of evidence and despite what your own investigation is telling you."

"So far!"

The captain rose from the chair and put on his coat.

"And I'm telling you to leave the man alone. You're the one gonna end up in trouble if you go around smearing his reputation in this community. If his name pops up during our investigation, we'll get him that way. And you'll be the first to know."

"And what about our investigation?" she shouted as she stood up, fists on the desk.

"This is not one of your investment scams. For once in your life, stop being so stubborn and be sensible about this. A man has been murdered here, and there could be ties to organized crime in a foreign country." He jammed his cap on his head and held up a finger. "In fact, I don't care if this guy Roche is involved. Your part in this is over. I want you out of it. I can't say it plainer than that."

"This isn't fair," she said. "You wouldn't even be this far if it wasn't for us. And now you're cutting us out? Damn you!"

Captain O'Daniel's massive hands stretched forward as if they could reach across the space between them and shake her. Instead he growled, turned on his heel, and stomped to the office door, punching his fist in his hand. He spun around.

"Why can't you show more sense? After all these years, your pig-headedness is still getting you in trouble. I thought you'd learned from your mistakes, but it's clear I was wrong. I've said it before, and I'll say it again: you two are bad for each other. Neither one of you has the common sense to come in from a thunderstorm. I've tried to help you out whenever I could, and this is the thanks I get. Damn you, too!"

The door shook for a few seconds to the sound of steam rising from the old radiators and Boston's head.

TWENTY-ONE

They had been sitting in silence for ten minutes.

"What's bothering you the most?" McBain asked. His partner had barely spoken since his arrival. He had deciphered through gritted teeth that her father had just left the office and that he could go to hell. She had also given the briefest of summaries of what the police had found in Maine.

Boston was leaning back in her chair with her hands folded on her lap. The sleeves of her black cashmere turtleneck were pushed up. This informal gesture rarely happened unless she was processing a puzzle or mentally working her way around a roadblock in the logic of a fraud case. But this time her eyes were open, narrowed, and staring straight ahead, not shut peacefully.

"Get it out," he said. "Talk to me. Which is it?"

He was reclining on the couch with his feet propped up on the coffee table, his suit jacket off and tie loosened, listening to Boston's terse description of her father's visit.

She inhaled and then exhaled with the vigor of a yoga instructor, still not looking anywhere but at the target of her anger.

"It's not just the fact that we're not getting any help from dad, or that he's cut us off from our sources. He's telling us to back off."

He nodded and played with an unlit cigarette. "I know what he's getting at, but it does make it a lot more difficult for us to get anywhere. What else?"

"Without any access to Lehmann's account information, we can't investigate the money angle any further or tie him to Roche or anyone else. It's bullshit. It's unacceptable. This could be a huge case, and he's just trying to box us out."

"I agree. I don't like the fact that they're looking to tie up the investigation with this convenient little identification of the car in Maine. There are too many dead ends in this related to our case for my taste, if you'll excuse the phrase. The Bakers dead. Lehmann dead. And now this link to Ms. Baker's accident to sew up that one. Maybe it's true, I don't know. I met the guy. He didn't strike me as the kind to have the balls to kill anybody. At least not in the open where he could get caught."

"And why won't he give us a list of Lehmann's patients?" she asked. "He knows it wouldn't do any harm, and we might help their case. We could be following different leads unconnected to the murder. He's trying to strangle our part of the investigation."

McBain pulled his feet off the coffee table.

"We talked to the Bakers' friends about Roche and Lehmann. Some of them might have been referred to Lehmann by somebody else. Maybe we can try to get some other names from them to build a bigger patient list. Do it the hard way."

Boston reached into a drawer of her desk and took out a white rubber ball with a Red Sox logo. She got up out of her chair and started pacing around the office, squeezing the ball and tossing it from hand to hand.

"Another thing about that," McBain said. "If there was a scam here, it didn't start with the Bakers. If Lehmann was part of a fraud scheme, there have to be others, dead or alive. This guy didn't change his stripes all of a sudden with this one couple. That's not how they work. He was probably doing the same shit here as he was everywhere else for the last twenty years. We need to know who his other pigeons are...or were."

His partner stopped and looked at him. Her eyes leaped between his and the ceiling.

"OK," Boston said. "OK. He's part of a group. And from your description, he sounds like a weak link. Maybe he's a predator, maybe a tool. Obviously in the hands of the kind of people who are willing to kill. This isn't just some run-of-the-mill Ponzi scheme or securities fraud. I'm sure there's big money involved. In which case, if I were him, I'd want to have insurance of some kind to make sure I didn't end up as an expendable part of the operation."

McBain smirked. "Well, it looks like either he didn't think like you, or whatever it was didn't protect him the way he'd hoped. Maybe whoever popped him found it before they left. They had to have looked."

"Maybe," she said. "Or maybe they just didn't know it existed, or what or where it was."

Boston went back to squeezing and pacing.

"I want that list," she said, her voice a low growl.

And McBain knew what he had to do. He stood up and went into his office. The room soon echoed to the sound of opening and closing cabinets. She followed him in to get a drink, only to have her eyes pop open. He had pulled a small backpack out of one of his file drawers and was looking through it. A black wool sweater with a high, zippered collar hung on his chair alongside black jeans. Digging into his desk, he found a pencil-thin light and placed in into the bag. He glanced up at her.

"Look, Boston, it's pretty obvious what we need. Lehmann was the linchpin here, the only connection to everything. You're right; we need to find out more, and it looks like we're not going to get any help from the police this time. I'll have to try to find it myself."

Boston lit up like the lights at a drag strip.

"About time," she said. She bounced the rubber ball on the carpet hard. "Let's do it."

McBain was waiting for this. He threw a set of thin black gloves on his desk and held his palm up.

"I need to do this without you," he said. "If anything goes wrong or I get caught, I don't want you involved. Tom is right about that. Plus, he'd kill me."

She didn't protest as he had expected. She didn't even frown. His partner folded her arms and looked at him with her patient but logical face, which told him that reason was not on his side.

"OK, McBain, fine. By the way, have you ever broken into a house before?"

He shrugged. "Well, no, but how tough can it be?"

"Have you ever detected or disabled an alarm system before?"

"No."

"Which one of us has actual experience at violating a police crime scene and getting away with it?"

He thought for a moment.

"You do?"

They left for the doctor's house after midnight.

The low-hanging moon was a furtive grin, and the passing front's cold edge lent a shimmer to the trees and stars as it carried the hum of distant traffic across the night. Bundled fashionably in urban black, the investigators parked three blocks away and wandered arm in arm up and down the sidewalk in front of the house. For good measure, Boston wore a black-haired wig with a ponytail under a baseball cap. They passed the high hedge three times while evaluating the grounds and the human presence on the block for signs of late-night curiosity seekers or insomniacs. There were none.

It took Boston less than a minute to disable the alarm system and open the back door to the house. They strolled down the walkway to the medical office as if on a Sunday jaunt in the park.

"You scare me sometimes."

"Thank you, Boozy. That's the nicest thing you've said to me in a long time."

They stood in the middle of the doctor's office and considered their options.

"So what are we looking for?" Boston asked.

"First, your list of patients. Then his insurance. That could be anything from a name to an account number to a full confession incriminating his associates. The police have his computer, as well as the file cabinets from his own office. That's where they found his financials and paperwork."

"Except that if he had a little side business," she said, "it wasn't likely to be in those files. Dad said they found loads of records and papers at the Maine house. The patient list is surely on the computer and encrypted, but my guess is he would have some kind of hard copy somewhere as his insurance. I'll check to see if there is anything at the receptionist's station."

"Also," McBain said, "he would have backed up his files somewhere. A network with public access that could be hacked is too dangerous. Probably a small storage unit or even a flash drive. The police didn't grab it, so it has to be here somewhere. What do you think? Hidden safe?"

Boston slipped the penlight out of her black wool pea coat. She gazed around the room. The heavy curtains were drawn across the window to the courtyard.

"Maybe," she said. "I hope not. You start poking around in here and the back rooms while I check out the front desk and start on the house."

The partners systematically combed the medical office space and the house for over two hours. They moved room to room, examining every drawer or suspected hiding area, concentrating on not-so-obvious places that could have eluded easy detection by the killers or anyone in a hurry. Noise was dangerous, but they tried tapping lightly on possible false fronts of secret compartments and moving furniture as quietly as they were able. With fingers and narrow beams of light, they pried into walls, vents, and floorboards.

When they rendezvoused back in the office, McBain looked at his watch.

"It's after three thirty, Boston. We can't stay much longer. What do you have there?"

She held up a manila envelope with a bulge in it.

"I didn't find any storage unit," she replied. "So I just grabbed the hard disk from the receptionist's computer—"

"Jeez."

"And rifled the files. I found the main file with the list of patients and took it. Pretty big list, I'm afraid. There was a small safe in the floor of the bedroom under the rug, but who the hell knows where the key is. Maybe he had it on him when they shot him."

He shook his head at the envelope. "I don't know how we're going to explain that one. Let's just hope we never have to."

McBain looked around the office.

"I came up empty," he said, rubbing sore fingers beneath his glove. "Damn. I doubt the receptionist would have anything on her computer, unless somehow she was in on it. Tom doesn't seem to think so. But where else would he have put it?"

The silence weighed heavily as they stood in the middle of the office. Their heads snapped to the curtains when a car raced by outside. Boston checked the ceiling, but it was solid, without panels. She leveled her eyes again.

"I wish I'd met him. Maybe I would have a better guess. He probably kept anything like that in the Maine house. I can try that on my trip up there, assuming the police haven't cleaned that out too. It's got to be hidden in some place that's special to him, but not so obvious that his associates would look there if they were under time pressure."

McBain nodded and racked his brain for original hiding places.

"You're right. But we got nothing from talking to anyone who knew him. Based on what I came away with, the only thing special to him in this room are the pictures of him and his important friends and clients."

She scanned the walls, then glanced at him.

"It couldn't be that easy," she said.

"We've got to hurry," he said. "I'll check the left wall with the degrees. You check the ones behind the desk."

Boston walked up to the wall. She swept over the pictures rapidly with her penlight. She focused on the middle row, reached up, and lifted a large photograph of Lehmann with three men on a golf course. The picture was different from the others. The doctor wore a wide smile on his face. She turned it over and removed the back.

Taped to the inside of the cardboard back was a small key.

"McBain," she hissed.

"Yeah." He turned and saw his partner holding the key in her hand under the penlight. "What the...? How did you...?"

"Easy—the most important guy on the wall. Former state senator and pretty powerful, based on what Dad told me. Figured he would put it there. Let's go."

She put the picture back in place, and they left the office. In less than a minute, they were kneeling over the open floor safe in Lehmann's bedroom. McBain removed several sheets of paper folded over and a small, felt-covered box about ten inches long that rattled slightly. Boston opened it and scanned the contents. She shut the box and placed it carefully in her small rucksack.

"Let's get the hell out of here. We got what we came for."

TWENTY-TWO

"How many are there?" McBain asked.

Her finger slid down the page.

"Thirteen," Boston replied. She took a stiff drink of the warm bourbon on the table in front of the couch. Two cold cups of coffee sat next to the bottle. "Jesus."

He sat close by her side, and his eyes switched from the box on the table to the pieces of paper in front of them. Everything blurred as they moved back and forth on the paper, so he blinked them hard and rubbed. Down the left side of the page was a column of names. To the right of each name on each row were several entries with medical terms in two columns.

"Weinberg. Brooks. Howard. Wadsworth. Goldman. Aaronson. This column to the right of the names must refer to their medical condition, maybe the cause of death. Pancreatic cancer. Brain tumor. Diseased lungs. Cirrhosis of the liver. But what's this last column? A treatment of some kind?"

She shook her head and fell back on the couch with her hand over her eyes. They were both drained and on fire, their bodies and spirits long past the point of exhaustion.

"I don't think so. Look in the box. There are a dozen glass bottles in there. I checked a couple of the labels, and they matched those drugs in that last column. I'll bet it has something to do with how they died. We need to get a medical expert to go through this list tomorrow...I mean today. Right now, we're too tired to work through it all."

McBain leaned back next to her and tried to focus his red eyes on the ceiling. Boston turned her head toward him and pushed away her hair.

"Boozy, did you see the last name on the list?"

"Yeah, I saw it."

"We're going to have to tell Christina Baker tomorrow," she said. "I think we'll probably have to get the process rolling for exhumation. If this last column is what we think it is, we should have someplace for the examiner to start looking. For once, I wish our suspicions had been wrong. This is just sickening."

He rubbed his cheeks.

"At least we know what his insurance policy was supposed to be," he said. "Too bad it didn't work. With enough time, we might have broken him. Or at least shaken him to the point we could have followed him and planted some bugs. Boy, would that have been nice to take to Tom on a plate."

"Yep," she said, then yawned. "He must have made the list to keep track of the victims as they piled up, the prick."

"At least now we have an idea of the scale of the operation."

She shook her head to keep her eyes open. "That list. Something about that list of names is familiar. One of the names, maybe..."

Boston pushed against his shoulder to raise herself off the couch. She stumbled over to her computer and began typing as she yawned again. Searching for a thread of some kind, she scanned again and again and then started over as her thoughts decoupled and drifted away from her eyes and hands.

After several minutes of silence, staring into the computer screen put her in a trance, and she barely snapped her head back before it hit the monitor. McBain roused himself.

"Stop, Boston. It's almost sunup. Open the foldout in the office, and I'll take the couch. Let's get a couple hours sleep and tackle this with some fresh eyes. Then we can figure out where on this list to start."

He half lifted his reluctant partner out of her chair just as her face was headed for the desktop again. He just made it back to the sofa with a blanket.

The light pried open his eyelids after a few hours, but it was the sound of softly tapping computer keys and the fragrance of dark roasted coffee that compelled him to roll over and look around. Boston was back at her computer, disheveled but determined. No longer sleep deprived, her mind jumped nimbly from screen to screen following a trail of links. She had the hungry look of the animal who has found the scent, taking the occasional note on a pad, the printer humming out pages every few minutes like breadcrumbs.

Without looking his way or asking if he was awake, she said: "I found it."

McBain rolled off the couch, put his jeans on, and swabbed his face with a wet towel. Then he grabbed a cup of coffee and pulled up a chair next to hers.

"OK, go."

Boston took her printouts from the machine and spread them across her desktop.

"Remember when we were first getting started and trying to figure out ways to dig up new clients?"

He nodded. "Sure. I ate a lot of hot dogs in those days. I didn't like it much."

"One of the tricks I used to resort to was to scan the obits for potential business. I recall you called me an ambulance chaser once."

"Sure, I remember that. You went through the *Globe* and the magazines on a regular basis looking for dead rich people. When the first person slammed the door in our face, I was convinced it was stupid. In hindsight, it wasn't the craziest idea you ever had. I don't think we ever got any hits, did we?"

"No, we gave it up after the first year. But my brain's working a little better with a few hours' rest and fresh coffee. So I went back into our files and checked on all the potential leads we had from the early days, including ones from the obits I looked at but never followed up on. Take a look at these two names."

He eyeballed two sheets of paper. They were copies of obituaries from the *Boston Globe* archives. The dates were four years old. "Grantham and Aaronson. They're both on Lehmann's list. You think?"

Boston put her coffee down and stretched her arms to the ceiling. "We won't be sure until we talk to the families. All I can tell you is that they were both loaded, and the cause of death matches the disease in the middle column of his records."

He refilled their cups and leafed through the pages she had printed out.

"That'll have to do, since they're the only leads we've got at this point. In that case, I guess we better grab a quick bite, work out our script, and get prettied up. I'll go out for the food while you figure out who—"

"Already done. Our first visit will be to Mrs. Grantham's sister in Cambridge."

McBain stroked his morning stubble. She leaned back in her chair with cup in hand and twinkle in her eyes.

"Don't give me that look," he said.

"What look?"

"That insufferable look that says, 'I just got an A on my homework; what did you get?' This is why I never come in to the office until I'm awake. You know I'm never at my best first thing in the morning."

He grabbed his wallet and sweater and headed for the door.

"Yes, I know," she said. "Don't forget I like my scrambled eggs soft..."

"Your bacon crisp, and your multigrain toast medium. I remember. Enjoy your smug mug of coffee and start thinking about our routine."

McBain's Range Rover crossed the Charles over the Anderson Bridge late Tuesday afternoon and was immediately surrounded by students as the pair paused at the light by Weld Boathouse. April was getting long, and the Harvard campus was packed with foot and bicycle traffic, a stream of humanity rushing to the end of the college semester. They hopped Memorial Drive and moved up JFK Street past the park and stores at a snail's pace behind a line of cars. All the while, Boston fidgeted and grumbled and scanned the street signs for the right turn that would take them deeper into Cambridge. They worked their way through the labyrinth for a good twenty minutes before wedging the

Rover between two cars amid the tight streets around the university, not far from the address they had been given by Mrs. Grantham's sister.

When they found the street number, they were surprised to discover that it was not a house. The door to the old four-story redbrick building was half open, with voices and laughter echoing from the rear of the ground floor. They walked down a half-lit hallway that opened on a small auditorium. Rows of metal folding chairs stood arranged in a rough semicircle around a raised stage. Scattered across the stage were assorted pieces of old furniture: a square wooden table with a pitcher of water and plastic glasses, a large, fluffy paisley couch, and three stark straight-backed chairs. Thick, black curtains hung from the rear ceiling as a backdrop.

Onstage, a half dozen young people were enacting, to the best that the investigators could tell, a scene from a play. A score of others observed the action from rows of seats in the front of the room, and it became obvious that this was a rehearsal rather than a live show.

"Well," Boston said, "at least it isn't performance art."

They found seats among the chairs in the back of the room. For the most part, the rehearsal proceeded apace without interruption. When an actor stumbled, a silver-haired woman in the front row halted the scene with comments or hand gestures. The teacher was full figured and flamboyant, hard to miss in a zebra-pattern scarf and red velour thigh-length jacket over a black dress. After fifteen minutes the session was over, and the future Broadway stars filed out past Boston and McBain. Most of them ignored the two investigators, sitting there casually looking like accountants. Boston wore a medium-gray suit with pants and wire-rim glasses, while McBain stroked his blandest rep tie underneath a worn blue pinstripe.

Boston made a point of evaluating each of them with a cold eye. A couple of students tried to glance condescendingly at the two strangers quietly judging them as they passed by, still too young to realize that until their brilliance was recognized, artists needed to be smart enough not to sneer at potential money sitting in the theater.

When the theater had emptied, the partners wandered up to the older woman stacking scripts on the stage table.

"Are we too late for auditions, Mrs. James?" McBain asked.

Theresa James tipped her half-glasses down a bulbous nose and eyed him with curiosity. The lines and age spots on her face suggested a matron pushing eighty, but her eyes evaluated him with the glint of passionate youth.

Boston extended her hand up to the woman.

"Hello, Mrs. James," she said with a polite smile. "I'm Ms. O'Daniel. I called earlier about your sister Mrs. Grantham. This is my partner, Mr. McBain."

"Ah." Mrs. James chuckled. "You had me for a moment there. I thought you looked a little old to be a student, Mr. McBain. Not that I discourage people of any age from taking my class." She scrutinized them. "I must admit in my defense you two don't look much like insurance people either."

He took her hand and kissed it.

"Enchante, Madame," he said. "I'm ready for my close-up."

The teacher smiled disarmingly. "I think that's my line, young man."

Boston elbowed her partner playfully. "Don't quit your day job, McBain. Thank you so much for taking a few minutes to see us, Mrs. James, especially on such short notice. I realize this was a somewhat strange and sudden request."

The teacher waved a ring-laden hand in a theatrical gesture.

"Not at all, young lady. I'm always happy to talk about Thomasina. It's been four years now since she left us, but we all enjoyed many wonderful years together. Nothing but fabulous memories."

She lowered herself to the edge of the stage while they took chairs in the front row. Boston held her folio on her lap.

"I wish we were here to discuss a more pleasant subject, Mrs. James," McBain said. "We'd like nothing better than to hear about your sister. If she was anything like you, I'm certain it was a great loss to Boston's social and cultural pulse. From what little we've learned, she led a long and interesting life, not to mention her patronage of the arts. It's an unfortunate part of our job that we don't usually have a chance to meet such people under the best of circumstances."

"I hope that her passing was not too painful," Boston said. "For her, or for the family."

Their hostess smiled benignly and pulled her coat closer as she folded her arms.

"After the illness took hold, Tommy was very sick and in some pain most of the time. But in the end, she went rather quickly, thank God. That part was a blessing. She had been so vibrant until her last year. And after her husband Alfred passed on, there really wasn't anyone close to her who could care for her besides me. Our brother Gerald was the oldest, but he was largely an invalid himself and unable to leave home. He left us a year back as well, you see, so I'm the last. I tried to be at the house as often as I could, but we came to depend on in-home care to attend to her."

"I trust money was not a problem for her?" Boston asked.

"Oh, no," Mrs. James replied. "Alfred had left a good amount of money behind. So we were able to manage the medical bills all right."

"Ah," McBain said. "You see, that's the reason for our visit today."

"Yes, Ms. O'Daniel explained on the phone that you had some questions related to medical insurance or something."

Boston pushed her glasses back up her nose with a pencil and cleared her throat.

"Just routine, Mrs. James," she said. "But I wonder if you had heard about the recent passing of a Doctor Lehmann in Brookline."

The teacher held a hand to her mouth as her eyes widened. "Oh, yes. It was terrible. I didn't actually read about it, but a friend called me who saw something on the news. You know he was Tommy's doctor?"

"Yes, ma'am. That's it exactly. It seems there are discrepancies in the long-term records related to a few of his patients, and we are working with the police and the insurance companies to clean up certain ones that appear to be unresolved."

"Goodness. What kind of discrepancies could there be with Tommy's records? She's been gone so long now. I don't think we ever had any trouble during her illness with medical bills."

"I'm sure it's just a matter of sloppy record keeping," Boston said, "or clerical errors by the company. But it's our job to confirm these things with all of the former patients on our list, just to make sure that everything was done properly. Insurance companies can be rather large and bureaucratic, you know. But boxes have to be checked and numbers have to match, or else the files stay open forever."

McBain flipped open a notebook.

"Mrs. James, were you ever aware—"

"My students are required to call me Mrs. James. You're old enough to call me Terry." She smiled back at McBain, and he thought she was pretty alluring for an eighty-year-old. Or maybe it was just the actress thing.

"Terry, do you recall any problems with any of the medical bills that were submitted during Tommy's illness? Any exceptional charges that might have raised an eyebrow, or seemed out of the normal procedures? Something that may have been questioned by someone? I realize this all took place four years ago."

She put her hand to her chin and thought for a moment before shaking her head.

"Not that I can recall," she replied. "I would have thought that if anything wasn't right, we would have been informed by the hospitals or insurance companies at the time. I'm certain I never heard of any questions about any bills. And my mind is still pretty sharp, Mr. McBain."

"I'll bet it is," he said. "I just watched you handle thirty college kids hanging onto your every word. What we are looking for is any kind of bill that might have been a one-off item or large enough that it might have stuck out, like a duplicate charge for a lot of tests or hospital care or something."

"I'm not sure I can help you with much of that. I don't really have a head for numbers, you see. Either Doctor Lehmann's office or Mr. Roche looked after all of those things for us."

"Mr. Roche?" Boston inquired with her pencil raised.

"Yes," Terry answered. "Mr. Roche took care of almost all of their financial affairs during the last few years. After Alfred passed away and Tommy got sicker, Mr. Roche was terribly helpful in making sure things worked smoothly. He helped manage their accounts so they didn't have to worry about money or the bills or anything. He set up several trusts for their favorite causes or charities so they would run according to Tommy's wishes. He assisted with the will and made sure that Gerald and I were included. He really was invaluable. Maybe he can help you with your questions."

McBain put his pen to his lips and smiled.

"It's nice to know that Tommy took care of you and your brother. Does this fellow help manage your finances as well?"

Terry James laughed. "Oh no, Mr. McBain, I don't have that kind of money. I don't need a man like him."

"I'm sorry," Boston said. "I would have thought Mrs. Grantham left you quite a bit in her will. You'll excuse me, but I gathered your sister was quite well off. Were there many other beneficiaries in the will?"

The older woman tipped her head back. "Well, I suppose after accounting for various causes and donations in her trusts, the estate really didn't amount to as much as we had originally thought. In fact, I think her attorney was a bit mystified by some of the final bequests. But I never really expected anything from Tommy's money anyway. Better it go to people who needed it more."

The investigators nodded approvingly.

He handed her a list of the patients from the Lehmann pages.

"I wonder if you could take a glance at this, Terry. We've been given a list of other cases that might also reflect some questions about insurance payments. We think perhaps some of the files or records might have been mixed up with one another. Do you recognize any of these names?"

Her brow furrowed as she put on her glasses and ran down the paper with a polished pink nail.

"I'm afraid not. I thought I knew most of Tommy's friends. I don't know any of these people." She handed the page back to McBain.

"Not to worry," he said. "I don't think there's any connection. We just have a lot of calls to make and thought maybe there was an easy way to sort out all the paperwork. We'll get to them all eventually."

They stood up, and Terry eased off the stage in one effortless movement.

"Thank you so much for your help," Boston said as they shook hands.

"I'm sorry I couldn't help you tick some of those boxes."

"Not at all," McBain said with a wave. "You've helped us cross a few things off our list and provided us with a new source. If we need anything else, our firm can always contact this Mr. Roche. It's been a pleasure. If we happen to have any more questions..."

"Call anytime, Mr. McBain." She offered her hand. He kissed it softly.

Boston's eyes and gait were percolating with energy as they left the theater. "I can't wait to talk to the Aaronsons tomorrow," she said, picking up speed.

But he paused at the doorway and looked back at the stage. Theresa James was packing up the last shopworn scripts and turning down the lights.

"What is it?" his partner asked.

"The play's the thing..."

"What does that mean?"

He turned his head back to her.

"Just a line from a very old story," he answered.

They hurried out into the growing twilight.

TWENTY-THREE

Christina Baker sat slack-jawed and pie-eyed as she stared at the white-board and absorbed what she had heard. The color drained from her cheeks.

"We thought you ought to be the first to know," Boston said.

None of them spoke for another few minutes. They sat around the stacks of paper on the table in the workroom while McBain and Boston sipped their burgundy. They had had a few days to take in the full measure of what they had discovered, sketching the outlines of the operation and filling in the puzzle as pieces of information emerged from the families. One by one: Grantham, Aaronson, Weinberg, Spenser, Morris. They were all on the board, down to the last of the names—Baker. With the help of Dee Dee Franklin's investigative resources, over four days the investigators had unearthed and interviewed relatives of all of the other victims on Lehmann's list and determined the lethal nature of the contents contained in the box of vials.

McBain broke the silence. "Ms. Baker, it's important that you understand. Your parents appear to have been victims of an extremely sophisticated, well-organized, and complex financial fraud. Just how complex we're only beginning to discover, but it's clear that it's one of the slickest and most successful that I've ever heard of. Anyone but the most savvy investor would have been taken in by these people, even among those who do this for a living."

"How..." Christina Baker began, then stopped.

"We don't have any information about how they moved money," Boston said. "To get that, we need access to account information for these families such as the files you've given us. And we won't get them.

But you probably put your finger on it that evening at the bar where we first met when you suggested checking offshore accounts. The police have already found evidence of those among Lehmann's files.

"What we do know is that there is a connection between Roche and Lehmann for each of these families. That they were all to one degree or another wealthy. And that the victim passed away rather suddenly from an illness. So our hypothesis is that Lehmann and Roche worked together to identify potential targets, maybe along with others. Roche was very likely in charge of tapping into the money and making it disappear without anyone being the wiser. Lehmann of making the person disappear from what appears to be natural causes without the family becoming suspicious. We know there is a professional forger in the group to help them with signatures and documents, not to mention people who are willing to kill."

"Could be the same person who used Lehmann's car to try to run you down put the bullet in him later," McBain said. "With their resources, a killer could easily move in and out of the country from Brazil, the Caribbean, or anywhere else."

"But my parents, they weren't wealthy. Not like that."

He rubbed his Euro stubble with the back of his fingers. "Without more detail, we can't know what these criminals used as criteria for their targets. From what we've been able to determine, the net worth of the other victims ranged from fifty million to nearly a quarter billion dollars at their peak. You parents were wealthy enough, it seems. According to the accounts, they lost almost fifteen million in investments, though some of that may be legit market losses. There's no way of telling how much the operation drained from each victim. But your parents are outliers for another reason."

"What do you mean outliers?"

Boston leaned forward over her wine glass. "Phillip and Sarah were in their early sixties. Most of the others were much older. And they all suffered from a serious illness before passing quickly. Whether this illness was natural or somehow introduced by Lehmann as their doctor we don't know. But we can be fairly certain he had some hand in accelerating their end for purposes of the scam. The timetable may have been orchestrated by whoever was in charge of the operation. But your parents were younger than the others and not obviously on death's door. So they were murdered in a way that made it look like suicide. That tells us that for some reason, the timetable was upset. Maybe they discovered they were being robbed. Maybe they came across one of the relatives of another victim and confronted Roche or Lehmann. Who knows?"

"It's even possible," McBain said, "that your mother's affair was a part of all this. It would make sense. Think of the secrecy about who her lover was. Maybe the group planted some young Latin type in her life to seduce her and keep an eye on things. He may have even had access to the house in order to place a poison in a way it was sure to be ingested."

Christina leaned forward on her elbows and put her face in her hands. The investigators looked at each other and wondered if their client was going to vomit, just as they had wanted to. It was a lot. They had gone over it again and again, not wanting to believe it themselves. She lifted her head and took a drink.

"But thirteen people," Christina said. "How could they have possibly gotten away with this? For how long?"

McBain pushed a sheet of paper across the table to her. Christina picked it up and read the list of names and dates.

"Assuming this is all of the victims," he said, "it goes back over seven years. Using your parents as a typical pattern, I would say that either Lehmann or Roche generated the original business and evaluated the potential victim for either health or financial reasons—probably both. Then, at the right time, he introduces the other guy into the equation based on trust, like Lehmann did with Phillip five years ago. Then they slowly gain control and support each other until such time as the opportunity to move money presents itself. The market meltdown must have come as a godsend to these guys. They time withdrawals to coincide with an illness that can lead to the demise of the victim without questions being asked. Make it look like nature just taking its course."

Boston said: "Among all the surviving relatives of the victims we talked to, there were one or two who grumbled about the size of their inheritance, but nobody had enough reason or evidence to take any action.

No one else was cleaned out totally the way you were. Roche probably managed the drainage so there was enough left in the estate to satisfy the surviving relatives. None of these families knew the others, so they must have carefully vetted clients so no one would be the least suspicious or have intimate contact with other families on the list. They kept each of them compartmentalized, which in our experience is pretty tough to do with rich people. No doubt that's one of the reasons none of your parents' friends who were patients of Lehmann had Roche as an advisor."

"Who knows how many others were in the pipeline?" McBain said. "They must have targets lined up with the idea of taking them out gradually down the road." He looked in his client's eyes. "You were the first person to ever raise serious questions after the death of a loved one. The first one to sink your teeth in and become enough of a pain to produce a viable threat to the scam. They must have thought you would eventually give up and go away. Guess they didn't know you very well."

She sighed. Her eyes were red but dry. "Now what? Can we have him arrested?"

Boston and McBain looked at each other and grimaced.

"For what?" they asked together.

"But surely," Christina said, "if we take this information to the police, if we get the other families to come forward, they can make a case."

"Yeah," he said. "Here's the thing, and here's our quandary. We don't have any actual proof or even any accusations yet, aside from yours. Everything we told you is what we've surmised from talking to all of these people. While we have confidence that we're correct, this only leaves us with a couple of choices. Boston?"

Christina looked at the redhead with a sense of foreboding.

"All right, Christina. We can take what we found to the police. Given the connection to their open murder investigation, they'll probably listen to us, take our information, and begin to question the other families and expand their investigation to include the securities regulators. If they genuinely suspect that these deaths can be ruled homicides rather than natural causes or unavoidable illnesses, they may start a long process that involves looking into Roche and bringing down this fraud and arresting the people they can get their hands on..."

McBain swirled his glass. "In which case Roche will probably be on a plane to an extradition-free time zone the minute he gets wind of it, closing accounts as he goes like slamming doors. As it is, we'll be lucky if he doesn't find out we were sniffing around any of the other victims. Once he gets on a plane, we'll never see him again."

"Even in a best case, the investigation will go on for years," Boston said, "involving legions of law enforcement and financial regulators, not to mention lawyers for the various families and their numerous trusts and other beneficiaries. And we haven't begun to consider the challenge of confirming the victims were killed through deliberate medical means, especially now that Lehmann is gone. Even if they can prove enough of it to arrest Roche—which is a long shot—he might still fall back on the old mismanagement excuse that he gave you."

Christina sighed as she shook her head. "Or? You said there was another choice."

Boston took it to her directly. "You hired us to get your parents' money back. We think we can do that based on the information we have, plus a little more proof and leverage. We think the odds are pretty good that if we confront Roche with enough pressure, he'll pay up to get us to drop the investigation. If McBain plays it right, he'll believe that he can settle with us without endangering the operation."

"How?"

"We blackmail him," Boston said, her face a deadpan blank.

"The fine line I have to walk," McBain said, "is to make him think we have enough to threaten his reputation with this case alone and that our snooping might expose the rest of their operation. At the same time, we don't want him to think we know he's involved with murder, or for that matter, anything beyond your case. They may very well think that with Lehmann dead and nothing happening these past few weeks, they've cut any link to the crimes. They pay you off to cut their losses, it goes away, and they get away with murder."

"You mean literally?" Christina asked. "What about the other families? We can't let them get away with that."

He turned to glance at the whiteboard and then back to her.

"With any luck, I'll be able to get him on record for the financial fraud. If we can hand him to the cops before he breaks for the exit, they might be able to grab him for fraud or an accessory to murder charge, turn him, and roll up the rest of the operation. It's a low probability, but maybe the threat of prison will wilt him. It does most white-collar types. That's our best and only shot. Either way, it will probably scare the crap out of him enough to put a stop to the whole operation."

Their client's features teetered between confusion and despair. She looked at the names again, her blood heating up. Boston could see it.

"Christina," she said. "You won't get him for murder anyway, your parents' or anyone else's. Lehmann himself took care of that part. Roche will never do time for that, even if he confesses to being the money man. We think this is the best deal we can get for you. Combined with Lehmann's death, it will probably put a stop to these people. We don't like it either, but those are our cold, clear options."

McBain watched her closely. She was wrestling with a range of emotions, some of them unfamiliar. He could see the rage fighting to emerge from the confusion in spite of their logic. He glanced at Boston, who shook her head once. He leaned forward over the table.

"Ms. Baker. Ms. Baker, look at me."

"Yes?"

"If we're going to nail Roche, there's something very important you can do to help us."

She lifted her head and tried to focus the fire burning in her soul. "Anything."

"We need leverage," he said. "We need to put pressure on Roche to try to open him up. To make him feel threatened enough to talk to us and to think he can trade his way out."

"My parents," she said. "An autopsy."

"That's right," McBain said with a nod. "We want you to begin the process. What's more, we want you to let Roche know it. Have your attorney shoot him a letter notifying him that due to the suspicious circumstances surrounding Dr. Lehmann's demise, you are having the bodies exhumed for examination. Make sure he mentions that the letter is just a formality. No accusations, no connection. We want him to sweat, but just the right amount."

"Meantime," Boston said, "I'll continue to pursue Sarah's affair. If it is connected to the scam, any mention of it ought to push the tick under his skin further. If it isn't, well, it couldn't hurt for him to think you think it is. He already knows you hate his guts."

Christina stared at the diagram on the whiteboard. "And you think that will be enough?"

McBain smirked. "Not quite. But when we have our little heart-to-heart, I'm going to ask him for a couple of things that should do it. He already knows you hired me to look at the records, so it will seem totally legitimate."

Boston looked at him with a raised eyebrow.

"What are you thinking?"

He glanced at her sheepishly. "I'm more than a little embarrassed that I only thought of it now as we were talking it through. There's a way he could have pulled off a con and raped the account without the Bakers or us picking up on it. But we would need to have another set of source documents to prove it. Know where I'm going?"

Boston scanned the table like a cat searching for a mouse. She steepled her hands and focused on the monthly statements from the financial advisor to the Bakers. McBain enjoyed his wine and waited.

"The trade confirmations," she said.

"Exactly."

Christina looked at them. "What are you talking about?"

"Once we started to focus on the possibility of offshore accounts, I should have immediately realized that there was something missing from your parents' investment records. Most people wouldn't give it a second thought, but it's a piece of information that's vital for enabling you to follow a trade or investment to ensure you got exactly what you wanted at the right price. Roche provided them with monthly statements that showed what they had in their accounts at any given time, and what it was worth. What that doesn't tell me is who he was trading with. He had control over when and how trades got done. You were right to suspect they were overcharged on commissions. But when I looked at the files, it appeared they weren't. There are a number of ways to fleece an account, especially if you're dirty and smart. The big-time guys set up their own company and execute the trades with that one, which gives them tons of room for manipulation. Unless you look closely, it all seems pretty normal, and you have to untangle a maze of accounting gimmicks to figure out your supposedly trusted advisor is working both sides of the street."

Boston paged through the investment files. "Nothing here."

Christina straightened and pushed the loose strands of black hair from her face. To McBain's eye, she looked haggard, like a boxer in the middle rounds of a losing fight. He had to keep her moving.

"OK, so we have a plan. Right, Ms. Baker?" he asked. "Boston stalks the affair angle, and you get the legal process rolling."

"I don't know. I wish there were more we could do to be certain he goes to jail. What if he thinks you're bluffing? Or he's afraid of his partners? As you said, you don't have any real proof."

Boston stood up and pulled out her phone. "I'll call my father now, Christina. McBain and I will set up a meeting with him and lay out our thoughts. He can advise us on our legal options and the best way to nail Roche. With any luck, we can get them involved from the beginning and have everyone coordinated on this. Agreed?"

Their client exhaled deeply and nodded. She left the room to fix them a late dinner. As soon as they heard water running in the kitchen, McBain turned to Boston. She put her phone back in her pocket.

"I didn't think so," he said.

"I'll call him when we're good and ready. And we won't give him a thing until we're in place and have Roche on the hook. Roche isn't the only one we need leverage against."

McBain closed his eyes and planted his face in his palm. "By the time this is over, one of us is going to be on Tom's shit list, and it's not going to be you."

TWENTY-FOUR

May Day in Boston arrived with a clear, blue sky. The days were getting longer and the layers of clothing thinner. The forecast looked promising, as life often does at such times.

McBain was feeling optimistic as he strolled along Newbury Street, shopping his way up the boulevard every few blocks. Maybe it was the new dress shoes. New shoes always made a guy feel good, probably because they were such a rare treat. And so was the type of case that moved along at some point of its own momentum. In the event, there had been no need to set up a meeting with the financial advisor. Richard Roche had called him within an hour of receiving the certified letter from Christina Baker's attorney.

At the ornate bronze canopy across from the Public Garden on Arlington Street, he turned into the Taj Hotel, his hands full with bags. At the top of the steps, he crossed plush maroon carpeting and a polished marble floor and wandered into the soft, dim lighting of the old Ritz Bar. He found the advisor seated at a table by the fireplace, far removed from the wide windows overlooking the street. Roche was impeccably coiffed and dressed in a custom-tailored herringbone suit, white shirt with French cuffs, and pink Hermes tie. His cufflinks were blue sapphires that caught the firelight.

McBain unbuttoned his suit jacket and took a seat with his back to the wall, facing the bar. He gazed around to the front of the lounge. It was Monday and just five o'clock. The crowd was thin.

"I miss the piano that was here when I used to come years ago," he said. "Almost as much as I miss being able to smoke in here."

231

Roche shrugged. "We old-timers have to learn to change with the seasons."

McBain nodded back. "Well spoken, sir. And thanks for calling me. I was meaning to ring you up in the next day or so myself."

"Yes, I thought you might," Roche said. "I was hoping we could talk about the police investigation of Doctor Lehmann's murder. And, of course, your work for Christina Baker, since the two now seem to be related. It seems the case isn't quite as closed as you suggested the last time we met. Oh, thank you, Milosz. What will you have, Mr. McBain?"

"Bombay Sapphire martini with an olive. In honor of your cufflinks. Shopping for clothes always works up a gin thirst for me."

Richard Roche chuckled and sipped his own martini diplomatically until the waiter returned. Several couples and a family trickled in for cocktail hour and took tables by the windows. Three businessmen headed to the bar.

Roche raised his glass. "To your good health. Now, I wonder if you were aware of a certain letter I received today from Christina's attorney."

"Letter? About what?"

"It seems that she wanted to advise me that she has initiated proceedings to have Phillip and Sarah exhumed so that another autopsy can be conducted. Apparently due to the doctor's murder, she now has questions about the nature of their deaths. You wouldn't know anything about that, would you?"

McBain clenched his teeth and drew in a sharp breath.

"Yeah, I might have mentioned something about that in one of our conversations. I didn't think she was serious. I guess the murder has her all fired up again. In fact, that was one of the reasons I was going to stop by your office. She's insisting we look at more detailed records of her parents' trading activity. I'm going to have to ask you for printouts of a few more things, like trade confirmations, customer agreements for investment strategy, and details of any cash withdrawals or transfers from their investment accounts. You know, the usual. Some of these things seemed to be missing from the files she had. This doctor thing has created a whole new level of paranoia, I'm afraid. I really was hoping to be done with this by now."

Roche was nursing his drink with pleasant disinterest, but his eyes were keying in on every word.

"As was I. Sadly, Christina continues to persist in her obsession with me after all this time. I suppose this latest tragedy is going to make her even more difficult to satisfy."

"Yeah, she is a pain in the ass, all right. I'm beginning to see what the last six months of your life must have been like. I hope she wasn't insinuating anything about you or the disagreement over her parents' investments in that letter."

"Not directly," Roche said. "To be frank, I'm not sure what she intended by notifying me, other than to signal to me yet again her intention to continue pursuing her accusations against me for the time being. She suggested as much weeks ago when she came to my office."

McBain shook his head and frowned. "To tell you the truth, I'm not sure what there is to be gained from this anymore. Based on my discussions with the police, they seem to be focusing on Lehmann more and more as the source of any criminal activity or missing money. The more they dig, the more it seems to me that if there was any hanky-panky going on, the people who killed him are probably behind it. Either that, or it must be linked to Sarah Baker's affair."

For the first time, he noticed Roche's dignified face fall.

"Sarah was having an affair? No. No, that can't be true. I assure you that she and Phillip were deeply in love."

"Maybe, but it didn't stop her. It seems women have needs that even a good marriage can't always satisfy. Who knew? Apparently she was pretty good at hiding it."

"I can't really believe that. Are you certain, Mr. McBain?"

The investigator shrugged and poked his olive with the toothpick.

"All I can tell you is what Christina Baker told me and the police. I don't know how she found out, but she's pretty devastated. The cops don't know whether it's connected to Lehmann or not, but they're putting it in their 'to do' file."

"My God," Roche said with a shake of his salt-and-pepper head. "My God. I'm sorry to hear that. Christina has been through so much already."

"This whole thing is just getting messier for both of us," McBain said.

Roche sipped his drink. "How so?"

McBain threw his hands up but kept his voice down. "The way this is going, if she continues to make a stink about her accusation legally, the next thing you know, your name gets tossed randomly into the soup with a murder and an affair, all the while she's screaming about how her parents were ripped off. You and I know the real story, but I'm sure your reputation doesn't need that kind of public insinuation.

"As for me, what was supposed to be a simple open-and-shut case of investigating some bad investments drags on and on, and I get nothing for my efforts but a hell of a lot more hours of slogging my way through hundreds of mundane transaction records that aren't going to tell me anything I don't already know. As I said, I looked at the files, and at the performance, and I'm willing to accept that you did your best and there's nothing further to be done. The lawyers get paid. The accountants get paid. And I get nothing but promises of a fee that I won't see for years, if at all. I mean, come on, the cops have this thing now."

The sparkle in the financial advisor's eye matched his cufflinks. "Yes, I see your point. This doesn't seem to be doing either of us any good." He paused, put his glass down, and glanced at McBain. "It is a shame there isn't some way to resolve this. I'm certain we would all be the better for moving on."

McBain put a finger to his lips and glanced at the tray of nuts on the table for a moment.

"I do have one idea," he said. "Given her current emotional state, I'm not sure it will work, but I've had good experience with this approach in the past."

Roche spread his hands apart. "I'm open to suggestions."

McBain leaned forward and plucked some pistachios from the tray.

"Hear me out. You offer to pay Ms. Baker some portion of the amount she claims is missing from her parents' account. Not the whole thing, mind you, just some fraction that helps ease the pain. You're not admitting any wrongdoing, just extending a goodwill offer based on your relationship with the Bakers and a certain sense of, I don't know, professional responsibility in the face of a market catastrophe. Not legal, we understand. Just a token of your friendship and sympathy. With that gesture, we take the money and you out of the loop. I can talk her down off the ledge by explaining to her that it's a fair offer, that the cops have taken over the Lehmann investigation now, and that her best option is to get on with her life with the knowledge that she has won something in her parents' name. Plus, it's a defensive move that demonstrates you're acting in good faith in case she does consider pressing it further in public. And I fully intend to sell it to her like that. She gets satisfaction, and you go on with your business without her annoying buzzing around your ear."

The gentleman put a hand to the knot of his tie. As McBain finished his pitch, the advisor took a sip from his glass and then placed it back on the table.

"That's an interesting proposal," Roche said. "Presuming we can settle on a nominal amount that is reasonable. Of course, if it works, you would expect to be compensated."

McBain tore a page from his notebook. He wrote one number on the paper for the settlement, and another below it. He pushed it across the table.

Richard Roche looked at the figures and smiled.

"Mr. McBain," he said. "I'm not a rich man."

"I think you can manage that," McBain said. "Look, the way I work is, I usually get a percentage of what I recover. In this case, you throw Ms. Baker a bone with a relatively small percentage of what she was originally asking for. But that reduces my cut. So you make up the difference I'm losing with her but save a pretty good seven-figure sum overall."

"Or I could pay nothing and simply hire my attorney to defend my good name."

"Or you could do that. I'm sure you've got an excellent, high-priced lawyer at your fingertips who is worth every penny. Your call."

The tranquil ambiance at the table was filled with the low buzz of chatter from the front of the lounge to their left and the bar to the right.

"How do I know that Christina will finally put a stop to all this even with your...suggestion? She has persisted in her accusations almost from the day her parents passed away. Six months from now, she could very well change her mind again."

McBain leveled his eyes at Roche, and a corner of his mouth rose. "Because she trusts me. You add it all up, and this thing is taking its toll on her. I know she's ready to stop. The only reason she's still going now is because of the offhand comment I made about an autopsy after the doctor died, and because she's so pigheaded. She wants to stop. Her husband wants her to stop. Probably the cops want her to stop. And so do I; I just want something to show for it. If she keeps pushing this, I get nada. So when I tell you that I can be very convincing when my own interest is involved, you know it will be the last you ever see of it. Whatever it takes, it goes away."

Roche tilted his head slightly with a look of friendly skepticism. "Are you certain?"

"You write up an agreement. I'll get her to sign it. Ask around. If you want, I can give you a list of dissatisfied customers. They hate my guts, but I expect they'll give you a straight answer on how I close my business. You'll find I'm a man of my word."

After another pause, Roche raised his hand, and a minute later, the check appeared. The investigator reached for it, but the older man waved him away.

"My treat, sir. I think I can write it off as a business meeting, after all."

McBain gathered his bags and walked out with Richard Roche. They stood on the sidewalk together for a moment. The tourists were enjoying the May sunset on the Public Garden, light and shadow stretching over the pond and ducks, orange-and-yellow streaks splashing on the young leaves and young faces. Several families posed for pictures around the massive oak trees and wrought-iron fence surrounding the park on a perfect spring afternoon. One young couple in formal wear stood with their backs to the street so the professional photographer could use the fence and Taj Hotel entrance as a backdrop.

They shook hands. "I'll consider your offer, Mr. McBain," Roche said. "But if you can deliver on your part, I think we might have an arrangement."

"I'll get to work on it tomorrow, Mr. Roche. You'll know I've made some headway if you hear she's called off the legal action to autopsy her parents. If I can get her to do that and persuade her to let the cops handle the Lehmann side of things, you'll know we're well on our way to putting this thing to rest."

McBain swung his bags as he strode home. Yes, there certainly was nothing like a good shopping trip to improve your mood.

On the other end of the scale, nothing sours a mood quite like the prospect of an unpleasant confrontation with someone who has explicitly told you not to do something. Before they called Captain O'Daniel to arrange a meeting, McBain insisted that it not take place at his office. He wanted to have the discussion a fair distance away from the nearest jail cell. Boston also did not want alcohol involved, so a bar was out of the question. Since they had already made contact with Richard Roche, they needed to take care in getting together with a police captain in any public location where they could be observed from any number of directions. So McBain laughed when she suggested the perfect setting for a clandestine rendezvous.

They arrived at the edge of Boston Harbor and strolled into the New England Aquarium separately in midafternoon. Most of the school tours had departed, and the line of yellow school buses outside the complex was diminishing. With the crowd thinning, the aquarium was large and open enough for them to determine whether they were being followed. Boston enjoyed the penguins in the massive first-floor attraction more and more each time she saw them. Camouflaged in a black wig and black jeans, pink high-tops and T-shirt, and a black motorcycle jacket, she managed to position herself by the railing in the middle of a group of Japanese teenagers to observe her partner when he wandered by twenty minutes later and headed up the spiral ramp that circled the inside of the building to look at the other exhibits. She held the video camera close to her face and used it to scan the entrance and crowd behind him.

After another quarter of an hour, she had her father's big frame in the lens, recognizable even without his uniform. Dressed in a navy-blue windbreaker and gray slacks, the captain walked right by the woman with the long black tresses streaming down the sides of her face and thick black plastic frames with tinted lenses. He strode up the ramp without bothering to linger at the penguins or pythons on exhibit. Boston smiled and lowered the camera from in front of her face. After taking more video of the birds diving into the water, she gradually worked her way up the spiral, stopping to peer into tanks of sea creatures at each of the four floors.

When she reached the top, Boston saw her father chatting with her partner at the railing on the far side of the concrete circle. There were a few other visitors gazing or pointing down into the four-story-deep ocean tank that rose through the center of the aquarium. None of them had followed McBain or the captain up, and they left soon enough. She drifted over along the railing until she bumped into her father.

He took a step back. "Excuse me. What the hell...?"

"Hi, Dad," she said. McBain laughed.

Captain O'Daniel looked her up and down, and then a little smile crossed his face. His pride and amusement showed, even when he quickly swallowed his grin.

"Not bad," he said. "But I like your green eyes better. OK, Mata Hari. Now why don't you and him tell me what's up with the cloak-and-dagger and why I'm standing at the top of a fish tank in the afternoon."

"Those are sea turtles, Dad."

"Tom," McBain said, "we wanted to talk to you about the Lehmann investigation and bring you up to speed on what we found out on our side."

O'Daniel scanned him with narrowing eyes. "Funny place for it. Why do I think I'm not going to like what I'm about to hear? What have you two been up to?"

"Just doing what you told us, Dad."

"That would be a first."

"We've continued the investigation to close the Baker file," McBain said. "Problem is, each time we tried, we came across a couple of coincidences that keep raising more complications and suggesting our case is probably tied in to yours. Closely tied."

"Such as?"

"Such as more than a few other possible homicides and the presence of Richard Roche," his daughter replied. "Such as a long-term affair Sarah Baker was carrying on with someone who took a lot of trouble to stay anonymous and who persuaded her to keep his identity buried. Such as a long string of forged signatures in the Bakers' financial records."

The captain's frown changed to a scowl. "I thought I told you to stay away from Roche."

"We did," she said. "Unfortunately, his name kept showing up in connection with a bunch of dead rich people over the past seven years."

"A bunch of...what are you talking about?"

McBain gave the police captain a rapid-fire summary of their interviews with the dozen families they had spoken to over the prior week. Boston chimed in with specifics while observing the entrance to the floor across the tank.

The captain leaned on the metal railing and listened silently until McBain was finished. The area was quiet but for the echoes of children yelling on the levels below and the soft hum of water filtration systems and pumps.

"And you concluded," O'Daniel said, "that each of these deaths was suspicious, despite the age and poor health of the deceased? Even allowing for the coincidence in their choice of physician?"

"Yes," McBain said.

Boston turned to the captain. "We asked all the right questions in the right way and accounted for that. Roche's name came up independently, without our prodding, with the very first person we talked to. After that, they just fell into place. Although the families don't seem to have suspected anything, the relative suddenness of each victim's death is a common denominator. Not to mention the fact that they were all on a list of names compiled by Lehmann for reasons you can guess. Each name had a medical condition and a specific medication attached to it."

The captain's eyes grew wider as she finished.

"So where did you come by this list of patients and medicines?" he asked.

"We found it," Boston replied.

Her father closed his eyes, put the bridge of his nose between his thumb and forefinger, and took a deep breath. "Found it where and how?"

She wanted to get the rest out fast. "Along with a box filled with a number of glass vials of specific narcotics that matched some of the items on the list that were given to each patient."

Her partner kept going. "The thing that wasn't on the list was the name of the financial advisor to each victim—Richard Roche. Like Boston said, that came up on its own. And that's the reason we're talking to you now."

The captain was shaking his head, his eyes still closed. "Jesus Christ. I should have known you couldn't keep your noses clean."

"Dad, we did just what you told us. We kept investigating our case and followed the money. Then we came across these names and screened them one by one. The trail led us where it led us—back to Roche."

A massive turtle pushed his pointy face and rough-edged green shell above the water, batted his eyes at them, and sank back below the surface.

"Tom, it's like I said weeks ago," McBain said. "We're out of our depth on this. We know we're up against something big here, something twisted, but we don't know what. So we're reaching out to you. It's our professional assessment that Roche was up to his eyeballs in an operation to swindle people out of their money. Judging by the number of victims that we know about and potential fortunes, we could be talking about up to half a billion dollars. The financial end looks well thought out and sophisticated, with planning horizons that take years and a methodical approach. Lehmann may have been the executioner, but Roche was almost certainly the money man."

Boston touched her father's elbow. "We don't know who else is involved or how many, Dad. But we know somebody's not afraid to kill innocent people. And who knows, with Lehmann dead, it could all be coming apart. The organization could have scattered by now, or be lying low until they find another doctor somewhere to pick up the pace again. Look at how Lehmann moved around the country. Roche is our only possible lead at this point, and yours. Be honest. Are you getting anywhere else on his murder? Have you traced what you found in Maine to anyone else?"

"We're not done chasing down the foreign accounts yet," the captain replied. "When we get the proper authorizations, we'll know more. We're waiting to hear back from the feds and the police in Brazil on the money trail and Lehmann's known contacts."

But Boston could tell he was thinking hard, mainly because he was still listening instead of yelling. She kept pressing.

"And they haven't generated any potential associates in this country either, have they?"

"Not yet."

"Aren't you the one who taught me that the more time that passes after a murder without anything else developing, the worse the odds of them being caught? Lehmann was the key. With him gone, they could very well move on from Boston if we don't act fast."

The captain turned to her. "Sure. If there is an organized operation here. And if Roche is involved, you could be right. But so far, Roche checks out as clean. We've looked at him, and we've talked to the feds about him too. All you've got is a coincidence that would barely make the cut as circumstantial evidence. Could be that Lehmann was fleecing these people himself. Based on what we found so far, he could have siphoned off money from these families through the accounts we found. We are checking his finances thoroughly, and his background. And as far as the Baker case goes, outside of a social introduction, there's no proven connection between him and Roche. Did any of these people you talked to accuse Roche of malfeasance?"

"No, but—" Boston replied.

"Exactly, which is why I told you to leave him alone. He could have known nothing about what Lehmann was up to."

"We did stay away from Roche, like you said," McBain said.

"Until yesterday," Boston added.

"I don't think I want to hear about it."

McBain described his meeting with the financial advisor at the Taj and his proposal.

"Roche is almost on the hook. He wants Christina Baker out of the picture. We figured if we had any chance of bringing it all together, we needed to work closely with you and the SEC."

The captain glanced left at his daughter, then right to McBain. He took a deep breath and exhaled loudly. At last he spoke. "You two were taking an awful big chance."

"Well," McBain said. "We gambled that Roche would think that we didn't find out squat about the scam and that we could tempt him into a meeting to put the Baker thing behind him. He's not like Lehmann; he's an ice-cold professional. With a little more pressure and your help, we were hoping we could turn him and get him to give up the rest of the organization."

O'Daniel grimaced.

"No, I meant selling me this at the top of a four-story fish tank. Up until a minute ago, I was about to throw you both in."

They wilted under his glare, and Boston bit her lip.

The big Irishman let them roast for a minute. "What do you have in mind? Talk fast; I'm getting hungry looking at all these fish."

"Sea turtles, Dad."

"Whatever. Get talking."

"Pretty straightforward," McBain said with a shrug. "We bug his office and record him confessing to me. You grab him, turn him, and roll up the rest of the operation in connection with the feds and the Brazilians."

The captain put his fingers up to the bridge of his nose again. "Contrary to what you two might think, wiretapping an individual who has not committed a felony is not 'straightforward' in this town, state, or country. If Roche is involved, and if you manage to get him to say anything that we can use to pressure him, it has to be admissible in a court of law to be of any value. Inconvenient as that might seem."

McBain thought for a moment. "OK, you tell us what will work on that end. Let me worry about getting something to record. In the meantime, we'll give you what we have for you to take to the DA and get a warrant."

"I presume you have a plan? A legal one?" O'Daniel asked.

"How tightly do you want to define the term 'legal'?"

Boston pulled her dad in her direction.

"Listen, Dad. McBain has already shaken him. Christina Baker let him know she is starting the process to have a new autopsy performed. If that goes ahead and produces anything in the way of evidence, it will give you grounds to approach the other families. If Roche is worried and jumps at the chance to settle after we get Christina to quote unquote 'change her mind,' we'll know he's on the hook and has something to hide. We know he was rattled when McBain dropped the bomb about the affair."

A soothingly aquatic voice sounded over the speaker announcing that the facility would be closing in fifteen minutes.

Boston continued: "I'm going up to Maine to check out a number of other possible places Sarah might have gone with her boyfriend. If I can get evidence of who she was with, McBain can use that description to put more pressure on Roche."

"To do what?"

"Try to buy me off," McBain answered. "Like I told you, I made him a pitch to settle with Christina Baker by paying her part of what she claims he stole from her parents. If I imply during the meeting that I just might have evidence there's more to it, I should be able to get him to confess to at least some part of the scam. Enough for you to bring him in on the spot and confront him with what we give you."

Captain O'Daniel stepped back from the railing and zipped his windbreaker. "Good thinking, McBain. If you're wrong about this guy, it means you're basically extorting money from an innocent man with a threat to ruin his reputation, all on tape in front of the DA. If you're right, you set yourself up to take a bullet."

Boston looked over at her partner. "See, McBain. I told you he'd understand."

"Well," O'Daniel said, a wry grin on his face, "how can I pass up a chance to get a ringside seat to either one of those? I'll talk to the DA and get back to you. And I want that list of patients and your box of drugs in my office by eight tomorrow morning. When will you be ready to meet with Roche?"

McBain put on his newsboy cap and buttoned his brown leather jacket.

"I should give it a day or two to make it look like I'm persuading Ms. Baker to call off her lawyer and not proceed with an exhumation. We'll see if he wants to make her an offer to settle. Then we go back and forth a couple times. By the time Boston gets back from Maine, we'll know whether we have any more leverage with the affair. Probably a week or so."

They walked over to the exit. Boston left first. Her father was preparing to follow five minutes later when McBain put a hand on his arm.

"It might be sooner, Tom. If I can make it happen while she's in Maine, I'm gonna go for it. I don't want her close to this if it blows up, whether Roche is guilty or not. I hope you can move fast."

Captain O'Daniel rubbed his chin and looked the investigator up and down.

"You know how mad she'll be."

He nodded. "Yeah."

"Look at you," the captain said, "doing the right thing."

McBain waited until he was out of earshot before whispering. "Don't get used to it, Tom."

TWENTY-FIVE

With the game in play, Boston and McBain shuttled between their office and the Baker house in Brookline finalizing their strategy, always apart and with one eye in the rearview mirror. Groomed by a mugging in New York, he was by nature always aware of his surroundings, at least when sober. With his focus now powered by adrenaline, McBain had no trouble throttling back on his drinking in order to keep his wits about him and his eyes sharp. As yet there was no sign that he was being followed.

Although Boston had never come face to face with Roche, the partners were taking no chances making presumptions about being observed. For her part, the redhead was not shy about nonchalantly exposing the Glock G19 she kept on her hip from time to time, both as a blatant warning to potential tails and to send a message to the organization should they be watching her. Her own experience shadowing previous marks and targets associated with their casework ensured that it was unlikely she would be caught unaware by any but the most experienced in the business.

The partners suggested to Christina Baker that she continue to carry on with her life and bookstore as if nothing out of the ordinary were occurring. The investigators gambled that it was the best approach to maintaining the ruse that no one suspected anything beyond what they had revealed to Roche. At the same time, the partners financed a rotating shift of off-duty police officers and detectives to shadow their client most of the time as a precaution.

As they had planned, three days after McBain's rendezvous with the financial advisor, her attorney forwarded a new letter to Roche indicating that Ms. Baker had reconsidered her decision to proceed with an autopsy and was interested in discussing a rapprochement in order to settle the dispute and move on with her life.

While they awaited his response, Boston prepared to travel the coast of Maine in a last-ditch attempt to track down the secret man in Sarah Baker's life.

"How soon do you think he'll come back?" Boston asked.

She was sifting through her book of Sarah's letters, underlining reference items and matching them against her trip notes one last time. She checked her watch. It was after business hours on Friday, and Roche had not called immediately. They would have to continue planning by phone after she left the next morning.

McBain looked up from the work table and pushed a stack of files and loose pages aside.

"I'm hoping sometime tomorrow or Sunday," he replied. "That way, we can dance back and forth a couple times on a number for the Baker settlement. I'll offer to negotiate on her behalf. He'll probably stall a couple days, pretending to discuss it with his lawyer and nudge me down. Meanwhile, he's either considering fleeing the country or asking for direction from his buddies. Then, when he's ready, he'll set up a meeting, hopefully in his office, where he feels secure. Anyplace else, he might feel vulnerable to being recorded. Speaking of which, what did Tom say today? Is he in?"

Boston blew out a breath and began to pack files into her leather briefcase.

"He's in, all right," she said. "Apparently the DA and the SEC both slobbered over the theory. We're not the only ones to get excited with the prospect of a case linking big-time financial fraud to mass murder of some of Boston's leading senior citizens. Somebody sees headlines in capital letters and a political payoff if we're right. Not to mention wrapping up this Brookline killing. If we're wrong, no skin off their noses. He's not enthusiastic about it, but he's got support for now, so he's willing to give us enough rope to hang ourselves. Or at least you."

"I'll bet. That's why you keep me around, partner."

"Stop it. I'm being serious."

"About what?"

Boston put her briefcase aside and sat down across the table from McBain. She folded her hands and leveled her green eyes at him with a face that said he was in danger of being fired. He hadn't seen that look since just before he had left his last job in New York.

"About what you and I talked about before bringing this to Dad. He's right, and we both know it. All we've got at this point is speculation, not evidence. We've got no idea who else we're up against or how Roche will react when you start pressing him. He strikes me as a tough mark. Not surprising for someone who smiles in your face while he and his partners are killing sick old people and raping their accounts. Even if we're right, he's not going to just wilt under a few subtle suggestions. As far as he knows, you've got nothing. And God forbid if by some chance we're wrong and it's just coincidence."

"You know that's not true."

"I know," she said. "But either way, I don't want you to push him too far when we've got no real proof to lay in front of him. If it looks like he's stonewalling, just take the check for Christina and walk out. If we don't have any leverage, we'll just hand what we found to Dad to use and hope for the best."

"You're right about him being unflappable," McBain said. "So far, at least. But I read him another way, too. He's pretty sure of himself, and maybe overconfident. Underneath those polished nails, he's full of himself. Want to know how I know? Because I've seen his type in spades. And because they've gotten away with murder for years. Maybe because he has some tough people behind him. You should have seen his face when I mentioned the affair. I could tell he was rattled. It might be the first time that anything has ever put their scam at risk. They thought they had the loose threads all tied down nice and neat when they offed Lehmann. Frankly, I don't think Tom or the feds are going to find anything tracing those overseas accounts. They're probably already dead ends.

"Roche clearly thinks I'm a low-life mercenary who can be bought off for the right amount. So what? So does Tom most of the time. This time, if I push that rep, it could pay off big time. In the first place, he'll probably think I'm nowhere near the cops on this. In his own mind, that'll reassure him that he can say what he likes in private. Who knows, maybe we'll get lucky and he'll talk about the scale of the operation and what they've done so he can threaten me into shutting our case down. Wouldn't that be great?"

"Shut up and listen to me," she said. "We're talking about people who poison dying elderly cancer patients without a second's hesitation."

McBain threw out his hands and chuckled.

"Boston, what's Roche going to do? I'm sitting in his office with the sun pouring in the window open to views from the next building at rush hour after the business day. The cleaning crew will be showing up any minute. He's gonna poison me, then say, 'Hey, would you just throw that out with the rest of the trash? Thanks, goodnight'?"

His partner was still glaring at him. She leaned across the table.

"You can be such a jerk," she said. "I'm telling you to be careful. We don't know what will happen. This is new ground for us, not our usual squeeze on some white-collar thief. I don't know how it's going to play, and neither do you, so don't get cocky. Or greedy. Or let your ego think you can bring down this whole operation with your smart remarks and insinuations about going public. For all you know, you could catch a shiv in the elevator on the way down. I bet Lehmann was pretty confident too. Did you already forget what he looked and smelled like with his head on the desk?"

McBain saw the serious logic in her eyes. She was right. She usually was, and it was a good reminder. More important, he didn't want his partner getting suspicious about how he might act in Roche's office. If she suspected he was up to something or leaning toward recklessness, her wheels would start turning, and his plan would blow up in his face. She would cancel her trip and be on him tighter than her black turtleneck, dropping herself into the same hot water he might be in. He couldn't let that happen.

His face softened into understanding, and he leaned in across the table until they were inches apart.

"I want this to go the right way as much as you do. And I don't want to end up in jail, or worse. I get the message, and you're right. We'll work out a strategy when you get back, and I'll stick to the script, just like always. We play it smart and close it the way we always do—carefully."

Boston frowned at him doubtfully for a few seconds and then stood up with her fists on the table.

He smiled up at her. "I know you love me."

She narrowed her eyes. "Asshole."

"When does Tom think they can be ready to keep me from digging my own grave?" he asked.

She glanced at her notes. "He wants to get the SEC onboard and briefed, so...four or five days. I'll be able to finish up in Maine and get back here to help you get ready. I only hope I can finally tie in Sarah's affair enough to give you some extra leverage."

Boston gathered up her last few files and started loading them into the briefcase. McBain watched her and considered their progress on that front, along with the odds that she would find anything to use against Roche.

"You realize there's a fair chance Sarah's affair may have nothing to do with this at all," he said. "We already know she had a long-running thing with Dennis Abbott. I don't care what he says, the odds are that after Phillip put a stop to that, she drifted into something new, maybe several."

Boston slowed her packing but shook her head.

"I don't believe that," she said. "My gut instinct tells me it has to be tied to this. Just too much effort went into hiding who he was."

"Maybe the affair was with some rich kid or young professor type at school," he suggested. "That would account for her keeping it secret from Phillip and everyone else. Also for the fact that the charges don't show up on her credit card."

Boston glanced at her partner and shook her hair dismissively. "Her Romeo wasn't any boy toy."

"Why do you say that?"

"Because I've read the letters and visited their hideaways. No man under forty is that smooth, romantic, and considerate. It's got to be an older guy with money. At least in his late forties, probably fifties."

"How would you know?"

Boston gave her partner a face that he interpreted as both "you poor egotistical sap" and "it's none of your damn business."

"Besides," she said. "Remember what Christina said about her mother when she first circled Dennis Abbott's name on the list? About the right kind of man?"

McBain thought better of inquiring further or debating the matter. Instead, her comments solidified the suspicion that had begun to germinate after his meeting with Roche. He lifted his eyes to the ceiling for a minute while he thought back on his conversation with Abbott. After a moment, he walked over to the side table and picked up one of the stacks of Sarah Baker's love letters that he had put aside to reference the few key elements that would help distinguish the identity of her lover. He paged through the stack, eyes searching for items he had circled or put checks against. One by one, he pulled out three of the pages and handed them to his partner.

"It's Roche himself," he said. "It's got to be. It makes sense now."

Boston looked over the pages. "Are you sure?"

"It's what we drank in his office. Sarah specifically mentions it three times as his favorite."

She nodded and gave him a smile of approval.

"Your drinking pays off for a change, McBain. An affair with Sarah would have put him that much closer to the Bakers. She would have trusted him implicitly with anything. Risky, but if he persuaded her to keep it all quiet from Phillip for the sake of his professional reputation, no one would have been the wiser. It's not one hundred percent certain, but it makes the most sense under the circumstances. Good eye."

"Thanks. Now we just have to prove it. If you can do that, it would give me some real leverage when I walk in to try to get him to confess something. Pull one string, you never know what will come out."

Boston reached into her briefcase and withdrew a thin file.

"I've got my work cut out for me. I'll get started early tomorrow for Maine. This time, I'll take some pictures of Roche with me as well. How's this one?"

The shots of Richard Roche exiting the Taj Hotel provided a full body perspective of the suspect as well as his distinguished profile. McBain nodded.

"How many places on your list for this trip?"

She looked at her portfolio and sighed.

"I've got eight spots to hit," she said. "A couple from receipts, but most we put on the list based on our profiles of coastal resorts or hotels from the letters. I'm guessing from the results so far that he paid all of the time, based on his style and interest in avoiding detection. Plus, we don't have any hotel payments on Sarah's records. Just a couple of stores that might or might not indicate the area. So I did a search triangulating based on our criteria and those places."

"How long do you think it'll take you?"

"I set aside three days tops. That allows for time to find the right people, ask questions, scratch it off the list or dig deeper. Problem is, the farthest one is Bar Harbor. They must have really liked Maine, or maybe there was a smaller chance they'd be discovered there. I'll start up north and work my way back down south."

He steepled his fingers and smiled at her. "Three days, huh? Are you sure you aren't budgeting in a little extra spa time here? Some of these are pretty posh resorts."

Boston kept her eyes on the list and rolled her left shoulder a couple times.

"McBain, these are long, hard days sitting in a car and trying to wheedle information out of people who get paid to protect privacy. But now that you mention it, I have been feeling a little bruised from class recently. Maybe a spa treatment would be just the thing. What better place to ask a few discreet questions?"

"Fine. Put it on the bill that we're never going to get paid."

She drummed her fingers on the table and looked around. The house was still.

"Since Ms. Baker isn't here, that brings up something else," she said.

It only took him a second. "Yeah, if we're right about this, she's going to be very upset."

Boston shook her head. "That's an understatement. If Sarah's affair was with Roche and we can prove it, she'll go ballistic. Better keep her away from any sharp objects, and him, when you tell her. Good thing she doesn't own a weapon."

"I'm actually a little more concerned about a different reaction," he said. "We're already asking a lot of her by keeping her involved. This stress may be taking her to her limit. This kind of news could trigger an emotional breakdown. She's tough, but this one hits close to home, again. So let's wait until we're absolutely certain....Wait, why do I have to be the one to break it? I thought you were so concerned about the tactful delivery of bad news."

Her cheekbones rose as she threw her hands up at him. "I know you're all about being up front and honest with the attractive female clients. I wouldn't dream of cramping your style."

"Can I get that in writing?" he asked.

"What do you think?"

"Yeah. Well, I'll just have to think of a way to break it to her easy. If you find anything, give me a call from the road so I can come up with something sensitive."

Boston reached into her briefcase and pulled out a holstered Beretta M9.

"Speaking of sensitive, do you want to keep this with you?"

McBain considered for a moment. When this was all over, he would need to get a license and learn how to shoot and actually hit something. "No, thanks. We're skating on enough thin ice with Tom. It'd probably do more harm than good."

"Fine," she said. "But while I'm away, watch your back and watch hers. The guys aren't always on duty when you're here at the house. Remember, the idea is that the police don't know anything about this, in case someone is watching you. So stay out of trouble."

Boston sashayed over to his chair and gently lifted up his chin with her hand.

"Any kind of trouble, *capiche*?"

TWENTY-SIX

When Boston hit the road that Saturday morning, McBain's private countdown began. He had three days at the outside to gather as much leverage as possible, get Roche to meet, and come up with a strategy to draw him into confessing something that the authorities could use to grab and hold him. And it had to happen even if Tom O'Daniel couldn't get his end of the operation in place. McBain was going, with or without the police. He could only hope Boston's rage would be mollified when she saw the extra cash he was squeezing out of the arrangement.

The table was cleared of everything but his tools:

A dozen pages from the Bakers' financial statements
Copies of the samples of forged signatures
A listing of the victims, medications, and causes of death
Notes on the Bakers' medical condition and original autopsy
Lehmann's bank accounts, both in the States and overseas
Sarah Baker's letters
Boston's sketch of the players and timeline covering all of the events

Now he had to use the threads to weave the tightrope to walk in order to get Roche to feel threatened enough to pay him off yet comfortable enough with McBain's unimportance to incriminate himself without knowing it.

Throttling back on his drinking wasn't a problem, but not being able to smoke in the house was. Though not a real smoker, he tended to go through a pack or two as he worked through his shakedown strategy. The first time he had tried to light up to be alone with his thoughts and notes in the workroom had drawn him an ugly lecture from his client. After that withering reprimand, McBain scurried outside to walk circles around the house. At least it gave him a chance to keep an eye out for strangers while he crafted his pitch.

Evaluating Boston's sketch, he knew that something critical was missing. These people were predators, but they were sophisticated and calculating. They were not sadists. Their planning reflected a methodical approach to looting their victims that amounted to years of careful identification and cultivation, gradual financial fraud that was probably channeled through complex offshore accounts and anonymous corporate vehicles, and the ability to close out each theft without attracting suspicion. Lehmann's file had only included fourteen Boston-area residents who were already dead. God only knows how many other victims there might be, or how many others were in the queue to be finished off.

Only one anomaly stood out from the system that had allowed these crooks to operate undiscovered for years. Why had the Bakers been murdered years ahead of schedule? That one loose end had in turn undoubtedly led to Lehmann's elimination. But despite the wealth of circumstantial evidence he had in front of him, there was no sign from anyone that the Bakers had had any idea that they were the victims of fraud. Yet they must have tumbled to the scheme somehow. Maybe Sarah had discovered something about Roche or overheard something she wasn't supposed to.

The thing that made the most sense was that Phillip had uncovered either the affair or that Roche had ripped them off. But Phillip didn't know anything about investment accounting, and there was no indication he had spoken one ill word about Roche to anyone, especially his daughter. It was certainly possible that after Abbott, he always had one eye out for cheating behavior on Sarah's part. Maybe he had confided his suspicions to Lehmann, who realized they had to eliminate him quickly before he sounded an alarm. So the doctor had to act fast and poisoned them both to make certain before he could talk to anyone else.

But that was just a guess, and he hated guesswork. Whenever they went for the jugular to corner a mark, rock-solid, exposable facts were the kind of leverage that guaranteed a winning confrontation. For all his bravado the night before, McBain didn't like the idea of going up against a professional like Roche without damning incriminating evidence.

The very time Boston's temperament would have counted the most, he couldn't involve her. The two of them always ran through their strategy and approach together, playing devil's advocate or throwing out new theories and scenarios for how a target might react. McBain took her warning the night before to heart, but thinking of her now only reminded him of how much he needed her. Not only her cleverness and devious train of thought, but her cold-minded logic in calculating exactly what evidence to use and how far the partners could take it. He had never had to work through this process without her skills before. He cursed himself that they had not gone through this before she left for Maine.

To make matters worse for him, Christina Baker was spending most of her time at the house. McBain was distracted and troubled by this. As part of their master plan, his client was supposed to be going about her normal routine. This should have meant keeping busy with her bookshop and other aspects of her life. He had expected that instead of padding around the house, she would remain at her residence in Beacon Hill, telegraphing a message of finality to Roche and company.

Her omnipresence in her Brookline home was testament that her deteriorating spirits were having the opposite effect on her schedule. It was also playing havoc with his concentration and emotions, putting the play in danger.

What he had said to Roche had been correct in some ways. He wanted it to be over for any number of reasons, including the frustrating certainty that he didn't want to care. His client needed it to be over too. And the more time she spent around the house, the more damaged and obsessed he perceived her to be. That was not a good thing for either of them.

In order to overcome both of his dilemmas, McBain tried to pull her into his preparations. He hoped in that way to keep her focused on something besides her parents' murders and the tragedies of this case by having her serve a purpose to their goal. And if that didn't work, she could at least serve as a sounding board for his scheming and clever delivery.

"Having you around is helpful," he insisted when she protested. "Boston and I always go through this rehearsal before we confront our suspects. Since she's not here, you can at least help me go through my checklist and let me know if an idea sounds too nutty. If I'm going to draw him out, I'll need to at least sound like we've got more on him than we do. Besides, I still need you to give me feedback on your parents' thinking. You never know what you could trigger."

On the other hand, he didn't need the gnawing guilt that came from pursuing his own best interest, regardless of whether that was what the facts dictated. What the hell, Tom was right. Boston was right. They weren't experienced or qualified enough to act like cops. The best thing to do was get the client some money, get paid, and get out. Let the police do the rest.

Stay focused on the outcome, not the client. Keep your emotions out of it and take home the paycheck. If all went as planned, he could at least comfort himself that he had arranged that part of the close well.

At least he had learned one valuable lesson from this experience already. Always vet your potential one-night stands carefully at the bar before getting too deep into a conversation.

A humming in his jacket pocket Saturday evening brought his attention back to business. He inhaled, then exhaled calmly.

"McBain," he answered. "Hello, Mr. Roche, good of you to call. Sure, now's a good time to talk."

The conversation was over in a minute.

"Excellent. I'm at Ms. Baker's house in Brookline now. I'll discuss the terms with her and give you a ring back tomorrow. We should be able to wrap things up the day after that at the latest if you're available. Good evening."

When he hung up his phone, the first thing McBain thought of was to check on his client. They were coming to the crunch, and he needed to focus on the meeting, not her sinking spirits.

He found her in the library. Christina was sitting at the writing desk, her face lit from below, the reflection of a lamp on white pages, her fingers drifting through a worn hardcover book. The French doors were open, the curtains billowing like sails in the cool twilight as the scent of cut grass and turned soil swept into the house from the freshly planted garden. As McBain entered the room, she looked up. At first she seemed not to recognize him, but after a moment, a smile crossed her lips. It was a weak smile, polite and empty.

"Got something relaxing there?" he asked.

"Just some French poetry. My mother used to read it to me when I was growing up. It would calm both of us. Not so much anymore. My French isn't as good as it used to be."

"Better than mine, I'm sure. I seemed to learn just enough to insult half of Paris when I went on business. Now I just do my bit for international relations by sticking to restaurant French and staying out of the country."

No response. The woman who had insulted him effortlessly on that first night was gone.

He held up his cell phone. "That was him. He went for it. We're going to meet in a few days to close the deal."

She nodded, then returned to reading her poetry. "That's a good thing, I suppose."

"You don't seem as excited about the prospect as I would have hoped."

Her face lifted from the page again. "Oh, you must think me ungrateful, McBain. Please forgive me; I'm not. I just hope you are able to get him arrested and find the other people who did this."

"I'll do what I can," he said. "At least you'll know you did what you set out to do: get part of your parents' money back. With the added satisfaction of knowing that their killer has already gone to his grave. And with any luck, the cops will take care of the rest. We'll do our best to make it happen."

Someday McBain would have to get Boston to teach him how to open his mouth and say these things without making their clients feel worse. Or maybe in this case, he just didn't know what to say that didn't feel intrusive. She had had that affect on him from the start in the bar.

"Come on," he said. He took her hand and lifted her from the chair. "I could use a cup of tea."

They went to the kitchen to sit at the long wooden dining table. Christina filled a stainless-steel kettle with water, and McBain watched the gas stove flame up. She rummaged in the cupboard and pulled down two cups; fixed a plate with water crackers, goat cheese, and biscotti; and placed it between them.

They sat in silence for a minute, not looking at each other or anything in the room.

"I hope Mr. Hilliard isn't too upset with us," McBain said. "Maybe since the doc's murder and our recent discoveries, he's had a change of heart about this whole investigation."

"He has had a change in attitude," Christina said. "But I'm afraid it hasn't been for the better."

"What do you mean? Doesn't he know we're getting close? It's almost over."

"He thinks this is even more foolish now that it's certain someone did try to run me over. David believes it is dangerous for us to pursue this in any way. He insists we should drop the matter and leave it all to the police. He doesn't want me putting my life in danger."

"He's right, you shouldn't. Nobody wants anything to happen to you. That's why we suggested you stay in Beacon Hill and not here. It'll make them think you're giving up."

"You're not giving up. And you could be in as much danger as I am."

"That's different. You're paying me."

Her eyes rose from the table to meet his gaze. "As you told me, you're financial investigators, not police. You didn't sign up for this."

"Maybe not. But we don't like to walk away from an interesting case without giving it our all."

"Is that it?"

"Maybe I still want to prove you were wrong about Roche and the money."

"That's an awful risk just to say 'I told you so,'" she said.

"I like to be right. And maybe I just want to hang around to make sure you don't fall off any more ladders. It seems to me you could use some looking after until this is over."

"And then?"

McBain listened to the pressure building from the tea kettle heating up on the stove. His glance shifted between the pot and the face of his client, worn and weary from grief and anxiety. Her dark hair was askew. It was unlike her. He wasn't sure whether it meant she was wearing down under the strain of the deepening investigation or just distracted. Either way, she seemed more vulnerable than he had ever seen her. If the affair did turn out to involve Roche, it was going to be another brutal blow. For now, her eyes still held a measure of that innate courage. And she smelled great, even across the table.

"Like I said, either we close the case with you getting paid something or the police squeeze Roche into turning evidence. Hopefully both. Then you're out of it as far as everyone is concerned. You keep your mind focused on what's important in the long term, and you'll do OK."

"That's surprisingly thoughtful of you, McBain."

"It happens sometimes. Don't get used to it. Boston doesn't."

Christina took the kettle off the boil and poured the steaming water into a ceramic teapot filled with Earl Grey. The design was modeled on the *Alice in Wonderland* tale, and he noted the face of the Cheshire Cat smiling out at him from under the spout. The grin said a whole lot of things.

"Speaking of which, tell me," she asked. "Why did you decide that Boston should investigate my mother's affair while you took on the task of examining these documents? After spending this time with you and observing you both, I'm still a bit unclear on the relationship in your partnership, but she seems to have a better knack for digging through these old records than you, not to mention matters of personal protection. Pardon my saying so."

"Maybe I just wanted to get you alone," he said.

"Because I'm so much fun to be around?"

McBain sipped his tea and thought for a moment.

"A couple reasons. Boston drives fast and can cover the ground ten times quicker than I can. You may have noticed she's better with people and more tactful than I am when it comes to eliciting the information we need from strangers. Plus, she's easy on the eyes and comes across to people as nonthreatening when she wants, and that helps in situations like this when you're asking a lot of questions.

"You're right, Boston is the accounting genius, though nobody seems to know why. She barely finished her second year at Boston College. I think it's some kind of innate talent that just makes the work second nature. I worked with numbers people on Wall Street with twenty years experience who didn't have the eye for mistakes and manipulation that she does.

"For my part, we're through a lot of the record sorting for now, and our eyeballs need a break. What I want to do is refocus on the financial side of things and figure out why and how they ripped off your parents. And how we can go about proving Roche is a part of it and getting him to say it out loud when I meet him. I'm going through the investment records and bank accounts again, along with the medical stuff, the doc's account information that the police gave us, and the letters. One of my many strengths is figuring out how and where money moved. There's a scam here and it's good, but I haven't seen the accounting sleight of hand yet that I couldn't figure out. We just have to keep looking at things from different perspectives. My time is better used calculating the angles and figuring out how to play Roche when we sit down face to face. It has to be done just right if we're going to bait him or bluff him into confessing. I also want to keep digging into the files and see if I can find possible reasons your parents might have been killed when they were."

His client tactfully nudged at the biscotti on the plate. "Oh, I thought it might have had something to do with your personal history."

He shifted a bit in his chair. "You mean my own divorce?"

"Yes."

"You know, I really like watching your mind work, Ms. Baker."

"What happened? She was unfaithful?"

"Hard to believe, ain't it?"

"Yes, it is," Christina said firmly. "It seems to me that when you focus on something besides drinking and hitting on women, you have some qualities that are quite admirable. I can't believe she didn't recognize that."

When conversations like these started, McBain inevitably ached for something stronger than tea and some witty remarks.

"Nothing quite so dramatic as Sarah's case," he said. "Just a familiar story. I thought I was in love. I thought I knew the person I married. Maybe we were just caught up in the whole New York scene. At any rate, at some point I started suspecting something. You never want to believe it at first. We always rationalize these things. Pretty soon, though, it wasn't even a matter of signs. Melissa was too self-absorbed to bother hiding the fact that she did what she wanted. She didn't want to talk, and she didn't want me. Then she got ugly. Then the lawyers took over."

"I'm sorry."

"The first couple years, I wondered what I could have done different. What I had done wrong that I might have changed. Strangely enough, I didn't drink much before I came to Boston, and I certainly didn't hit on other women after I met Mel, so it was neither of those things. It took a while, but I finally came to understand. In a way, it was almost comical. Like a version of the old 'it's not you, it's me' line that she gave me at first. Because it really was her, not me. There wasn't anything I could have done differently that would have mattered. And that's what hurt most of all."

"I don't think I understand."

"People talk a lot about having your heart broken for the first time," he said. "Like it's some kind of rite of passage to becoming an adult. But I think there's something worse. When you come to realize that you have had absolutely no impact on someone who meant the world to you. That her life would have gone on exactly the same if she had never met you. You were interchangeable, like a car or mobile phone. When she can walk away hurt-free, without any effect, you know you were just an insignificant stop on the road. You know she doesn't think about you or have many memories she'd recount with friends. When you realize that, some fire goes out inside you. Maybe it's called growing up; I don't know."

"I'm sure you're wrong. There must have been something between you."

"No, I'm not wrong." He smirked and grunted once. "Imagine being George Bailey, and when the angel takes you back, you look around and find out that taking you out of the picture had zero effect on the world you loved. That's a terrible truth to know. But to move on with your life, you have to accept it. It's not a good feeling, but maybe it's healthier in the long run. It doesn't mean you're a failure. It just means you made a really bad choice in life. So if you're smart, you can learn from it and go forward making better choices. Anyway, it all happened five years ago. I try not to dwell on it now."

She poured them both more hot tea.

"Is that why you drink so much?"

"No, I drink because I like it. And because it gives me the chance to meet hot married women like you."

Christina pushed her black hair away from her eyes. They were full of pain but still pulsing with the faint beauty of distant stars. "If it's any consolation, if I weren't married, I would have let you buy me dinner."

"I think I like you better when you're a pain in the ass to me, Ms. Baker."

She sipped at her tea. "I notice that since you took my case in the bar that night, you always call me by my surname."

"Kind of a rule we have."

"Did Boston institute this rule?"

"We both did," he said. "Keeps me focused on the specifics of the case without personalizing the issues. Particularly if the client looks like you."

"Thank you. You two work so well together and think so much alike, I thought perhaps there was a more personal side to your relationship. I don't believe I've ever seen a more functional couple in my life."

"We're not a couple, we're business partners."

"Your partnership certainly works well. From all appearances, it seems to be quite enjoyable."

"Yeah, it's fun working with a hot-tempered redhead who can kill me a dozen different ways in seconds."

Christina was grinning like the cat on the tea pot.

"Well, fortunately for me, I didn't respond to your overtures at the bar."

"Look, Boston and I are partners. We've been together four years. Nothing has ever happened between us, and nothing ever will. Strictly business, not romance, if that's what you were worried about."

Her eyes narrowed, and she put her chin on folded hands.

"No, it's something else. I've watched you together. You're not like lovers. There's some kind of deeper, more permanent intimacy there than romance. Almost like you have been friends forever. But it's more than that. You make me think of stories people tell about soldiers who have been through war together."

"I always said you were pretty smart, Ms. Baker."

"So are you going to tell me what it is between you two?"

He finished his tea and headed back to the war room.

"Smart enough to know there's a point to stop asking questions and never mention the subject again. Let's get back to work. If you're up to it, we can talk about the terms of your settlement with Roche."

In contrast to the subtlety of breaking bad news, when it came to bluntly changing a subject, McBain's conversational skills were excellent. He liked to think he had taken something of value with him from Wall Street.

TWENTY-SEVEN

Boston cruised toward the sea with the window down and the Miranda Lambert cranked up. Spring had allegedly started in late March. In Maine, traces of winter linger even in late April and early May, like an ex-boyfriend who hangs around long after he's been told to drop dead. The Shelby swung south out of Portland on Route 1, and as the road to Port Elizabeth rounded a rocky curve and passed a stand of trees, the full panorama of the Maine coast opened into view. On Highway 77 she slowed the car, and as the sun emerged from a cloud, the distant white-caps sparkled like diamonds. Boston pulled down her Ray-Ban aviators and turned down the music, taking in the breadth of the seascape. The afternoon sun beat down on white sails, sand, azure sea, and sky.

There, on the edge of a wooded promontory perched above the cove, loomed the Inn by the Sea, her last stop of the day. Unlike the small B&Bs and cozy hotels she had visited, the sprawling, three-story, gray-and-white buildings and cottages stretched across a wide green lawn with an aura of casual luxury, wings reaching out beyond the tree line in search of the beach and ocean.

Boston checked into her room and pushed open two framed windows. Her gaze followed a stone walkway across a wide lawn, past rows of flower beds and white Adirondack chairs toward a crescent beach. Couples wandered the grounds and sand holding hands or relaxed on the grass drinking in the view, a good read, or a glass of wine. It certainly looked like the hotel referenced in Sarah's letter.

"Another goddamned freakin' romantic paradise."

The investigator sighed and unpacked. While she was hanging up clothes, she checked in with McBain, who confirmed that he had called

Roche back with a counteroffer but was still waiting to get a meeting scheduled. Then she put on her smiley face and roamed the hotel for two hours with her story of impending connubial bliss and picture of Sarah. By seven o'clock, she had come up empty for the third day and eighth resort in a row.

Boston had come to view gluing the bridal grin to her face as an achievement worth rewarding with an early cocktail hour. At least then she could have a drink while she quizzed the bar and restaurant staff. On the other hand, according to their brochure, and if Sarah's letter was correct, the Inn boasted one hell of a fabulous spa. Boston scheduled an hour of downtime as a present, regardless of what emerged from her scouting trip. The stress of this entire case and the frustrations of her road trips simply demanded it.

At 7:05, she was at the spa wearing a plush white terry cloth robe and a body coiled with tension. For the next sixty minutes, the private room echoed with yells and groans as a deep tissue massage attacked the past year's worth of aches, bruises, knots, cuts, and tears in her muscles and joints. The scent of aromatic herbs, nutritional oils, and soaps permeated the massage room. The blond masseur did not look that old, but he certainly knew his craft. She hadn't had a massage like this...ever. It was almost over, and she didn't want it to end. She began to wonder if it was right to want to date a guy just for his hands.

"This is worth a year's salary, Sven," she said. Sven hovered over a collection of little bottles, deciding on one last therapeutic oil. "Just what the doctor should have ordered. You've got the Midas touch."

"Thank you, Miss O."

"God, I have to come back here more often. Like every week. You available?"

He laughed. "Of course. I have been here for years. And you should come back again soon. Perhaps tomorrow. I can only do so much in one session, even with a body like yours."

She barely raised an eyebrow. "Thanks, I think."

"I only meant that you have an exceptionally physical body. Perhaps you are dancer or trainer? But you need massage more often. Your back muscles have many knots. And your neck and shoulders—so tight. And I can see you have some bruises that need to heal. You have amazing feet, but two of the toes were broken, yes?"

"Bad rock-climbing experience," she said.

"Oh, you come up to Maine to climb?"

She exhaled deeply as his hands kneaded her lower back.

"Ugh. No, I'm up here looking for a resort to host my wedding later this summer."

"Wonderful, Miss O. You keep coming back to Sven. I make sure you get relaxed for wedding. No bruises on the back or arms at all. You will look beautiful in your wedding dress."

"Thanks Sven, that's a deal...uuuhhnnnn. That's perfect."

And it was over. Boston felt so fabulous she was almost able to purge her mind of the reason for her trip. Tension had been physically exorcised from body, mind, and soul. Why ruin it? But what the hell, it was worth a shot. She felt so good she had nothing to lose, and she had come all this way. She sat up and pulled the towel around her.

"That was unbelievable. Better even than I heard. My friend's mother recommended this hotel and your spa. She's been coming here off and on for years with her boyfriends. She hasn't been back for a least a year, but she loves the place. Now I see why."

She reached into her wallet and took out a picture Christina had given her. "Her name is Sarah. Did you ever do her?"

"Oh yes," Sven said. "I never forget Sarah and her friend. Couple years ago, but we never forget people who get a customized Sweet Surrender."

Boston was so dumbfounded that she nearly forgot her act. She fumbled for a few seconds. "Sweet Surrender? What...?"

Sven stepped back and extended his muscular arms as if to take in the warm, brown walls of the room.

"Perfect for you and your husband," he said. "Begin with the sooth-ing hot tub together in your own honeymoon suite. Then an hour of customized massage from not one but two of our professional staff at once. Masseur or masseuse, whatever you like. All set to soft candle-light and the soothing music of your own choice. It is so completely... sensual. We use variety of massage treatments and techniques. Deep tissue, Swedish, reflexology, whatever you prefer. You must schedule one for yourself and your husband."

"Sounds wonderful," Boston said. She shed her towel and slipped into her robe in one smooth, choreographed motion. "And you remember Sarah had one of these special massages?"

Sven was man enough to enjoy the view and professional enough not to show it. Boston appreciated that and filed it away under too good to be true or gay.

"Of course. Not many people ask for Sweet Surrender. I was there for Sarah, and Helena for the gentleman. I am surprised she did not tell you about that part."

"Oh," Boston said, putting her hand to her mouth. "I wonder if that was the surprise present. My friend was telling me Sarah and her friend were going to buy us something unique during the weekend here. Damn. He's a great guy. I think it's him anyway. I better not put my foot in my mouth."

She reached into her wallet again and pulled out Phillip Baker's photo. "Is this him?"

He shook his head. "No, this man was little younger looking, more distinguished. Very European looking."

She tried again with the other picture. "Oops, I was afraid of that. That was her ex. Perhaps this gentleman?"

"Yes, that is her friend. A fine man. He arranged for the Sweet Surrender and the music as special weekend."

Boston put the picture back in her robe pocket with her wallet, exhaled deeply, and closed her eyes. For once her blood was not rushing with adrenaline, as it might. Instead, the tension in her entire body had drained away, replaced with a sensation of one of the most satisfying hours of her life. Perhaps this was what Reggie Jackson had been talking about when he described the feeling of hitting a home run.

"Thank you, Sven. Like I said, you definitely have the Midas touch."

After throwing on some jeans and an oversized cream wool sweater, she sat at the bar and dialed up McBain. As if a magic door had opened, while she was waiting for him to call back, the bartender recognized Richard Roche and Sarah as well. They had stayed at the inn over a long weekend two years ago at this time of the season. Although they were not regulars, the barman recalled seeing Sarah draped all over her friend during a late-night after-dinner cocktail, and it stuck in his memory.

"And he says she was all over Roche like a cheap suit after one too many glasses of Sambuca," Boston said to McBain. "He couldn't miss them. Not hard to believe. A couple drinks after the massage I just got, and you could pour me into bed too....Are you kidding? It was great. Best money I've ever spent on a job....No, not a woman, a man....No, big blond guy, like the ones who work for the villain in the James Bond movies....I don't think he was gay....Just a towel....Oh, McBain will you focus? This is what we've been working to get on him. Have you heard back from him yet?...OK, then I'll see you tomorrow night sometime. Reward yourself with a drink. I'm going to finish another one, get some dinner, and crash for about twelve hours so I can enjoy this feeling.... Thank you, partner; that's sweet of you to say. Goodnight."

"Great work, partner, the best you've ever done. This should clinch it. See you tomorrow. Goodnight, Boston." The call ended, but he kept staring at the phone in his hand. Predictable as it was, the confirmation about the affair was terrible news. But the day couldn't have ended any other way.

It had started well enough. Christina Baker seemed to return to her old annoying self for a few hours as she paced the workroom and mulled or rejected his ideas about how to handle Roche with her best guess as to how he would react. The intelligence and confrontational wit that had lacerated him from time to time parried most of his shallow arguments into the wastebasket of dead ends with her well-ordered mind and penchant for common sense. He thought that with the right training, she might make a first-class extortionist.

Roche called back in the afternoon to confirm he would be prepared to meet the next day after work. McBain felt a sense of immediacy and picked up the pace of the back-and-forth with his client. At last he felt he was ready to close out the case with the best deal he could get.

But inevitably, the more they honed in on the facts that he would use against the con man, the more the conversation began to center on the

Bakers themselves. As the day progressed, she began to walk McBain around the house. Her mind wandered, and the conversation flagged as they talked, her efforts veering between puttering and reminiscing. The investigator could sense her slipping back to depression, threatening to drag him with her.

The pictures were what made it the most real for McBain. What made him feel. And as they shifted from living room to hallway to bed-rooms to kitchen, Phillip and Sarah were becoming for him what they still were to Christina: living and laughing, writing and loving, hearts still beating. Despite his best efforts, they were evolving from ghosts to people. His memory reengaged with the stories from their friends and colleagues about the parties and the late-night debates. In the library, he listened to Christina's recollections of her efforts to prod them into using e-mail and the computer. How they loved to write by hand and type on that antique machine.

The pictures told the tale of the marriage, and of the family. Phillip and Sarah as young parents with their toddler in the park, sunburned faces grinning like fools sailing off the Cape without a care in the world, standing with pride by the graduate, raising champagne glasses in the front of the bookshop and the sign that announced Grand Opening. The pictures, as unfaded as memories, gave them life as surely as blood and air had done.

By dinnertime, the talk had turned to holiday meals and their last Thanksgiving together. Christina cooked chicken and pasta primavera, but neither of them ate or drank much. When the phone rang and he left to take Boston's call, McBain was tired of thinking, tired of feeling. He just wanted it all to end. More, he wanted to take her pain away as well, so that neither of them had to feel it.

Instead, now he had to make it worse for her. He lifted up his cell and dialed again.

"Tom, it's McBain," he said. "That's right, I just talked to Boston. She'll be back tomorrow night. I spoke to Roche earlier today and set up the meeting for tomorrow late afternoon. I can't wait any longer; I've got to go."

He listened for two minutes and then signed off. And he noticed his heart wasn't racing anymore. His mind was clear and ready. He knew what he was going to say and do. He walked to the bathroom, rolled up his sleeves, and filled up the basin with cold water. The touch of the water was supposed to help him feel clean as he threw it against his face again and again. The hand towel hung on the wall, but he ignored it. He stared in the mirror, letting the cool droplets fall from his forehead and chin.

When he turned and saw the open door, he had no idea how long she had been standing there watching him.

"I'm meeting with Roche tomorrow after the markets close," he said.

She looked at him with curiosity. "I thought you were going to wait until after Boston got back from Maine. She said that you needed to know more about who might have been with my mother. To prove it was a part of the plan to swindle them."

He shook his head. "Change of plans. I just talked to the police. They want to move now in order to try to nail Roche with what we've got. They're getting nervous that he might bolt and leave the country."

McBain thought it would be easier if he just said it fast. Or maybe he just didn't know any other way.

"Besides, that was her on the phone earlier. She found out who your mother was with in Maine. It was Roche himself. It was part of the con. He was using her to set your parents up."

Christina didn't say anything. She walked back to the living room and collapsed in an armchair. He dried his face and followed behind her.

"My mother...and Roche," she whispered. "Is she sure?"

McBain let her cry quietly for a minute, then sat on the arm of the chair and put his arm around her shoulders.

"It wasn't your mother's fault," he said. "You have to know that. It was all part of a very good act, a con by a pro. It wasn't her fault."

He looked around the room for something to put on, music or a television. Christina covered her eyes with her hand.

"All this time I told myself it couldn't be true," she said. "Ever since you found the letters, I didn't want to believe it was possible. Part of me kept saying it was a fantasy of a kind. A story she wrote to herself. Then, after Boston's trip to Vermont, I wanted it to be some stranger, or some old boyfriend. When I thought it was Dennis, it was still unbearable, but at least it didn't have anything to do with their deaths. With all this. And now, you tell me it was him? For years they were together? This is a nightmare. A nightmare without an end."

He hated himself for being the one. He hated not being good at this. And he was beginning to hate Roche. That wasn't useful.

Christina sat back, defeated, her hands listless in her lap. "It was all a lie. My whole life, my parents' marriage, everything. They didn't love each other. They just put on a show for me all those years."

McBain knelt in front of the chair and grabbed her fingers.

"Stop it," he said. "You stop right there. This whole day, you and I have talked about Phillip and Sarah. I've seen pictures of the three of you together, and the two of them. I've spent weeks with you in this house and hundreds of hours with their friends, and gone through their lives on paper getting to know your parents. I may not know much about love, but I know the real thing when I see it. There was no bitterness in those letters, no resentment of Phillip. And whatever happened between them, whatever con Roche pulled off to charm Sarah away once in a while to some secret getaway, I damn well know she always came home to the man she loved. I know that because I spend my life around liars and parasites and people who never appreciate what they've got. I make my living finding out the truth. And the truth I've discovered in this case is about a family who loved one another more than anything most of us could imagine. So don't you even start thinking that way. Your parents deserve better, and I won't let Roche or anyone else take that from them."

He stood up. Christina put her head back on the chair and composed herself. Finally she opened her eyes and looked up at him. He stared into the dark pools in search of the person who had enchanted him that first night at the bar with her beauty, sass, and intelligence. She was still there. Almost broken, but not quite.

Without the strength to get up, she reached out and grabbed his wrist.

"Will you stay with me at the house tonight?" she asked. "I just need company."

And there it was. It would be the easiest thing in the world to just pull her over the edge. An extra bonus fresh out of the blue for his consideration, with no one to know except the two of them. No commitments beyond one night of comfort that she would view with gratitude the next morning, though not much beyond. A secret she would keep regardless of what happened next, just as Sarah had kept hers.

McBain reached across with his free hand, took hers, and held it.

"I can't," he said. "I'm sorry. I've got something I have to do at the office tonight. To get ready for tomorrow."

"What is it?"

Despite himself, he leaned forward and kissed the top of her head. Grabbing his blazer, he headed for the front door. At the doorway to the living room, McBain turned and took a last look at his client before heading out.

"I told you," he said. "You'll be OK. You go home to Beacon Hill tonight. Tell Mr. Hilliard it's over. I'm going to make sure of it."

He closed the door a little too hard for his own liking and headed back to Boston.

TWENTY-EIGHT

The elevator stopped at the tenth floor, where most of the passengers got off. The investigator stepped to the back. Two men remained, both dressed in suits and standing in the front of the car. Two buttons were lit on the panel besides the one that McBain had pushed; one below his floor and one above. That meant that the two men could exit at either or both floors. Neither of them looked Brazilian, or for that matter particularly physically fit.

For now, he wasn't worried. As Boston had so graphically pointed out, if there was any danger lurking, it would play out after his meeting with Roche. That gave him all the confidence he needed. As the next man exited on the fourteenth floor, McBain glanced at his watch. He would be on time for his five thirty appointment, assassins notwithstanding.

Alive and relatively well, he knocked on the office door on the sixteenth floor, and Richard Roche beckoned him in. The financial advisor stood behind his desk with the phone in his hand, dapper as ever in gray pinstripe suit, French cuffs, and purple Hermes tie.

"I'll be off in a minute," he whispered.

McBain took a seat across the desk and unbuttoned his suit jacket. Roche was discussing the stock market close with a client. While the investigator waited, his eyes surveyed the adjoining buildings in search of office workers or high-rise residents who were within eyeshot of the office with reasonable views. There weren't many. From where he sat looking out over the harbor, the desk area seemed to be the most exposed to view from the outside. His head swiveled to examine the table in the client meeting area, then over to the credenza holding investment books, brochures, and newspapers. On the top of the credenza sat the silver tray with ice bucket, crystal tumblers, and several bottles of liquor.

"Mr. McBain," Roche said as he put down the phone. "Thank you for being on time. I'm sorry about the delay. Unavoidable client business, you understand."

He waved it away with a smile. "Not a problem. This is my most important appointment of the day, Mr. Roche."

The older gentleman walked over and poured himself a Scotch on ice from the bottle of eighteen-year-old Macallan. The bottle hovered over a second glass.

"Can I offer you a drink while we conduct business to seal our agreement?" he asked.

"No, thanks."

The white teeth were perfect. "Don't you trust me?"

"Certainly. As much as you trust me."

Roche laughed. "Touché. But you needn't worry." He took a healthy drink from his own glass. "You see—harmless. Pity to pass up good Scotch."

McBain smiled back. "Fair enough. Pour me a couple fingers with no ice, and I'll get to it in a few minutes. I'm a little hung over from last night. Started my celebration early. I'll perk up after we get down to business and talk about the settlement."

"Excellent," Roche said. "I gather that Ms. Baker is satisfied with the number I suggested and is ready to close out our disagreement with a signed acknowledgment of my lack of culpability in the matter of her parents' investment losses."

"I wouldn't go so far as to say she's satisfied," McBain said and chuckled. "In my experience, she never is. But as I said, she trusts me and took my advice to settle. She had her lawyer look over the document you faxed to my office and put her pen to it, so we're just about done. Legally that precludes her from ever suing you over this matter in the future."

He reached into his briefcase and handed the signed agreement to the financial advisor. Roche took it, sat behind his desk, and put on his glasses to examine the pages.

"Nicely done, sir," he said as he finished.

"Thanks. Boy, I don't mind telling you I'm more than ready to put this one behind me. This is the most bizarre piece of business that's ever crossed my desk. Serves me right for walking up to a pretty woman in a bar. Next thing you know it's all business, then I find out about the parents' suicide, then Lehmann gets killed. Jesus H. Christ, all I wanted to do was get laid. Excuse my language."

Roche leaned back and sighed. "Ah, to be young and full of energy. I'll agree, Christina is certainly a beautiful and determined woman. I'm just glad we are all able to put this tragic matter to rest and move on. I'm sure she now accepts that it's for the best."

McBain loosened his tie and collar, exhaling loudly.

"I'll say. The parents were tough enough. I just can't believe this whole thing about Lehmann. The cops are convinced he was into some real shit with some nasty people. Who kills a doctor in Brookline? Plus, I heard they've unearthed some overseas accounts. They're thinking some kind of big-time medical fraud scam with him as the key player. I'm sure you must be having an even tougher time with it, since you actually knew the guy."

Roche was shaking his head. "Yes, you're right. I still find it hard to believe myself. Though I didn't know him well, he certainly seems to have fooled a good many smart people. And trust is such a fragile commodity these days."

McBain frowned as he rubbed his chin.

"Still bothers me, though. I know the cops and insurance people think Lehmann was behind some kind of major con. But I met Lehmann. He didn't have the balls or brains to set up offshore accounts or worm his way into society. Unless he was an incredibly good actor. C'mon. Bank accounts in the Caymans and Mauritius? Lehmann didn't have that kind of savvy."

The financial advisor put a finger to his lips. "I'm afraid I gave the doctor advice on setting up some offshore accounts. But solely in relation to their tax benefits and diversifying his assets overseas. He had asked me about them years ago. Naturally, if I had known what he was going to do with the information...I'm just glad I wasn't directly involved with establishing the accounts."

"Good call on your part," McBain said. "Looks like he used the information you gave him to juice up his operation with his friends. They had a pretty good thing going for a while there. Who knows who else they were ripping off? The cops don't have any ideas yet. But there have to be others out there, right? My guess is I shook him up pretty bad when I showed up asking questions. Then Christina Baker told him about the legal action she was initiating against you, and he began to worry about an extended case that might result in more scrutiny on his relationship with the parents. I mean, hell, he was the Bakers' doctor. Who knows what might have come up? You know what I mean?"

"Yes, I think I do."

"In a way, I almost feel responsible for him getting shot. That's another reason I'm glad you and I are well out of this case. I could be putting you in danger just by being around you. Who needs to take chances?"

"Indeed. It seems bad things can happen to anyone connected to the Baker case. It's good that you're through with it."

"On the other hand, I have to give credit to these people." McBain leaned over and picked up the tumbler of Scotch from Roche's desk. "With Lehmann gone, it looks like they might get away clean. From what I've seen, the cops can't seem to come up with anything else but those accounts. Or any*one* else. Yet."

"Well," Roche said, "it's only been a few weeks. I'm sure the investigation will go on for some time."

"I don't know," McBain said. "In my business, I've come across some pretty sophisticated financial frauds. And I've got to tell you, this is the smoothest and most thorough I've seen. Most of the guys I negotiate with rely on some kind of Ponzi scheme or con job, talking the suckers into investing in some kind of crap. But this one was seamless, like a well-run business. The Bakers didn't seem to even know they were being slowly shafted. By the way, we found some expertly forged paperwork among the Baker files."

"Forged? What kind of forgeries?"

"I suppose I should tell you in case the cops come calling, since it may impact your connection to the case. Turns out some of the signatures on the Bakers' investment transactions were forged—mainly withdraw-als, authorizations for wire transfers, things like that. The cops figure Lehmann had a real pro doing the work. Used it to transfer money from their accounts without them knowing. Pretty sophisticated. There's no way you could have known, any more than the people at the bank or broker. The transfers eventually flow through some domestic accounts to the overseas ones. Pretty slick, huh?"

"My God," Roche said. "I've read about such things over my career, but never imagined any of my clients would be victimized. I assure you I went over every major transaction and transfer with either Phillip or Sarah..."

McBain put the glass back down and held his palms out.

"Whoa, nobody's accusing you of anything. I already told the cops the Bakers never had any problems with you. They've traced some of the cash to Lehmann's accounts anyway. Nothing for you to worry about there. They'll probably just want to verify things with you as their investment manager over the past five years."

"That's good to hear; thank you."

McBain picked up his glass and swirled the Scotch around. "I'm sorry, could I get a couple cubes in here?"

"Of course."

"Yeah, after all, I wouldn't have expected either of the Bakers to pick up on anything like that to begin with. Neither of them knew squat about money or investing. Hell, they probably didn't even bother check-ing their statements or any of the investing information you sent them. They trusted you to handle all of that for them. Completely."

"Well, I wouldn't say—"

"So they wouldn't even know the right questions to ask, let alone wonder who they were trading with. You see, that's the glaring missing piece even I didn't pick up on at first. Of course, that was probably the case with all of the others too."

The financial advisor leaned back and crossed his legs. "Others? What others? You are confusing me."

"Didn't I mention? I got hold of a list of some of Lehmann's pa-tients, separate from his files, along with various diseases they suffered from—'suffer' being the key word. The police don't know about it; don't worry."

"I'm sorry. What is that to me?" Roche asked as he sipped his drink, the glass held delicately with ten fingers.

"Turns out this was a list of old people, all deceased, and not unlike the Bakers, they died with a lot less money than they should have. Funny thing was, when I talked to all of them, your name came up as the family financial advisor. That was quite a coincidence, don't you think?"

"Yes, it is, but I have many clients who are still alive, some of whom also knew Doctor Lehmann. Not all of them geriatric or wealthy, either."

"Do you have love affairs with many of them? I have to give you a lot of credit. Some of those women were in their nineties."

Richard Roche put his glass down, seemingly perplexed.

"What is this all about? I can assure you—"

"Mr. Roche, I'm just a two-bit shakedown artist. I'm nowhere near your league. You conned some of the richest people in the city out of tens of millions, and they didn't even know they'd been taken."

Roche pushed out his lower lip and leveled his gaze at the investigator. "I don't know what you're talking about or inferring," the advisor said. "But I resent the implication that I was involved with Dr. Lehmann or anything illegal he was doing."

McBain leaned forward and put his glass on the desk again.

"I'm talking about a very sophisticated strategy to transfer hundreds of millions of dollars from sick and dying people over a period of years so they would never miss it. People who wouldn't know an option from a preferred stock but would trust their investment advisor with their financial arrangements. Are you saying you don't know anything about that?"

As they stared at each other, the room was suddenly very quiet, deaf to any sounds in the hallway outside or the street below.

The advisor's face took on an amused expression. "I don't suppose you're wearing a wire of some kind?" he asked with a curl of his lip.

"I'm basically shaking you down for cash," McBain said. "Considering the nature of our transaction, I don't think I want to record anything we say to each other. Maybe I should be asking you that question. But you can frisk me if you like."

"Point taken," Roche said.

"Besides, I'm not interested in putting anyone away; you know that about me. For me, it's the con itself that's so intriguing. I'm all about learning every trick in the book so I can be better at my job and make more money next time. And you're a master."

For a minute, as Roche sat silently measuring him, he thought it just might work. The man had that subtle smile on his face that was itself an act of acknowledging the achievements of hard work and cleverness that mark a skilled, self-assured craftsman. McBain had seen that smug look of superiority and satisfaction at one's success countless times before.

"I'm afraid I can't help you, Mr. McBain." His face remained impassive. "And I thought we had come to an agreement about your involvement in my business."

"I'm a man of my word, Mr. Roche. When I walk out of here, it's all over. But personally, if I were you, I'd go to the cops now. As you just said, it's early in the investigation. The closer they get, the more they're going to focus on you as the money man. And if a simpleton like me can figure that out, so can your partners who put a bullet in Lehmann. You've got a nice life. If you make it, you could be looking at accessory to murder charges, or you could help the authorities out and probably enjoy some of the millions I'm guessing you've hidden away at some point."

The financial advisor smoothed his silk tie and inhaled. He reached into the center top drawer and tossed a white envelope across the desk to the investigator.

"Here's your 'advisory fee,'" Roche said. "Thanks for the advice. But I'm certain I don't know what you're talking about. I resent what you are implying, and if you continue this line of innuendo and false accusations after today, I assure you I will go the police and take legal action myself."

McBain took the envelope and examined the checks inside. There was one made out to Christina Baker for three million dollars, along with a separate payment to McBain for five hundred thousand. He unfolded the single sheet of letterhead that held them. It was a hand-written note to Christina expressing regret at the passing of her parents and the unfortunate market circumstances. He read it over. Something didn't sit right about it, so he read it again.

"Looks good, Mr. Roche."

He stared at some of the words for a few seconds. Finally, he folded it over and put the letter and checks back inside.

"As promised," McBain said as he pocketed the envelope, "the Baker case will be closed as far as you and I are concerned. Since that's the case, I'm sure you wouldn't mind telling me how long you and Sarah were having an affair."

"McBain—"

"I know it was you, so you might as well admit it. I talked to some of the staff at Inn by the Sea. I just wondered where that fit in to the picture. Hey, you put in five years on this account. That's quite an invest-ment. All the bills you picked up for high-end resorts and hideaways. The time, money, and effort on Sarah. All while a guy like you could be scoring a hot, thirty-year-old trophy wife or socialite girlfriend."

McBain held up his hand. "Don't bother to deny it. I have a stack of copies of the letters she wrote to you, along with a couple of hotel employees who can put you together at places and times she described in her letters. I'm sure she kept it quiet, just as you asked. She may not have named you in the letters, but it's been verified."

Roche turned to the window for a minute, coughing twice into his hand. He cleared his throat.

"Does Christina know? Anyone else?"

"Just me."

He swiveled back to face the investigator. Something in his eyes was different. McBain thought he detected the faint stirrings of a cornered animal.

"Yes, I did see Sarah for a couple of years," Roche said. He smirked. "But I can assure you that that was entirely separate from my profes-sional relationship. Sarah was a wonderful, vibrant woman, and she and Phillip...well, you understand."

McBain laughed.

"Well I certainly understand that some in our business might consider that a breach of ethics. Not me, of course. Hell, you're preaching to the choir. I was trying to nail the daughter. But someone less broad minded could think your professional relationship might extend to something more substantial with Doc Lehmann and some of his friends."

Roche stood and buttoned his jacket.

"Our business is concluded here," he said. "Good-bye, Mr. McBain."

He didn't offer his hand.

The investigator didn't move.

"Sarah was poetic," McBain said. "She was an elegant and romantic writer. She also had a keen sense of perception and eye for detail. The aroma of the logs in the fireplace in a cabin in the dead of an icy winter. The orange and soft pink of the sunset viewed from a sailboat off Newport. The brand of Scotch her Romeo preferred at special moments to celebrate occasions."

The eyes narrowed, and the inscrutable smile flickered for a moment. The older man glanced at the bottle of Macallan on the credenza. He put his glass down on the desk and took his seat, clearing his throat again.

"You know, it's amazing how little these people who clean our buildings make," McBain said, picking a piece of lint off his pants. "They work long and late hours, taking out the trash, mopping floors, and dusting off shelves with no thanks and only a pittance for compensation. Most of them are so grateful for a little bonus and all too happy to take a night off. Good thing you keep your liquor supply locked up. You never know who might get into it."

The mask fell.

McBain watched Roche's eyes shift between the bottle of Scotch and the near-empty tumbler on the desk. The chair swiveled, and his glance swept the window as he looked outside. The investigator suspected he was searching the nearest buildings. When the chair swiveled back to the front, Roche's expression had changed so much it was like seeing a different face.

The cool demeanor gone, McBain watched his eyes and saw his mind at work calculating options, wondering whether he was being told the truth or bluffed by another con artist.

"All right, McBain," he said. "What's this all about?"

"It's about fourteen people. And it's about time."

Anger was overriding the older man's patrician calm now. McBain sat back and guessed his host was about to make his last move. Roche wouldn't know what he had used, but he would know his time was limited. His own heart rate picked up in anticipation, so he inhaled and exhaled deliberately. As he had expected, Roche took a key from his suit pocket and opened the desk drawer that the investigator had found locked the night before.

When his hand reappeared, it held a small automatic pointed at McBain's chest. He didn't know much about guns. He knew enough to recognize that at this range, Roche couldn't miss. Besides, he suspected the financial advisor had experience.

"Start talking," Roche said. "What did you put in it?"

"I forget."

Roche pulled the slide back and chambered a round, all pretense of sophistication gone from his voice and demeanor. "Don't test me, you little shit. With your reputation, I could kill you right here in full view of anyone, and my attorney could make sure I never spend a day in jail."

In his heart, McBain considered how true that was. Until this moment, he had never thought about that aspect of his work. Maybe it was even appropriate, based on some of the things he had done. But it didn't matter much now. His eyes focused on the end of the barrel. Despite the size of the pistol, the black hole grew larger until it opened like a freshly dug grave. In all the times he had seen guns on TV or in the movies, that was something he had never realized until now, as he sat across from a man willing, able, and eager to pull the trigger. He fought against the numbing cold spreading through his stomach and chest into his limbs. Drawing in a deep breath, he pulled his eyes away from the muzzle and looked at Roche.

"Go ahead," he said. "Pull the trigger. I may be a shit, but I'm the only one who knows what you just drank. Nobody else could get here fast enough. And there's no way you'll discover in time where the counter-agent is hidden in this office. I can get to it in seconds. What's it gonna be?"

To keep his eyes from the gun, he glanced at his watch, then back to Roche, who remained as silent as a judge.

"From what I remember about the dosage I put in the bottle, I'd say you've got fifteen minutes tops—maybe ten, judging by the color of your face. But I'm not real good with drugs. Better talk fast and make me believe every bit of what you say is true. And just remember, you don't know how much I already do know."

He didn't dare look at the barrel. Instead, he kept his eyes fixed on the older man's face and kept his breathing steady. McBain could see the confidence melt from his visage as if it were passing into the beads of sweat that were forming. He watched the fear begin to infect the man's decision making.

"Take all the time you want, Roche. Just remember, the clock started ticking the minute you took the first sip."

The advisor's hand went to his throat for a moment, and he swallowed. McBain could tell he was thinking about it as he began to feel the first effects. Thinking about the different drugs they had used on the victims, guessing which one it might be, and whether it was lethal. Wondering if it was worth the gamble.

Roche put the gun on his desk, still within reach.

"All right," he said. "What do you want to know?"

"Everything," McBain said. He leaned forward in his chair and put his own glass on the desk. "But since time is money, let's focus on the highlights. What happened with the Bakers? Why did you and Lehmann kill them?"

"I didn't kill them," he replied. "And I'm not incriminating myself for crimes I didn't commit."

McBain could see from his posture Roche was going to play hardball. The man must have been an incredible gambler and trader. He had figured out he was being recorded somehow, and he didn't feel sick enough yet. He was still confident, and more afraid of his partners than jail or McBain. The investigator was willing to bet that would change very soon.

"You've got one chance. Get protection from the cops and give them all up."

"And what do I get in return?"

"Well, to live, for starters. The rest is up to how much you cooperate. Not my call."

From the look on his face, McBain knew the financial advisor was calculating his options, not liking any of them. Thinking fast. Getting his story straight.

"Lehmann killed them," he said. "Phillip had become suspicious about the losses. Lehmann and I talked about it, and he became nervous. He acted without permission. He poisoned them to keep them quiet and then covered it up using their medical records. He used something that immobilized them and then slipped them something to fake suicide. That's all I know."

"How did you rip them off? You set up the offshore accounts yourself, didn't you?" McBain asked.

"Most of the losses were due to the market, I swear to you. The rest I was able to move by having the account trade with entities I set up, just as you said."

"I want the account numbers. Now."

"The Lehmann accounts are the only ones. Everything went through there, then on to the foreign banks and Brazil."

"Don't bullshit me," McBain said and pointed at Roche. "I can set up a secret account in an offshore tax haven in my sleep. The accounts the cops found were only for Lehmann's use, and you set him up for that. That was for his share of the profits to keep him onboard. I want to know where the real money is. The big money that you funneled from those other twelve victims."

The advisor gritted his teeth and shook his head. "McBain, it wasn't what you think. They were close to dying anyway. They were in terrible pain; you saw the diseases. What Lehmann did was a blessing. Besides, they had so much, they never missed it."

"The accounts, locations, and numbers. Now."

"I can't," Roche insisted. "Not until—"

"I want the names of the other people involved too," McBain said. "Write them down on that legal pad."

"I don't know...all of them...later."

"I'll make it easy for you to save time. Log on to that computer and write down the passwords I need for any e-mail and bank accounts."

Roche was tearing at his collar now, his breathing a tight wheezing sound. As fast as his trembling hands were able, he logged on to the laptop.

"I'll tell you what you want to know. Please, there's no time...hurry... I'm feeling sick."

McBain glanced at his watch.

"We're almost there. Why did they kill Lehmann? Didn't you still need him?"

The advisor ran a sweat-covered hand through his salt-and-pepper hair and blinked.

"I...I mean they...after he tried to kill Christina Baker with his car, they decided...he was too much of a risk."

"When Lehmann tried...Lehmann really did try to run her over?" *What the hell...?*

He sat back for a moment, his thoughts now shifting between Roche slumping lower in the chair and the separate parts of the case. The police had found Christina's DNA on the doctor's SUV in Maine. But they had all finally presumed another killer had driven it and then taken it back to Maine after the assault in an attempt to frame the doctor. Lehmann had killed the Bakers. McBain flashed back to the sight of Lehmann's head on his desk that morning. He looked at the gun on the desk.

In the few seconds that his eyes were closed, he attained the clarity of the mathematician that had eluded him since the beginning of the case. The last piece clicked into place as he thought of his partner: three days and nine locations. *They really must have loved Maine*, she had said.

Suddenly it all came together, brutally clear.

McBain stood up. Keeping his eyes on Roche, he backed up to the door to the office. He turned the lock until the metallic click of the dead bolt filled the room.

He took a deep breath and walked slowly back to the desk. Lighting a cigarette to calm his nerves, he stared down at Roche pulling his shirt-front open. McBain's jaw was tense. The fear was gone, and he felt his blood warming. He walked around the desk and slapped the gun to the side of the room, then took two steps back.

"It was you."

"What...you talking about?" Roche gasped. His eyes were wandering and getting bleary.

"There's no fucking Brazilian gang." McBain almost whispered it.

No response.

"There never was. It was just Lehmann and you. You killed those people yourselves. Then you killed Lehmann. He wasn't the weak link. He was the only link."

"Please...call...a doctor."

"A doctor. That's funny. I thought I recognized that handwriting, especially the little r's. You did the forgeries yourself, didn't you?"

The financial advisor didn't respond, but twisted in his chair.

"You had access to all the accounts and information about their health. You're pretty quick with a gun too. Even if you didn't have access to his house, he would have agreed to meet with you at home in the dead of night. I'll bet you set up all the loose files the cops found that pointed the finger at Lehmann in his office and the house in Maine. Messed up the house like someone was searching for something. Made it look like some kind of organized crime ring killed him. Most of all, you had the cool and the guts to do it."

Roche could only look away and cough.

McBain put his hand in his pocket and touched a slim vial. "Go on. Keep talking, and I'll tell you when to stop. If I believe you, I might even tell you where the antidote is hidden."

The advisor was still aware enough to know he had nothing left to bargain, and little time.

"What happened at the Baker house that night? Phillip found out about the affair, didn't he? The truth."

"Yes, Phillip found out," Roche said. He was out of time, trying to live now, his voice barely a croak. "He threatened to fire me and report me to the SEC for unethical...behavior. They didn't know about the money. I had been giving them phony statements, and...I had to stop him, don't you see? He wouldn't listen to reason. Lehmann didn't want to do it, the coward. I told him all he need do was cause a heart attack in Phillip. The threat would have been enough. If he had done that, I could have persuaded Sarah to keep quiet."

"So you did it yourself?"

"It had worked with the others. They died peacefully...natural causes..."

"Except it didn't work out that way with the Bakers. They were too young. So you had to come up with a way to make it seem like a suicide. And since you and Sarah were having an affair, that fit in easy.

"You knew the Bakers' schedules. You knew when they wouldn't be home, and you probably figured it a pretty good bet the door wouldn't always be locked. You knew their favorite drinks, so you could spike the bottle ahead of time with the drug that would immobilize them so you could shove the poison down their throats.

"Thanks to Lehmann, you had intimate details about Phillip's budding heart problem and the medication they were taking, both of them. You knew just what to give them that would finish the job and not look like anything out of the ordinary for two people who might have been distraught enough to kill themselves. Didn't you?"

His head back, Roche gave a small nod. "Yes."

"While they were dying, you made sure you got rid of anything you could find that might have led to you, right? You knew where they kept their investment records, so there was no problem replacing the old statements with the new ones. All of a sudden, the real losses magically appear, and it looks like they were so depressed they couldn't take it.

"And once you got away with that, you figured Lehmann would be an even weaker link than he already was. So you watched him carefully and got a plan together."

Roche was struggling to talk now.

"Why did you kill Lehmann?" McBain asked. "Why not just threaten him or buy him off?" He forced himself to focus. Control was important now. He had only a couple minutes at most.

"The fool panicked," Roche croaked. "He tried to run over the girl...That's when I knew...he was about to crack. He called, uh, after he found out about her legal investigation. I told him to keep calm...he wasn't implicated, and I could ride it out. But he worried about another autopsy. I had to...had to..."

"Sure, but that was easy. You had that planned all along. You set up the accounts for him, didn't you? A guy as smart as you had to have his contingency ready to go, and Lehmann was always going to be the fall guy."

"...Yes."

"You must have had information on Lehmann. You had him by the balls. A weasel like that would never have had the guts to pull this off."

Roche coughed but nodded, then answered.

"I found out his background years ago. I blackmailed him. I knew about his license problems here and in Brazil. I threatened to expose him...unless he helped me."

"Of course," McBain said. "So Lehmann tees up the potential pigeons based on their age and medical history, and you run the numbers. Together you find rich patients who are going to die soon anyway, so no one will be suspicious. You just help them along the way a little early based on his inside information. It all happens naturally."

"They were...sick...in pain..."

"Once Lehmann was dead, there were no other leads to anyone. The odds were always good that nobody would have ever found his list, his insurance policy, even if he threatened you with it. And if they did, it wouldn't mean anything. By the time people started asking questions, you'd be long gone. You were home free except for one thing: Sarah.

"Since Sarah was so close to you, I'm sure you knew where the personal diaries were too. You probably casually quizzed her over the years to see what they kept a record of. You knew what obsessive writers they were. But you didn't count on Sarah lying to you. I'm sure you never wrote back, for safety's sake, but it never occurred to you that she would have made copies of her love letters. Problem was, she was too much the romantic. She treasured those times too much not to have anything written down to have as a keepsake. The funny thing is, if you had written to her, that probably would have been enough. Then she would have shown you those too, and you could have destroyed them while she was gasping her last breaths.

"Instead she cherished them, even as she hid them from Phillip to keep from hurting him. In the end, they were a testament to her love. But not for you, for Phillip."

McBain pulled the glass vial with the counteragent from his pocket and held it up for Roche to grasp at with his tearing vision.

"What was it like, watching them die together, those two people who trusted you for years? The woman who had lain next to you in a loving embrace? Did they struggle at all? Did they have the energy to fight while you forced the drugs and booze into them that were going to kill them?"

Roche groaned, his hands twitching.

"I'm sor...unh."

"So how does it feel now? This is how they died, all of them. How does it feel?"

The urge to attack, to beat the older man, was beginning to overwhelm him.

"You piece of shit! They trusted you. And you killed them. All of them. For what? For more money than you can ever spend?"

His face turning ashen, Roche reached out his hand for the vial, imploring.

"We're supposed to stand for something. People don't just give us their money. They trust us with their future, with their lives and their dreams. They believe we can make it better. And you took that and twisted it into something hideous."

The approaching thunder of footsteps echoed in the hallway outside the office door. The door handle shook.

"You're going to die, you son of a bitch. You're going to feel what they felt in their last painful seconds and pay for every fucker who ever stole a dime instead of honoring that promise."

"McBain," someone shouted from the hall. His brain registered the voice of Tom O'Daniel. "McBain, open the door. Now, goddamnit!"

He didn't move, didn't care. His eyes were saucers of hate. His face was shaking with suppressed violence, his mouth leering with bloodlust as he loomed over Roche.

The door flew against the wall with a violent explosion, and the Boston police poured in. Tom O'Daniel came in behind the detectives, several police officers, and a small platoon of agents from the SEC and FBI. The office could barely hold them all, some frozen in place with their eyes on Roche slumped in his chair, some with their weapons pointed at McBain.

The financial advisor could barely breathe. His throat was closing up, a gasping, rasping gurgle from down below all that remained of life. Soon he wouldn't be able to swallow.

None of the officers moved except for the captain. He eased to McBain's left side and spoke with authority.

"Give him the antidote."

McBain held the slim vial in front of his own face, his fingers gripping the glass tube to the breaking point, the tension bending the slender cylinder. The rage gripped him with ferocity so tight all he could see was the faces of the elderly victims as they breathed their last. All he could hear were the words and memories of their families. Roche deserved every moment of this.

Tom O'Daniel moved closer to him and looked at his face. Recognizing the perilous nature of the moment, the captain touched him on the arm.

"McBain...Boozy," he said calmly. "It's over."

"Fucking bastard." McBain spat on the dying killer. And it was broken. He tossed the vial with the antidote onto the desk in front of Roche. One of the detectives quickly poured the liquid into Roche's mouth. It would take a few minutes, but he would live.

The police lowered their weapons. O'Daniel gestured to the detectives on either side of Roche. "Read him his rights as soon as he can understand them."

McBain pulled his gaze away from the broken figure slumped in his chair, shirt ripped open and soaked with sweat, his breath shallow and wheezing, the tie hanging loosely around the neck like a noose. His eyes finally saw Tom O'Daniel staring at him. The captain was inches from his face.

"Guilty or not," the captain whispered, "you almost killed a man right now. I could have you thrown in jail for attempted murder."

McBain was recovering, his own breathing and vision returning to normal.

"I don't care. You heard him, Tom. He deserves to die."

The captain grabbed his arm and pulled him toward the door and away from the others.

"Are you crazy? Did you hear what I just said? Think for a minute. Take a deep breath and think."

The investigator shook his head and looked straight at the captain.

"Is this what you were talking about, Tom?" he asked. "Is this what you people have to deal with every day? How do you not go home and vomit every night? How did you ever let your daughters leave the house?"

The big Irish cop nodded at him, his eyes rich with a lifetime of hard experience. McBain looked at him and finally understood some things he had never appreciated about what Tom had tried to tell him. About the danger, and about being a cop. Not just the physical danger, but the risk of losing a part of yourself that could never be recovered.

"Yeah, McBain. This is what I warned you both about. Maybe you'll listen to me next time and leave his kind to us. We'll need you at the office to debrief tomorrow. For now, just go home and get loaded. Try to let it go. You got him. You got him for all of them."

McBain took one more look at Roche in the chair, at the detective reading Roche his Miranda rights as the bastard began to move his hand to his throat. He grabbed his briefcase, took a deep breath, and headed for the door. Suddenly his legs felt wobbly, and his face was beginning to fill up. He had to get out of that room and be by himself. Now that it was over, all the emotions that had pushed and pulled him through the Baker case over the past weeks flooded his system, replacing the adrenaline and rage that had powered him like an out-of-control freight train right to the edge. For the first time in a long time, he needed a drink badly. And he hated himself for it.

"Oh, and McBain."

"Yeah, Tom?"

"Put the envelope back on the desk before you leave. All his assets belong to the courts now."

TWENTY-NINE

Tremont Street was alive with color again, welcome proof that winter always ends, even in New England. The office windows opened out onto fragrant flower beds of pansies and geraniums under blue skies; bicycles and pedestrians; and the music of French horns from a studio downstairs competing with car horns. Crisp air carried with it the feel of cleaning day. McBain was enjoying it all so much he refrained from tossing a half-smoked cigarette down on the courtyard and shoppers below.

So, he thought, life goes on after all. He left the window open and strolled into the front office, hands in the pockets of his beige cotton pants. For the first time in weeks, he felt something akin to rested.

"Ready for lunch yet?" Boston asked.

She was lounging on the couch, red soles of her black Christian Louboutin pumps and gray wool pinstripe pants up on the coffee table. Her favorite ruby pendant was draped over a black short-sleeve blouse, her toned arms glowing with an Irish tan. Boston also looked more comfortable than she had in months. The headline of the paper parked in front of her face no doubt contributed to her mood.

"Boy," McBain said. "Dee really ran with it. I know we gave her a lot of raw material, but man, that woman can turn a phrase. You'd never think a business paper would print a story with this kind of drama. Still, you don't have to keep reading it. It's not like your name is in there."

Boston lowered the paper and smiled her prize-winning, freckled smile.

"I can live with it; can you? Besides, we agreed it was best for business—"

"Like I had a choice."

"And for the sake of giving the feds and the department credit for the legwork so they'd be in a forgiving mood. It's probably the only thing that kept you out of jail. Let's see: extortion, attempted murder, breaking and entering, withholding evidence, violating a police crime scene, theft, illegal possession of medical narcotics, impersonating an insurance investigator. What am I forgetting?"

McBain fell onto the couch next to his partner.

"General moral turpitude. Are they able to use any of what they got on tape, or did I screw it all up?"

"Dad's not sure yet," she said. "The DA is not happy, but apparently the law can be a little vague on one civilian trying to poison another to extract a confession, even if the police have a surveillance warrant but are unaware of how stupid the civilian is prepared to be. Depends on how much cooperation they get from Roche now that he's recovering from the unfortunate mistake someone on the cleaning crew made."

"So I'm not out of the woods. Did Tom at least tell you anything yet, or is he punishing us?"

She threw the paper down on the table so that the headlines trumpeted the major details. Serial Killer. Hundreds of Millions Missing. Fraud. Conspiracy.

"He's feeling generous, with all the attention Dee and the media hounds are showering on him. The Boston district attorney has contacted all of the other families and begun to work back through the histories. The SEC and FBI and whoever else is jumping in have found all of the offshore accounts and begun tracing the trail. I think the US Attorney's office is trying to argue for jurisdiction as well. So far, they all seem a bit stunned with the scope and complexity of what they could be looking at, all devised by one man. Roche was quite the magician. It helped that apparently he'd left his computer on and files open when he was arrested."

"Yes, that was considerate of him."

She looked at him with her best teacher's frown. "Don't feel so smug, partner. You did something really stupid and got away with it. Oh, and when were you going to tell me about the gun? I had to hear it from my father. You didn't know about that, and it could have got you killed. The man was a psychopath."

"I tried the drawer when I got into the office that night," he said. "I figured that's what he might have in there, considering. Of course, it didn't occur to me then that he was the whole operation. If I'd known he'd had the cool to put a bullet in Lehmann's skull, I don't think I would have been quite so sure of myself."

"So how long had you been planning that stunt?"

"Not long. But the first time I left his office, I recognized the name of the cleaning contractor that the building used. So I contacted Marco and kept him on call just in case we needed to get in on short notice. I didn't really know what I was going to do until that night. After I got your call about Roche and Sarah, something just...happened."

"You know what I mean. You deliberately made sure he met with you while I was still in Maine, didn't you?"

"Yes."

Boston shook her head and looked away. "Why did you do it?"

"You know why I did it. You of all people know."

"I think I do, and it scares me. Because I can't even ask you to promise it won't happen again." She turned her head back to face him. "But I don't need you to protect me anymore. We're partners, and we've built this business together. We've come too far in the last four years for you to do this."

McBain bit his lip, and guilt was only one of the emotions that overwhelmed him. "I didn't mean for it to go that far," he said. "I was going to put a stop to it as soon as he opened the files. But then, I realized it was him...just him. He and Lehman killed all of those people. I couldn't get it out of my head. All I could see was each of them fighting for life in their last few breaths. Especially Phillip and Sarah. After these last few weeks, it's like we knew them. Like he had killed our friends."

"So it's just like dad said. You couldn't stop."

"You should have heard him. Even when he was dying, he couldn't bring himself to feel sorry. He rationalized killing and robbing those people, like they were some kind of angels of mercy. It made me so angry."

She reached over and touched his hand.

"It still doesn't make sense to me."

Their fingers interlaced and fingertips merged.

"I'd be scared if it did," he said.

"No, I mean killing the Bakers. Just because of an affair? So what? They go to the SEC. Even if they had eventually discovered that they had been cheated, even if he had stolen the money or lost it through sheer incompetence, he had legal authority and signatures. The lawsuit would have lasted years, even if they wanted to pursue it. Why did he have to kill them?"

He shrugged, leaned over, and picked up the paper with his free hand.

"Who knows?" He pointed at the headlines. "Maybe he'd gotten away with so much for so long he figured he could get away with anything. Maybe he just didn't want to take the chance of them opening up a can of worms that would lead to the others. Could be he always thought Lehmann would crack under the pressure."

Boston put her other hand to her pendant and cleared her throat. "Speaking of cracking," she said, "how's the tooth?"

McBain dabbed at a small purplish bruise to the left of his mouth where his lower molars would be. He worked his lower jaw back and forth carefully.

"Ugh, OK for now," he answered. "The dentist says it wasn't too bad. The permanent crown should work out fine. Doc said he couldn't understand how it broke so quickly since the last visit, even with the bruising. Told him my wife hit me, but I had it coming. I guess I'm lucky you weren't wearing your emerald ring."

"Sorry."

McBain squeezed her hand and turned to her. "Me too. I was wrong."

"Boy, I'll bet that was tough to say."

"Yes," he said. "But I'm learning. Things like trusting my partner. Always being honest with her."

"Wow," Boston said. "Maybe you'll even be a real boy someday, Pinocchio. If we stick together long enough."

They leaned toward each other until their foreheads touched, each with eyes closed, savoring the moment of peace and success. His hand reached up and caressed her cheek.

"I'm not going anywhere," he said. "Somebody's got to help you with your anger management issues."

Boston straightened up and pulled a lock of red hair across her lip into a nefarious mustache. He thought it went great with green eyes and freckles.

"You're tongue's sticking out a little again," he said, and grinned.

"Don't push your luck, Irish."

McBain threw his hands up in front of his face with a yell.

"Well," she said, "as my penance, I spent most of the morning straightening out the paperwork here so that we can return these to Christina. I put everything that wasn't already at the house into boxes and labeled them."

He glanced down at the coffee table and cardboard boxes around it. Bending over, he picked up one stack of paper without disturbing the rest.

"What's this last group of charges on the table?" he asked, puzzled over a pile of credit card receipts.

"Oh, that's the stuff I used for the road trips to track down some of the places Sarah stayed with Roche. I know it's anal with the case over, but I wanted to separate the ones from Sarah's credit card and from Phillip's. You were right, there was some overlap. In fact, one of the things that threw me was that a couple of bills from his card showed up near one or two of the inns. It confused my trail at first, but then I re-membered Christina mentioning how absent-minded they were about accounts."

McBain paged through the stack in his hand. The forensic accoun-tant in his brain sorted, processed, and organized the information intui-tively, the way it had on the trading desk when he had needed to react and make decisions in seconds. He had already gone over most of the items in the past several weeks, but now his mind analyzed them in the context of what he had learned from Roche.

"What are you looking for?" she asked.

"I'm not sure," he whispered. "Something...I don't know..."

She wandered to her desk to wait. Over the years, she had learned when to disappear and leave her partner's mind to its own peculiar, meandering ways. The question itself would have to form, then the answer would present itself in good time. Since that time might amount to weeks, she saw no reason to go hungry, so she started paging through her phone for lunch possibilities.

"We still don't know," he mused out loud, "how Phillip found out about the affair. I should have pushed him on that one."

"You had other priorities, remember?"

He nodded, but he wasn't replying just to her.

"For some reason it seems important. I think it goes to the question about why. Maybe I'm the one who's being anal now."

"And you think the answer is in there?"

The room fell quiet for ten minutes while McBain went through several stacks of credit card statements and receipts. Fortunately, Boston's system had all the old papers organized and prepared for Christina Baker to keep or dispose of.

"The overlap," he said. "I wonder. Did Phillip follow her? Did he stumble across her name accidentally at a place he had been to?"

"Maybe he saw something on a credit card statement," Boston said. "Something that didn't make sense to him because she used his credit card instead of her own."

"Yeah, maybe...where's your timeline?"

She pulled the document out of her files and handed it to him.

He scanned the list of significant events and participants in the case. His mind assimilated the dates along with the receipts in front of him and thought about what Roche had said. Phillip had been angry enough to turn him in, so he didn't just suspect, he knew. There was no debate—he was going to report Roche to the regulators.

In fact, Roche had given him two stories about what had happened at the house that night. Separately they contradicted each other, but taken together, they confirmed that Roche had killed the Bakers intentionally, and it wasn't over the money. They hadn't known about the money. It was over the affair. And Boston was right, it didn't make sense. They had talked to dozens of people about the Bakers, and it didn't fit with their profiles. So what would have made Phillip so angry? It wasn't as if this was Sarah's first affair.

McBain closed his eyes for a minute, and his stomach tensed as a new thought occurred to him. Just as in Roche's office, he thought of an old adage a former engineer on Wall Street had used to admonish him: to every equation there is one and only one valid solution. He exhaled as he opened his eyes.

"We were wrong all along, Boston. Holy shit, how could I have been so blind?"

Her eyes swiveled back and forth over the ranks of receipts in front of her, then at the other piles of documents on the desk. Bewildered, she shook her head at her partner.

"Boozy? What's wrong? What are you talking about?"

McBain thought quietly as he roused himself from the couch. He didn't want to be right; he just was. Grabbing his blazer, he absorbed Boston's questions and thought about her reaction. And then he thought about Christina Baker.

"I think I know someone who can tell us for sure. Let's take a walk. I'll explain along the way. You're not going to like it."

The crimson door to the brownstone opened, and McBain once again noted the weathered sadness of Dennis Abbott's features. The face was not so tanned now after weeks back in New England, and the hair seemed thinner. Despite the spring morning, he was dressed in a pale-green wool sweater and held a book with a worn leather cover, the kind that McBain had observed in abundance weeks ago in Christina Baker's shop and on the shelves in the library in Brookline. As he had on McBain's first visit, Abbott greeted them without any outward sign of emotion and led the way to the garden behind the house, where he offered them coffee.

"Mr. Abbott, this is my partner, Ms. O'Daniel. Since you're a good friend of the Baker family, we wanted to speak to you personally about the closure of our investigation."

Abbott's head bowed in a barely perceptible nod, though to McBain's eye, it might have been simple weariness.

"I read the newspaper and watched the reports on TV. I called Christina to tell her how sorry I was to hear about what happened. It's still too impossible to imagine. That Phillip and Sarah were murdered for their money...that Doctor Lehmann was part of that gruesome plan and all those deaths..."

The old man stopped for a moment and stared at his hands. They were smaller than McBain remembered them, more stained with brown spots now that the tan had faded. The investigators let him continue.

"How is it possible that Sarah could have had an anything to do with a murderer like Roche?"

McBain shrugged. "I'm in no position to pass judgment on Sarah Baker, or anyone else, for that matter. Roche was a professional at what he did, as a forger, a thief, and a charmer. We all make bad choices. The price isn't always this steep."

"I read the stories, and I still can't believe it," Abbott said. "All those people taken in and murdered? And he used Sarah in the same way to rob them too. Then killed them to cover up his crimes." He shook his head.

"Except that it isn't the whole story," McBain said.

"What do you mean? I thought—"

"So does everyone else," the investigator replied. "And that's the way it's going to stay. But even the police didn't get it exactly right. My partner finally hit on it while we were cleaning up our records this morning. That's when the light bulb went off in my head."

"The Bakers never even knew that they were robbed," Boston said. "It took me a bit to get that part, because it happens so rarely. Roche had been giving them dummy records the whole time that showed their portfolio holding up well, even in the downturn. He wasn't thinking about killing them for a long time. All of his other victims were of an age and ill health that never really aroused suspicions. In the case of the Bakers, he had to accelerate his timetable. He only replaced the fake statements with the real ones that showed the losses after he killed them. That's why none of their friends ever heard a bad word about Roche from either Sarah or Phillip."

Abbott had turned pale, and his face was absorbing her every word. McBain could tell he knew what was coming.

"Then why? Was it about the affair?"

"Yes, he killed them because of the affair," McBain said. "We thought it was the affair with Sarah. But it wasn't, was it?"

McBain could sense the pain radiating out from Dennis Abbott. He watched as it spread throughout his posture and filled his eyes. The old man's face softened, but the lines of age seemed to grow wider and more fractured, the investigator's words draining life from his cheeks. McBain felt a sense of guilt and shame as he spoke. He had never hurt anyone before. Not like this.

Boston looked at him and then dipped her eyes.

"They weren't killed because of the money, Dennis," McBain said. "They were killed because Phillip was gay."

Abbott began to shake and collapse, his legs failing him. He turned and barely reached a seat on the bench. McBain had never seen a man so completely overcome with loss. They sat down on either side of him to steady the old gentleman. He and Boston sat quietly next to a gentle man in agony, respecting both his age and his love.

After a few minutes, Boston uneasily put a hand on the back of his shoulder and spoke: "Did you know?"

Abbott lifted his hands from his face to push back his white hair.

"I suspected," he whispered. "The day you first came here and told me about Sarah's letters, I suspected the truth. I lied to you about an affair with Sarah to protect Phillip. To protect my relationship with him, and his privacy. I didn't want to believe he was capable of that, though. I couldn't believe that Phillip could throw away what we had for a monster."

McBain lit up a cigarette because he needed one.

"Roche was more of a monster than anyone imagined," he said. "Our best guess is he started the affair with Phillip five years ago, when he pushed you aside. Then, at some point a couple years later, he wormed his way into Sarah's heart somehow in order to cover all his bases and make sure he had complete control over the finances and an intimate knowledge of both of their lives and habits. But of course he made sure to emphasize to each of them the importance of absolute secrecy about their relationship. He probably figured he could milk the account dry and then make excuses about the market dive far into the future when it didn't matter."

"It worked fine as long as Phillip kept his mouth shut," Boston said. "We know Sarah didn't tell Phillip, at least not until the very end. Her letters were hidden, and up to the last, there was no indication of any break with Roche, or that she had told her husband. Phillip must have found out somehow and confronted Roche, threatened him with exposure, probably in the last day or so. That threat meant he and Lehmann had to act right away. If Phillip was angry enough to out him in public, his reputation in this town would have been ruined, not to mention his scam. Some of the relatives of the other victims might have gotten wind of it and come forward. The authorities would have opened an investigation into the charges and discovered who knows what."

"The one thing that allowed him to get away with it for so long was Phillip's need to keep his own life secret," McBain said.

Boston shifted uncomfortably in her place. The air in the garden was still and empty. Even the birds were missing. She coughed and cleared her throat.

"I'm still amazed," she said, choosing her words carefully. "With all of the information we looked at, all of their friends who we spoke with, there was no indication that Phillip was homosexual. In this day and age, even with a marriage that was a front for so long, how could no one have known about him? Or about him and Roche? Everyone today is so open about these things."

Abbott was struggling just to control his emotions as he listened, so they waited a long time for him.

"You have to understand," he said at last. He could only speak slowly. "It wasn't Phillip's fault. You have to understand what it was like for him. For men like us. But I never imagined it would lead to this."

He rubbed his nose with the sleeve of his sweater, his voice hoarse with despair.

"For many of us, it just wasn't possible to come out into the open. Younger men today still don't have it easy, but compared with what we went through, it is a different world. You might think it a simple decision now, that keeping your life private isn't necessary any longer. Gay marriage. Gay pride. Openly gay actors. But being a high-profile person or celebrity is one thing. For them, society might have put that prejudice behind it.

"I remember, when we first met, Phillip told me what it was like at his house when his father first suspected his son was gay. The man began to grow colder and watched him constantly as he matured. Phillip was gradually ostracized until he almost felt hated. The day he told the truth to his father, the man beat him, almost to death. Soon he lost his family, his friends, any support he had from the whole world. Back then there was no support network, no open place to go to find other men like yourself. When that's your foundational experience, you learn how to hide who you are."

Boston stood up to pace around the garden.

"But," McBain said, "he was a highly regarded professor at a prestigious college. In one of the most liberal areas of the world. Even here? And now?"

"It scars you for life, Mr. McBain. As much as any other horrible experience from childhood can scar us. Not everyone is open minded and tolerant. Not even here, not even now. At any rate, Phillip never felt he could take that chance. In a way, he was still trying to win back his father's approval. He told me once it was the reason why they were so careful never to tell Christina. He didn't know how she would react. He wouldn't take the chance of losing her."

McBain nodded. He could imagine that feeling.

"What about Sarah? What about the marriage?"

"Of course Sarah knew, from the beginning. But she loved him anyway. They were best friends, compatible in every way. I always joked with them about being the perfect couple. When Christina was born, the perfect family. Their love was real. That's why no one ever suspected the truth. Phillip and I were careful to remain discreet all of our years together. And if Sarah had any affairs at all, she kept them secret too. That's why I lied to you. I wanted to keep their secret for them. Keep it in our family."

Boston crossed her arms, gazing off into the trees. "So that was the reason Sarah was able to take so many long trips away from home. Phillip probably didn't care who she was with as long as she was quiet about her affair."

"Yes," Abbott said and nodded. "He wanted her to be happy, so he never asked, especially after Christina was grown and out of the house."

"I guess we'll never know how Phillip found out," McBain said. "Maybe he recognized something that Sarah said or referred to from time he spent with Roche himself. Whatever it was, he and Sarah were both honest enough about their relationship that they must have talked about it and realized that they had both been taken. Once the scales dropped from their eyes, they were certainly smart enough to figure what it was about: their money. They both must have been furious and confronted Roche, forcing his hand. They never imagined what else he was capable of."

McBain got up and stood by Boston's side, holding his fedora. The proper thing to do was to leave Dennis Abbott to his feelings, thoughts, and friends. Any further presence on their part would be too personal an intrusion.

"Thank you for coming here, Mr. McBain. Thank you both for telling me. I'm sorry, you must think me a weak old fool."

McBain put out his hand, and they shook. "No, I think you're a man who has been blessed with a rich and long love. We're very sorry for your loss, Mr. Abbott."

The partners turned to go.

"One more thing," Abbott said. "Does Christina know?"

Boston glanced at McBain and shook her head.

"No, sir," she said. "Not yet."

The old man pulled his sweater close around him and shivered. "I don't know how to tell her. I've never had to do something like this before. I love her so much, and I'm terrified she isn't prepared to hear it. But she deserves to know the truth. I think Phillip and Sarah would have wanted it too. The lies have cost so much."

"They usually do, Mr. Abbott," McBain said as he straightened his hat. "Don't worry, I'll do it. She's my client."

THIRTY

McBain parked the Range Rover in the driveway in Brookline late Saturday morning. Christina Baker answered the front door in a light-blue sweater and jeans, holding a pair of white cotton work gloves in her hand. The dark hair was pulled back into a ponytail and only slightly mussed.

"Well, hello," she said. "I was just going through the library, taking an inventory. Or should I say a new inventory. I was wondering if you were going to come by. We haven't spoken since that night. When Boston called to tell me about the boxes, she said you might be here today. It's nice to see you again."

She welcomed him in, and he noted that the large work table in the front dining room was cluttered with the cardboard boxes they had shipped over and the boxed-up records they had used. Otherwise, the room had returned to a semblance of normality, the paintings returned to their rightful places on the wall. Once again it was a house that felt lived in, filled with pictures and family treasures, not whiteboards and faceless numbers.

"I've been going through some of the rooms upstairs. I'm beginning to sort through my parents' things and organize items for storage or sale."

"Making some changes?" he asked.

"Gradually," she replied. "I suspect we'll get the house ready for sale sometime in the next year or two. I'm not moving too fast, but with all this behind me, I know I'll be ready at some point. Searching through the closets and hallways again over the past few months has shown me how much work it needs. We lived here a long time. But now that my parents can rest in peace, I can begin to think about fixing it up and finding the right people."

"It's good," he said. "You should be thinking about the future, not just the past."

The enduring spark of life was back in her eyes, and Christina Baker radiated more energy and enthusiasm than she had in weeks. McBain could see flashes of the woman who sparred like a champion and had survived unspeakable tragedies and assaults on her world over the past year. It would be a long road back, and she would be changed, but she would get there.

"Boston has called several times since they arrested Roche," Christina said. "I thought maybe you were going to have her wrap things up. Have you moved on to another case already?"

"You know me better than that," he said. "You didn't think for a minute I'd leave without saying good-bye...Ms. Baker."

He caught the same look of amused confidence that he had first seen leaving the bar that night. The same laughing eyes, a little the worse for wear.

"No, I didn't," she said. "But I was wondering if I was going to have to keep getting my news from the television or Boston. We haven't talked about what happened during your meeting that day with Roche."

McBain shook his head.

"No need to go into that now," he said. "It went down pretty much as you and I rehearsed it before the meet. Except, of course, the whole part about him being behind everything himself. The police heard enough that they were able to arrest him. Now it's just a matter of the DA and cops taking him apart. Well, and the feds. I guess you'll have to talk to them about your money. I had the check in my hot little hands, but they grabbed it before I could leave his office. Sorry."

His client did a double take. "Sorry? Are you serious? You brought a sick murderer to justice. And I still don't understand why you and Boston aren't in the news stories, even though she explained it to me. I'm not supposed to mention your names and involvement to any media people, but I don't think that's fair."

"It's for the best, believe me. Please, honor our request. You'll be helping us out. We like to remain anonymous, like the Lone Ranger and Tonto, Batman and Robin—"

"Bonnie and Clyde?"

McBain almost smiled. "That's good. She'll like that one."

Her gaze fell to the floor for a moment. "I also wanted to thank you," Christina said. "Thank you for what you did for me that last night here."

McBain glanced up the stairs and then back at her face.

"I usually hear that the next morning," he said. For long seconds, their eyes joined. "Just don't let it get around. I have a reputation to maintain, you know."

"I promise it will always remain just between us."

They wandered into the library. The French doors were open, and the scent of rose bushes, upturned soil, and mulch wafted in on the spring breeze. He tossed his coat and fedora on an ottoman.

"Please sit down. We can talk while I clean."

"No, I'll stand, thanks. I just came to give you a final report on the case. It's part of our job."

"So formal, still. Yes, I recall from your visit to the bookstore weeks ago. I promise not to get up on any ladders while you talk. But I thought I already knew everything. Do you have more news from the district attorney's office, or the police?"

"In a way," he said. "The news has been full of what the police and authorities think it's important for the general public to know. For reasons relevant to the case, they have felt it necessary to keep certain things under wraps. Also, they have to make a solid case yet, and that means gathering all the facts about how and why Roche did what he did. Plus, one last piece of information has come to light that's not going to be in the papers."

"All right."

"I'm going to tell you the rest of the story, because you deserve to know."

"What are you talking about?"

"This is going to be difficult, so I'm going to say it straight out," McBain said. "Roche killed your parents because they were going to turn him in to the SEC. But they didn't even know about the money. He replaced the fake records showing profits with the real records after they died."

Once again, Christina Baker stood dumbstruck in amazement.

"I don't understand," she said. "That doesn't make sense. Then why did he kill them? Why were they going to the authorities?"

McBain forced himself to look at her when he said it.

"That night I told you we discovered that Roche was the one having the affair with Sarah. Somehow Phillip found out about the affair with your mother. When he did, he and Sarah talked about it, and Phillip was furious. He was furious because he had been having an affair with Roche too, for five years. He was going to turn him in for unethical conduct. Roche killed them to keep that quiet."

A kaleidoscope of emotions were cycling across her face.

"What are you talking about? An affair with my father? My father...my father was not homosexual. Are you insane? Are you stupid, McBain?"

"It's true," he said. "We spoke with Dennis Abbott, and he confirmed it."

"Dennis Abb...what does Dennis have to do with this? You said he had an affair with my mother years ago."

"He lied. He lied to protect you. But the truth was that Abbott and your father were in love for over twenty years. Roche came into the picture and deliberately maneuvered him out so he could get close to Phillip and rip them off. That's why Dennis removed himself from all of your lives. Then, at some point, Roche decided to cover his bases by luring Sarah into a relationship. That was the one in the letters."

McBain saw it coming. As the emotional wheels turned from confusion to denial to bewildered rage, the power of her anger swelled.

Christina slapped his face as hard as she could. Then she slapped him again. He staggered but stood his ground, his face bright red. He kept talking.

"Phillip was jealous and angry. After he and Sarah exchanged stories with each other, they both felt betrayed and used. They must have figured what he was up to and told him they were going to the authorities.

Roche realized his reputation would have been ruined, and he would have lost other clients based on that alone. The fact is, he killed them because of that. They didn't even know they had been wiped out yet. He killed them to prevent an investigation that would have revealed everything he and Lehmann had done in the past and outed him as gay. At the very least, his career in this town would have been finished. An investigation by the SEC probably would have discovered the other clients at some point and the link to their deaths."

She wasn't swinging at him, but she was boiling mad, her whole bearing filled with contempt and scorn.

"You're wrong. You're lying. You can't possibly know that."

"You're right, I didn't know for sure. So I spoke to Captain O'Daniel after talking to Abbott, and had him get the story from Roche. He confirmed everything. Roche begged them not to make it public. Which is fine, because that's what I told the police I wanted before I talked to them. There's no reason it has to go any further, and since Roche is scared of it, we can still use it as leverage against him."

Christina Baker retreated and tumbled into a leather chair. The ticking of the grandfather clock in the hallway intruded with the echo of a hammer while he watched her. McBain didn't expect her to reply. You don't expect someone to thank you for destroying her life.

He pulled out a cloth handkerchief and put it to the corner of his mouth. It came back bloody.

"You should talk to Abbott," he said. "He really cares about you."

Barely able to speak, Christina glared up at him. The defiant rage at the relentless attacks on her family and reality blazed from her face.

"Get out of here, you bastard. Get out of our house."

And she broke. Her head fell onto her arm, and she began to weep inconsolably.

McBain picked up his hat and coat and left. Walking to his car, he realized something for the first time about this business he had chosen. Sometimes the wrong people got hurt no matter the outcome. And sometimes he was the one doing the hurting.

THIRTY-ONE

D oyle's Café was rocking to sports season and the superiority of the Boston machine. The Patriots had made it to the Super Bowl, both the Bruins and Celtics were no doubt headed for championships, and the Red Sox, despite their terrible early season record, were certain to redeem themselves later in the season. Some things Boston fans just took in stride. The town was a living testament to the human failing that allowed hope to triumph over experience.

With the Baker case finished, at least their part of it, Boston and McBain treated themselves and Tom O'Daniel to an early cocktail hour on Saturday afternoon. Their corner booth was as far away from the flow of traffic as a person could get in the packed restaurant. They had to raise their voices to be heard among the raucous symphony of sports announcers, glasses, and drunken college students.

The partners hunkered down to enjoy the first weekend in a long time without work to focus on. That was for others now.

Boston, jeans stuffed into her cowboy boots and hourglass figure stuffed into a white T-shirt, worked her way back from outside and slid past a gaggle of staring students into the booth.

"Dave had a message for you," she said.

"Let me guess," McBain said. "He doesn't like working weekends."

"Something to the effect of 'thanks for nothing' was the gist, but in more colorful language."

"Ingrate. Probably something to do with those thirteen back cases of fraud that are sitting on his desk now. Dave doesn't like being the focus of high-profile media feeding frenzies either."

Boston sipped at her gin.

"Unlike certain limelight-hogging police captains who shall remain nameless."

Captain O'Daniel shrugged.

"Well, you didn't want the publicity. Somebody has to coordinate all the media coverage. To use your phrase, baby girl: just doing what you told me to do."

"Aaargh!"

A couple of college guys bumped their table and paused for a moment to grin at the redhead...until they saw the size of the captain's eyes and fists. "So," she asked after they hustled away. "Where does it stand at the moment?"

"Roche confirmed all of it," her father replied. "Just as you guessed, Phillip and Sarah confronted him. Phillip had known his wife was seeing someone for some time, and he was looking for something in his records when he picked up on one of Sarah's trips that looked familiar. They talked and finally figured out he was playing both of them. They were bright enough to suspect he was going to rip them off and told him they were going to the SEC. The murder played out pretty much like you described it in the office. Roche is a sick creature."

"I don't imagine you were able to use a lot of what you got on tape," McBain said.

"Enough," O'Daniel said. "Enough to keep Roche locked up without bail."

"And he's talking to you?" Boston asked.

"You'd be surprised. Mister Sophisticated is a changed man ever since his brush with death. I'm not sure if he suddenly realizes what's going to happen to him, or thinks he's going to be some kind of celebrity criminal, but he's cooperating, all right. Or it could be he's also concerned about some of his potential roommates. Apparently word got around among the hardcores about him poisoning a lot of sick, dying elderly people. I told him we can't be sure how much longer we can keep him isolated."

McBain shook his head.

Boston lifted her glass to the sky. "And people ask me where I get it from. Don't think you're joining us when you retire."

"Sure," her father said. "As if you'll be able to stay out of trouble that long. Speaking of which, let's talk about what we got on tape, some of which I've managed to persuade the DA to forget he heard for the sake of the case."

"Um, you're welcome?"

"Stow it, funny man," the captain said. "You know what I want to talk about. When we talked before the meeting, you and I discussed your strategy—"

Boston's eyes widened. "You knew he was going without me, and you didn't say any—"

"And I don't recall any mention of using narcotics to influence the discussion. It was supposed to be straight and simple: bait Roche into confessing just enough for us to pull him in. What exactly were you thinking? You might very well have blown any chance we had, not to mention your own position."

Doyle's was boisterous enough that there was little chance of anyone else caring about their conversation. Still, McBain had wanted to avoid being buttonholed by Tom O'Daniel into explaining himself. He just hoped it would make sense.

"Tom, I bad-mouth the business a lot, but I like to think that I took a couple of useful things away from my time there. As a trader, you learn how to read the flows of the limited amount of information that you have and take a calculated risk. That's what I did.

"The best traders aren't the ones who throw it all on one stock or think they're smarter than the market. Those are the idiots who look like superheroes for a moment if they get lucky, but who hang. The good ones are experts at managing the risks. They gather as many facts as possible, figure the odds. They have the discipline of a block of ice in the arctic. They cut their losses, they take their profits. They know exactly what their target is. Those are the guys I learned from and study. You'll never hear most of their names, and that's the way they like it. It's not about ego. It's about making sure you have as much information as possible, finding your advantage, taking a calculated risk, and winning."

The captain was sipping his beer and eyeing McBain with skepticism.

"So, what's all that mean in terms of Roche?"

"I'd met with him a number of times and done my research. I knew he was going to be incredibly cool, and maybe impossible to break. I also knew we were in the dark about too many things, with very little proof of anything. While I hoped I could bait him out, I figured it was a long shot. The odds were all in his favor, and it turns out that since there was no gang, it was even worse than I imagined."

"So you decided to cheat."

"That's right, I cheated. I rigged the odds in my favor by spiking his drink. Sure, Roche is a sicko, but he's also very smart, and he'd had years to get his story ready. It put time pressure on him and forced him out of his comfortable, relaxed game where he had time to think and evade. Roche had worked long enough with the doctor and drugs, and seen their effect on people, including the Bakers, that I guessed it would scare the truth out of him. I figured it was my only chance at making sure he gave us what we wanted, straight and undiluted."

"He could very well have shot you and taken his own chances, just like he threatened to do."

"Once again, a calculated risk," McBain said.

Boston elbowed him. "Based on an incorrect psychological assessment of the mark, partner."

"Exactly," the captain said. "As it turns out, he could have just decided to go out shooting. The man had already killed a dozen people. Not to mention the fact that he's mentally unbalanced. Nice calculation, genius."

"Like I said, incomplete information."

"And you're telling me you didn't plan to kill him, huh?"

McBain took a belt from his drink before he replied. "No, but let's put it this way: I knew he might have a gun in the drawer, since I couldn't get it open the night before. If I wasn't walking out of there, neither was he."

Boston gulped the last of her martini and lasered her thoughts at him when he glanced at her, half raising her fist. But Captain O'Daniel pushed his daughter's hand down and stared at McBain in consternation.

"You're damned lucky I figured out what was going on in that office," he said. "Two more minutes, and you would have been arrested for murder."

"Thanks again, Tom. For saving me from myself."

"And how did you know he wasn't gonna drink that Scotch before you got there? Or worse, share it with a client of his in the middle of the afternoon?"

When McBain met his gaze, he saw that the captain already knew the answer.

"I didn't know. But my read on him was that he saved that bottle of Macallan for special occasions. I was counting on him saving it for me."

"But you could've been wrong," O'Daniel said.

"Dad..."

"That's right, Tom. I could have been."

The thick red eyebrows were the tips of flames over the edge of the captain's beer mug. He emptied the glass and lowered it to the table. "You're a son of a bitch, McBain. You might have put my little girl in danger, or some other person who was completely innocent. You want to play Russian roulette, you do it on your own time and outside of my cases. If you ever do anything like that again, you'll need more than a dentist. I'll put you in a cell so dark and deep the doctor you'll need will never find you. You understand me?"

"Yes, sir." McBain nodded once.

They all took a minute to let it go and sat back sipping water. Doyle's was lively. A couple of off-duty cops dropped off another two rounds at their table for the local heroes. The televisions filled the bar with baseball and basketball. It was as if none of it had taken place. For all of the individual souls here and on the TV, it was just another May afternoon.

"How's Ms. Baker doing?" O'Daniel asked.

Boston stayed quiet and looked out at the crowd.

"How would any of us be?" McBain answered. "Pretty bad, I expect. She won't return our calls. I can't blame her. What did we do when our world changed? Get up each day and put one foot in front of the other until the bad stuff goes deeper, and you just get on with it. She'll harden, hopefully not to the point that she loses herself or her memories of Phillip and Sarah. But I think they did a pretty good job with her. She'll see that and remember the love. She's got lots of character and a good husband. She's smart and tough. With a lot of luck, she'll move past that petty stuff and get back to some kind of normal as it all fades. Once the new autopsy is done, that should help. Then if the damn reporters would leave her alone. She's had enough people prying into her family's past and privacy for a lifetime."

"I hope so," Boston said. "I like her. It's nice to feel that way about our client for a change."

McBain nudged his partner.

"Oh, by the way, speaking of homophobic bigotry, I appreciate you keeping your hostility bottled up while we were talking to Abbott."

The O'Daniels threw up their arms in a pretense of objection over their cocktails and plates. Boston sounded wounded.

"McBain, I told you before I do not hate gays....I'm just not entirely comfortable with it."

"Look," he said, "I'm not condemning you. We all know how you both feel. Why give me a load of PC shit? You are who you are. It took me five years of living in the Village to be gay friendly. It's not everybody's cup of tea."

Her father slammed a shot glass down on the table.

"Fine, McBain. While we're on the subject of bigotry, I got an earful of your opinions about people on that tape. And don't be thinking just because you got away with something this time, it gives you license to go trampling the rights of every slimy money manager who comes your way in the future. This guy was scum and a psycho, and you have my thanks for what you two did. You were right about him, and your instincts paid off. Just remember what I said about his kind last time. You've burned through about as much good luck as any one man can, and when you talk about odds, just think about what your odds are now given past events."

Captain O'Daniel shifted his gaze from McBain over to his daughter.

"And what about you?" he asked. "You got what you wanted: your first murder investigation. Was it as glamorous as you'd hoped for?"

Boston shook her head.

"No." She poked at the ice in her glass. "I thought we'd seen some real shits in our work. I never imagined something like this, that people like Roche really existed. Or Lehmann. They weren't even sorry. They just rationalized murdering those people as if they were undertakers measuring them for coffins. And Roche cleaned up his trail in their own house while the Bakers lay dying. Do psychiatrists even have a name for people like them?"

"I don't know," the captain said. "He was a predator, the kind we see every day. Just because he wore a suit and tie and preyed on people with more money doesn't make him any better or more special than the ones we see in any poor neighborhood. In this case the Bakers, just like the other victims, walked willingly into his trap."

Boston slumped in her seat. The illusion of glamour had worn thin, replaced by the numbing reality of the devastation wrought on so many families. As they had for McBain at the house that night, for her the numbers and papers had morphed into smiles and laughter, the reality of Phillip and Sarah Baker. And their lifelong search for love and belonging.

"All they wanted was a chance at a better future for their daughter," she said. "Maybe some grandkids. And it got them killed."

McBain finished his martini and pulled over another.

"Every time you think you've seen the bottom..." Boston said, and sighed.

"This is new territory for us, Boston," he said.

Their eyes joined, and they read each other's thoughts, but it was Captain O'Daniel who said it:

"New, but not exactly unfamiliar, right?"

Boston raised her glass in front of the two men.

"A toast."

They touched her glass with their own.

"To family," she said.

There is something about a wet, gray evening and a live piano player that makes a man want to drink bourbon. So he ordered a Perfect

Manhattan, up and cold. With the coming of May, the winter's chill had departed for good, but the skies were still pregnant with spring rain. Despite the weather, or perhaps because of it, he had come out to meet his client one last time, at her request. McBain could only hope that meant she had worked through her anger issues. On the other hand, there was a lot of glass in a bar.

Christina Baker arrived on time, as expected. And as usual, with more style than any woman in a rainstorm had to right to. Looking like an old-time movie star, she walked into the Holiday in a Burberry raincoat, with a tote bag and plaid umbrella, and there was hardly a dark hair out of place as she removed her wide-brimmed hat. She closed her umbrella and took off her coat before sitting down, which he took as a promising sign.

"Thank you for meeting me, McBain."

"Always my pleasure, Ms. Baker."

She ordered a martini and loosened her silk scarf.

"I spoke to Dennis Abbott yesterday," she said. "We talked for a little while. He's going to meet me for dinner tomorrow night to talk about my mother and father. Dennis and I have quite a bit of catching up to do. There are a lot of things I want to know about my parents."

"I'm glad to hear that. Abbott's good people. See, your family's getting bigger already."

She played with her ring for a minute.

"I want to apologize for hitting you, McBain."

"That's OK, I'm getting used to it," he said. "I would have been surprised if you had reacted any other way. Regardless of how you feel about it, nobody likes to find out that kind of family secret from a stranger. They probably should have told you themselves a long time ago and trusted they raised you right. But I'm not going to pass judgment on their decision. It was theirs to make. Good to get some anger out of your system, though, so you could think things through."

An icy glass slid across the bar to sit in front of her.

"Thank you, Michael," she said. "Yes, I've had a lot to think about. I've found out so much in the last few weeks. About my parents. About life and what some people are capable of. Even about myself. It's almost more than a person can take in at once."

McBain nodded. "It can be a strange and ugly world. I'm still learning how ugly. Nobody should have to face what you did. You came through it a hell of a lot better than most people. Now you know why I drink so much of the time. Cheers."

Christina's fingers touched his arm, and he looked over at her.

"I called Boston. She told me what happened with Roche. Why did you do it? You could have lost everything. You could have gone to prison or been killed."

As he often did when faced with a raw question, McBain sipped thoughtfully at his drink before answering.

"A lot of reasons. When it came down to it, I needed to know the truth as much as you did. Maybe because I thought it was the only way to make sure he could be stopped. Sometimes I just think I know what I'm doing, but I'm really winging it. Mainly because he deserved it. Some other reasons that I'd rather not talk about."

She nodded but kept her hand on his arm.

"Is everyone like that?" she asked.

"In the investment business?" he replied. "No, not at all. Most people work hard and try to do the right thing by their customers. Lots of them like what they do and understand the responsibility. It's only the ones who cross that line or make the big headlines who give the business a bad name. And like I said before, when times get bad, they seem to come out of the woodwork and make everybody else look corrupt too. It's not fair. But you already knew that."

They drank together wordlessly, observing each other in the long mirror behind the wall of bottles. The bar was not crowded yet, and Michael kept his distance.

"Can I ask you something, McBain?"

"You can always ask me anything you like."

"Why do you both do it? It must be so depressing to be in a business where you have to deal with people who lie and steal from the ones who trust them. Maybe if you went back to advising people about their money or something, you wouldn't see so much of the bad side. You could treat people like they're supposed to be treated. Then you wouldn't need to drink so much."

He shook his head. "Nice idea, Ms. Baker."

"You can call me Christina now, you know."

"I don't think so." He tried to say it lightly. It didn't work. "No, for some of us, there's no going back. Once you cross a certain line and see what we've seen, you can never look at people with clean eyes again. Boston feels the same way; it's one of the reasons we work so well together. Otherwise we would have quit long before we came across something like this. Now, with this one, it makes it even harder."

He looked at her lovely face. The physical bruises, at least, had faded away. "Plus, the money's pretty good."

She held his gaze for a moment before stirring her martini sheepishly.

"I'm sorry I'm not able to pay you your fee yet," she said. "I've been told by the district attorney and police that recovering any money will take quite some time now, especially given the number of families that are involved and the scale of the investigation. Apparently they haven't even finished fighting over jurisdiction in the cases yet."

McBain shrugged. "That's OK. Boston and I are in good shape. And even though we're trying to keep a low profile and give the cops and SEC all the credit for solving the crimes, word will get around. Dee Dee and Dave will see to that. We'll do fine out of the whole thing. You just pay us if and when the courts work things out for you."

Christina reached into her tote bag and brought out a familiar rectangular shape, wrapped in silver paper and tied with a blue silk bow.

"In the meantime, I brought you a gift."

"What is it?" He smiled as he took the package.

She smiled back, for the first time with her whole face. It was a wonderful thing to see.

"You can open it now if you like, or you can wait."

He found the seams of the paper, gently unwrapped it, and looked at the cover. McBain's stomach and chest tightened for a moment. He swallowed hard and took a long drink to stop his lips from trembling.

"Thank you," he said. "That's the nicest thing a client's ever done for me. It's one of my favorite movies, but I didn't know it was based on a book."

"Yes, by Jack Schaefer," Christina said. "It's a first edition from 1949. I think it's appropriate."

"I'm not sure I deserve that."

"I am."

At times like these, McBain enjoyed being in a bar with a piano. Sometimes it was good to just shut your mouth and listen. To feel the emotion coursing through your veins telling you that you were still alive, that you had done something decent for a change, and that maybe you were not as bad as you thought you were. He turned in his chair to face her.

"I apologize, Ms. Baker. I was wrong. Your instincts were right on from the start about Roche, and about your parents. You had something most of us don't have: faith. I should have trusted that. I made a mistake. I'm sorry."

Her dark eyes glistened as she touched his hand. "I was wrong, too."

"About what?"

"You were worth every penny."

"But I didn't get your money back."

"You did more than that. You got justice for my parents. And for those other families who were robbed and had their loved ones taken from them and didn't even know it. And because of you, Roche and Doctor Lehmann were stopped before they killed anyone else. That's a lot. This time, you made all the difference in the world. It's probably the best thing you've ever done with your life."

McBain looked for his past in the dregs of his bourbon. "Maybe."

Before McBain could stop her, Christina left her chair and threw her arms around him. For a minute, neither of them moved. They just held on with eyes closed.

Her voice was a whisper, the ghost of a last farewell: "I will never forget you, McBain."

"I think that's about the finest thing a man could ever ask of a woman," he said.

Without another word, Christina pulled back. She put on her raincoat and hat, picked up her umbrella, took her bag off the arm of the bar chair, and walked away.

The echo of traffic racing by on the wet pavement poured in when she opened the door. Though his eyes barely lifted from his glass, he could see in the bar mirror as the heartbeats crawled by that she hung there a moment, framed in the entrance of the doorway by the failing light of a damp gray rush hour in the city of Boston. Then she turned her head a little, her profile reflected at the edge of the mirror outlined like a silhouette in a cameo.

"See you around, McBain. Take care of yourself."

And she was gone.

"Good-bye, Christina."

McBain drained the last of his drink and listened to the rhythmic melodies of the rain and the piano keys. A trumpet player arrived and joined the piano. More people wandered into the bar.

Michael came over and slid a tall glass of ice water in front of him. The barman looked down at the novel by the empty cocktail glass.

"Hey, I didn't know *Shane* was a book."

"Yeah, go figure," McBain said. "I wonder if the ending is the same."

"Another drink, Boozy?" the bartender asked. "This one's on us. After what you did, you deserve it."

McBain didn't want another drink. Not now, not ever.

"Sure, Michael, why not? Just like in the movies, we should always get what we deserve."

Made in the USA
Middletown, DE
07 June 2017